DAMNATION GAMES

EDITED BY
ALAN BAXTER

First published by Clan Destine Press in 2022

Clan Destine Press
PO Box 121, Bittern
Victoria, 3918 Australia

National Library of Australia Cataloguing-In-Publication data:

Editor: Alan Baxter

DAMNATION GAMES

ISBNs: 978-0-6453168-4-1 (hardback)
978-0-6453168-5-8 (paperback)
978-0-6453168-6-5 (eBook)

Cover Design by © Luke Spooner

Design & Typesetting by Clan Destine Press

www.clandestinepress.net

Contents

Introduction

The themes I return to time and again in my work seem to always revolve in some way around horror and crime. I've said before that I consider horror to be the genre of honesty. There's no shying away from brutal reality to supply a happy ending with horror. Even when the evil is overcome, it rarely happens without cost. Survivors are rarely unscathed. Horror looks into the darkness and doesn't turn away, but confronts it.

In many ways, crime stories are often horror stories too. There *are* victimless crimes, and white collar crimes that only hurt faceless corporations (which, let's face it, are often no better than organised crime syndicates themselves), but on a personal level, crime is dark and nasty stuff. Murder, manipulation, kidnapping, stalking and more go hand in hand with burglary and car-jacking and cons. All these things, in one way or another, cast their perpetrators as predators and the victims as prey. And that's where crime is horror, because being something's prey is probably the most deep-seated fear any of us have.

Being eaten by something else is a genuinely terrifying concept. Perhaps being eaten alive is second only to being buried alive as a source of fear, and even then only because the latter takes longer. And while someone stealing your wallet isn't quite the same as being literally eaten, it does turn us into the victim of a predator, and that's a horror story.

Desperate people can be driven to crime to survive. Again, we find the predator and prey dynamic, where one person will predate on another simply to continue existing. Does that make them a bad person, though? What if they're not only trying to save themselves but also protect their family? Is it more okay to kill an innocent adult if that will directly save the lives of innocent children? What about killing someone else's children to save your own?

Crime, by its very nature, is usually horrible, and generally involves horrible people. But not always. It does, however, almost always involve morally grey people, and what is horror at it genesis if not an exploration of the morally grey, human or otherwise? This is where, for me, horror and crime are so inextricably linked. You can probably see why I find these themes so juicy for fiction.

So when Lindy Cameron of Clan Destine Press approached me and asked if I'd be interested in editing together an anthology of horror stories, I said I most certainly would, but I asked, "What about supernatural horror and crime, combined?"

Lindy said, "Hell, yes!" and thus was the concept for *Damnation Games* born.

It's no secret to anyone that I'm a huge fan of Clive Barker—his work has influenced mine more than anyone else—so I wanted this book to draw a subtle reference to that passion of mine, and it came out in the book's title. The name is a nod to the debut Clive Barker novel, *The Damnation Game*. But that only plays a tiny part in what I hoped to achieve with this. That novel revolves around an ex-con gambler and his entanglement with one of the wealthiest men in the world, who happens to have made a deal with the devil. Barker's stories often also feature crime at a much more urban and intimate level, like his story, "The Forbidden", from his collection, *The Books of Blood*. You may think you don't know that story, but if you've seen the movie *Candyman*, you know it better than you think. The film was an adaptation of Barker's short.

I took huge influence as well from comic books of the same era (we're talking the 1980s here) and things like Jamie Delano and Garth Ennis writing *Hellblazer* made a huge impact on me. There we have all kinds of supernatural and magical occurrences matched with gritty urban stories and unsavoury characters.

Then there's William Hjortsberg's 1978 novel, *Falling Angel*, which was brilliantly adapted into the movie, *Angel Heart*, starring Mickey Rourke. In that story, private investigator, Harry Angel, is hired to find a popular singer named Johnny Favorite and becomes embroiled in strange and frightening occult shenanigans.

I could go on and on about the various things like these that have enthralled me over the years, but I'll stop there for now. I could talk about this stuff for hours. Regardless, you can see the core of my passion, that delicious combination of the supernatural, the horrifying, and the criminal. It's found its way repeatedly into my own work with novels like *Devouring Dark* and *Sallow Bend*, and stories like those in the *Tales From The Gulp*.

So of course when I was asked to edit an anthology, that's exactly where I went. I asked a slew of amazingly talented writers if they would send me stories and I couldn't believe how many said yes. I also had a limited open submissions for members of the Australasian Horror Writers Association (of which I'm currently President) and I got two incredible stories from there as well.

I asked the authors to interpret the theme as widely as they pleased. Those examples above should give an idea about how broadly this theme *could* be drawn. I was keen to see stories from a variety of locations and eras, drawing from the incredibly wide churches of crime and horror. What I received was better than I could have imagined. From English cosy mysteries to urban monsters, from Victorian mathematicians to contemporary lawyers, from near future police procedurals to outback ghost stories, and more, this book, I guarantee, will surprise you. And it'll scare you and entertain you.

I hope you have as much fun reading it as I had pulling it together. But all credit goes to the authors, who made the task simple. They are amazing. Thank you to each and every one of you who wrote for this book, and thank you to each all of you now reading it. I hope you enjoy these Damnation Games.

Alan Baxter
NSW August 2022

A Bitter Yellow Sea

GENEVE FLYNN

'LUCKY YOUR *GONG GONG* DIED SO MANY YEARS AGO,' GOH MIN LEI'S grandmother said as she rearranged the oranges in front of her husband's urn. She sighed as she straightened. 'Too bad I won't have such dignity when I pass on.'

Min Lei surreptitiously checked her phone. Hunar, her colleague from the police technology department, had sent an alert about the fifth missing child. Nothing had come through yet. 'You know the UN emissions tax is too high, Poh Poh.' They had had this conversation many times. But until Singapore lifted its ban on cremation, her grandmother, Ah Lam, would have to accept a government-sanctioned burial in Jurong Island Memorial Park, the now-defunct petrochemical processing plant off the coast. Min Lei peeked at her screen again.

'Go on.' Ah Lam flapped her hand. 'I know you want to get back to work.'

Min Lei's phone vibrated in her pocket and she gave her grandmother a gentle hug. 'I'll come by again tomorrow. I'll bring you some congee from Market Street.'

'Go. Go.' Ah Lam turned and shuffled towards her recliner, leaving Min Lei to let herself out.

As the lift travelled down to ground level, Min Lei tapped on the notification. The link that popped up showed an online auction for a Just Like Me Doll, a wildly popular fad that allowed kids to have a plaything created to look just like themselves. A cold current raced down her back. The doll in the listing had a pointed chin, a dimple on the left cheek, small, single-lidded eyes, and a page boy haircut: exactly like April Teo, the missing seven-year-old. She'd suspected the cases were linked to a possible trafficking operation and had asked Hunar to search for anything that looked like a call to possible buyers.

Min Lei tapped on the details of the listing. An address and a name: Solomon Chow.

The apartment smelled like goat. It was mid-level in the Breakwater Tenements, only two floors away from the artificial community green space in the atrium courtyard below. Min Lei thought of Solomon Chow watching from the shadows as children played on the Astroturf.

'The doll is almost new,' he said, holding it up reverently. 'Do you have a daughter?' He grinned and bobbed his head. He had a round, nondescript face: one you might pass every day on the street and forget as soon as you saw him. His thick arms and barrel chest suggested physical work. 'She must be pretty, just like you.'

Min Lei forced a smile. 'It's a pity the doll has already been personalised. Was it your daughter's?' She glanced around the living room, even though she had previously noted the shabby couch and rickety coffee table in front of the television. There were no toys around, no pictures of any daughters who might resemble April on the walls, only large, framed photos of an older woman who bore a close resemblance to Solomon.

His face fell flat and anger simmered behind his eyes. 'My daughter wants nothing to do with me.'

'I'm sorry. That must be difficult.' She took a steadying breath. 'You said you found it?'

His sunny expression returned, as if a switch had been flipped. 'Someone left it in the green space. Can you believe it?'

'You didn't see who?'

Solomon stared at her and drew the doll back to his side. 'Why are you asking all these questions? I didn't steal it, if that's what you're implying.'

Min Lei held up her hands. 'Forgive me, Mr Chow. I chatter when I have an urge to shop.' She laughed girlishly and was relieved to see his shoulders relax. 'I'm very keen to buy.'

'Well, all right then. The list price is two hundred dollars.'

Min Lei winced inwardly but reached into her pocket and drew out the money. 'That seems fair. The doll is in very good condition.'

Solomon beamed and exchanged the doll for the notes. 'Yes, she's perfect.' His fingers brushed hers. They were doughy and clammy, despite the air conditioning. 'You're lucky. I had *many* other interested buyers.'

Min Lei nodded, careful to keep her expression pleasant. 'Thank you.' She carefully tucked the toy into the bag she had brought, praying there would be transfer—hair, skin… anything she could test against the database. It was a long shot: a doll that looked like a missing girl wasn't enough to get a warrant, never mind an arrest. And just because Chow had the doll in his possession didn't mean he had taken April.

She took a step towards the entry and he hurried to open the door for her.

Her back prickled; she could feel his eyes on her as she passed.

'Goodbye, miss,' Solomon said. 'Tell your daughter I said hello.'

The hum of the monorail to the Jurong Island Memorial Park was the only sound as Min Lei continued to search on her laptop. The families, couples, and singles visiting their late relatives sat without speaking. Although the government had made the facility as welcoming as possible, there was nothing comforting in travelling to an industrial island and heading a hundred and fifty metres below ground to pay your respects.

The petrochemical plant had been rendered obsolete with the global shift to greener technologies, and the massive underground storage caverns were ideal for housing the deceased. With every inch of the mainland earmarked for development, space was a premium the families of the dead could not afford to pay. Even cemeteries were being churned up to make way for industry.

According to Chow's Citizen Connect profile, he had been a maintenance worker at the park since 2026. He was divorced and had lived with his mother until her death a year ago. Mrs Chow had been interred in one of the crypts on the island.

Min Lei frowned and closed her computer as the monorail glided into the station that fed directly into the memorial park. None of Chow's neighbours knew him well, and although they had seen him at the green space, he rarely spoke to anyone. The man had virtually no online presence; apart from the details she had already trawled over, he was a ghost.

The doors opened and quiet murmuring started as people assisted elderly relatives and small children to exit. Min Lei stood, grateful that the cocoon of glum silence had broken.

The foyer was a holdover from when the facility had processed millions of litres of crude oil and naphtha. Severe, industrial and grey, it echoed with footsteps as the visitors made their way to the front desk to register.

'Detective Goh Min Lei.' She held up her ID for the receptionist to check. 'I have an appointment to speak with Supervisor Zeeshan Bhatt at two.'

Zeeshan Bhatt was a trim, brisk man in his fifties. He approached with a small computer tucked under his arm and spoke as quickly as he walked. 'I hope you don't mind talking as I do my inspections, Detective,' he said, leading the way to the lifts. They entered and he pressed a button to take them to the lower levels.

'Not at all,' Min Lei said. 'I haven't seen the storage caverns before.'

Bhatt's face lit up. 'Ah! You're in for a treat.' He turned to her with a cocked head. 'You said on the phone that you wanted to talk about Solomon. What is this about, if I may ask? Is he in trouble?'

Min Lei's ears blocked as they descended. She held her nose and blew, then shook her head. 'We're just asking some preliminary questions.'

The lift halted with a slight judder and the doors opened. 'That sounds like police-speak for "Don't ask".' Bhatt strode out into the vault.

Min Lei gaped then hurried to catch up. She had seen the brochures and infomercials, but nothing compared to seeing the facility for herself.

The access tunnel was large enough to house a Boeing 777. The floor was smooth, painted concrete, but the walls were unfinished rock and lit with halogens at intervals. Five immense, well-lit spaces opened up at the end of the tunnel.

They passed a similarly large shaft to the right which angled further down into the rock. It had been sealed off at the entrance with a heavy steel gate.

'What's down there?' Min Lei asked. The extra tunnel was not in the advertising.

'That's Gallery Number Six. JTC Corporation tried going deeper when the caverns were first excavated, but there was a catastrophic collapse. Don't worry. It's been shored up and, as you can see, sealed off from the public.' Bhatt pointed towards the five caverns ahead. 'These are the jewels in Jurong Memorial's crown.'

The caverns had to be at least three hundred metres long and thirty metres wide. Walls of concrete crypts marched back towards the rear of each space. Metal pipes ran along the length of the ceilings; they had once provided water curtains to soak the walls, keeping the liquid hydrocarbon contained. Now they funnelled any seawater seepage.

Workers moved up and down the aisles, replacing browned flowers, emptying stale water from grave vases, and sweeping the floors. Families knelt in front of panels on the walls here and there, bowing over electrical joss sticks. Although she understood the need to avoid naked flame, the ceremony felt empty without the sweet smoke. Soft music played in the background and ventilators whirred quietly. The scent of lilies filled the air, but couldn't quite disguise a faint chemical reek.

Bhatt led the way to the left-most cavern. 'Welcome to the Lee Kwan Yew Gallery, named, of course, after our first prime minister.'

'Mr Bhatt, what can you tell me about Solomon Chow?'

Bhatt slowed and faced her. 'Not much. He's an exemplary employee. Never tardy, very hardworking, keeps to himself, rarely needs to be written up.'

'Rarely?'

He hesitated then lowered his voice. 'Look, he's harmless. It was nothing.'

Min Lei waited.

'It was a once-off. He's never done it again.' He glanced around to check they were alone. 'If word got out, it would look bad for Jurong Memorial.'

'Mr Bhatt…' She weighed the risk. 'I'm investigating a missing children's case. Please. If there's something you know—'

'Oh goodness! No, no. It wasn't anything like that. He was caught changing some of the memorial plates around. He said they were in the wrong order. Of course, they were in the correct place. We check our records very carefully before burial.'

Min Lei deflated a little. Being a nuisance didn't condemn the man. 'Thank you for sharing that with me. If it has no bearing on the case, the incident won't be made public.' Still, she wondered how many families were paying respects to the wrong remains. The thought of her grandmother, one day, lying lost in one of these enormous vaults made her uneasy.

Bhatt ducked a bow. 'I would appreciate that. We do our best to honour the dead.'

'One final thing, was Mr Chow at work during these dates and times?' She showed him a list of the approximate timeframes the children had gone missing.

He pulled out his computer and called up a scheduling program, then nodded. 'Yes, like I said, Mr Chow is an excellent employee. He clocked in all these times.'

Min Lei let herself into her apartment and wearily toed off her boots. She had stopped by the station but there had been no further news on the children, nor on the forensics for the doll. Hunar had gone home for the night. She sank into her sofa and stared at the plastic bag containing takeaway noodles. It had been hours since she had eaten but she still had no appetite.

Her grandmother would scold her if she knew.

With a sigh, Min Lei drew out the chopsticks, tore the gold paper off and snapped the sticks apart. As she peeled the lid of the container, she stopped and stared at the wrapping. Pulse quickening, she put the container down and fished her phone out of her pocket. She scrolled to the link Hunar had sent her.

There.

Tucked beneath the doll was a faded yellow piece of paper. She had been so focused on April's face that she had missed it. What on earth was it? She enlarged the image and could make out some red logograms. She swore. Chinese was not one of her strengths. She debated sending a message to Hunar then checked the time. Finger hovering over her phone, she paused. It was after ten and he had a young family, and it was probably just another false lead.

It could wait until the morning.

The next day, Min Lei was still no further along on the case. The doll had returned no conclusive evidence that linked it to April Teo, nor any of the other missing children. The only strange detail was the traces of petrochemicals on its clothes. However, as Solomon Chow worked at the memorial park, that was hardly surprising.

The piece of paper was only partially visible in the photo, and Hunar could only say that the writing was something about protection.

Min Lei brought up the listing of the doll again. It now showed that the item had been sold.

It also showed a new message: the seller had another doll available.

Solomon Chow's apartment was deserted when she arrived. She cupped her hands around her face and peered into the front window, but apart from the same drab couch and coffee table, there was nothing to see.

'Damn it,' Min Lei muttered.

A child's cry echoed up from below and she hurried to the railing. Two levels down, in a corner of the atrium green space, a young girl backed away from a hulking man with a round head and a barrel chest. They were the only two people in the playground.

'Leave me alone!' the girl cried.

Min Lei dashed for the stairs. She clattered down, her boots barely making contact as she took each corner at a run. She hit the level two below Chow's apartment and sprinted towards the open area. Chow had the girl's thin arm in one meaty fist and was hauling her away. The child clawed at his hand and screamed, her toes just scraping the Astroturf.

'CHOW! PUT THE GIRL DOWN!' Min Lei bellowed.

He spun, dragging the girl in a stumbling circle. She cried out in pain.

'You!' he snarled. 'What do you want?'

'PUT HER DOWN!' Min Lei's hand inched towards her baton. She couldn't risk stray gunfire in such an enclosed space.

Chow yanked the girl against him. 'This is none of your business.'

Min Lei slowly reached into her jacket pocket and flipped open her ID. 'Police. Let the girl go.'

Fear flickered across his face. He shoved the child away and rushed at her. She stepped to the side, whipping her baton out and across the back of his knee. Chow collapsed with a howl. She landed a knee across his back, tugged his arms behind, and snapped cuffs on his wrists.

'Wei! What are you doing?' A woman shouted. 'Felicity, come here!'

The little girl shook her head and cowered at the other end of the playground.

Min Lei pushed to her feet. 'This man was trying to abduct your daughter.'

'Abduct?' The woman's face twisted with fury. She charged at Chow and fell on him, slapping and punching his face and head. 'Solomon, you fucking bastard! You'll never see her again!'

'Get her off! Get her off!' Chow screamed.

Min Lei dragged the woman back. 'Solomon? You know him?'

The woman swung her foot and connected solidly with Chow's side. He coiled over with a groan. 'Of course I know him,' she spat. 'He's my ex-husband. Worst mistake of my life.'

'Chow isn't going to press charges.' Min Lei's supervisor, Michael Tan, scowled from across his desk. 'But I've had to issue a *very* thorough apology.'

'I had reason to suspect he—'

'What? That his daughter—who he told you he had a difficult relationship with—was on a court-appointed visit?'

Min Lei clenched her jaw. 'She was screaming and he was hurting her.'

'The child has a history of behavioural issues. Family disputes are not our jurisdiction.'

'And what about child safety?'

Her supervisor raised a finger. 'Don't.' He sat back with a heavy exhale. 'I know this case is sensitive, and I know you're doing the work of two. Departmental cutbacks are affecting everyone. But you need to keep a level head. Understand? Do the work. Don't get emotional.'

Min Lei bit her tongue and nodded. 'Yes, sir.'

The congee was cold by the time Min Lei arrived at her grandmother's apartment. After visiting Market Street, she had stopped back at the station to check again on forensics and if Hunar had learned anything more about the writing on the yellow paper. But there was nothing new.

'Have you eaten yet?' her grandmother asked with a critical eye. 'You're no use to anyone if you waste away to nothing.'

Min Lei began setting out the containers. 'No, I wanted to eat dinner with you, Poh Poh.'

'Hah.' Ah Lam reached up and gave Min Lei's cheek a searching pinch. 'You'd better take the bigger bowl. You need it more than I do.' She picked up the container and shooed her away. 'This needs heating. Sit, sit. Tell me about your day.'

Min Lei sat with a sigh. 'What's to tell? I spent the day chasing my tail feathers.'

'Well, I'm an old woman with nothing much to do. Tell me anyway.'

The rhythm of her grandmother's pottering was soothing and Min Lei found some of her frustrations easing as she spoke. Ah Lam soon turned the simple rice porridge into a feast, with diced century eggs, stir fried greens, and sliced shallots. Min Lei's stomach woke with a grumble and she was about to take up her chopsticks and spoon when a thought occurred to her.

'Poh Poh, can you read this paper?' She brought up the photo of the original listing, magnifying the image.

Ah Lam shuddered. 'Ugh. Why would you give this thing to your child?'

'What about the paper?'

Her grandmother squinted at the screen then recoiled, staring at Min Lei in horror.

'What?' Min Lei cursed herself. She quickly tucked her phone away and put her hand on her grandmother's arm. 'Poh Poh, I'm sorry. I shouldn't have involved you.'

'*Jiangshi*,' Ah Lam whispered.

'What's jiangshi?'

Her grandmother was white as a funeral sheet. 'The spirits of those who are lost.'

Once she had managed to get her grandmother to eat a little and got her settled in bed, Min Lei pulled out her laptop and began searching. Ah

Lam would say nothing more, only that the yellow paper was some sort of talisman against the jiangshi.

Singapore was once a melting pot of cultures, with superstitions from all over Asia. The government had stamped out much of it, proudly proclaiming that the city state was at the forefront of scientific thought. Still, she managed to piece together what had frightened her grandmother.

The myth of the jiangshi—hopping vampire—had risen from the two-thousand-year-old practice of returning the deceased to their village when they had died far from home. The bodies were transported upright, strung on bamboo poles by walkers, giving the corpses the appearance of hopping. The pale, greenish complexion likely came from decomposition, and the long teeth and nails, from flesh that had shrivelled and receded.

The claims grew more outrageous after that. Taoist priests had been supposedly called on to reanimate the dead for the journey, and the yellow talismans were used to control them. Sometimes, the jiangshi became devoid of their souls and never returned home.

Min Lei's grandfather's shrine never had a speck of dust on it, and her grandmother placed fresh offerings every day. Ah Lam spoke often of living with her husband in the afterlife. The thought of wandering forever lost and alone after death must have been terrifying.

She stretched and felt her spine pop, then bent and continued to read. The next site claimed that jiangshi hunted people by their breath and fed on their *qi*—life force.

Jiangshi are created in many ways. Some were people who died of violence, or who had unfinished business; others return from death when a pregnant cat jumps over their grave.

Min Lei snorted.

Some were poor souls who were improperly buried.

She straightened. Solomon had been caught switching the memorial plates in the vaults. Did he have some delusion regarding the jiangshi? How was it related to the missing kids?

Min Lei pulled up Solomon Chow's listing. There was no yellow paper in the picture, only a doll this time. Another plaything that looked like someone's child somewhere. This one had been modelled after a boy of about eight: a happy open smile and a mop of black hair.

She searched the missing children's register, blinking gritty eyes as she peered at one photo after another. There were no cases that matched the doll in appearance. She closed the database and stared at the listing again.

Her stomach clenched. Chow had taken another child. *This* child. She could feel it. Michael told her not to get emotional, but there was no denying it: Solomon Chow was guilty.

Before she could change her mind, she tapped out a quick message, putting in a bid. Then she sat back, heart thrumming.

A moment later, a notification popped up. She had won the auction.

'No hard feelings, eh, Detective?' Chow limped over to the table where the doll was propped. 'Sorry for making you come out so late. I have to start work early tomorrow and my child support payment was due today. I really need the cash tonight. And, well, you've seen what my ex-wife is like.'

Min Lei glanced around the apartment as she trailed him, hoping for something that would be enough to warrant a search. The place was just as impersonal and joyless as before. 'Thank you for understanding, Mr Chow. Again, I apologise for any injury I caused you.'

He picked up the doll and held it out. 'Here, you can have a look. Make sure it's worth the price.'

She hesitated. What if he was just a strange, lonely man? She glanced at the doll and imagined the boy who owned this toy hidden somewhere that only Chow knew, crying, terrorised, alone.

She reached for it. Perhaps this time, there would be trace.

Chow's hand clamped on her wrist, swift as a viper's strike. The doll fell to the floor with a clattering thump. She twisted for her gun but something sharp drove into her forearm. Burning cold pumped beneath her skin and she saw the syringe empty as the room spun away.

The city lights played across her face as Min Lei slumped in the backseat of Chow's car. They drove over a speedbump and the shimmer across the windows danced. In a distant corner of her mind, a hazy alarm was sounding but she had no urge to do anything about it; instead, she watched the sparkling refractions and drifted.

They pulled to a stop outside the Jurong Island Memorial Park. She stared, entranced as the letters on the sign swam in dizzying circles. Chow climbed out and, using a portable computer that looked identical to his supervisor's, he opened the gate. A dim flicker: that must have been how he was able to clock in when he was busy doing… something. Her thoughts fractured again and melted away.

He got back in and glanced at her. She tried to ask him where they were going but only saliva dribbled out the side of her mouth. Chow reached back and wiped it away. She turned her head, too slow to avoid the taste of his fingers. He started the engine and drove in to the underground car park.

He heaved her onto his shoulder and Min Lei vomited helplessly. The half-digested congee flooded her nose and dribbled down his back, bitter and sour and savoury. She coughed and shuddered, working a tongue that felt too thick and unwieldy to clear her mouth.

'God damn it,' Chow muttered and shrugged her higher up.

Her stomach and ribs cried out and she batted at him weakly.

They entered the elevator and he nudged a button. Min Lei heard the doors close and felt a sudden, disconnected urge to cry.

When the doors opened again, Chow marched across the enormous tunnel that Min Lei recognised from her interview with Bhatt. They were heading towards the memorial vaults. What was Chow planning to do? Would he prise open one of the crypts and shove her inside? Perhaps he had emptied one in readiness to bury her alive. Perhaps he hadn't bothered and she would share the tiny, lightless, airless space with a corpse. She would suffocate, arms and legs pinned and useless, and he would change the memorial plate. No one would ever find her. This final thought broke her daze and she screamed, squirming.

Only an airless whistle came out.

He delivered a numbing punch to her thigh, then veered towards the steel gate that closed off the darkened entry of the sixth, collapsed tunnel. He drew out a key card and swung the gate open, then struggled down the stairs, leading them to a second gate, which opened to his card. He slid her off his shoulder, grazing and bruising her front.

They were before a mass collapse of stone and rubble. Chow lay her down then wrapped his arms around a large rock and, with muscles straining, slid it out of the way, revealing a man-sized opening.

Chow scooped her up and carried her through, like a grotesque groom bearing his bride across a threshold. He laid her on her side several feet inside the entrance on the levelled stone floor and disappeared into the bowels of the space. Faint putrescence, air deodoriser, and the sharp reek of formaldehyde filled her throat. The only source of light came from the gap they had come through, and she could just make out scattered rock and large, tumbled slabs here and there.

She forced herself to breathe, slow and deep. Her sour breath echoed back to her, giving the impression of a space much smaller than the galleries above.

Then she saw the shoes.

Min Lei blinked, heart tripping and stumbling, waiting in agonised stillness for her eyes to adjust fully.

They were women's heels, scuffed and furred with white mould. Her gaze travelled higher and she stifled a moan. Legs, mottled green, extended up from the heels, their upper half hidden in darkness. Was this one of Chow's victims? Did he take women as well as children?

Chow's footsteps echoed to the right. Min Lei tested her arms and legs cautiously; her muscles trembled but she felt a little stronger. She fumbled along the ground, found a fist-sized rock and quickly tucked it close against her stomach.

Light flared from a battery-operated lantern. He travelled first up one side of the cavern, then down the other, turning on lamps.

Min Lei reeled. *Oh God. Let the rock above crash down and bury them all.*

The shoes belonged to one of the many corpses standing upright and facing the body of an old woman tied to an ornately carved wooden chair, which was painted gold and inlaid with a red cushion. The corpses, green-tinged and unearthly still, were all shapes and sizes, men, women, and children, all in their funeral best, all with yellow paper talismans tacked to their foreheads.

He had pulled the dead from their crypts to create an underworld court.

The old woman looked like the empress of the court atop the golden chair, except beneath the ropes that crossed her body, she wore a fashionable jacket and skirt with a large fake chrysanthemum pinned to her lapel. She, too, had a faded piece of paper stuck on her face. Her unnaturally black hair had been permed but it was awry, as if she had slept on one side and forgotten to set it upon waking.

Several small, shrivelled bodies lay discarded on the ground at the old woman's feet, desiccated as cicada husks. One of them had a pointed chin and a page boy haircut.

April Teo.

Hate and terror flooded through Min Lei. What had Chow done to them?

Bowing once, Chow peeled the talisman from the old woman's forehead.

Her eyes opened, first one, then the other, milky and blank as dusty marbles.

Min Lei bit back a scream.

With a throaty hiss, the old woman peeled her lips, blackened jaws yawning wide as she stretched towards Solomon like a sunflower seeking bright nourishment. He gently patted her age-spotted wrist. 'Don't worry, Ma. I brought something for you.'

He went to a darkened corner and picked up a limp bundle. The small head lolled and Min Lei saw, with a breaking heart, the mop of dark hair. The boy moaned softly and Chow's mother lunged against her restraints, seeking the source of the noise, nostrils flaring.

Min Lei pushed herself up onto her hands and knees, inch by inch. Chow regarded his mother with reverence and seemed not to notice.

He lay the boy across the old woman's lap and raised his small face to hers. She snuffled hungrily, mouth working across his cheek like the foot of an ancient mollusc. The boy squirmed and whimpered.

The old woman clamped her lips around the boy's mouth and nose, neck corded with sudden strength. He gave a muffled shriek and thrashed, but Chow held him firm. The roundness in the boy's face deflated, his eyes sucked inward.

Min Lei lurched to her feet and charged clumsily. Chow's eyes widened as she brought the rock down with a crack on his temple. He grunted and collapsed to his knees, clutching his head as she stumbled and crashed beside him. The boy hung from the old woman's mouth, no longer struggling. Min Lei pulled herself up and tugged at him but the old woman hunched over his body possessively, eyes rolled back as she fed. Min Lei grabbed the rock again and smashed it into the old woman's face, shattering her eye socket. Pale ichor exploded from her milky eyeball and she released the boy. Min Lei caught him as he tumbled, loose-limbed. He weighed no more than a paper doll and his eyes were half-open and lifeless.

Chow staggered upright and stared at his mother in horror. 'Ma! No, no, no.' He cradled her face with trembling hands then turned on Min Lei 'You ruined her!'

He tore the boy from her arms and dragged Min Lei before his mother. The old woman inhaled hungrily through browned teeth. Min Lei clawed at his hands, kicking at his legs. He slammed a fist into her stomach and she folded to the ground, mouth opening and closing uselessly, all breath driven from her body.

Chow tugged at the ropes tying his mother to the chair. 'You'll pay, you stupid bitch.' He yanked the last knot free and stepped back.

His mother slowly stood, scenting the air.

Min Lei tried to push upright. Her gut and chest were on fire. Her head thudded. She desperately sucked for breath.

'Punish her, Ma,' Chow whispered.

The old woman rolled her good eye towards her son and lunged for him.

Chow wailed and together, they crashed to the ground.

'No!' Chow cried. He fought to keep her mindlessly gawping mouth from his, cupping his hands around her head. 'Please, Ma. Don't I look after you?'

Min Lei's diaphragm unlocked and she sucked in a mighty breath of putrid air. She pressed her hand over her mouth and rolled away, scrambling as far as she could from Chow and his mother.

The old woman reared back and dove at his face, cracking her forehead against his nose. His hands slipped and she clamped her lips over his. Chow screamed and battered at her with powerful blows, knocking her loose. He hurled her away, and with no instinct to preserve herself, the old woman struck a rock slab like a doll; her arm and leg snapped. The leg bent back at a terrible angle as she twisted and clawed towards him.

'No, Ma.' Chow wept bitterly, scooting back. She reached for his ankle and pulled herself arm over arm towards his face. He sobbed and pushed her away, but still, she sought his mouth. He scrabbled for a rock and brought it down. Keening, he raised it over and over, pulverising his mother's head, shattering her skull, matting her hair with grey curds. 'I'm sorry. I'm sorry.'

Min Lei scrambled for the exit, reached it, and slammed the gate behind. She spun, sure he would be right at her heels.

Chow had not moved. He gently pushed his mother's body off his legs and got up. Tears dripped down his chin as he hauled barrels from the back of the cavern, positioned them every few metres, twisted the lids open, and kicked them over. The sweet, heady smell of petrol flooded the area. The jiangshi stood motionless.

'Solomon, what are you doing?' Min Lei asked. 'These people deserve to be buried.'

He turned to her and drew out a lighter from his pocket. 'Burn in hell.' He flicked his thumb over the flint wheel.

Min Lei turned and ran for the first gate. There was a *whomp* behind her and a hard, hot shove at her back. She sprawled, skinning her hands and chin. A klaxon sounded and water burst from the ceiling. Sprinklers flooded the tunnel and water gushed from the floor above. Min Lei spluttered, tasting seawater. One of the pipes from the upper galleries must have ruptured. The heat from the cavern evaporated as hundreds of litres doused the fires. She grabbed the rail and held on as more and more water fell. Finally, the sprinklers sputtered to a stop and the flow eased.

Whimpering echoed up from the tunnel. Min Lei struggled back down. The gate was almost fully submerged and Chow clung to the bars, shuddering uncontrollably. His head was seared bald, and his skin was black and white and pink and hideously raw.

'Solomon, give me the key card! I'll open the gate!'

He shook his head.

A rectangle of yellow paper floated past him. His weeping eyes followed its slow passage and he moaned wordlessly.

'Solomon! Hurry!'

Another talisman drifted past. Then another and another, until the water became a sea of yellow. Hands reached for him, blackened and clawed from the heat. Gaping mouths yawned from beneath the water. Solomon Chow let go and allowed them to take him.

The Question

ALAN BAXTER

"DADDY," MAX'S VOICE WAS A WHISPER. "WHERE DO WE GO WHEN WE DIE?"

Carl stared at his son's pale, thin face. At the tube running from his nostril, taped to his cheek. His frame under the light sheet was skeletal. Machines blipped and hissed around the bed. Carl clenched his teeth, held in tears. It wasn't the first time Max had asked.

"I don't know for sure, kid." He reached out, stroked Max's soft, dry brow. He remembered when strawberry blond curls used to cover it. "But what I *do* know? We go somewhere beautiful, so peaceful, where nothing ever hurts. You're never hungry. You *never* get sick."

Carl had no idea if he really believed that. He certainly never used to, but what the hell else could he tell a seven-year-old? The cold brutality of the boy's sickness belied any chance of a benevolent creator, so why would there be anywhere to go? Or was that the ultimate test? He'd hate any being who might devise such cruelty, but the simple truth was, he didn't know. No one *knew*, no matter what they did or didn't believe. So he held onto the possibility, because without it, he was untethered, lost and adrift with no hope of ever being found.

Despite the disease, Max's eyes remained the same, and they were full of tears. If Carl did his best to ignore the rest, focused only on those wide, innocent, frightened eyes, he remembered the wonderful, energetic, vibrant boy Max had been.

"But I'll be on my own," Max said, tears breaching.

Carl felt as if he'd been punched, unable to hold his grief any longer. No child should die like this. No parent should watch their child waste away in fear and confusion. He clasped Max's cool hand in both of his. "You'll want for nothing, my sweet boy. I promise."

"I don't want to be by myself. Daddy, when I die, will you die too? Please? So I'm not there alone?"

Carl's tears flowed unchecked. He leaned forward, kissed his son's cheek, his lips, his forehead. He pressed his brow against Max's. "Of course, darling. I'll take care of you."

What other answer was there?

Sandra came back into the room a while later, found them like that, Carl's forehead pressed to his son's. Max had fallen asleep again. Sandra sat beside Carl, lay her arm across his shoulders.

"He woke for a minute," Carl said.

"Enough to talk?"

"A few words."

Sandra smiled, but there was only pain in her eyes. "I missed it." She sucked in a quick breath. "You need to rest?" she asked.

"Not right now." He reached out, one hand holding Max's, the other on his wife's knee.

They sat that way for hours, a tiny, grief-laden family. Eventually Carl moved to the armchair nearby and slept. Sandra switched with him the following morning.

Max didn't wake again.

Sandra's brother took both her hands in his. "Love you, Sis."

"Thank you, Pete. You've been a rock."

Pete glanced at Carl, slumped in the armchair, eyes half-closed. "You going to be okay?" he asked. "At least… you know what I mean."

"I'll be all right." She swallowed tears, knew she could let go later, in private.

"He going to be okay?" Peter nodded towards Carl. "He drank a lot today."

"Drinks a lot every day," Sandra said. "Since Max went."

"Anything I can do?"

"Just be around. It helps."

"Okay. You need a hand tidying up?"

Sandra looked at all the cups and glasses, plates and bowls strewn about their home. *The wake of a wake*, she thought. "No, thanks. I have energy to work off. Sitting through the service was… hard."

"You're not wrong. I can't imagine how much harder for you and Carl than the rest of us."

Sandra went up on tiptoes to kiss her little brother's cheek. "You get home. Back to your clan. We'll see you soon."

"Call. For anything."

"I will."

As the front door clicked, Sandra began the clean-up. This marked the end of it. Now they were Sandra and Carl, not Sandra, Carl, and Max.

Carl stood, weaved a little left and right, then went for another bourbon.

"Honey, be careful," Sandra said.

He grunted, poured a measure, swallowed it in one. Poured another. He staggered back to the armchair, glanced up at the ceiling, like he was listening, winced. He sat sipping while she tidied. By the time she was done he'd passed out. She went to bed.

Sandra leaned on the doorframe between the garage and house. Carl hadn't noticed she was there. He stared up into one corner, the engine part he'd been cleaning forgotten. He wore an expression of discomfort, something close to pain.

"Max?" he said softly. It was a question.

Something in Sandra's heart pulled tight. She glanced up to where he looked, saw nothing but a dusty cobweb.

Carl's face scrunched up a little more. "I'm sorry!" His tone was plaintive.

"You okay, love?" Sandra asked.

He flinched, looked over. "I guess."

"I miss him too."

Carl nodded. He held her eye for a moment, as if he might say something, then just nodded again and returned his attention to the engine part.

"You going back to work on Monday?" Sandra asked.

"Suppose I should."

"It's not so bad, you know. Being back at work, I mean." She'd been back a few days already, like an automaton. Acting like herself, some stilted puppet play of normalcy. She figured if she kept acting the part, perhaps it would eventually come true. Why couldn't Carl? She didn't want to be angry with him, but she was. Even though the raw, aching, wound of Max's absence filled her mind to its limits, she still thought around it as much as possible. Forced other activities, despite the all-consuming black weight. Carl should do that. They should do it together. "It gives you something else to occupy your mind."

He didn't answer. After another few moments, she slipped away.

Sandra looked towards the bedroom door, frowned. "I don't think so, Steve. Sorry."

"I don't want to be a dick," Steve said, struggling for the right words. "Only it's been three weeks."

"I know. Can you give us a bit longer?"

"Sure," Steve said. "I'll wait until next Monday, but if he's not back then… well, that's a month. We can't carry over for so long. I'll have to get someone else in."

"I get it, Steve. Next time I'll *make* him come to the phone, talk to you himself."

"You do that. I'll verbally kick his arse."

"Someone fucking needs to." Sandra sucked in a quick breath. "Sorry, that's not fair on you. It's not your job. Neither is hearing my anger."

"It's okay, really. I'm so sorry, Sandy. I mean, for everything. Fucking hell, if I could afford to hold his position for a year, I would."

"I know, mate. Thanks."

Sandra hung up, went to the bedroom door. She supposed she should be grateful Carl had made it to bed this time, but the thick alcohol fug that hung in the room made her cringe. "Honey, please get up? I have to leave for work, but do something today, yeah."

"What's the point?" His voice was gravelly.

"We have to try—"

"Try what?" he snapped, leaning up on one elbow. Hair in disarray, eyes dark and sallow, red-rimmed. "Try to go on like normal? Live our lives? Pretend like he's not dead?"

"Yes, live our lives, Carl, but we'll *never* pretend he's not dead. How dare you! We'll always remember him. Honour him." Her rough and tumble like bloke, all giggles and attitude. Rambunctious, her mother always called him.

Carl just stared at her, and that made her grind her teeth. She had enough grief for both of them, shouldn't have to babysit the man who was supposed to be with her in this.

"We can honour his memory by *living*, Carl. I've been looking into setting up a charitable trust in his name and—"

"I hear him, you know."

"What?"

Carl sat up, though his spine slumped like a weak sapling needing water. He looked at her with hollow eyes. "He calls me."

Something softened in Sandra and she moved to the bed, sat beside Carl. She tried not to let her horror at the smell of him show. "Honey, it's grief."

"No, it's not. He's alone. And he's scared."

"We don't know—"

"I know you don't believe. Me either. So secular, aren't we? We brought Max up that way, question everything, don't believe people who claim to have all the answers. But you're right. We *don't* know. I know you think it just ends. Life. Like a light switching off, that's it. Before now, that was my thought too. Seemed most likely. Feels like hubris to think differently." Carl looked up, maybe realised he was rambling. It was the most he'd said since Max died. "But I *hear* him, Sandy."

"What do you hear?"

"He's calling for me."

"Oh, Carl." Despite the odour, she leaned her head against his. "I miss him so much, it hurts."

"Me too."

They cried together for a while, then Carl said, "I need to tell you something."

"Okay."

"The night before he died, he woke briefly."

"I remember." She'd missed her little boy's last words. She'd asked Carl what Max had said and her husband claimed he couldn't remember. She knew that wasn't true.

Carl nodded. "He asked me again where he would go."

"Oh!" Sandra sobbed, unable to hold back the tide of grief that threatened to drown her.

"I told him it would be somewhere beautiful, peaceful, where no one would get sick. But he said he'd be alone there. And he asked me to die too, to be with him."

"Carl!" Sandra sat back, eyes wide. How could her beautiful little boy ever be expected to deal with thoughts like that? And why the hell had Carl not told her until now?

"And I told him I would!" Carl almost wailed.

Carl's admission sent him deeper into darkness. At first, Sandra thought maybe unburdening himself of the guilt of their last conversation would help him move past it. What a thing to agree to. The weight of it had to be soul-destroying. She would have told Max the exact same thing, of course. Despite knowing it would make no difference now, she would have agreed as well.

"I mean, nothing's really changed my mind about death," she told her brother over takeaway coffee in town, sitting on a bench in the sunshine. "But even if there was something else, surely our little boy would be all right there, without us. Without Carl. Surely."

"Of course," Pete said. "I don't know what I believe, but I think if there is something after this, no one would be lonely there. That doesn't… well, it doesn't make sense, does it?"

"Can you imagine Cody or Charlotte dying and…" Sandra stopped herself. "Sorry, I shouldn't even suggest hypotheticals about your kids."

"I get it. And no, if they died, I don't think I'd imagine they were alone."

"Of all the shit we've dealt with," Sandra snapped. "Now he's doing this. I'm the one who feels alone here, you know!" She ground her teeth a moment. "Shit, I shouldn't say that."

Pete put an arm around her shoulders, pulled her tight. "Without

Carl's support, you are alone. And that's not fair. It's okay to be angry. At Carl, at death, even at Max."

"Carl's given up even the pretence of a life. He'd spent a couple of weeks bumbling around the house after the funeral, fixing things that had been let go, tinkering with his old Holden in the garage." Sandra sniffed, wiped a sleeve across her eyes. "Despite avoiding any real conversation, he still moved around. But now he just stares at the TV and drinks."

"You want me to come around? I don't mind kicking his arse if I have to."

Sandra laughed despite her anger. "I don't think we're at that point yet."

It's only when I'm properly drunk that I can't hear him any more! he'd yelled at her the night before, his words an almost incoherent slur.

He's not really calling you! she'd shot back. *You have to let him go!*

The words had stung her, but they hit Carl like a bullet. He refused to say more, swallowed bourbon, and was unconscious within minutes.

"Then again," she said to Paul. "Maybe you talking to him might help."

"I'm happy to. And maybe he needs professional help."

Her boss was generous, gave her the day off. It was Friday, after all, he said. Take a long weekend.

"It comes and goes," she told him, scraped empty inside by Carl's continuing slide. "Some days are harder, you know?"

"Of course. I'll see you Monday."

Carl was already drinking again, liquid breakfast now. He was dropping weight fast, hardly eating, barely moving. The parallel to watching Max waste away through no fault of his own made her furious. She wanted to be sympathetic to Carl, but he was doing this to himself. Why couldn't he try harder?

But I hear *him, Sandy.*

Could it be true? Even as she thought it, Carl stiffened in the chair, looked up, then around himself. He caught her eye, his brow tightened. "You hear?" he asked desperately.

She shook her head, lost for words.

"You really can't hear him? Calling for me?" Carl drank, straight from the bottle. He hadn't used a glass in days.

"We need food," Sandra said stiffly. It was true, even if Carl wasn't eating. But more, she needed to be away from him. She drove to the supermarket, imagined him there drinking the bottle dry. She'd stopped buying alcohol, but he ordered it online, delivered right to the door.

She wished she *could* hear Max. Carl had spoken to him one last time and she'd missed it. Now Carl claimed to hear him still. It wasn't fair. Just once more, his high, beautiful voice. Just once more hear him say, "Mummy!"

She went back to work on Monday and Carl continued drinking. His job was gone. They would soon start to struggle on only one income.

When she got home at six he was out cold, stretched along the sofa, a pool of vomit on the floorboards beside it.

"Fucking hell," she muttered, went to get a mop and bucket.

As she cleaned, she saw his jeans were stained with piss. He was nearly as dead as Max, she thought. Maybe that was it, trying to kill himself with drink. See through his promise.

The next morning she physically pulled him from the couch to thump onto the floor. He cursed and complained and she yelled and insisted he shower and change and shave. He stumbled around, numbly complying. She cooked toast and scrambled eggs while he cried in the shower, then she went to get him. She screamed at him until he came downstairs and ate some food.

Vaguely restored by the wash and the sustenance, he watched her across the table as she stared at him in fury.

"I'm sorry, Sandy."

"Are you? Why are you leaving me to deal with all of this? We're supposed to be in it together."

He hung his head. "I need to die."

"You do not!" she snapped. "You need to *live*. For him!"

"I need to *die* for him!" Carl shouted back. "I promised I would! But what if they're right and I go somewhere else?"

"What? Who?"

"Religion. What if religion is right? They all say suicide is a sin. What if Max is lonely, needs his Daddy, but I go to hell and he's still alone? Huh? What then?"

"Carl. You're not making sense. If there is something after, Max is okay. The whole idea of an afterlife is that people are okay. Your dad is already there, right? Max loved his Gramps." It sounded absurd, but by Carl's logic, wouldn't that help?

Carl looked up sharply. "Then why do I hear him?"

"It's in your mind. It's grief."

"He's so scared, Sandy. He calls for me over and over again and he says, 'You promised!' and the betrayal in his voice is like knives."

Sandy sucked in a steadying breath. "So what can you do? If you carry on the way you're going, you'll drink yourself to death. You *know* that's what you're doing. That's suicide."

His face fell, eyes suddenly bereft. It hurt her to hurt him, but she was so angry, and so tired.

"Pull yourself together, Carl. You can't kill yourself, so what *can* you do?"

"Sandy, he needs me!"

She shrugged. "Stop drinking. Go to work. Maybe Steve will still let you back, perhaps he hasn't filled the job yet. And hey, maybe you'll be lucky and get hit by a bus on your way. Just don't step out in front of it deliberately, because that's suicide too."

Red hot with rage, blackened by grief, she stood and strode from the house.

He was less drunk than usual when she returned, but far from sober. His face was drawn, eyes sunken. He looked up when she came in.

"Everything I can think of works out to be suicide!"

She frowned. "What?"

"I've spent all day trying to think of a way to join him, but every single thing I come up with comes down to suicide in the end. Dangerous sports, going to a war torn country. Every option is me trying to find death and that fundamentally boils down to suicide. I can't take the chance. I can't even ask someone else to kill me because that's the same thing! Isn't it?"

She wouldn't debate this madness with him. "So you have to live."

Tears poured over Carl's cheeks as he looked at her. "He's been calling for me *all* day, Sandy!"

"I've made you an appointment with Doctor Rada Yevshenkova." Sandy held up a hand to forestall his protests. "I don't want to hear a word about it. She's a very well-respected psychiatrist and specialises in grief counselling. You *are* going to see her. You have a session on Wednesday afternoon, another on Friday afternoon, and you're going back to work on Monday. Steve said he can find you something."

She drove him, taking another afternoon off herself. Her boss was accommodating, but she knew she couldn't push him much longer. She sat outside while Carl was with the doctor, then drove him home again.

"How did it go?"

"Nice lady. I expected someone older, she's only about thirty."

"Did it help?"

"She's very good. We talked about grief and how to start getting on with life despite the pain. She talked about how we can use the pain as a focus, not try to deny it, but accept it and move with it."

"Sounds like it makes sense."

"Yeah. Like I said, very good."

Sandra felt a glimmer of hope. The first flicker since palliative care for Max had been declared. "I'm glad," she said, putting a hand on Carl's knee. "And you'll see her again on Friday. Hopefully cement some of that down?"

He looked over at her and she glanced across as she drove. Tears glistened on his cheeks. "Max cried for me the whole time I was there."

She began to wonder. What if Carl was right? He'd been a stable man all his life, all the time she'd known him. When his father died, Carl had been broken by grief for a time, but he was stoic too. He made arrangements, comforted his mother. He functioned. And his father hadn't been especially old, the man's death was unjust, really.

Of course, to lose his son was entirely different, incomparable, but all the way up to the night Max had died, Carl had been his reliable self. They cried and raged as Max's cancer progressed. They had been bereft and inconsolable, but they persisted together, held each other up. Carl functioned then too.

Right up until Max asked that question.

Will you die too?

Was that single request enough to break a man into pieces?

Time passed, and Carl grew more and more empty inside. He continued to see Yevshenkova. He returned to work. Once he fully realised that any other option was suicide, and therefore unacceptable, he fell forward through life. But he became a shell of himself, hollow and tortured and utterly convinced Max was alone and scared and calling for him. Every day, he said, their boy was crying for his father. Carl's eyes sank, he grew thin and unsteady, convinced he was failing his son over and over.

Steve rang her, assured her he was glad to see Carl back at work, but he was worried. "He's only sorta half-here."

"I know," she said.

"I'm worried he's going to cause an accident. Hurt himself. Or someone else."

"I get that, Steve. But please, give him a chance. He's trying to find his way back." She wasn't sure she believed it.

Steve was quiet for a while, just his soft breathing over the line. "Okay," he said eventually. "For now. But I have to watch him all the time. It's… not sustainable, you know?"

"Thank you, Steve. I'm sorry."

What if Carl was right? What if their son *was* lost and alone and scared? Even if there was a heaven, Max was a frightened seven-year-old boy who needed his parents. Maybe that's why Carl suffered so much, because it *was* real.

"It's constant, Sandy," Carl said one night as they lay in bed. "How can you not hear him?"

"What should I hear?"

"He's just sobbing and quietly saying, 'Daddy, Daddy, please!' over and over."

"Does he ever call for me?"

"Sometimes. He cries and says 'Mummy', like he misses you. But I made the promise. I'm the one he's expecting. The one failing to do what I said I would."

Carl shuddered in a breath. He seemed to cry all night, every night. He still drank, he barely slept. There was no joy left in him.

"How can it be real, honey?"

"I don't know," he managed. "I don't understand. I don't *want* it to be this way. But it is!" He leaned up on an elbow, face dappled by moonlight leaking through the curtains. "I'm only forty-four, Sandy. What if I live another forty years? Or fifty? Max will be alone all that time!"

She gathered him in her arms and held him. What else was there to do?

In the depth of the night, Carl slept. Sandy woke, unsure why. A distant voice drifted through the dark. "Mummy? *Where's* Daddy?"

She started, heart pounding, wide awake.

It must have been a dream. Surely.

"I know it's only ten Ks away," Sandra said. "But it's about hanging out and having fun, you know? Just a couple of days."

Carl tried to smile. "It's a good idea. A fancy spa like that? We're lucky to have it so close by."

"Thank you. We'll get massages and manicures and all that shit, but mostly we'll drink and gossip. Make ourselves feel special."

"You are special."

She knew he meant it, but it came from a blank, ashen face. He glanced up briefly, listening, winced, then took her into a hug. Had she heard a whisper too?

"Have fun," he said.

"Don't drink too much, yeah?"

"Sure."

The Hyacinth Day Spa and Holistic Retreat was in a fancy sandstone building with a long, tree-lined driveway. She went through the motions of enjoying the time with her friends, but anticipation made her stomach churn. A little after midnight she slipped from the window of her ground floor room and walked the long driveway, all in black. She wore a balaclava rolled up into a beanie, black leather gloves on her hands. Ten kilometres, only ten minutes' drive on the country roads, would take around two hours to walk, according to Google maps. She'd be back in her room well before dawn.

It turned out the map was generous. She got to her house around 1.40am. Her heart raced, her mouth dry. Without pausing to think, she used the butt of a large bowie knife to smash out the small window closest to the deadlock on their front door, hoping he wouldn't hear. She reached through, opened the door, went in. The new bottle of Jack Daniels she'd left in the kitchen stood on the counter, almost empty. Had he suspected?

Her legs were jelly as she climbed the stairs, pushed open the bedroom door. He snored. Tears soaking the wool of the balaclava now pulled over her face, she pushed on his shoulder to roll him onto his back. He grumbled and said something, muffled and lost in the thickness of drunken slumber. His eyes flickered and half-opened.

"I love you, Carl," she said. "Be with him."

And the knife came down with a meaty *thock* into his chest, again and again.

Miss Jam

CHRIS MASON

IT WAS TWO IN THE MORNING AND RAINING STEADILY. SENIOR CONSTABLE Lois Grainger stepped to the edge of the giant hole in the ground. She shone her torch over old car bodies, mattress springs and tyres, fridges, fence posts and tangled rolls of rusted wire.

"What do you think it is? A sinkhole?" asked Ben Miller, her junior recruit.

"No idea," said Lois. Half the size of a soccer field, the open pit appeared to be as deep as it was wide. The drop over the side where Lois stood went straight down. In the bottom, rising from a lake of muddy water, was the mound of hard rubbish. The back walls of factories, tall windowless slabs of brick and concrete, bordered the hole on three sides, with barely an arms width between the walls and the drop off. It made Lois feel like she was looking into a box. Behind her was the overgrown backyard belonging to the property they'd been called to. A rotting wooden fence covered in ivy, the palings either loose or missing, provided little safeguard to anyone unaware, from wandering in and plummeting to their death. On the far side of the property, making no sense at all given the ease of access through the yard, was a laneway; a dark corridor of cobblestones contained within a high brick fence with broken glass set into the top. At the end of it was a three metre, padlocked iron gate. From the street, the hole in the ground was completely hidden from view. Lois thought it a sinister version of a secret garden.

"How deep do you think the water is. Do you think it gets wider at the bottom? It goes back under where we're standing?" asked Miller.

Lois shrugged. "Dunno. I think I've seen enough."

"What if someone's down there." He peered into the darkness.

"I doubt it. Only way in is the way we came. I don't see footprints, any other sign of entry, do you?"

"No, but–"

There was always a 'but' with Miller. "You hear anyone calling for help?" asked Lois.

"No."

"Can you *see* anyone down there?"

"No, but I think—"

"So, you're thinking now? That's a first." Lois sighed. She was at that late stage in her career where she had close to zero fucks left to give. What she did have, she certainly wasn't wasting on Miller. She'd never considered herself a great cop. Probably wasn't much of a good one either if she were honest. Not anymore. Forty years on the force, most of it working night patrol in the northern suburbs, had blunted her soul. Three years ago, she'd asked for reassignment—desk duties and daylight hours—but been denied. The best thing on offer had been a transfer to the western division to babysit new recruits. Apparently, her age and owning a pair of tits gave off a maternal vibe. Lois cut her losses. Her knees weren't up for running, nor was her ticker. She was tired most of the time. At least, she'd thought, she could sit in the car while the young pups did all the leg work. Not so with Miller. He rarely gave her any peace.

He went on, clearly fixated with what he'd found. "Everything is old. The cars are vintage. And see that wringer washing machine? My gran had one of those."

"Fabulous," said Lois.

"Hang on." Miller held up his hand. "Do you hear that?"

Lois listened. It was difficult to hear anything with the amount of rain falling. But she could hear something… a bicycle bell? She frowned. No, water dripping on metal, that was all. She directed the circle of light straight down and caught what looked like a figure crouched atop the hood of a car. Lois blinked and it was gone. Shadows. Too many shadows. The place was fucking with her. "I don't hear or see anything. Let's go."

Miller pointed to an area near the gate where the ground sloped rather than fell away. The angle was steep, but it wasn't the suicide drop they were looking over. "I bet I can get down from over there."

"Why?"

"Get a better look."

"At what?"

He waved his torch at the pit. "All this stuff. The cars alone must be worth a mint."

Great. The real reason he'd dragged her out here in the rain wasn't because he was concerned for public safety, but because he had a hard on for a car wreck.

Lois put a hand on her spine and arched her back. Her muscles were tight. The cold wasn't helping. "Here's an idea, why don't you come back in the morning when you're on your own time."

Miller took off, edging his way along the fence line to where the gate was.

She wondered why she bothered. In her job, Lois had seen a lot of stupid, but it never surprised her how often it showed up wearing a uniform. The new generation of cop was a different animal to what she was used to. They came with an unhealthy combination of arrogance and ambition, a lack of critical thinking, and the inability to cope with the fact Lois didn't adhere to the rulebook. Some were just basement level dumb. Either way, it was a rare bird who got past her bullshit filter. Lois gave them all plenty of rope to hang themselves. Failure, according to the gospel of St Lois, was the best leveller. She broke them all in the first six months. It was the one thing she was good at.

Constable Ben Miller had been with her five and a half months and hadn't come close to breaking. The kid was made of Teflon. Another few weeks and he'd be let loose in the community. *God help us all.* Lois hadn't made her mind up yet what was going to get him killed. All she knew was that day, without a doubt, was coming.

"Yeah, I'm right, this looks like a good access point," Miller yelled. "Are you coming?"

Sure. Slide right on in there and skewer myself on a piece of rusted pipe then freeze my arse off in the dark, while I wait for help. Yeah, nah. Not going to happen. All she wanted was to get home, have a hot bath, and order in pizza. Maybe a couple of beers in front of the TV. Then sleep. After that, she was going to have a long hard think about retirement. She couldn't keep doing this shit.

Lois blew into her hands to warm them up. "All yours, sunshine. I'll meet you back at the house. I want to check we haven't missed anything."

What she could have said… perhaps should have said, as his supervising officer, was *get your arse back here now or your probationary report won't be worth shit,* but she didn't. Which was why things ended up the way they did.

Lois ducked through the gap in the fence. There was an orange tree in the yard. The fruit had been picked over by birds, and what was on the ground chewed by rats. The smell of citrus lingered, sickly sweet. Lois wondered why anyone would put a house so close to a rubbish dump. The hole was practically in the backyard. She stepped through tall grass and onto the back porch of the pre-war worker's cottage. It was one of two remaining in the street. The rest of the neighbourhood had been invaded by light industry, warehouses, and automotive repair shops. Why on God's earth was anyone still living there?

Glad to be out of the rain, Lois searched the house again. It had a simple layout. There were two front rooms, a kitchen, a small bathroom, and a washhouse with a concrete laundry trough. A hallway—the front door at one end and the backdoor at the other—ran right through the middle. The place was derelict. There were cracks in the walls you could put a hand through, the floorboards were rotted through in places, and paint flaked from the plaster like bad dandruff. In the corner of the kitchen, the ceiling had given way, exposing rafters coated in pigeon poop. The rooms were all furnished, albeit everything covered in a thick layer of dust. There were books on shelves, cups and bowls and decorated plates in the cabinets, biscuit tins and cutlery on the kitchen table. Crocheted cushions sat on every chair. Framed photos adorned the walls—sepia faces from a distant past. It was if time had stood still. There was no power connected. Viewed in snatches of light from the torch, the house looked just as creepy as the hole out back. As far as Lois could tell there were no signs of recent habitation. Yet an emergency call had come from this address. A woman saying she had an intruder in her house.

In the bedroom, floorboards creaked—the sound of weight shifting. Someone was in the room with Lois. Hand on her gun, she spun around. An elderly woman dressed in a pink candlewick dressing gown, her silver hair plaited and wound tight around her head, squinted up at her. Her open mouth was all gums.

"Where did you come from?" said Lois, startled.

"Sorry, didn't mean to scare you."

"Are you the lady who called 000?"

"No dear. I live across the road."

"Why are you here?"

"I saw the police car pull up out front. I said to myself, must be trouble at Miss Jam's again."

Lois relaxed. "And you are?"

"Olive Langmore."

"And this… Miss Jam… do you know where she might be?"

"She ought to be resting."

Lois had checked the whole house twice over and not found anyone. "Resting? Where?"

"Centennial Park."

"The cemetery?"

"That's where they put her."

"The owner of the property is deceased?"

"She died in 1946."

"1946?"

"Yes, dear."

Lois bit into her bottom lip. If this kept up, it would be a long night. "So, who lives here now?"

"If you don't count possums or pigeons... no one. This house has been empty since they found Miss Jam in that big old hole out back. She jumped you know."

"Ms Langmore—"

"You can call me Olive."

"Olive, how long have you lived across the road?"

"Eighty-six years. I was born there."

"You never left?"

"No, I never did. Inherited the house early and decided I liked it well enough to stay. The council wants to kick me out, but I got me a lawyer. He says until they offer a good amount I can stay put. Tell the truth, I don't want their money. I'd rather keep my house. The council's trying to get this one too, but it's heritage listed because Miss Jam's family owned all the land around here once. Won't stop the buggers though. They'll find a way to rip it down, you wait and see."

"And you live alone?"

"Always have. Never needed a husband. Too much like hard work."

Lois tried not to smile. "Olive, we received a distress call from someone who said there was an intruder in this house. Do you know who made that call?"

Olive's head turned towards a black Bakelite rotary dial telephone. It sat on top of a pile of mouldy magazines on the dresser. "Miss Jam's up to her old tricks again by the sound of it."

Lois picked up the handset. There was no dial tone. "Well, it seems someone's playing tricks." What she couldn't figure out was whether it was Olive or not.

"Every time a call comes from that phone, there's trouble," said Olive.

"What kind of trouble?"

"Boys go missing."

"I see."

Olive wagged a finger at her. "Now don't you go giving me that look."

"What look?"

"Like I'm senile. Like I don't know what I'm talking about. No one ever listens. I've seen her."

"I'm sorry, Olive, but I'm having difficulty understanding what's going on here." Lois replaced the handset. "Who has gone missing?"

"Let me think for a minute."

Lois noticed the hem of Olive's dressing gown was splashed with mud. Her slippers were the same.

"That boy, Wayne Sutter for starters. Only fifteen when he disappeared."

The name didn't ring any bells. "What makes you think Wayne got a phone call?"

"I heard from the butcher this house was on Wayne's paper round. Why? It's empty. No-one ever explained *that* did they?"

"And when did Wayne go missing?"

Olive pursed her lips. "My memory isn't what it used to be, but I think it was back when Bob Hawke was Prime Minister."

Lois nodded. "Okay. Well, thank you for all your help, Olive. How about we get you back home where it's nice and warm?"

"Didn't anyone have the sense to tell you about Miss Jam?"

"I'm afraid not."

Olive shook her head. "Well, they should have. You get a call to come to this house, best you ignore it."

"I'll remember that for next time." Lois directed the woman into the hallway.

"I always said they'd find the boy in the pughole if they cared to look."

"The pughole?"

"Where the brickworks used to dig out their clay."

"Are you talking about the rubbish dump out back?"

"Yes, dear. All the rest of the clay pits around here got filled in. But not that one. That one got forgotten." Her voice dropped to a whisper. "It's where she puts them."

"Who?"

"Miss Jam."

Lois pinched the bridge of her nose, took a breath. "And who is 'them'?

"The boys. The boys Miss Jam calls to the house. They can't ever stay away from that hole in the ground. They always want to know what's down there. And if they do go down there," Olive sniffed, "Miss Jam makes sure they don't ever come up again."

Lois's head pivoted to the back door. *Shit. Miller.*

The rain eased to a drizzle as Lois hurried to where she'd last seen Miller. Mindful not to slip in the mud that now caked her boots, she swung her flashlight from side to side, looking for a sign her partner had changed his mind about investigating the pit. When she failed to find him above ground, she trained the beam below. White light picked up bumper bars and sheets of corrugated iron, a tricycle with a bent wheel.

"Miller, are you down there?" Lois called.

No response.

She pushed wet hair back from her face. *Fuck*. She didn't want to request backup. Not yet. If Miller turned up, they'd both look like half-drowned idiots. She called again. Where the hell, was he?

She sensed movement back towards the fence. Olive had followed her. She was between the gap in the palings, one bony arm raised, her finger pointing at Lois.

"Go back to the house," Lois shouted.

Olive kept pointing, insistently. Her pink dressing gown had turned the colour of old blood. If she stayed out any longer, she'd be soaked through. An invitation for pneumonia.

"Nothing is ever easy," Lois muttered under her breath. Now she'd have to call it in, request paramedics for Olive too. She reached for her radio and stopped. What if Olive wasn't pointing at her? Miller? Lois turned, holding the torch at shoulder height. Something crawled, spider-like, across one of the factory walls. It dropped to the edge of the pit, landing on all fours, then stood. The figure was small and feminine with a delicate pale face and long dark hair dripping over narrow shoulders. Lois stared at it, and for a moment the creature stared back, eyes reflecting the light like a cat. Head cocked, it made a strange clicking sound. Lois didn't have to think too hard to understand she was in the presence of something dangerous. It looked human, but the pretence was shallow. Lois unholstered her gun. Before she had a chance to raise her weapon, the thing stepped over the side of the pit and disappeared into the darkness.

In the silence that followed, a hundred things went through Lois's mind. Did she trust her instincts? *Yes.* Was it over? *No.* Safety off, she positioned the gun above the torch, right hand fisted over her left, and slowly turned back towards the fence. A ghostly face met hers. It was both beautiful and tortured, the mouth split with rage. A frigid blast of air hit Lois. She reeled, losing her balance. Teetering on the edge of the pit, arms pin-wheeling, Lois fired a shot. Reflex, nothing more. The bullet went nowhere. She held ground just long enough to be thankful she wasn't at the other end where the drop was straight down. Then her heels slipped, and she was flat on her back, sliding head-first down the steep incline like she was on some whacky waterpark ride.

Sticky clay coated her from head to toe. It matted her hair, clogged her ears, oozed into her socks and down her collar. She clawed her fingers, splayed her arms and legs, in an attempt to slow her descent. Something sharp collected her shoulder. She felt it dig in and tear first through fabric then through skin. Far above, all she could see was a line of light cutting through the rain; her torch tumbling after her.

A roll of chicken wire saved Lois, cushioning her fall after she flew out over the moat of muddy water when the slope gave way to a two-metre vertical drop. The wire cut her hands up, scratched her face, but it hardly mattered. She'd missed a star dropper by a hair. Her torch came to rest on the roof of a car. The light revealed Miller hadn't been so lucky. He was wedged between the car bumper and a fridge, a length of rebar protruding from his thigh.

Miller stared up at her, his face milky white. His mouth opened and closed like a goldfish. He was in shock. He'd lost blood. From what Lois could tell, the rod had gone through muscle and not a major artery. Something, at least.

"Hang in there, kid," she said, thumbing the call button of the microphone that was somehow still strapped to her shoulder. The device was dead. She felt for the connecting cable. It came up loose in her hand. She pulled the radio from its pouch on her belt and wiped the screen. The unit crackled to life, but every frequency she tried gave her static. Miller's radio didn't work either.

The pile of metal beneath Lois groaned and shifted. She had the feeling she was sitting atop a scrap metal Jenga. Carefully, she crawled over the car wreck, grabbed her torch and shone it upwards. Her only hope was the octogenarian who'd tried to warn her had not gone back to the house as instructed.

"OLIVE!" she shouted. "Olive, are you up there? Get help. I have an officer down."

She took off her jacket and uniform shirt. The shirt was, for the moment, dry. She used it to wrap Miller's leg. She put the jacket back on. *Keep warm, stay sharp*, she told herself. She felt around under his leg to get an idea how long the piece of rebar was. Ten centimetres down, it went into a lump of concrete. *Damn!* Moving him was not an option.

Miller started to shake. She held his hand. "You've got to breathe, kid. Do it with me, yeah. Big breath in… now slowly let it out. And again."

From somewhere below came a tinkling sound.

"Listen, I need to go get help," said Lois.

Miller's eyes widened. He found his voice, "You can't leave me here… not with her."

"I don't have a whole lot of choices. I can't move you."

"She'll eat me alive," he sobbed.

Lois ran her hand along his belt. "Where's your gun?"

"I don't know."

She looked around and couldn't find it. She had no idea where her gun was either. It must have fallen when she did, ended up in the water. His torch was gone too.

FUCK!

The tinkling turned to jangling, like tin cans being pulled on a string. The sound grew louder. A discordant orchestra of metal.

Miller whimpered as arms snaked out from under him, wrapping tight around his waist. Lois clawed at them to no avail. He jerked backwards, his body folding in on itself. She grabbed his other hand and pulled hard. The leg that had been speared by the rebar buckled in against his chest, tearing away from the block of concrete. His other leg flailed. Lois wedged her feet under the car bumper to anchor herself and kept pulling. It made little difference. It was as if Miller was being sucked into a compactor, his body disappearing bit by bit into the mound of metal.

"Give him back, you bitch," Lois screamed. She fought with everything she had. Found strength she didn't know existed. Miller wasn't her favourite person in the world, but she was damned if she was going to let him be taken. Not like this. Not by a vindictive spirit. Lois did have her limits.

By the time only his face remained visible, the fear had gone from his eyes, replaced by stunned confusion. "Mum?"

"I'm here," said Lois. She cupped a hand behind his head, stroked his brow. "I'm here." In the end it was all she could offer, before he disappeared altogether.

Lois waded through hip deep water. She trod carefully, unable to see below the muddy surface. It was tough going, constantly losing her footing as her boots slid into crevasses, big and small, between drowned junk. The rain had stopped, although she hardly noticed. Tears poured down instead.

Above, clouds parted, and a half-moon cast a grey wash over the pit. As she moved closer to the side the water got shallower. She spotted a milk crate and wrangled it free from a coil of pipe. It gave her enough height to shimmy her chest then her stomach up onto a low spot in the clay bank. After that it was a slow climb to the top, digging the toes of her boots into the mud to get traction, and using her fingers to drag herself forward. It had been a quick ride on the way down. Lois took almost half an hour to get back up.

When she was at the top she called out to Miller. He didn't answer. She didn't expect him to. Miller was gone.

Olive wasn't in the house when Lois returned. There were no lights on across the street. She hoped the old woman was tucked up in bed with a hot water bottle. She'd check on her later. One thing at a time. *Get yourself together first.* Her brain was foggy. Her throat burned. She had pain in her chest. She fumbled for the keys in her pocket, opened the car, and used her knuckle to punch the call button. Then she puked.

While she waited for Special Tasks and Rescue, Lois went back into Miss Jam's house. She took a blanket from the bedroom and wrapped it around her shoulders. At the kitchen sink she squeezed mud from her hair and wiped her face clean. She checked herself over. There was some serious bruising to her ribs, and a laceration on her right shoulder—not deep, but it stung like hell. The pain in her chest had dulled. Now it felt like there was a boulder resting there. Lois didn't know what was worse—she was having a heart attack, or Miller had got to her. *Mum.* He'd called her *Mum.* In his last moments, the kid had found a way to break her.

The scene looked different in daylight. The hole at the back of the Jam house was indeed a clay pit; orange-brown mud sculpted into a deep bowl. Lois counted thirteen car bodies among the tower of scrap metal, household appliances, and builder's rubbish. Somewhere below it all was Miller.

The STAR unit set up in the backyard of Miss Jam's house. The Water Operations Unit were there too. As were Forensics. There was an excavator on standby in the lane. There were also dog handlers, already down amongst the rubbish hunting for Miller.

Lois went over the details of the callout with the detective assigned to the case. He wore a crumpled brown suit with a tie only the colourblind would choose. She kept it simple. Something had attacked them. Miller had fallen into the pit. She'd attempted a rescue but failed. Then she recounted her conversation with Olive. His face was stony.

"I can talk to her again if you like, maybe get more sense out of her this time?"

"That won't be necessary."

"Someone's checked on her already?"

"Are you fucking with me, Senior Constable?"

"No Sir, I am not."

"Wait here."

She watched him exit the house and speak with her commanding officer. The detective didn't return, instead it was Senior Sergeant Moore. She'd known Patrick since the early days. He'd organised her transfer from Elizabeth LSA to Western Adelaide. He'd always been in her corner. Even when she hadn't made it easy for him.

"What's going on?" said Lois.

"You're being stood down."

"What?"

"The Chief Inspector has suggested a psych assessment."

"For Olive?"

He sighed. "No, for you."

"I don't understand."

"The woman you spoke to…we found her wandering at the end of the street. She has a bullet wound."

"How did that—"

"She said you shot her."

Shit. Lois felt her knees give, struggled to stay upright. "Is she okay?"

"She's in a serious condition. They've taken her to hospital"

Lois went to speak, but he stopped her. "Don't say another word. To anybody. Go home, get some sleep, and get your story straight."

Patrick called by her house later that evening. He wasn't in uniform.

"Can I come in?"

"This a social visit?"

"Kind of."

Lois waved him in. He took a seat on the faded sofa by the window.

"I've been to see Olive Langmore."

"How's she doing?" Lois sat opposite. She picked at a hangnail.

"Fine. Bullet went straight through her wrist. Chipped some bone on the way through. Main thing is they got the bleeding under control. Tough lady. She's giving the nurses a hard time because she wants to go home already."

"Sounds like Olive."

"I took her statement. She's adamant her getting shot wasn't your fault. Says it was an accident."

"Yeah, well it shouldn't have happened." Lois sighed audibly. "For what it's worth though, I did tell her to go back to the house."

"Exactly what Olive said." He rubbed his chin. "She's an interesting character."

"She is."

"I think we need to talk."

"Off the record?"

He nodded. "We've known each other a long time."

Lois smiled. "Some might say too long."

"Shit, you know me better than my wife does."

"Which one?"

"Ouch." He paused. "Maybe I—"

"Don't go there. No point."

He looked at the ceiling then at Lois. "Seen a lot of weird stuff too."

"That we have."

"Ah, fuck. I just need to know what I'm dealing with here, Lois. According to Olive some freaky arse shit went down last night. It's hard to know what to believe."

"I can tell you the truth but I'm not sure you're gonna like it."

"Try me."

Lois didn't hold back. She told him everything. It felt good to let it out, even if she did sound as crazy as Olive. When she was finished, she sat back and waited for a response. He made her wait.

"We can't find him," he said, finally.

"That's bullshit."

"I don't know what else to tell you."

"*Tell me* you won't stop until you *do* find him. I promise you Miller *is* down there. You just need to dig deeper." She couldn't stop Miller from being taken, but she'd be damned if she was going to leave him down there in the pughole… with Miss Jam… or whatever the fuck it was. "*Please*. Do this for Olive. For me. Do it for Miller. Do it for who knows how many others down there. *Dig deeper*. And when you've found them… all of them… you need to do one more thing."

"What's that?"

"Fill that fucking hole in."

It took another week of excavation before they found Constable Ben Miller. His body was under five metres of mud. He wasn't alone. Twelve young men, preserved in clay, were recovered. Their disappearances dated back over seventy years. There was not one reasonable explanation as to how they'd got there. Miller was a special conundrum. It wasn't humanly possible to bury a body so deep and then put tonnes of rubbish on top in only a few hours. Lois was off the hook.

She took a month's leave before returning to the station. They gave her a job on the front desk. By lunch time she'd had enough. At 5.30 P.M. she cleared out her locker and handed in her resignation. Patrick didn't question it. She didn't know what she wanted yet, but she knew it wasn't that.

Before the year was out, the pughole was filled and both Olive's and Miss Jam's houses bulldozed. The Council gave the greenlight to a property developer with plans for a home maker centre and factory outlet complex on the site. The first step in redeveloping the area. In time, the factories would go too, replaced with apartment blocks and cafes. History lost in almond milk lattes and vegan menus.

All but one item from the demolition of Miss Jam's house ended up at the Wingfield dump. On the night Miller went missing, after she'd called for help, and before she warmed herself under a blanket, Lois had collected the black phone for safekeeping. It sat in a lockbox in her basement. She'd grown sick of it ringing.

The Resident

PHILIP FRACASSI

JAIME STANDS RIGID, FISTS CLENCHED, HIS BACK TO THE HOUSE. ROB methodically places strips of packing tape over a ground-floor window, the room beyond occupied by nothing but heavy dark. Both men wear black jeans, black hooded sweatshirts, black gloves. Smears of face paint. Jaime twitches when Rob's elbow connects with the window; a muted crack splinters the night. A moment later his brother pulls the glistening skin of tape and broken glass toward him, dumps it in the tall grass.

The house has no alarm system, no dog and, as far as they knew, no hidden cameras. The family had departed earlier in the week, leaving the brothers a finite window of time.

"I'm telling you, they're gone," Rob said over the phone a few nights prior. "I followed their car to the airport myself, parked with them in a long-term lot, walked behind them to the damn security gate. Their kid was crying, the wife looked like shit and our friend, Mr. Drake, didn't look so hot himself. I got the feeling it wasn't a planned trip."

"Well, it was. Drake told me himself they were going away. I'm just surprised they left so abruptly," Jaime said, struggling to recall any details he may have missed.

"Maybe someone died, they had to burn to catch a funeral," Rob said thoughtfully. "Regardless, they're gone, my brother. We gotta move now."

Jaime wasn't sold on the wisdom of rushing a plan months in the making, but he couldn't deny the opportunity. And if the family left in a hurry, it could bode well for them. Folks got sloppy when they were hurried, especially when it was a last-minute trip.

We just need to make sure we're *not sloppy,* he thought after hanging up with Rob.

Regardless, he must admit—so far, so good.

They arrived on foot, having parked a few blocks away. The house had been dark. *Completely* dark. No interior lights on timers. No porchlight. No security light popping on as they approached from the rear, their entrance hidden by dense trees on all sides.

Sloppy, Jaime thought as they'd jogged soundlessly toward the rear of the large Victorian.

Rob slips through the window, carefully cleared of any stray, narrow daggers of glass.

With a final exhale, Jaime follows his brother inside, sliding headfirst through the black mouth of open window to land softly on the wood floor. Despite their knowledge of the house being empty, he's still caught off guard at the density of the dark, the weight of the silence. He finds it oppressive. Unsettling.

After taking a moment for their eyes to adjust, the brothers move silently out of what appears to be a dining room. They would find what they came here for on the second floor, hidden behind a painting—the portrait of a woman—in the master bedroom.

That's where Mr. Drake kept his valuables, important documents, and—for a few more minutes, anyway—fifty thousand dollars in cash, all of it stacked in clean, untraceable, hundred-dollar bills.

Jaime knows this as fact, because it was Jaime who'd handed Mr. Drake all that money in the first place, just like he'd done the first of every month for the past year; ever since Drake and his family had moved into town and occupied the old Victorian.

"Don't spread this information around, but I pay all my vendors in cash," Drake—who owned several lumber mills throughout the northwest—had confided a few months before. He winked as Jaime counted the bills. "Works out for both sides."

"Well, I hope you have someplace safe to keep it," Jaime had said, doing his very best to sound disinterested. He'd been given orders from his brother to extract as much information as he could from the man, but without creating suspicion.

But really, if you can't trust the bank, who can you trust?

"Oh, I do, don't you worry," Drake replied carelessly. "The house came with a handy feature." He leaned in, lowered his voice. "There's a hidden safe in my bedroom."

"Those old houses are full of cool stuff like that," Jaime replied, ignoring his quickening pulse. "I bet it's hidden behind a Van Gogh or something, huh? Or an old portrait, like in those gothic novels."

"Not too far off the mark," the man said, then frowned. Jaime sensed he'd hit a sore spot and was going to let it go, but Drake offered a sad, tepid smile. "It's a portrait of my mother, actually. God rest her soul."

Jaime nodded casually, putting the last of the money into the briefcase they always used. "Sorry to hear that," he said. "About your mother."

It wasn't unusual for a teller and a client to make small talk during the larger transactions, but Jaime noticed—or perhaps only imagined—that Drake stiffened as he took the briefcase.

"You have a nice day, Mr. Drake," Jaime said, flashing his most careless, professional smile, already nodding to the next customer in line, as if he couldn't give a single shit about Drake's day, his dead mother, or the painting in his bedroom.

Jaime had siphoned other information out of Drake over the course of their dozen or so transactions. He knew the Drake family had moved into the old Balkis place, a stodgy Victorian that seemed to change owners every few years.

He therefore knew that Mr. Drake's safe, like the house itself, was *old.*

"My boy could probably break into the damn thing with a stethoscope," Drake said during a bank visit a few months prior, before giving a nervous laugh. "And we should probably install a security system one of these days. Everything about that place is so ancient..."

And, just over a week ago, Jaime handled their monthly transaction once again, for what turned out to be the last time.

"Need a bit more this time," Drake said as he handed Jaime the withdrawal slip, which showed double his normal amount.

Fifty-thousand dollars.

"No problem," Jaime said, fighting to keep his voice even.

"Have to leave town in a couple weeks, so I need to settle two months at once," Drake replied, scratching roughly at an unshaven cheek.

Desperate to know timing, Jaime took a calculated risk. "You wouldn't rather withdraw this when you return?"

"No," Drake snapped, then wiped a hand over his mouth. "I mean, it's fine. My bookkeeper will come for it at the end of the month, once my family and I are gone. Make all the payments. Until then..."

"Mother will keep it safe."

Drake's eyes snapped up, narrowed with uncertainty.

"The portrait," Jaime added lamely, internally cursing himself.

"Oh... yes, of course." Drake seemed to relax, then fell silent.

Jaime counted out the cash like always, keeping it professional as he stacked and banded the bills, barely able to suppress the thrill of knowing it would all be returning to his hands in a couple short weeks.

And now, finally, here they are, standing in the master bedroom, the narrow beam of Rob's penlight cutting through the dark to settle on the painted portrait of a dark-haired woman, her brown eyes wide and searching, her skin pale as snow.

Those blood-red lips seeming to frown at the two intruders.

"She don't look so friendly," Rob says quietly, and Jaime huffs a laugh in response.

Bitch looks downright wicked, he thinks. But keeps it to himself.

It's time to work.

While Rob holds the light, Jaime steps closer to the painting. Close-up, the woman's face is even more haunting. Her hooded eyelids make her appear bored, or irritated. Her cheeks are sallow pits of shadow, her frowning lips slightly pursed. The brushstrokes overall, he notices, are heavy and frantic, as if the painter—Drake's father, apparently—was hurried. Or, perhaps, nervous.

Scowling back at the woman, Jaime feels along the edge of the gaudy gold-painted frame, the carved wood twined like heavy roots. The portrait is wide, at least two feet, but when he grips the right edge and gives it a tug, it glides away from the wall easily as a cabinet door, the hidden hinges silent and smooth.

"Holy shit, Jaime. There it is."

Jaime gives Rob a quick glance, then studies the face of the safe recessed into the wall. It's smaller than he'd expected, maybe a foot high and wide, but plenty big enough to hold the cash and whatever else the odd businessmen stored there. To his delight, there's a classic combination dial and a small release handle. No electronics. No keypad. No gadgetry.

A cakewalk.

Rob steps closer, eyes squinted in concentration.

"How long?" Jaime asks.

Rob sets his toolbox on the carpet, opens the lid. "Half-hour maybe. I'd say ten minutes to drill, maybe another twenty with the borescope." He stands up, holding the end of an extension cord. "You see an outlet? And check the windows, yeah?"

Jaime pulls his penlight free from his pocket, twists it on and moves it around the base of the walls. "Outlet," he says, pointing to a spot about ten feet down, near the bed.

As Rob plugs in the cord, Jaime moves to the room's two windows, careful to cup a hand over the penlight until he's sure the windows are closed, the curtains drawn. "Windows are good, brother. Get to it."

Rob pulls more tools from his kit. "Why don't you check the rest of the house, make sure there's nothing else worth taking."

Jaime nods and, keeping his penlight pointed down to the weathered hardwood floor, steps into the hallway.

By the time Jaime is searching the last room of the second floor, having found nothing more interesting than a jar of silver dollars in the kid's bedroom, along with a half-finished model airplane and a smattering of clothes thrown across the floor (*they really did leave in a hurry*, he'd thought sourly, noting the tube of uncapped glue next to the scattered model pieces), he could hear the whine of Rob's drill digging through the metal of the safe.

By profession, Jaime's brother was a self-employed locksmith, having learned the tools of his trade while spending eighteen months in a state penitentiary. Rob had been caught stealing a lightly used Honda, one he could strip for parts and walk away from with an easy five grand, give or take. But luck wasn't with Jaime's big brother that day. The cops rode him into a ditch, trashing the car and sending Rob upstate to learn the craft of jimmying locked car doors, replacing doorknobs and, yes, even bullying open the occasional home safe. He often referred to his time in prison as 'free trade school' and, after his release, actually played it straight for a couple years.

Right up to that first day Mr. Drake walked up to Jaime's teller window at First National Bank and Loan. On that fateful day opportunity didn't just knock, it pounded on the door with both fists, too loudly to ignore, hammered away until the brothers had no choice but to answer.

Finished sweeping the upper rooms, Jaime sticks his head back into the master bedroom to check on Rob, who continues drilling steadily, a small worklight aimed at the safe from the floor, his dark goggles reflecting the hot white face of the steel surface. Jaime figures he's still got some time to explore and decides to check out the downstairs.

Cupping the end of his penlight as he heads down the steep, twisty staircase, he first goes to the front door, checks to be sure it's locked, then peeks out one of the two narrow windows bordering the door.

The front yard of the house is swallowed by murky, moonless night. Even straining his eyes, Jaime can't see a thing past the gray bannisters of the front porch. He's surprised to feel a chill run up his spine, burrow beneath the skin at the back of his neck. He can't fight the feeling that he's not staring into an oversized yard bordered by a weathered iron fence, the pickets marching along the perimeter topped by pressed spears, their tips corroded with rust (a deterrent as worthless as the ancient locks on the warped-glass windows), but an abyss. A sucking, all-consuming void. Cold and deadly as outer space.

As he's puzzling over this, there's a spattering of footsteps from behind.

"The hell?" he says, spinning away from the door.

He catches a flash of bare feet, the blur of a light-colored dress as it disappears down the hallway.

"Hey!" he yells, moving toward the hallway, following the direction of the woman he saw running past. He debates running up the stairs to get Rob but knows there's no time. She could be popping out a side window any moment, screaming into the night, waking neighbors with cries of alarm.

Without further debate, Jaime sprints down the narrow corridor after her, his shoes pounding on the hardwood, his penlight held up before him, the soft eye of the light's path crawling in jerky movements along hallway walls constructed in dark, molded oak. He angles the light to point straight up ahead, where he catches a glimpse of that pale dress darting through a door at the end of the hall before it slams shut with all the nuance of a meteor strike.

"Hey, God damn it!" he screams and, without pause, slams his shoulder full force into the closed door. It offers little resistance, and he stumbles awkwardly into the room before coming to an abrupt halt, his breaths heavy, the point of his penlight weakened by the total darkness, the skinny beam bullied by heavy shadows.

As his heartbeat steadies, he hears it, obvious and close.

A woman's stifled, panting breaths.

Staying near the doorway to ensure she doesn't slide past him into the house, he runs his light over the walls—sees bookcases, wood paneling; a large, framed painting done in abstract, a confusion of color and space.

There are no windows.

She's trapped, and she knows it.

"Just relax, okay?" he says, feels along the wall for a light switch, finds it, flips it on.

Jaime is surprised to find himself standing in a large office. A massive mahogany desk sulks at the far end of the room, an overstuffed leather chair askew behind it. The front of the desk is an engraved slab of shining wood that reaches the floor, hiding the cubby where a person's knees and feet would reside while working. There's little other furniture—a bland couch along one wall, a wooden chair backed against another. To his right, built-in shelving supports framed photos of innocuous, dreamy faces, leather-spined books with gilt titles, worn with time. A closet door.

He takes a step toward the closet, then hears a rustle of fabric from the far end of the room. A stifled gasp.

She's behind the damn desk.

"Look, I'm not gonna hurt you. I don't know who you are, or what you're doing here, but I'm not here to hurt anyone. Why don't you come out and we can talk?"

A beat of silence, then a thin, timid voice. "I'll see your face."

Jaime scoffs. "Lady, in about three days the entire police force is gonna know who was responsible for this. It ain't complicated. But I don't plan on sticking around, okay? Once we're done with that safe upstairs, my brother and are out of here. As in, goodbye America. So don't worry, you describing my face is the least of my concerns." He pauses, rotates the top of the penlight so the beam goes dark. "I'm no murderer. I'm a bank teller, for chrissakes."

He waits another beat, not wanting to drag her out. For all he knows she's found a pair of scissors to shove at his guts, or a letter opener to stick in his eye. He wants no surprises. "Come on, lady. Please."

Finally, slowly, the woman rises from behind the desk. Visibly shaken, her black hair hangs loose over half her face. Her dress is frilly and cream, almost formal. She's young, younger than him, and he puts her at twenty-three, twenty-four-years old. Twenty-five tops.

"That's right," he says, spreading his hands wide. "Look, no knife, no gun. I'm just here to rob a safe, that's it."

The woman watches him closely, large brown eyes focused warily on his, her sallow cheeks splotched with red from the exertion of running, hiding. The adrenalin of fear.

"Good," he continues. "Now, what's your name? What are you doing here? You're not one of Drake's kids, 'cause he's just got the boy. You the maid or something? Nanny? What?"

She offers an almost imperceptible shake of her head. "I live here," she says, soft as a whisper.

Jaimie thinks about this a moment, wondering who this woman could be and what the hell he was going to do with her. Rob, he knows, will likely want to put her down, stuff the body in the cellar. Buy them time. "I don't think that's true," he says slowly. "No one lives here but the Drake family. Unless you're visiting? An aunt or something? Oh!" he says, snapping his fingers. "I got it. You're housesitting." He looks around the floor, as if waiting for an animal to appear at ground-level. "They got a cat or something you take care of?"

The woman shakes her head again, brow creased in confusion, or annoyance. "I live here," she repeats, louder this time, as if emphasizing the truth of it.

"Okay, okay." Jaime isn't liking this situation. Not liking this woman.

Maybe she escaped from a mental asylum, he thinks. *Been living in the walls like a rat. Or locked in the basement. Maybe Drake's some kind of rich psychopath.*

"Just come over here, okay?" he says, putting a little more steel into his tone. "And open your hands so I know you're not gonna stick me with something."

Obediently, the woman raises her hands, steps around the desk.

"Fine," he says, scanning the room until he sees what he wants. "Now sit in that chair, and don't move. If you run, I'll catch you, and things will go bad."

Keeping her eyes on him warily, she steps toward the chair, studies it a moment, then sits down, hands resting on the wooden armrests, head turned to watch him.

"Great. See, we're all friends." Jaime closes the door behind him, then plucks a lamp with a stained glass shade from a small table next to the couch. He yanks hard on the cord running behind the couch. There's a muted *snap* and it leaps toward him. He jerks the other end of the cord from the base of the lamp, then tosses it to the ground, ignoring the cracking sound of the multi-colored shade.

"That was Tiffany," the woman says blandly.

Jaime approaches her slowly, winding the cord in his hands. "Yeah? I guess you can bill me. Now keep your hands still, I'm going to tie them to the chair," he says, pulling a pocketknife from his pants and flicking it open.

The woman's eyes widen for a heartbeat, then settle into a careful watchfulness as he cuts the cord in half, puts away the knife, and winds a cord around each wrist. He ties it tight enough that it digs into her skin, but not so much to cut off her circulation. He hopes, anyway.

"There, I'll leave your feet as they are. That chair looks heavy, so I don't think you're gonna get up and run around. Just don't kick me."

Jaime goes back to the door and opens it, the house beyond silent and dark. His eyes, now adjusted to the light, see the hallway as a murky void. He brings out his penlight once more. "I'll be right back. There's no way out but the front door, and I'll be standing at the bottom of the stairs, so no point tiring yourself out."

He's halfway down the corridor when it clicks for Jaime that there's something wrong. Something it takes him a beat to get a finger on.

It's the silence.

For some reason he doesn't understand—because there's no way in hell Rob could be through the safe that quickly—the drilling has stopped.

Jaime glances back down the hallway, toward the rectangle of light coming from the open office door, then takes a few steps up the stairs.

"Rob?" he yells. "We got an issue down here."

Jaime waits for a response. Hears nothing.

"Jesus Christ," he mutters, gives one more glance back to make sure his prisoner isn't chair-hopping down the hall, then runs quickly up the steps. He turns for the bedroom, not wanting to leave the woman unmonitored for more than a minute. When he steps through the open door, he notices the portrait is still swung wide, the safe still closed. Rob's worklight shines dumbly from the floor, set next to an unmanned drill, an open toolbox.

Rob, however, is gone.

Jaime spends a few minutes searching the bedroom, calling out his brother's name. He confirms the windows are still locked from the inside, then quickly searches the other second story rooms, frantic, opening closets and double-checking exit points. All the windows are locked, the curtains drawn. The rooms, empty.

The first stirrings of panic swirl in his chest as he takes the stairs two at a time. At the bottom, he glances to his right, sees the open door of the office. A beacon in the dark. Furious at himself for leaving the woman alone for so long, he sprints the length of the corridor, toward the light.

Inside the office he finds her, sitting in the chair, hands securely bound. The look of fear in her eyes, however, has diminished.

"Problem?" she says, arching one eyebrow.

"No," Jaime replies, and takes off once more down the hall, checking the other rooms, calling again and again for his brother. He makes his way back to the broken window, expecting to feel a cool breeze blowing in from the outside, but stops a few feet short. He stares at it numbly, his brain temporarily knocked off its moorings.

The window is whole. His silver-lined reflection stares back at him.

His heart thumping faster, harder, he studies the rest of the room. "I must have the wrong window," he mumbles out loud. But there *is* no other window in the room. *This* was their entry point. *This* was the window Rob smashed and pulled away. The one they'd both slid through like snakes.

"Rob!" he yells, louder now, no longer caring if he's heard by a neighbor, or a passerby. He needs to find his brother. Needs to find out what—what the hell exactly—is going on.

The front. He must have gone out the front.

Jaime sprints to the front door, grips the brass knob, and twists.

The door doesn't budge.

"What?" he says in disbelief, and yanks on the door again. He checks that the deadbolt is clear, that there is no obstruction at the door's base. He jerks back on the handle, teeth gritted, muscles straining.

Nothing.

Jaime runs his hands through his hair, mind spinning, vision tilting as if he were drunk, or drugged. Not knowing what else to do, he heads back to the window they'd come through.

You mean the one that's somehow whole again? his mind says, taunting him.

"Shut up," Jaime mumbles. He turns on his light and searches the room for something heavy enough to smash the glass but sees nothing of use. "Fuck it," he says, and takes two steps toward the window. He raises one steel-toed boot and kicks the glass.

His foot bounces off and he falls awkwardly to the floor. He stares at the window, wide-eyed. He stands and—more carefully now—kicks it again. It's as if he's kicking a stone wall. The thin glass doesn't even tremor.

"No..." he stutters, mind shrieking, hands shaking. "What is this…?"

A distant voice breaks through his thoughts.

"Jaime?" the woman calls from the end of the hall, her voice ethereal in the dark, empty house. "I think you and I should have a chat."

Jaimie stares at the (impossibly) unbroken, impenetrable window another moment, rubbing his chin with a finger. He takes a deep breath, nods his head once, assures himself that all is well. That all is *normal.*

Then he turns and leaves the room.

A chat? A sudden, savage fury flares in his chest, burning away the confusion and worry over his brother. The fear.

Yes, he thinks, murder on his mind. *A chat sounds fucking lovely.*

Jaime enters the office, squinting against the light. The woman is still tied to the chair. He notices, with a pinprick of pleasure, that her hands are bone-white, her fingers curled painfully, as if cramped. *Good,* he thinks. *I hope it hurts like hell.*

He steps in front of her, staring down, his face twisted with rage born from fear. She stares back, defiance in her gaze. He wants to slap her. To grab her hair and bounce her stupid head off the wall.

As if reading his thoughts (and apparently not worried about them in the slightest) her mouth curls into a smile, bright red lips slinking up her pale cheeks like blood in milk.

"Something funny?" he says, fighting to keep his voice steady as his anger builds.

The woman shakes her head. Her eyes glance to the desk. "What you're looking for is over there."

Jaime looks to the desk, confused, expecting to see... what, exactly? *A key? A safe? A pile of money?*

On top of the desk, dead center of the massive, smoothed wooden surface—as if it were being presented on an oversized platter—is a book.

Flustered, he closes his eyes, takes a deep breath, and focuses once more on the woman tied to the chair. "Look, I don't know what's going on here, but my brother is missing, and I can't..."

The woman's smile widens. A hint of white teeth. "Can't what, Jaime?"

Anger rises in him once more—anger at being afraid, at being left alone in this house, at not understanding who this woman was, and why he, why he...

"Can't get out," he says softly, like an exhale. "I can't get out of this house."

The woman nods, pursing her lips. "I see. And your brother? He was opening the safe, am I right?"

"That's right!" he says, his voice too loud, too shrill. He takes a step forward, kneels so they're face-to-face. "What happened to him? Do you know? You do, don't you."

Her brown eyes study him and her smile settles into a dispassionate frown, as if she's suddenly grown bored.

"Open the book, Jaime..."

Jaime stands, digs his fingers into his hair in frustration. "How do you know my name?" he yells, spittle flying, his face hot.

Suddenly, it feels to him as if the office isn't an office at all, but an oven, and some unknown force has closed the door and is turning up the heat, slowly cooking him from the inside out. "How!" he screams again, spinning on her, one hand clenched into a fist, *wanting* to strike her, to beat her until she answers him.

The young woman's eyes regard him calmly, then she shrugs. Relaxed. His threat of violence insignificant, as if he were nothing but a spider climbing along a wall, and she was having an internal debate whether to ignore it, or crush it to death.

"The book," she says again, her tone that of a patient teacher speaking to a thickheaded pupil. "The answers to all your questions are in that book. I promise."

Jaime studies her for another beat, then stomps to the desk, circling behind it. He pushes aside the leather chair and snatches the book from the desktop.

It's small, thin. The cover is soft, worn leather the color of red wine. Or blood.

"Go on," she says, watching him.

Jaime flips open the cover, revealing an unlined page covered in neat black handwriting.

March 3. The house is bigger than we thought. Mary and I have room to roam, and Dean has taken to it quickly. We never had this much land in the city, and tomorrow I promised him we'd explore the rear acreage, find the source of the bubbling water we can hear coming from the woods late at night. Perhaps a creek big enough for fish, I'll have to...

Jaime looks away from the page, back at the woman. "What is this? A diary? Drake's innermost thoughts?" he says angrily. "You think I give a rat's ass?"

The woman eyes roll up and away, as if considering, then settle back on Jaime. "I understand. Maybe skip ahead to a more recent date."

Jaime glowers at her a moment more, then roughly flips through the book until he arrives to a page dated in October, the current month. With a frown, he can't help noticing, as he turns the pages, that the handwriting—so neat in the beginning passage—grows wilder as the days fly forward. Sloppy, even. As if written with an unsteady hand.

October 2. Time is short. I have to keep my thoughts clear, or God help us. Clear on the task at hand. On what must be done so we can GET OUT, all of us. Leave and never look back. Dear Christ I wish this had never... that we had never... but it's all settled now. The plan is set. If this book is found, and my family, if we don't make it please know we tried, I tried, I tried!

Jaime turns the page, but the writing is indecipherable. He turns another and is surprised to see the date jumping ahead to mid-October.

Last week.

It's all set! All set! Just a matter of waiting now, just waiting for the rats to eat the cheese. My GOD they better come, they better have some goddamn BALLS and do what I need them to do because if they don't then we're good and fucked. Then we're the food. WE'RE THE FOOD. But we have a deal, and she won't go back on it. She won't she won't she won't. We have a DEAL! Come, rats, come! Come get the cheese.

Jaime wants to drop the book to the floor. Disgust rises in his throat like acid. This doesn't make any sense. What the hell was wrong with the man?

Was Drake mad? Mad, and I didn't realize?

The woman's voice cuts through his thoughts.

"Caught up, are you?"

Jaime glances up at her, then does a double-take.

Is she closer?

He glares at her a moment, brow furrowed.

Could she move that chair without me hearing? No… impossible.

"Caught up, yeah," he says. "So what? Guy was a nutjob. Totally off the rails."

"Perhaps," she murmurs thoughtfully. "Regardless, I think," she says, and he sees a glitter in her dark eyes, an obscene curling at the corner of her lips, "you should continue. Turn toward the back, where he's written the rest of it."

"Rest of what?" he says, teeth gritted, wanting to throw the book at her smug face.

"The rest of what you need to see."

Jaime, not knowing what else to do, and fighting the urge to beat the damn woman half to death, sighs in annoyance. He flips through a half-inch of blank pages until he sees more handwriting.

These pages, however, are not filled with diary entries.

At the top of the first page, in all capital letters, and underlined heavily beneath, are two words.

THE WAITER.

"What the fuck is this?" he says, staring at the page in confusion.

"It will make sense if you keep going," she says quietly.

Jaime sees scribbled notes below the headline. A name he doesn't recognize. Other names beneath. Random words thrown around the page.

Too young?

Not very smart.

Violent past.

Jaime turns the page, sees another headline scrawled across the top.

MARY'S MECHANIC.

Again, the random names. A phone number. Lines connecting different groups of people, some scribbled out, others written in their place.

Bankrupt.

Criminal history.

Manslaughter.

Jaime feels a cold tickle of terror settle on the nape of his neck.

This isn't right, this doesn't make sense...

"Turn the page, darling." The woman's voice is gentle and close, as if she were somehow standing just behind him, whispering into his ear. His nervous eyes dart up, but she's still in her chair, watching him closely, that smile now replaced with... what? Something he doesn't like. Hate, maybe. Or...

"Turn the page," she repeats. A command.

Jaime turns the page. Breath shoots out of him like a cough. His eyes water, his chest constricts.

No… NO! Impossible.

At the top are two words:

THE BANKER.

Below are many notes. Much more, he realizes, than on the previous pages. He notices his own name right away. Below that, his brother's name. The name of his locksmith business. The years and place of his imprisonment. There are many numbers and dates. Deposits, he thinks. Or... no... withdrawals. His eyes dance over the page, picking up stray words filled with meaning:

Mention the safe. The brother can...

Not too much at once.

No alarm. Leaving town. What else?

Violent history.

Killer.

Wife beater.

Children gone. Run away.

This is the one.

RATS.

Jaime drops the book onto the desk. Suddenly, he feels incredibly hot; his cheeks wet with sweat, his eyes burning. A tear slips from one eye, runs a cold finger down the side of his face. "I don't..."

The woman stands in front of the desk. She looks older. The light, perhaps... or... he knows her. Yes, yes. He *knows* her.

"The painting," he mumbles, his body numb, his face slack. "You're the woman in the painting."

The woman raises an eyebrow, as if impressed. She lightly places her (now very much untied) hands on the edge of the desktop. "I get so lonely, Jaime," she says, her lips pouting girlishly. "I can't do it myself, and I don't feed on children." She sighs, then laughs suddenly, loudly, and Jaime takes a step back. "One of my stupid rules, I suppose. Plus, you know, it draws suspicion if good families who buy nice homes… well, disappear. People would talk."

Jaime notices, with an almost detached sense of understanding, that the woman is rising, slowly, almost imperceptibly, into the air... a few inches, then a few more. Black smoke slips behind her like liquid seeping into paper, eating the light.

Her face is so bright as to almost glow, and her eyes are wide... too wide... and he knows now, knows what he saw in them.

That indescribable expression.

Hunger.

"Where's my brother?" he says, but her smile only widens, the darkness behind her expanding, stealing into corners, the light of the room dimming, dimming...

"Oh, I'll get to him, don't worry. One at a time, Jaime. No need to be greedy. And besides, there's no hurry, is there?" She looks down at him, licks her lips with a blackened tongue. "We have all the time in the world."

Jaime falls back into the chair, stares in terror as the darkness behind her forms wings—wings that are slowly closing.

"Tell me," she says, her voice deeper, older. "Have you ever seen a snake digest a rat?"

"I'm no rat," he says, lips quivering. "I'm no rat."

The woman's eyes appear large as plates, swirling, abyssal black.

"What *are* you?" Jaime whimpers as the wings close around him, icy cold against his flesh. He gasps with the shock of it.

"I told you," she whispers—and now the voice is most assuredly inside his head, burrowing into the soft tissue of his brain like a bloodthirsty tick as his flesh dissolves inside an ancient, starving mouth.

"I live here."

Kookaburra Cruel

AARON DRIES

DOWN BY THE RIVER WATCHING WATER SLEEK BY. RIPPLES FEEL predetermined, as if everything was meant to flow this way, and no other. It confirms what I already know. I'm meant to be here, on this day, dodging wombat shit, watched by preppy kangaroos that grunt in my direction before bouncing into the scrub. I finger the gun in my raincoat pocket. It's April 11, 1991.

And I'm scouting for the perfect place to blow my brains out.

Picture my blood running in the snake belly black water after I pull the trigger. See the snails tic-tac-toeing my cheeks with slime where my body fell by the riverbank. Twigs in my hair. Spiders crawl from burrows in the earth to hide under my shirt. I see all this, and more. So clear. But then the corpse opens its eyes and sits up to look at me, brain oozing from the bullet hole, down its cheeks, between its lips. Snails stick to its skin, wet eyes googling.

"Are you sure you want to do this, Detective?" it says, gurgling on grey matter.

"I'm not a detective anymore," I imagine myself saying. "And you know it."

"Chantal..." The corpse sounds like my mother—not that I've heard her voice in years. Time is a thief. The resemblance is in the schooling, in how small it makes me feel. *"If you're doing this to be with Matthew, know this: he isn't here with us. Not as you remember him, anyway."*

I slip my hand into my pocket where the gun barrel is icy to the touch. Shaking. Kookaburras laugh at my lack of conviction, at the cliché I've become. Rain patters my coat, drums the leaves. Thoughts no longer align—they are torn things that sting when re-wired into order. A pulse in every inch of me. My heart is trying to convince me I'm whole, still alive. That I have a choice here.

My finger on the trigger loosens.

Kookaburras cackle louder. Three share a branch in a nearby tree. A gutted snake dangles from one of their beaks, the flesh pink as rosewater. They laugh again to let me know this is their territory. My body will be theirs to claim should I die out here. Don't look to the kookaburra for sympathy, no matter the warmth of its laugh.

"No, not yet then," I say aloud, and look back to my corpse.

Relieved, it nods and reclines on the mud. She looks comfortable. Grass grows up through her skin, which is sun-spotted from too many years doing grunt work on the beat, knitting her in green until she's no longer there. Just a mound of nature for the wombats to dig up later. Flowers bloom on her chest, petals opening to free pollen-streaked spiders.

"Soon, though."

I head up the hill to the cabin. My legs are heavy. Everything is heavy. It's dusk. Kookaburras call after me but I don't look back.

Dooling, the owner who lives on the other side of the huge property, has left a basket on the doorstep. I hadn't locked up before heading to the river. Doing so didn't make sense. I wonder if Dooling came inside when I was out, if he snooped. Distrust is an old cop reflex. Given the chance, I would have snooped, too. It's in my nature to pry where I'm not wanted. The ability to do so without being noticed was what made me good at my job.

Step over the basket. Draw the sliding glass door open. Stick my head into the small room.

It doesn't *feel* different inside.

Strangers dislodge the puzzle pieces of a space without noticing. They shift air and shadows, indications of where they have been, and if you look hard enough, what they did within that space presents itself. And why. Out of whack shadows. A scent where there was no scent before. The condensation ring on the tabletop that's one inch to the right of the glass. Strangers get carried away and overlook details that incriminate them later.

Cabin shadows are where they should be. Everything smells the same, just danker. The glass hasn't moved.

My body starts to unclench.

Suspicion comes easy to people like me. Considering the cases I've worked, I don't run myself over hot coals for this. My ex-husband did that enough for the both of us.

I retrieve the picnic basket, knees popping as I bend. Mum had Arthritis, too. All the women in my family had it. I'm the last now. A note is tucked between a loaf of bread wrapped in a tea towel, and a bottle of red wine.

Sorry, Chantal. Ran out of time to bring this down earlier. You were out. There's a bottle opener in the bottom drawer to the left of the sink. Bread is homemade. You should have everything you need to enjoy your stay. I don't imagine our paths will cross. Leave the key under the doormat on checkout. All the best, Dooling.

I read between the lines. What's there is evident. Some things I add.

Don't worry about me dropping by again. You don't want to see me, and I don't want to see you. It's like I'm not even here, Chantal. This is a transaction. For all intents and purposes, you're alone way out here in the scrub. A million miles away from anyone, really. And if the wind is blowing away *from the homestead, or if there's thunder…*

…I won't hear the bullet at all.

Wind pushes eucalyptus leaves into circles on the veranda, tightening circles. Gumnuts bounce on the wooden boards. A chill climbs my back. I step into the cabin I rented on a whim because my home in Canberra has become a poisonous place. Yank the door shut. The basket is lighter than expected—or maybe I'm stronger than I give myself credit for. Look back through the glass. The vegetation is thick with veiny branches. Faces in the tree trunks all sad or screamy. Flickers of gloomy sky like scratches on an old skillet after too much scrubbing.

The thought of food makes me ill, so I pour myself a gin and diet ginger ale instead. Dooling's wine can wait. It's almost five thirty. My toiletries bag is on the counter with my lipstick and foundation inside, the clamshell mirror I look at only when I must because I hate what I see. Hiking boots smothered in mud by the door. I'm sure it won't be long until I'm back in them and wandering outside. These walls are closing in again. There's the book I brought out of habit. No television. No radio. The clothes in my suitcase are all too big. The past year has taken a toll on my body. I'm fifty-six but look older. Police work does that. I'm hardened but had hoped I'd still be of use to someone. Nobody wants me. Nobody calls. This woman here is tainted goods. Her son is dead. Husband run off. What good is the gold retirement watch if there's nobody around to ask her the time anymore?

Another drink. It burns all the way down. Good.

You deserve to burn.

The rental is nice, just small. It's all I need. The perfect place to suicide. I don't want to do it in my house. I've spent too many years keeping the floors clean just to flood the place with gore. I'm being glib but sue me. I don't want to die in the house I shared with my men.

The cabin is neutral ground. I've always loved the mountains.

Bogong moths the size of mice tap at the window trying to get in at the lamps. I feel their kamikaze strikes against the glass in my shins, in my tooth fillings. I hate them. The fluttering of their wings reminds me of how we kids used to peg playing cards to the spokes of bikes and the sound they made as we rode. *Fft-fft-fft-fft-fft.* My bike riding years are behind me. And most of my friends are gone.

I don't eat. Consider killing myself again. Think, no, not tonight. I'm too annoyed by the moths at the windows. I came up here to feel calm and they've got me agitated. I decide to go to bed instead. It's early but who cares. What is time to someone like me? Time is a punchline and I'm the joke leading up to it.

The mattress is in the corner of the cabin to the right of the front door. I flip back the blanket and hear something strike the floor. It isn't loud. It doesn't seem heavy. It isn't one of my things. It is alien.

A silver earring sits on the hardwood floor. It's small, delicate, almost handsome in design. At first, I think it's the shape of a star. Reach down. Pick it up. Turn it over in my hand. No, it's a starfish. The corners are curled, as though propelling itself through water, against the channels and currents of my palm wrinkles. The hook is thin, clean. It snatches light from the bedside lamp and glimmers. I roll the earring between my thumb and forefinger, wondering who it belonged to, and make a mental note to pop it in an envelope for Dooling or the cleaner, whoever finds my body.

Hi there. Found this earring. Could be yours or maybe it belongs to the last person to rent the place. Hope you find the owner. It's a pretty thing. All the best, Chantal.

PS: sorry about the mess! Hope you're insured. Those stains are going to be a real bitch to get out of your curtains.

I place the earring on the bedside table and take a swill of water from the glass I'd left there. Soon my reflux will kick in. It always does after heavy drinking. Ease off my readers and turn off the light to study the ceiling in the dark. Memories creep in on cue.

Matthew has been dead for two-and-a-half years. My husband left me eight months ago.

I've had time to process Neville's abrupt departure. But I will never recover from the loss of my son. He saved me once. At the time, everyone told me suicide is murder—Neville, my colleagues at the department. They saw I'd had reasons to do it, means to do it, and had set aside the time. Nothing else mattered to them. Everyone except Matthew.

"Mum, what are you *doing*?" he cried when he came into my bedroom and found me on the bed. He'd later tell me he came over because his father was away for work, and he knew I'd been put on stress leave. I hadn't answered the phone in two days.

"No-no-no-NO-NO!"

I was awake enough to feel shame. Shame is a physical hurt in the flesh. Coloured pills and the numb forever the CAUTION labels promised didn't come through, empty as an 'I do'. Cut to the vomit when they pumped my stomach in the ambulance. I wanted out of this world at forty-seven, and somehow found myself alive with my adult son in the back of an ambulance instead.

"It's okay, Mum," I remember him saying.

"Sorry. So sorry. Sorry..."

"You're going to be okay."

There are other memories from those following days, all equally acute. Neville walking into the room where I was being treated and the bird-like way he perched on the mattress beside me. His red eyes. His red nose. His red capillaries. "Christ, Chantal. How could you be so stupid." It wasn't a question. He lifted his head, biting his thin red lower lip. Just one more word to silence me.

"Selfish."

That night in the hospital, I looked at the white walls and saw Amanda Lu.

She was the sister of the girl who had been murdered a year before I went to the medicine cabinet seeking bottles with warnings stickers. Amanda died because I didn't pick up on certain clues. She was murdered like her sister. Their killer stabbed them both forty-three times, cut off her hands and feet. I know the bastard's name but don't say it, hardly ever think it. My mind is a carousel of victims. Every face is remembered. It's my way of honouring who they were, not how they looked on the slab. With Amanda's assistance, we were closing in on our prime suspect. But he got to her first. I think he did it to send me a message. In a cruel cheat of fate, he was struck by a passing truck after fleeing Amanda's apartment. The knives were still on his person, as were Amanda's hands and feet. I could hardly believe it when my partner told me. It only seemed real when I saw the bastard's outline on the bitumen, chalk running in the rain. The lesson had been taught. I was—am—a failure of unforgivable magnitude.

Amanda Lu.

I couldn't save her, or her sister. And my son isn't here to save me a second time. Perhaps that is for the best.

The cabin is mine for five days. It even has a name. 'Kyle'. I saw the holiday rental advertisement in The Canberra Times classifieds. Dooling is over the hill, through a forest of pine trees, on an alpaca farm. I walked that way earlier, rain dripping through the canopy, cartoonish red and white toadstools everywhere. At a bluff, I passed between a gap in the boulders to peer at the owner's house down there in the valley. Nice place. Two storeys. Neat garden. Alpacas chewed grass in their pens. I went to the river, fingering a trigger every step of the way. My goodbyes went unheard. I no longer feared death, only pain. Pain, I'd seen up close.

The Matthew I used to know:

Handsome and tall, the spit of my father. A popular kid who grew into a sporty adult fond of a beer, and with a laugh that carried through the house when he visited from Sydney. He loved his mum, and only to me disclosed shades of the life he kept from us. Shades were enough. I didn't push my questions. I tried not to make assumptions (hard to do for most people, but harder for cops) and separated my hopes from his hopes for fear of him resenting me as he did others. He appreciated that. When Matthew looked you in the eye and smiled, you felt alive, like you had someone on your team. The dimples in his cheeks that called back to the boy he used to be. His hard, calloused hands. Workman's hands.

Versus Matthew at the end:

A skeleton wrapped in a sheet of skin with no fat or muscle between. Shitting himself. Vomiting blood. And then in the final months, the way he stared at me and didn't know who I was. Dimples stretched away. Silver rings slid onto the mattress because his fingers were so bony. In the night, he screamed the names of men I hadn't wanted to know about, and he never wanted to disclose to me. I wished I knew who these people were, and hoped they knew I would welcome them at our doorstep where I cared for him should they knock, that I would keep them safe from Neville. With time (not a lot of it, though), Matthew became less a man than a Condition with a capital C. So, when I held him and kissed his fingers, I had to acknowledge my love for The Condition. That was all that was left: the plague which seemed to target men born a certain way, men like my son. The invader that had overtaken this country of a person, burned his crops and enslaved his people. I loved The Condition, the disease, in the hopes I could gain its trust and control it. This was a foolish thing to invest effort in. One of many wasted moments. It got to the point, alone in the house with Matthew, where I had to whisper at him to let go.

"Stop fighting, my son. You're free."

Neville must have been searching for reasons to travel. He was hardly around, especially towards the end. A queer kid had never been easy for him. But to have that queer go out because of the plague… *that* he couldn't handle. The diagnosis confirmed something in Neville, that he'd been right to hate all along. It got to the point where others—family, the occasional friend—were too afraid to hold our son for fear they would catch it. I held him. I kissed him. Bathed him. Mopped his shit and blood. I wore rubber gloves. Scrubbed my hands until the skin cracked. His skeleton rose through his skin as though trying to climb into the grave. Kind eyes turned black. My boy was better than this. I used to think, *what a waste*. And that's what I told him when he sat me down and said he was sick. I regret saying this. It's a foolish thing to merit time in what you don't get as opposed to what you do. I'm happy to have had what I was blessed with. Though I hungered for more—still do. His absence, the nothingness of his non-existence, is a weight in my day that will never ease. He is with Amanda Lu. I do not want their weight on me any longer. Better a flash of light and a bang. Then whatever comes next. I've never been stupid enough to believe in God. I wish I could be that easily fooled.

Moths kept trying to get in all night long.

Fft-fft. Fft-fft-fft-fft. Fft. Fft-fft-fft-fft-fft-fft.

Sleep must have claimed me at some point because dawn breaks and the kookaburras are laughing. Groggy, I reach for my glass of water and touch something warm and foreign on the bedside table instead. Snatch back my hand. Put on my glasses. Jolt in the bed.

"Jesus Christ!"

The earring is still there.

Only now it's threaded through the lobe of a human ear.

Fine hairs along the rim—if that's what you call it. The outer ear. Tiny hairs rise as though capable of sensory reaction. I place the remains (though, in all honesty, it feels more like the beginnings of something and not the leftovers) on the dining table next to the guest book and a map of walking trails. Rain announces itself on the tin-roof. I sip my tea and rub my chin, glancing from the ear to the gun I set by the toaster and Vegemite.

How truly odd this is, I think. *There really is no other way to put it.*

Odd.

Another me, maybe the married me, or the motherly me, might have been fearful of finding an ear. I'm not those people anymore. Why should the appearance of a body part shock me when parts of my body have been numbing out, bit by bit, piece by piece, for months? I am zombie, a necrotic thing. The only difference is that I carry my dead bits and pieces with me.

So, what the hell do I do with it?

The lime green landline beckons from the wall. Dooling's number is printed on a laminated card bound to the keys he left out for me the prior day. How would that conversation go?

"Uh, sorry to bother you, but did you happen to leave a magic earring in the cabin? It seems to have grown an ear overnight. Do you, uh, want to come down here and take care of it for me? I've got enough on my plate. Thanks!"

Maybe I should flush it down the toilet, as I did one of Matthew's dead canaries when he was a kid. The bird died while he was at school. Neville and I told our son that Nero got out of his cage and flew home to be with the other canaries. There were hundreds, even thousands of them in the sky, calling out to him. And Nero listened. It wasn't anyone's fault.

"But how did Nero open the cage from the inside? Nero doesn't have hands!"

Smart kid. Always was.

"I think something happened to Nero, and you and Dad don't want to tell me because you're worried about how it'll make me feel," he'd said with tears in his eyes, sounding so even-tempered and adult it aged me years within a second. "Well, I'm sad. I'm just really, really sad."

Sighing, I place the ear on the table. Leave it there. Pick up my umbrella. Climb inside my raincoat. Put the gun in the pocket. Take to the hills to think—and maybe more. I don't lock up. There's nothing in the cabin worth stealing because I value nothing. There are crows in the sky. Sparrows here and there. No canaries.

I come home five hours later to find that the ear has grown a head.

It blinks, mouthing words yet unable to speak, having no lungs with which to breathe, no throat to muscle out the noise. The head tongues the roof of its dry mouth. I go to the fridge by the sink and wrestle an ice cube out of the tray. Offer it to the head, and when he blinks twice at me, tongue extending, I slide it into his mouth. It sucks for a bit and then crushes the cube between its jaws.

"Don't chew!" I say, extending a hand. "You'll hurt your—" The hand stills. "Teeth." Drops. Jaws no longer grind. I grip my rising and falling chest. Every inch of my body is vulnerable. Exposed. This is who I really am. I am a mother who hungers for someone to parent. And this thing on the counter now has me by the short and curlies.

No, not a thing. This is a man.

He's younger than Matthew when he died, maybe twenty-three, twenty-four. Caucasian. Handsome. Sad, skittish deer eyes. Sallow cheeks. Lips like a Roman statue.

I'm not sure how long I sit and stare. Long enough for the light to change. Fatigue settles in. Emotions I can't name niggle with a hundred tiny mouths, but not even this is enough through the wall of numbness. Not yet. It's good to feel something. It might be shock, but sleep is something I need above all else. Unfortunately, I always wake. Cops never die in their sleep. That's just the way it goes.

I can't have the head looking at me while I nap (I might be far gone but I'm not immune to the creep factor), so I roll the head over. "Sorry," I say, touching it gingerly—all fingertips, no palms. The mass of meat faces the microwave and Dooling's basket. I run my fingers through the man's duckish hair. Should he have lived to be in his forties, I imagine he may have been bald. He's warm.

Who are his parents? Do they know what became of him? How would his mother feel knowing he's here with me?

I lay my head against the pillow.

My eyes bolt open at a voice within the room.

There are still a few hours of light left in the day. I squint against the glare that has crept through the port hole in the slanted ceiling, stalking the floor and onto the bed. I haven't moved, and my bones grind as I lift myself up off the mattress.

The head has grown half a torso.

"Okay," I say. Take a breath. "Here we go."

Rubbery lungs inflate and deflate beneath the man's broad shoulders. Veins slither across the tabletop, slow roots in search of soil. Flesh glimmers around the edges as it crystalises and then grows lax, undulating, each flex expanding outwards in new growths, a tide of meat drawing closer to shore with every wave. And I'm that shore. It's me he wants.

"You're awake," the man says, voice a rasp. *"Please, lady, you're in danger."*

"W-what?"

"Turn me over so I can see you."

You don't attend as many crime scenes as I have without developing the gall to handle a John or Jane Doe. I scuttle off the bed, go to the table, and take the chunk of man by the shoulders. My grip is tenacious, more *me*, this time. Roll him over so he's earring side up. He's feverish. Bright blue eyes peer into me.

"Thank you," says the man.

"You're, um, welcome."

"Can I have another ice-cube?"

I oblige him. "You said I was in danger?"

The man pushes the ice from one side of his mouth to the other. Hot breath over the cold cube makes his words steam. *"What day is it?"* he asks. *"What date?"*

"April twelfth."

The man blinks. Tears in the corner of his eyes. He prepares to speak, maybe taking a moment to absorb where he is and what has become of him.

"I was killed five days ago." His brow furrows. Confusion muscles into a frightened kind of hope. *"That means my friend might still be alive."*

Now is as good a time as any to take a seat. I'm light-headed. My hands interlink on the table. Gears shift. My detective voice kicks in. "What's your name, son?"

"Scotty."

It's as if in saying his name, acknowledging who he used to be, the man has given himself permission to cry. Tears appear silver in the cool light. His loss is confirmed for both of us now.

"Scotty McLain. I'm from Canberra. I came to this cabin with my friend. We were asleep when someone came through the door in the night. We're in the middle of nowhere, we didn't think we needed to lock up. The bastard got in when we were sleeping."

Something in me thaws. I think of the cases I didn't solve, the wrongs I didn't right. Amanda Lu and her sister and how their body bags protruded at all the wrong angles in the morgue. All those closed casket funerals I watched at a cop's distance, where you appear to be paying respects but are scanning the mourners for suspects because killers are compulsive creatures who feed off suffering. The situation facing me now isn't about whether I believe the man or not. Rather, if I still believe in my own abilities. Perhaps this is a test. But who—I can't help wondering—is the teacher?

"The intruder. Who was this man?" I ask.

"It's the owner," Scotty says, quick as thunder close to the strike. *"Burly fella. Sickly looking, but stronger. He's so tall. Like a giant. His name's Dooling."*

My mind leapfrogs to the note in the basket. The neat handwriting—careful, considerate, swishes and flicks.

"How do I know you're telling me the truth, Scotty?"

"I..."

My eyebrow raises. I need to challenge him. Need to know.

"I can prove it."

Scotty closes his blue eyes, which are so like Matthew's. There's that same sympathy in them, a fish out of its bowl *I-can't-believe-this-is-happening-to-me* naiveté. It's enough to make me burst. *I don't want this. This isn't how things are meant to go.* Numbness is what I need, numbness more than anything because numb is safe.

"Oh, you can prove it, can you?"

I'm laughing. The sound has a kookaburra cruelty to it. I hate myself.

The dead man nods, so much as he can nod, right temple against the tablecloth. He shivers and coughs. His mouth opens. Eyes pinch. My pulse quickens with expectancy, a feeling that everything is slipping off keel.

Scotty regurgitates up a human pinkie finger. It flops on the table beside his mouth, webbed in greenish strands of saliva. The second knuckle is tattooed with the letter E.

I stumble backwards. "Fucking hell!"

Scotty clears his throat. *"He's only got four fingers left on his right hand."* His voice is clearer now. *"I bit this one off when he attacked me. I swallowed it whole."*

Bile slips up my throat and I swallow it down. There's a part of me that wants to dive to the raincoat by the door, pull the gun out, shove the barrel in my mouth and do what I came here to do. I'm not doing that, though. I don't know *why* I'm not doing that.

Scotty speaks again.

"Don't," I say. "Don't—"

"Matthew was wrong."

"Shhh."

"When things were really bad, when you were caring for him at the end, he told you he was afraid there was nothing…beyond."

"I don't want to hear it!" I cover my ears. Scotty's words cut through. My stomach turns again, nerves in riot. The arthritic pain twists and clenches and splints in elbows and knees and shoulders. It's everywhere.

"If only there was…only the pit."

I glare at the man on the table. In his eyes, I see refractions of light cast from some other place. My ticket to that place is in the chamber of the gun. That light is both cold and hot at once, and I hate that my son—that all sons and daughters—are lit by it in the end.

"There is no love in the beyond, Chantal," Scotty tells me. I hear the mourning in him. *"Where there was love there are only cogs. And we all turn. We all have a place. Cogs on cogs on cogs, all of us powering the machine. Powering It. We all turn."*

"You can't tell me this, Scotty. You can't. It's not right."

"I escaped, but they'll know I'm gone soon."

"Close your mouth."

"Help me, Chantal. While there's still time. I can hear them turning."

Gin burns all the way down. The muddy boots are tight about my ankles. I set off for the house on the other side of the hill, through the boulders, across the valley. The folds of the rubber slicker wisp as I march over uneven earth, crushing mushrooms.

The image of the severed finger with the letter E tattooed on its knuckle probes my brain. It knows my will is squishy. It knows that it is *inside* me now, and the only way to purge it is to see this through.

It's four thirty in the afternoon. Evening will fall soon. There's hardly twilight at this time of the year. Night eats day and then we live in its belly until it shits us out again. We endure this over and over, and each time we wake, there's a little less of us left. This is what it is to get old. I know I was—no, *am*—right to want no more of that cycle.

That little slip into past tense makes me uncomfortable.

The *was.*

Do I stop every so often to reconsider my decision to pursue this? You bet. But my legs keep moving, step after step, a beat in search of beat, my body, my soul, and my need for answers. Even here at the end of who I used to be, I still have to know. Because I've been faced with a mystery. I sense the mystery as to why Scotty came to me is old and cosmic. Within that mystery lies a secret. And secrets are man-made.

According to Scotty, the man on the property did the worst thing a man can do.

So, detect, Detective.

I peer over the ridge. It would take me half-an-hour to reach the house below. All going to plan (ha—what plan?), I'd be trekking back to my cabin well after dark. There would be no light with the clouds as thick as they were in the mountains. I sit on one of the rocks and shake my head. Of all the cabins I could have rented, it had to be Dooling's.

The kookaburras are laughing again.

"Hey there, mate," I say to the enormous man bent over in the garden. He also wears a slicker, only his is garbage bag green. The rain has petered off. Just little spits every now and then. The garden would be soft. A perfect time to turn blood and bone. Alpacas bray in my direction, their pelts knotted and slimy with oil and water.

I hold my ground.

Dooling stands and faces me. Scotty was correct. The owner is a giant of a kind. Easily seven feet of bulk, a mixture of muscle and fat. A moon of a creature. He wears heavy duty gardening gloves on both hands, gripping a three-pronged trowel in his right—it looks comically small compared to the rest of him.

"You're the lady in the cabin, yeah?" he says. His voice is buttery.

"Chantal."

"That's right."

"And you're Mister Dooling?"

"Just Dooling," he says, nodding. His eyes are small and round in his face. I hear him breathing from where I stand, half a dozen yards away, the space between us full of sun-bleached pinwheels stabbed into the grass. There is mucus in his throat. It rattles. I want to cough for him.

"I'm just out walking, Dooling."

"Weather for the ducks," he says, gesturing to the sky. It spits again in reply.

"I was wondering if you could help me with something?"

Another phlegmy inhale, followed by the rattle of breath fighting its way from his thick throat. The air we share vibrates in his presence, with the exertion it takes for him to keep living. His stormy energy. I'm afraid of him. The numbness has receded now. Coming here was a mistake. I wonder if he can taste my motive on the wind. If he's who I think he is, what he is, he already knows I've come to cause him grief.

"You should have used the phone in your cabin," he says. The crown of his bald head is sweaty—or maybe it's just from the rain. "Whatever you needed, I could've arranged and saved you a walk."

Alpacas stir. A crow calls.

The pinwheels are turning, turning.

"You know," he continues. "Brought you whatever you need. Even if it was after dark. I've got a torch."

I wonder if, five days earlier, in the dark, that same torch illuminated the earth between his house and the cabin he rents in The Canberra Times classified section. I believe it did. I believe he turned the torch off before stepping into the clearing. I believe he waited for Scotty and his friend to turn off the lights. And I believe Dooling waited a while, out in the trees, until it seemed the right amount of time for a person to fall asleep. I believe he could have waited longer, just to be sure, only Dooling couldn't wait. He is impatient. His boots would have crushed the dewy grass as he stepped closer to the cabin, that his heaviness would have made the veranda floorboards creak. This sound would have alerted Scotty. And the end would have come fast and blunt. I believe Dooling may have put the torch in his huge mouth, the plastic tight between his teeth, to light the way back through the trees, across the valley, as he dragged Scotty's friend home. I believe that it would have been after dawn by the time Dooling got back to clean the mess he made in the cabin. Scotty was buried in sunlight. But by that time, Scotty was in the beyond. He was turning.

We all turn, Scotty told me. And even though I didn't want to believe that, too, I did.

"I'm sure you do have a torch," I say. "I didn't think. I'm a feet-first kind of gal."

Dooling studies me. "How old are you? No spring chicken. Sorry, I don't mean to be rude. I'd hate for someone like you to fall, is all. There's lots of foxholes. Roll an ankle in weather like this, I might never have heard your calls."

I look at his hands again. Five fingered gloves on each.

"I'm a widow," I lie. Well, sort-of lie. This is an indication of age, or at least as much rope as I am willing to gift him.

"A widow."

"Yeah."

The man drops his guard. "Me too. House sure feels empty without the ole girl around no more."

"Sorry to hear," I say.

"So, what is it?"

"What's what?"

"What do you need?"

"Oh," I say. "Sugar. Can't have my coffee without it. When I was younger, I'd never have a cuppa this late in the day. But you don't need as much sleep when you're older."

"There's sugar in your cabin right above the—"

"Ants."

"What?"

"Ants got to it. Little buggers."

"Damn things. I'll have to spray the place again."

The wind picks up, making the alpacas cry. It sounds like a warning—not that I need one. Rain comes down harder, sluicing Dooling's oily face. He is a golem of a thing, an assembly of parts, all different sizes. His trowel is like a third, arthritic hand that reminds me of Mum at the end. How she held me even though it hurt to hold me.

Where there was love there are cogs.

"I'll get you some sugar," he says, limping towards the front door of the double storey house. I follow close behind, but not too close. A safe distance. Though, from my time on the beat, I've learned there's no such thing.

Dooling tosses the screen door open and slips inside. He shifts sideways to fit. That's how broad he is.

The giant.

I'm sure he must have expected me to wait on the veranda. Rain on the tin roof masks the sound of my feet as I glide into the house. It is warmer inside than I'd expected. An awkward, sweaty kind of heat, like climbing inside someone else's jacket. The house smells like mice. I make sure to keep an eye on the door.

Playing with fire was one thing. Willingly allowing yourself to be burned alive was another.

I glance down the hall. Hear the shuffling of Dooling's heavy feet. The thud of a cabinet door opening. The rasp of crockery over wood.

Take another step.

There is a staircase on my right. My shoes squelch over the tiles, and I almost slip. I grip the balustrade. The wood is cold.

Hold steady, Detective.

Did Dooling's wife polish the balustrade when she was alive? Was she the house-proud kind? Speculation worms deeper, deeper. Did the ole girl know of her husband's proclivities? Was she aware that beneath the polish there was rot at the heart of her home?

Was this *her* secret?

I see you, I want to tell her. *I see everything.*

Dooling emerges at the end of the hall with a round clay pot in his hands—Pooh Bear with his honey. The gloves have been removed. He bows his head to fit through the kitchen architrave. The light is dim in the hall.

"Didn't know you came in," he says.

I say something about the rain, as if this will do. The cool wind presses against my back. Water trickles beneath my shirt. Icy beads course my skin, down the rise and fall of my spine, down my chest and between my breasts. Tingles. Goosebumps. My flesh is alive. These sensations are a welcoming, and for the first time in a long time—well before AIDS took Matthew, before Amanda Lu came into my office—I *know* I am alive. Every ripple of air between Dooling and I feels predetermined, as if everything was meant to flow this way, this way and no other. I'm meant to be here, on this very day, walking into a monster's lair, led here by things that live when they should be dead. It's April 12, 1991, and if the giant gives me reason to, I'll blow his brains out.

"Yeah," he says. "The rain."

His face is in shadow except for a splash of glow reflecting off a photo on the wall. It lights his eyes. They are bile yellow where they should be white.

My heart skips a beat when something thumps behind a door to my left. Dooling doesn't look in the direction of the sound—an indication

I should not look either, that whatever is behind that door does not exist. But it does exist. I know it. And he knows I know it.

Wind whips the screen door. My slicker ripples on my frame.

Dooling smiles, revealing dentures that don't sit right. Horse-like teeth in a sloppy hole. He takes a step into the light, a boot coming down too hard on the tiles. I peek at the sugar pot he holds. Dooling's knuckles are tattooed. The right hand, letter by letter, reads LOVE. And the left would read HATE, had he still his pinkie finger. The stump has been cauterised. No bandages. All scabs.

Another thump from the room on my left.

Followed by a muffled cry for help.

The fake smile on my face remains in place. My hand dives into the pocket of my raincoat and withdraws the gun. I level it at the giant, his lips slinking back over those oversized teeth.

"Stop right there," I say. "Back it up. Into the kitchen now."

"What are you doing?"

I lift the gun higher. "Thought you said you lived alone, Dooling."

He scowls. "I didn't say that. I told you I was a widow."

"Who's in there?"

Dooling licks his lips. "Spot," he says. "Such a good boy."

At those words, I fire a warning shot into the ceiling—enough to send Dooling backpedaling down the hallway. The pot strikes the tiles and shatters. Sugar explodes in every direction. Wind catches the grains and sweeps them into the air in a fine mist that catches the light. Dooling dips as he scuttles into the kitchen.

I kick the door on my left. The bones in my body lock and shudder, pieces of me cracking inside. No regrets. The door wasn't locked and swings open.

The words fall out of me. "Sweet Christ, no."

A naked man is on the bedroom floor. He shuffles forward to the extent of the chain about his neck. He's starving. A foot strikes a silver bowl on the ground, raw chicken wings flipping onto carpet covered in newspapers. The chain reaches up to a hook in the ceiling—giving the man enough room to move around but not reach the door or window. Gnarly whippies of shit in the corner. Blood on the walls. His hands are bound behind his back. A gag in his mouth. The colour of the gag is poison mushroom red, the colour of Neville's lips the day he told me

I was selfish. The man howls. He rolls, exposing the cut marks across his back and buttocks. Rolls again. Slices to his navel and cock and balls. The man bounds upright again and runs at me, snapping backwards at the taut pull of the chain.

I spin in time to see Dooling re-emerge with a shotgun. My vision flowers with light, my light, my gun. This isn't my first rodeo. I fire a second time. My aim isn't as good as I'd hoped it would be either time. The first bullet missed completely and the second caught Dooling's arm. That is enough. Just. The shotgun falls from his grip as he lands on his side, thrown onto the chequerboard linoleum in the kitchen. I run towards him, Spot keening in his room-cage at my back. Dooling rolls onto his feet with a nimbleness that spits in the face of everything I know about men of his age and size.

Widow power, I think. *Alone power.*

In the time it takes me to get to the kitchen, Dooling has already snatched up a knife. He rushes at me, swinging the cleaver in an arc. I attempt to spin away in time, rewind my steps, heft the gun—only nothing is quick enough. The blade carves the length of my right thigh, through slicker and jeans and flesh. Adrenalin dulls the pain for now. The force behind the giant's attack keeps the knife coursing downwards, inertia dragging the giant to his knees, revealing his bald crown. Opportunity. Knife strikes linoleum. The giant cranes his neck. His eyes meeting mine. I level the gun against his forehead and pull the trigger. The detonation is incredible. Brains sludge across my chest. Bone shards spear my lips and nose. I smell his sick thoughts on me.

Dooling hits the ground so hard the house shakes. He's not quite dead yet. Limbs shudder, his boots squeak-thump the linoleum at my feet as he bleeds out. His mouth opens, closes, opens, closes, the dentures coming unstuck from his gums to clatter in a boney kookaburra laugh in the pit of his throat. I watch Dooling slip away and go still. The moment something dies, it is immediately dead. So dead, so inanimate, it's hard to imagine it ever lived. I've learned this as a cop. But I lived it first as a mother. Something glimmers in Dooling's eyes for a moment, a flicker of light, but then it, too, vanishes. He is cogs now. That and nothing more.

I rip the belt off Dooling's blood-stained trousers and fashion a quick torniquet above my thigh. I limp up the hall to Spot, who is rocking on the floor with his head between his knees. I approach him slowly with the gun in one hand and Dooling's cleaver in the other. The boy lashes out in defense.

"Everything's okay," I say. "Let me help you. It's over. He's dead."

I look upon this chained man and see my son on his hospital bed, flanked by nurses who tell him it's okay to let go. And he had a lot to let go of, too. So much anger. Anger at the principal of the school he taught at who fired him once he learned Matthew was gay, worried he'd conscript the kids into the fold. The men and women who called my police department to report when my son went to the local pool where his sarcoma bruises were on display for prying eyes. His father. I choose to believe Matthew let them go, there on his death bed at the end, more tube and machine than man. He gestured at me to come close, his lips parting, wanting to tell me something. But he died before he had the chance. I watched him ease. Saw the monitor turn to lines. Heard that no-pulse whine. Nurses swooped in. A sheet drawn over a face I'd watched change since birth. But the chained man on his knees before me is someone else's son—which isn't to say I'm not proud of him, as I'm sure Scotty would be, too.

Today, this man will live. He has no place on my carousel of the dead.

I rip off the gag. I feel his heat when he puts his brow against my neck and weeps. Scotty told me his friend's name before I left the cabin.

"Are you Proctor?" I say.

He looks up at me. Nods. "He called me Spot."

I cup his bruised cheek and tell him nobody will ever call him that again. "You need to come with me, Proctor."

"D-do you know Scotty?" he asks. "Did he send you? Is he okay? My god, I thought he was hurt. Scotty fought. He bit him. The screams—"

Trying to keep strong, I grip the young man by the chin and make him stare into me. "Scotty doesn't have long, I think. He's at the cabin. There might not be much time. I don't know how this works. I just need you to be stronger than you've ever been. This—" I search for the right words. "This is a goodbye."

It is an awful thing to watch a heart break. I've delivered many death notices over my years on the force, innocent boys and girls carved up or run down or lost. Nothing compared to this honesty. Like so many other things in this world and the next, we must continue to turn. Each and every one of us.

"How are you going to get me out of these chains?" Proctor says.

"The old-fashioned way, honey." I lift my gun. "Cover your ears."

Proctor is under one arm. I've dressed him in my raincoat. He's still weighted by his manacles. Tender feet pinch inwards. We cross the stretch of land between the house and the rental, lit by a torch—*the* torch, maybe—I found on a bench in Dooling's kitchen. The hill fights us. The pine forest wants to eat us. But the clouds pull back to reveal stars. They shine bright. The battery in the torch winds down and dies. I'm thankful for the quarter moon that lights the rest of the way.

We emerge from the trees, into the clearing.

Proctor stops us both. He quivers under my hold.

"There," he says, and points.

I lift my gaze to the cabin and see someone standing at the bottom of the stairs. This figure is whole now, and glows with the soft iridescence you sometimes see in a curling wave by night. That glow is elemental. And fleeting.

"Go to him," I tell Proctor. "It's Scotty who saved you. Not me. Not really."

Proctor grabs my shoulder. "Thank you, lady," he whispers.

I nod. It's all I have left to give. Teary, I fight to keep my voice pitched low. "When you're done, I'll take us to the hospital. We're not in good shape, you and I."

"How will you explain what happened?"

I let him slip away from me. My body tingles.

"I honestly don't care," I say. And then I smile. He's not at the smiling stage yet. He may never be. So, I smile for the both of us.

Proctor turns to Scotty, who waits, upright and whole, naked and proud. The light is on inside and the bogong moths launch themselves at the sliding glass door again. I can't blame them. That light is warm.

I watch the two men stumble close to one another. They stop. Proctor lets the yellow slicker grease off his shoulders and pool at his heels. They embrace, flesh to flesh. Cock to cock. Their kiss is deep with history.

It's like the cool valley wind, blowing from behind, wants to usher me closer. I maintain my cop's distance, though there are no suspects here. The gun is still gripped in my bloodied hand. Dry blood. I let the gun go. It makes a soft padding sound against the earth. My shooting days are over. For now, at least.

No promises.

The two men draw apart. Clouds recede further, letting in more moonlight. Voices carry on the breeze.

"Don't go," Proctor says to Scotty. "You can't leave me again. Please."

It is too late.

"Baby, no—"

We both watch Scotty come apart, sliding into pieces like lumps of clay. There is no blood. No pain. This is a return to earth. Proctor cries quietly. He doesn't drop to his knees and try to scoop his lover up. No theatrics. He lets him go. I find this brave.

It's time. I cross the clearing to touch Proctor's neck. "Let's leave this place," I tell him. The pieces of Scotty have become mud at the foot of the stairs. I catch sight of the small starfish shaped earring in the mess. Proctor sees it too and picks it up, rolls it between his thumb and forefinger. "Ha," he says. The memories tied to the earring are his. I do not pry. That life is his. That life has merit. I learned this from my son. Matthew is the teacher. He always was.

Proctor stands, tells me he's ready, and we approach my car parked next to the cabin. I stop. "Oh, I need my keys," I say, leaving him. "They're just inside. Give me a minute."

I step away and approach the cabin for the final time. I have no intention to gather the last of my things inside. They have no value or relevance to whoever I am now. My eyes shift to the door. Through the glass. The keys on the table inside right where I left them.

Bogong moths pound at the door. I grab the handle and slide it open.

"Go on," I say to them. "Now's your chance."

But they do not enter.

The Zoo

GEMMA AMOR

I KNEW I WAS IN FOR A ROUGH RIDE LONG BEFORE I SAW HOW MANY PEOPLE were camped outside the London City Zoo's main gates, which were cordoned off by the time I pulled up in my brand new Mercedes-AMG GT. I knew it because I felt a sense of dread building in my bones. Hard to describe, but that's the best I can do. My bones, on fire. Not in the same way that old women say their bones ache before it rains. More like my bones don't feel pain, but they *are* pain. I am made of it, the closer to the echo of a bad thing I get. Like my skin is stretched across a scaffold of suffering.

I felt it from several miles away, this particular bone-bad, so I knew I was letting myself in for something truly terrible this time. I knew, and I went anyway. I chase the money, see. What else is there worth chasing? Only charlatans claiming to be Psychic chase glory. The best thing we can hope for is that someone takes us seriously, that those we choose to open up to can discern between the genuine ones, like me, and the crackpot scumbags who only pretend to have powers so they can soak up adulation and profit from the pain and suffering of others.

The false ones are those who lap up the limelight, beg for attention however they can. Insert themselves into missing person's cases and the like, uninvited.

I don't operate like that. I'm a consultant. Legitimate. Payrolled. I stay away until I'm invited. Bit like a vampire, I guess. I can't come into your house of pain until you specifically ask me to. Until you invite me across the threshold. Even then, it's up to me as to whether or not I accept. A man at this stage in his career can, and should, pick and choose his clients carefully.

That being said, I never turned down the Metropolitan Police when they came calling. Money, see. They had it, despite what they told the world at large. Not many could afford my rates, which were calculated to accommodate not only my unique skillset, but my discretion and silence, which was more valuable than my abilities to some.

In the belly of my car, a handcrafted 4.0 litre V8 biturbo engine strained at the leash, making a noisy entrance, which was exactly the point: I'd paid for the noise. I paid for all the extras, too. Customised interior painted and stitched in red and black, the most aggressive colours I could think of, LED lighting, accessories coming out of every goddamn orifice. *Look at me,* this car said. *I've fucking made it.* I fucked a lot of women in that car, they seemed to like the leather interiors, the noise of the engine. Those seats had been deep-cleaned more times than I cared to admit, even though I'd only had the car a few weeks.

I parked a good distance away from the furore, choosing a quiet spot on the street with no passing traffic. All those people milling about meant scratches on my paintwork, and I couldn't be having that. I'd worked hard for this sexy sleek polished beast, a vehicle that finally fit the sort of person I was trying to be, outwardly at any rate. None of those idiots craning their necks trying to see into the crime scene would have any understanding of how hard, exactly, I worked for it. How much I suffered. They didn't need to know, either. I didn't need anyone's approval. I just needed my fat paycheck after the job was done. That was approval enough.

I buffed a smudge off the bonnet of the Merc as I passed, feeling genuine pride. People who grow up with money don't understand this sort of pride, the sort that comes with finally being able to afford something you've always been told was out of reach. *Not for people like you, wealth is a privilege,* they teach you, from the youngest of ages. Well, fuck that. Wealth is a man's right. He just has to reach for it, is all.

There must have been a hundred onlookers crowding around the taped off area in front of the Zoo as I approached. I almost turned around, then. People made me itchy in large numbers, but that wasn't the reason. The undercurrent of something foul and foetid was the reason. It was overwhelming. My teeth vibrated. My bones sang furiously the closer I got.

I pushed on through anyway, throwing dirty looks around like confetti. *Go home, you fucking losers,* my face said, but I kept my mouth shut. I never understood rubbernecking. When something bad happens, my instinct is to run the other way, avoid seeing what I don't have to. The bone-bad means I can sense chaos before I see it, and so I choose not to. See it. I can't fathom why people *do* seek out violence deliberately, why onlookers slow down when they pass a car accident. Why would you *want* to see that? Wreckage, pain, blood? I suppose it's the same ancient gene that drew our ancestors to public executions or the Roman Colosseum. The whole world is a stage, and all the men and women merely players, even in death. I hate that.

I used my elbows to get to the front of the crush, drew some sharp breaths which quickly died when the recipients saw the badge I brandished like a priest wielding a crucifix at an exorcism. It didn't match my suit, but I could live with that. For now. Maybe at some point I'd get a customised leather wallet. Embossed with my initials, perhaps. Chrome trim. Small compensation for having to put up the shit I do.

This close, the Zoo gave off what I liked to think of as a 'funky brain smell', which made no sense to anyone but me, but that was okay. I was used to nobody ever understanding what went on in my head. It was lonely, but simpler than trying to explain what being a Psychic actually meant.

I stepped over a fresh puddle of vomit near the ticket office, squeezed through the turnstile, and ducked beneath another line of fluttering tape as the reporters and bystanders behind me jostled each other for a better view. *How did they always know?* I wondered. It was eight-thirty in the morning. I never ceased to be surprised at how fast the British press got hold of things. At how quickly they could mobilise in the hope of nabbing a scoop.

Well, there wouldn't be one: this was an old-fashioned inner city zoo, built by the Victorians, with high surrounding grey stone walls and a chunky wrought-iron entrance gate that, once closed, completely sealed the compound off from the outside world.

I was thankful for this, later.

Fleur Orwell met me inside. Usually a nice normal colour, she was white as a sheet. My heart sank further when I saw this, which was saying something, because it was already down by my screaming knees.

'Alistair,' she said, in a hoarse voice.

'Fleur. What...' I trailed off. Partly because of the pain, partly because I realised I couldn't hear, or sense, any animals. Not a single one.

But wasn't this a Zoo?

I swallowed, my throat dry.

'What have we got?' My voice sounded a good deal less competent than I would have liked. 'Your call was pretty cryptic...'

God, my bones. My poor, poor bones. The pain got worse by the second. It was like a crushing fist. I steadied myself against a wall.

Fleur looked at me with pity in her eyes. It wasn't the usual pity she held for the freak who saw things with his mind that no normal person should be able to see. Rather, it was a type of pity reserved for someone who had not yet seen what she was desperate to unsee.

Fuck, I thought. It had to happen sooner or later. The few homicides I'd been brought onto had been clean and easy, as far as murder went. One strangulation, one poisoning, one smothering with a pillow. Nothing too...messy, not yet. Painful to be around, but not a bit like this.

Fleur echoed my thoughts.

'I've...I've never seen anything like this in my life before,' she admitted, throat working strenuously. I wondered if hers had been the vomit outside. Orwell was of strong stomach usually, a cool, collected detective who liked to take her time with things. It took a lot to ruffle her feathers.

I fervently wished that I hadn't eaten such a large breakfast.

'Are you wearing Armani again?' Fleur blinked at me. 'At a time like this?'

I refused to feel sheepish.

She shook her head. 'You're going to regret it,' she said, mournfully.

'Show me.'

'We'll start with the bird enclosure.'

'Alright,' I said, but it wasn't.

Fleur shivered as she led me away from the main gates, around the ticket office and towards a large, netted and fenced-off compound that traditionally housed flamingos. Access to it was via a system of metal and wire swing-gates. The inner gate wouldn't release and open until the magnetised latch of the outer one was closed, to prevent the birds from escaping, I assumed.

Only once I was through the gates, there were no birds anyway.

Not of the avian type, I mean.

Instead, I found a half-dried up concrete-bottomed lake coated with a brownish meniscus of algae. Around it, some tired landscaping: boulders that didn't come from anywhere geographically nearby, scrubby grasses, bulrushes in the scummy water. Pink feathers scattered everywhere like raggedy little blossoms. Some natural, some not. No flamingoes though, not in the lake.

Just two human bodies, dead in the centre. Positioned like a fucking water feature at a sculpture park.

Their blood still dripped into the nasty water below.

'Jesus,' I said, covering my mouth with my hand. A sheet of white hot panic slid over me. My bones were melting, so badly I could barely walk straight. My knees semi-buckled. Fleur grabbed me just in time to stop my legs folding completely.

'What?' she said, beyond the obvious. 'What do you see?'

I couldn't reply. I couldn't speak.

I just looked with wide, unbelieving eyes.

The bodies were hoisted up about four feet into the air upon tall, crudely sharpened stakes inserted via the rectum, exiting through the victim's backs, just between the shoulder blades. Like meat roughly thrust upon kebab sticks. The stakes were painted dark pink, mimicking the pink of a flamingo's leg, and bent backwards awkwardly in the middle at a realistically depicted raised ankle joint. To reinforce the illusion, one of each of the victim's legs was folded sharply and taped, ankle to buttock, to imitate the stance of a flamingo standing on one leg, the other tucked safely beneath. Broad membranous appendages had been attached to the victim's feet, flappy webbed abominations fashioned from what later turned out to be surplus human skin (from where, we never found out) and sticks. Painted pink, of course.

Both corpses—a man and woman in their twenties, perhaps, hard to tell, all things considered—were smothered in a thick, pasty glue that had dried hard and was decorated with thousands of carefully placed synthetic neon pink feathers. Decorative, frivolous. They riffled as a light breeze swirled around the enclosure, disturbing the long, curved beaks with bulbous tips that were bolted to the victim's heads. Fashioned from wood, meticulously painted and fully articulated, they flapped open, revealing two traumatised, slack-jawed faces beneath.

I wobbled again, but kept my balance. The longer I looked, the more I wished I didn't see, both inside and outside of my mind.

How long had this taken? I thought, blurrily. I felt a seeping sense of ritual and craftsmanship, the same feeling I associated with someone doing a jigsaw puzzle with laborious dedication, or embroidering cross-stitch or painting a very detailed picture. Tongue poked out slightly in concentration. I sensed intense focus and pride. Not the pride I felt when I looked at my new car. Instead, a warped pride for a thing well-made, for a thing created to exacting standards, not for something earned, but for something the creator hoped other people would appreciate.

An image swam to me: a childish, wounded shadow, seeking approval.

Look at the Flamingo People, Mummy, a voice said, but I knew there was no Mummy. Not for the abomination behind this scene. That was part of the root of it. Whoever we were looking for, had been…

Had been…

Abandoned?

I couldn't focus. A barrage of other people's thoughts and experiences and memories assaulted me.

'They were alive when she did it,' I gasped, unable to help myself any longer. Tears ran down my face. I was awash with torment. My bones told me a story of splintering vertebrae, of ruptured skin, of inhuman strength, of immense, intense suffering and fear and trauma and…

I couldn't help myself. I threw up.

They had been alive when she'd speared them right through the middle.

One had watched the other die, in brutal, indescribable agony.

Fleur neatly sidestepped the steaming puddle I made near her feet (poached eggs on toast with avocado and toasted pumpkin seeds) and retched again herself as she caught a whiff. She'd already emptied herself earlier, so she managed to get control more quickly than I did.

'Alive?' She said, breathing heavily.

I saw flamingoes flying free across the rooftops of a nearby housing estate. The perpetrator had set them free, presumably. Along with all the other creatures.

How?

How?

'We need a profile,' Fleur said then, as I knew she would.

I shook my head.

'Not yet,' I mumbled. 'I can't.'

The gate behind me swung open. A team of white-suited forensics filed past, carefully manoeuvring themselves around the lake. They had been waiting for me, I realised. They knew I liked to be one of the first on the scene. It reduced the risk of mental contamination. Too many chefs spoil the broth, and all that. Too many threads of disgust and shock and revulsion to untangle make things messy. Put me on the scene before all of that, like a dog getting a scent when it's fresh.

Although the all-pervading stink of the Zoo would take years for me to shake off, I suspected. It wouldn't have mattered had I been first on the scene or last, not this time. The memories of what happened here were tattooed into my soul from the second I set foot in the place.

Fleur gently steered me out of the enclosure. I appreciated her patience. She needed what she needed from me, but I could only give her that once I touched one of the bodies, which I couldn't bring myself to do. Not yet. I couldn't physically withstand the pain of contact. I was on the verge of fainting as it was.

I felt a moment's relief as I left the Flamingo People behind, until I realised the detective was ushering me towards another destination.

'There's more?' I whispered, knowing the answer already.

'Oh, so much more,' she said, sadly.

It all blurred, after a while. A nightmare there was no escape from. Even when I left, I knew I'd have to see the Zoo People every time I closed my eyes.

Like the poor small boy in the monkey enclosure. After that, I never ate a banana or even looked at one again, which was a shame, because I'd always loved bananas. Great energy foods, especially for someone like me, who burns calories three times as fast as a normal person.

Or the skinny lad in the giant tortoise pen, who lay completely crushed beneath the weight of a giant boulder crudely painted like a shell and dropped from what looked like a huge height square onto his back. His arms and legs and face stuck out around the edges, smeared with thick mud, now dried and caked to look like the old, wrinkled skin of the reptile he was meant to represent. Blood and entrails seeped into the soil around his splayed form. I could only assume that beneath the boulder, he was pancaked, split wide open like a stepped-on gooseberry. The overall effect was convincing. He looked like a tortoise, nobody could argue otherwise.

In the butterfly pen, expertly flayed skin caught the light of an increasingly warm day in place of gossamer wings.

And over in the sloth enclosure, an elderly gentleman's arms and legs had been dislocated at every possible joint so they hung long and loose, and then bound at the ankles and wrists around the branch of a tree, where he hung upside down like a pig carcass. Two long, curved and sharpened bones that looked like knives had been jammed into the backs of the man's hands to mimic sloth claws, three in each foot. He was zipped into a furry one-piece with a hood drawn tight around his face to complete the absurd aesthetic.

In the deer park, a whole family had been arranged in various cervoid poses, held in place with wooden frames and synthetic fur and metal staples liberally applied. All of them were crowned with bloody antlers, daggered into their skulls with a force that was staggeringly brutal.

There was more, but I stopped seeing it after a while. The brain can only deal with so much. The last thing to break through the milky opaqueness of my gathering pain-fog was the snake pit. God, the snake pit. A middle-aged woman, rolled out like a soft clay log and stuffed into a thin membrane, sausage meat in sausage skin. Her mouth stretched wide, and her eyes bulged above the matted fur of a dead rat jammed halfway down her throat. Only the rodent's tail dangled out over the top of her swollen, blue tongue. That tongue had been snipped in the middle, with shears or scissors, to make a fork, just like a snake tongue. Something about this last detail got to me so deeply I forgot my name for a little while.

Thankfully, I had Fleur to remind me.

'Alistair,' she said, not unkindly. 'I know this is a lot. I can't imagine what kind of pain you're in right now. But…we need a profile. Profiles? We need…' She scrubbed her hands through her hair. 'We fucking need *something.*'

'I can't,' I said, feeling woozy. 'I just…'

I staggered out of the snake pit, which was heated to tropical temperatures, and sat down abruptly on the floor outside as the cooler air hit me. I put my head between my knees. I felt like a snake myself. My bones had disintegrated. I was putty, I was molten. I would never know comfort ever again.

'Who are all these people?' I asked.

'We don't know. We can't even begin to ID until we have them… back in a normal state,' Fleur replied. De-costumed, she meant.

'How is this even possible?' Sounds and smells and other sensations came at me from all directions, a charging herd of sensory bison.

Fleur handed me a bottle of water.

'It shouldn't be possible,' she replied, in a flat, dull voice. 'But then, neither should the things you're able to do be possible. I guess our definition of possibility needs a rethink.'

I raised my head a little but continued to stare at my shoes. Flecks of drying vomit marred the burnished leather. I itched to rub them away but lacked the energy to do so. Sick had also splattered onto the neat creases of my Armani pants, just like Orwell had known it would. I distantly thought about adding the dry cleaning bill to my final invoice.

'It would take a small army of people to do this many awful things to this many victims,' Fleur continued, softly. Her priorities were in the right place, but then, she didn't have to deal with the reverb of the dead and dying in her mind, did she?

'But we've checked the security footage from all the cameras. There are a lot. Of cameras, I mean. State of the art system, installed last year. No dead zones in the Zoo. Every inch covered. In high definition. I guess they take animal security seriously.'

'And?'

'Nothing. Not a thing out of place. No activity beyond the animals, who were simply there one minute, and then…'

'Not,' I finished, wearily.

My nose started to bleed. I didn't even try to stem the flow. I let it drain down me, a hot, vile trickle. I knew what it meant. It meant I was reaching tolerance.

There was only so much longer I'd be able to stay before suffering a brain haemorrhage.

'Nobody came or went that we could see during the night,' Fleur continued, handing me a fresh, folded napkin. It was like she'd come prepared with an Alistair Repair Kit. 'Nobody climbed over a wall or broke in through the front gates or dropped in from the fucking sky like a parachuter. Nobody. It's…'

'Impossible,' I said, knowing that nothing was impossible, not really.

'The logistics of getting into the zoo aside…All of this…it had to have been done off site,' Fleur continued, thinking aloud. 'And the bodies transported here. The …costumes…' She struggled for the correct word. 'The stuff used to turn the victims into animals…the fake feathers, for example. The glue. It had to have been done elsewhere.'

'Forensics?' I was trying to find any excuse I could to avoid touching the bodies, but was running out of time and reasons.

'Forensics will comb every single inch of this place, but what are they going to find? Dozens of sets of fingerprints, hundreds of footprints, countless discarded hairs and fingernails and tissues and blobs of chewing gum and scraps of litter and…it's a Zoo, for fuck's sake. People in and out by the hundreds. Post mortems on the bodies will give us more, but that takes time and…the *scale* of this, Alistair. The scale. It's deranged. It could happen again.'

The implication: whether or not it happened again was now my responsibility.

'The strength it must have taken…the sheer force applied, the scope of violence...I am completely fucked. Completely. I may as well resign right now, this morning. We'll never solve this without you. There is nothing *to* solve. Nobody came, nobody went. It's like someone… clicked their fingers and manifested a…a…'

'A human zoo,' I replied, and threw up again.

I felt better after the second time. Like vomiting relieved a little pressure, somehow. Or maybe the physical sensation blotted out the pain of my bones momentarily. Either way, it gave me ten minutes of breathing space. I stuffed the napkin into both nostrils and hoped it would be sufficient.

'What do you need from me?' I said, knowing full well.

'A profile. There must be at least two, if not more people involved. Terrorism? Animal rights?'

I gave the detective a look over the blood-soaked material. 'I think animal rights activists have limits, Fleur. Besides, that doesn't feel right. The sense I get is not of anger. No rage. No...lessons to teach. No organised sense of justice.'

'What does feel right?'

I put my head back, opened my mouth, put my tongue out to taste the air.

'Child's play,' I murmured.

'What?'

'It feels like a kid, playing. You know little kids? How rough they can be? It...it feels like that. There's a lack of awareness of any wrongdoing. Enthusiasm. Like...it's a game.'

'A game?' Two indignant spots of colour bloomed on Orwell's cheeks.

'A game of dolls or dress up, you know? "Let's play Zoo".'

'But that doesn't make any sense. How could a kid be responsible for this?'

I shrugged. 'You asked. I'm just telling you what I feel. And the animals...the real ones. All missing, right?'

'So far. Which is also impossible, in and of itself. You'd think we'd be overrun with reports of lions stalking the aisles of the supermarket, lemurs hanging off of lampposts. But there's been nothing, so far.'

'The point is, why. Not where they are now. *Why* they are missing? Set free, presumably.'

'Why should that matter?'

'Because it does. It fits. An impression of impulsiveness. But also a backwards sort of...compassion.'

Fleur was silent for a long time, trying and failing to make sense of this. Then she placed her hands on her hips.

'Well,' she said, firmly. 'Can't put it off anymore. Which one are you going to touch?'

I thought about it. I knew I couldn't go back in the snake pit, not ever again.

I opted for the deer family, for the father of the group, arranged like a stag rampant, thinking only of the physical injuries, which, by comparison to the other Zoo People, were not as heinous. I felt it would be the easiest to bear because of this.

I realised too late that only thinking about the physical pain, and not the mental, was idiotic.

For he had not died alone, had he? He had died with his children in front of him, his wife next to him. I hadn't considered that until it was far, far too late.

I touched him, and the world ceased to exist.

All that remained were things I lacked the capability and language to fully articulate.

I told Orwell, after I woke up in the hospital, that the sensations had been so strong I'd not been able to work up a profile. This was a lie, but I was an exceptional liar, and she bought it. Dejected, she stayed with me until I checked out anyway. The doctors, mystified, told me my symptoms resembled those of a man who had suffered a massive stroke. By the time they fed me this information, my vitals were back to normal and there was nothing demonstrably wrong. Rather than stick around and suffer scrutiny, I discharged myself between check-up rounds.

Fleur drove me home, told me not to fret about my new car, she'd had another officer take it back already. That was the thing about Orwell: she cared. Colleagues, victims. It made her a good detective, because it made her tenacious.

I felt bad about lying to her, because I knew what it would do to her career.

But some things, even for me, are bigger than prospects.

Once the door to my penthouse was firmly closed on Detective Orwell, I scrambled to get down on paper what I'd seen in the few incandescent moments before I'd fainted in the deer enclosure. It was tough, because I'd blacked out almost immediately after touching the Stag Man, but I gave it my best. I drew on a large sheet of baking paper.

That was all I could find in a hurry. What I'd seen had not been easy to visualise, but I did my best. I drew a small child, curled up in the corner of a dark, cluttered room. I drew an old house, with a lamp post outside. I drew things I didn't fully understand: shapes and lines and patterns. I drew sticks and stones and bones. I drew dolls and blood and entrails like sausage links. I drew until my fingers were numb, then I stopped.

I took a shower, binned my blood and vomit-stained suit and shoes. Put on something softer, less formal, something that wouldn't intimidate a small kid.

I ran the sketches I'd made through a reverse image search engine. I had to keep adding details and re-scanning, dredging up more features from my recollections slowly, like cognitive fishing. Bricks, a deep red in colour, except around the window casements, which were a light cream. Trees lining the street: mottled bark, distinctive leaves. A wrought iron fence surrounding the property, with unusual detailing welded at intervals. A porchlight with a fleur-de-lis depicted in cracked stained glass. Terracotta mouldings on the columns holding up the porch. An old tarnished brass letter box, shaped like a gaping lion's mouth. A faded set of painted daises on a peeling wooden door. I used the image engine, street view and a variety of other online searches until eventually I got a hit. A red-brick Edwardian mansion block near Marylebone.

I took the car. Finally, its horsepower had some function.

I had to get to the Kid before she did it again.

The Daisy Chain Children's Care Home was housed in a decaying mansion, the outlier in an otherwise affluent district I knew well. An eyesore, to many, but for the kids inside, a home, of sorts.

I flashed my police badge, fabricating a complaint phoned in by a concerned member of the public. Scared of repercussions—scared just in general—the manager of the home ushered me upstairs to the top level, the level just before the attic. It was stuffy and quiet, and smelled damp.

'She's up here alone?' I asked, knowing the answer.

The Care Home manager looked at me with haunted eyes. I could see shadows beneath them. She was terrified of the Kid, I realised. With reason.

'She isn't like other children,' the woman whispered.

'She was abandoned?'

'Left at the Zoo by her mother when she was two years old. She was too young to have any memory of it...but...'

'These things last,' I said, knowing exactly how it felt. Years of rejection because of what I could do. Because I'd been different. Backs, turned. Conversations, cut short. Relationships severed. It was why I liked money as much as I did. Money never let me down. Money never rejected me.

'She's in there.' We'd reached a small, dingy door at the end of a hot, narrow corridor. It was locked. She gave me a key. Our hands touched, and a bolt of fear transferred: cold, greasy. The woman was a coward.

'You can stay out here,' I replied, knowing what needed to be done, not wanting any interference. Not that I thought she'd stop me.

And I fully intended to go through with it, before I saw the child.

I fully intended to kill her. Especially when I saw the things she'd made, in that dark, cluttered room she had all to herself. I saw dolls, fashioned from sticks and clay and fabric and skin and fur. I saw bones, I saw Zoo People in miniature. I saw scissors and glue and feathers, stones, scraps of material and plastic and leather, I saw the City Zoo's gates, made from wire and plasticine, I saw the wall, a ring of pebbles held in place with superglue.

I had every intention.

She was a monster.

Someone who could make things in the musty recesses of a rotting house in the suburbs and somehow manifest those things onto or into real people, real locations. Like puppetry, only worse. Much, much worse. Because I don't think she knew that what she crafted here in the shadows was somehow enacted outside in true, grisly proportions. How could she have known? She never left the care home, the room. She was locked in here because nobody knew what else to do with her. She was lonely and dangerous, powerful yet unfettered by the constraints of adult regulation.

She was a nightmare waiting to be unleashed upon the world at large, and for that reason, she had to be killed.

Except when I saw her, my heart did something strange. It beat faster and deeper than it had for many years.

She was scrawny and small, like I'd been. Seated cross-legged on the floor, she was making another Zoo Person. A kangaroo lady. There was a pouch, with a tiny baby stuffed inside. She'd stitched a long, fat tail to the model, who looked a lot like the Care Home Manager. Probably why the woman had been so frightened: subconsciously, she sensed it was her turn soon. That meant the victims in the Zoo must be people the Kid knew, somehow. Perhaps an adoptive family that had sent her back. Relatives, teachers, other people in the system who had let her down. I didn't know, I didn't care.

She looked up from her work slowly. She'd been fully absorbed. I saw the pink tip of her tongue, poked out between her lips. Focus. She found peace and solace and pride in what she was making.

Our eyes met. A wall of latent grief and longing hit me like a bat to the head. Hope flared in her eyes. It was unbearable. It was enough to stop me doing what I'd meant to.

'Are you my new Dad?' she asked, in a soft, young voice.

I stood there, stripped down to a bare, piteous nub of a man. My bones were singing a symphony of a life about to change beyond all recall. But this time it was not bone-bad, despite the circumstances. It was bone-good, although nobody but the two of us would ever understand that.

I was unable to answer right away.

The Faces in Morgan Alley

RICK KENNETT

THEY WORK QUICKLY, QUIETLY AND EFFICIENTLY IN THIS ROOM BUILT FOR one function, because that one function is to be performed early tomorrow.

Standing on the stepladder and holding a length of chain in his left hand he reaches up with his right to slide back the pin in its steel bracket. This bracket is bolted to the underside of the oak beam running athwart the room. He slips a link marked with chalk onto the pin then slots the pin back into the bracket. The chain depending from the bracket is six feet three inches long, the length calculated by dividing one thousand by the weight of the subject in pounds.

His assistant hands him up a coil of rope with the regulation length of twelve feet. It has a pear-shaped brass eye at one end though which he shackles the rope to the end of the chain. He jumps down, his shoes thumping hollowly on the metal of the trapdoor. The rope, its other end looped through a similar brass opening, is left coiled on the floor while they leave to fetch the sandbag.

There was something off, something self-conscious about her movements. He couldn't pinpoint it, but she seemed like she was walking down the street for the purpose of walking down the street, and it bugged him. There were tassels on her skirt, peacock patterns on her blouse and a feather in her hat. She was supposed to be a flapper. Couldn't she *flap* a bit?

Passing a darkened alleyway she was pounced on by a figure, indistinct and blurred in the viewfinder. She fell back with a cry, arms flailing.

Yes, that's better. Struggle. Yes, yes. Struggle. Yell.

Although the yelling was unnecessary—the mic was muted to eliminate ambient noise—it helped. Sound would be dubbed later. Struggling and unnecessarily yelling, she was dragged into the alley, her kicking black stockings on her thin legs disappearing into the dark.

He glanced up and down the city lane off which the alley ran. Morning sunlight slanted in, shining into this slot of tall buildings one side, boutique shops and a little café just opening for business on the other. Nothing stirred among the long shadows. The Sunday streets of the city were empty for the moment, which was just as well. Moss hated rubber-neckers.

He zoomed his phone's camera in on the woman's black leather bag lying on the pavement, then did a slow tilt up to the sign on the wall: *Morgan Alley.*

He turned off his camera. "OK. Thank you." He opened the phone's address book, selected 'Weird Beard' and emailed the video file.

From within the alley a man's voice said, "Ups-a-daisy," followed by a grunt of exertion. A young man of somewhat stocky build, thin face, dark hair, emerged. Dressed in high-waisted trousers with old-time braces over the shoulders of his white woollen shirt. A round faced diminutive woman of twenty or so followed immediately behind, brushing at her loose skirt, blue-grey and tasselled.

Moss put his phone away in the pocket of his suit which was clearly tailor-made—though clearly not for him and not recently—and brought out a pencilled list headed 'Scenes to be Shot'. Half the lines were crossed out. He crossed out another that read: *nat passes alley entrance owen attacks nat.* "That's that done," he said with satisfaction.

"Don't you want to do another take?" said Owen. "You know, just to make sure?"

Nat, straightening her hat, gave him an evil look as if not welcoming the thought of another drag into a dirty alley.

"It was all right in the viewfinder," said Moss. "It'll do."

"That sounds the sort of thing Ed Wood might've said."

"Ed who?" Moss dragged out his phone again, dabbed at its screen, opening Facebook.

"You're the wannabe Spielberg and I'm just your layabout house-mate press-ganged into playing a bit part," said Owen, "but even I know Ed D Wood Jnr, world's worst director of the world's worse movie, *Plan Nine from Outer Space.*"

"Sounds sci-fi," Moss sniffed. "No one's interested in that sort of thing."

"Aren't they? Have you noticed what some of the most commercially successful films are these days?"

But the wannabe Spielberg was on a roll. "What's we're doing here is the real thing, what people are really interested in. What we're doing here is history, raw emotion and ultimately the mystery that is death."

"What we're doing here," said Nat, "is a student film, and from what I've been seeing while editing it, not a particularly good one."

Moss gestured to his phone. "Weird Beard's just posted on Facebook. He likes the vid we just shot. 'Your delve into surrealism is eccentric brilliance, reminiscent of the early work of David Lynch.'" He made with a self-satisfied smirk which quickly morphed into a thoughtful frown. "Surrealism?"

"Your film professor would find eccentric brilliance in a Cornflakes commercial," said Owen.

Moss made to say something, stopped and stared at Nat. "That's it. That's why I thought you looked wrong. You don't have a bag. No flapper out and about in the 1920s would walk down the street without her purse or some—" He stopped again, stared again, this time at the empty pavement behind his actress. "Where'd the bag go?"

Nat didn't even bother to turn around. "If by bag you mean the one I suggested I carry while we were coming here? My own crocheted woollen bag? The one you said looked too modern? That bag?"

"No, I'm talking about the black leather bag you dropped at the corner."

"How can I drop a bag I don't have?"

But Moss wasn't listening, didn't even seem to be aware he'd just contradicted himself. He scanned the alley paving stones, then glancing up thought he glimpsed someone at its far end, a flash of colour in its drab depths, an impression of a shortish figure, there and gone. He turned back, searching again for a bag that wasn't there. "I thought it a nice detail you added because dropping her bag was exactly what Jinny Lee did when Josh Brannic attacked her."

"I had no bag," said Nat pointedly.

"Time for breakfast, don't you think?" said Owen.

Using a block and tackle attached to the oak beam they haul the sandbag up through the open trap from the pit below. It has been secured to the loop of rope and left overnight. Carefully measured, the rope is found to have stretched almost an inch.

The twin leaves of the trap are closed by pulling the release lever back which is then secured by slotting a cotter pin into place. The stepladder is returned to the centre of the room and ascended. Adjustments are made to the chain to accommodate the stretch in the rope.

Two sturdy planks are brought in and placed either side of the trap. Two long ropes with their ends balled into fist-sized knots are attached to hooks in the ceiling so that their ends hang at shoulder height above the planks. The rope attached to the chain is gathered up, its loose coils tied together with light twine so that the loop is now positioned at head height.

Their work for the moment is done and there's the pleasant smell of brewing coffee and frying bacon. As they exit they pass those tasked with laying the seagrass matting on the steel decking of the gallery.

Nat stirred her coffee with a plastic spoon and from her seat outside the café looked down the city lane. "Bet this place has changed a lot the past hundred years."

"Over there," said Moss, pointing across to where a driveway swept down into the basement of a modern office block, "was where Brannic was standing in the door of his pokey little draper shop early on the morning of November 16, 1922 when he saw Jinny approaching on the other side of the lane. He darted across and hid in Morgan Alley to wait for her to pass."

"Creepy," said Nat.

Owen glugged his coffee in one go then got out his phone to Google Josh Brannic. This produced what was likely a police mug shot of a man with shallow cheeks and unshaven face, untidy black hair, an unmistakable look of terror behind his dark eyes.

"Something like me," Owen observed.

"Which is why I asked you to play the part. And because you work cheap," said Moss.

Owen gave his empty coffee cup a significant look. "Yes, I must remember to declare it next time I'm paid my unemployment benefits." He studied the photo of Brannic again. "That's a troubled face if ever I've seen one."

"By the time they took that he had reason to be troubled."

"Why was Jinny walking alone in this lane so early in the morning?" asked Nat.

By now Moss was fiddling with his phone again, trying to locate the video file he'd sent to Weird Beard. "She'd been to some gala affair in town and had had an argument with her boyfriend and stormed off," he said off-handedly, then glanced up, frowning. "Haven't you two done any research on the people you're playing?"

"We're not …" Nat paused, searching for a phrase that eluded her. "What do you call those theatrical obsessives?"

"Method actors?" Owen suggested.

"Yeah. We're not method actors, Moss. I mean, I'd never even heard of the Morgan Alley Murder till the day before yesterday when you asked me to do some editing for you."

"Which I greatly appreciate, but I sometimes wish you two would make more of an effort." He began again searching through his video files.

"We got dressed up," said Nat. "Owen and I spent all yesterday morning going through op-shops and vintage bazaars. That's effort enough. Anyway, why didn't Jinny just cross the street if she saw him enter the alley she was about to pass?"

"Maybe still pissed off with the boyfriend and didn't notice," said Owen.

Moss swiped at his screen again. "Actually, no. Jinny worked at Josh Brannic's draper shop so they knew each other. If she saw him cross into the alley ahead of her it wouldn't have seemed creepy at all. She lived with her widowed mother in the next suburb east," Moss pointed along the lane towards the morning sun, "so this was her usual way home. Anyway, the story goes that there'd been some sort of romance between Jinny and Josh Brannic, but when he saw her coming up the lane so early that morning he guessed by the way she was dolled up that she'd been out with someone else, so he killed her in a jealous rage."

Owen conjured up an image of Jinny Lee on his phone and showed the screen to Nat. "Looks something like you."

Nat studied the black and white round-face of the long-dead young woman, lace collar, hair in curls. "Poor girl."

"The police had their motive and their moment of opportunity too," said Moss. "It didn't help Brannic's case that he had her blood on his hands. He said he'd found her body, but of course he would say that. The newspapers of the day stirred up public opinion against him. I mean, illicit love, passions raging, a grubby shopkeeper with a vaguely foreign sounding name, the rape and murder of a young and pretty innocent. There was also a confession to a cellmate while he was awaiting trial."

"An unverified 'He told me he done it' I bet," said Owen. "Heresy confessions are not evidence."

"The judge in Brannic's trial thought otherwise," said Moss.

He went back to searching his files, muttering and swiping. After a couple of moments of this Nat said, a little touchily, "Moss, don't tell me you've deleted this morning's video. I really don't fancy being dragged into Morgan Alley again to be ravished and—" She broke off with the realization the waitress was there beside her with their raisin toast.

The woman stared at them. Owen and Nat—Moss was too preoccupied with his phone—stared back.

"We're making a film," said Nat in the awkward silence.

"OK," said the waitress. She clattered the plates of raisin toast on the table and fled back into the café.

"Great," said Owen. "Now she thinks we're a bunch of weirdoes shooting a hard core porno in a back alley."

Moss, oblivious to what had just happened, had finally found that morning's video and was now watching it with a growing look of confusion. At last he looked up, a curious expression on his face. "I want you to take a look at this," he said in a curiously strained tone. He slid his phone across the table to them. "I want you to tell me exactly what you see. Describe it, if you don't mind, rather minutely."

Nat and Owen put down their raisin toast in mid-bite and peered down at the swirls of pixels and light on the phone screen.

"It's Morgan Alley," said Owen, carefully, not sure what was expected of him. "Your initial establishing shot before Nat comes into view. There's a sort of smudged form at the corner of the alley, sort of like oily smoke. Is that me? No, can't be. Too small. Odd that it's out of focus yet everything else is sharp enough. OK, here's Nat walking into shot … no, no, it's another smoky shadow … it's just reached the shadow at the corner … and it's stopped. Now you're panning across and … yes, here's Nat walking into shot and now you're tracking with her to where the two shadow blurs seem to be … there's a lot of bending and twisting about them … Now they're coming into focus a little … I can see them clearer now. Looks like a man and a woman struggling or gesticulating. The man seems to be wearing some sort of striped blazer and the woman is wearing … green?"

"Yes. Green," said Nat."

"OK, now it looks like they've changed positions and the man has the woman against the wall … thought he had a hat a moment ago but it looks like it's fallen off."

"Think she just pushed him. Not sure. I've just stepped in front of them and obscured them. All right, here's Owen jumping out of the alley and dragging me back in."

"Yes, I drag Nat in and the shadows are revealed again … oh shit!" Owen flinched back from the phone screen. "The guy in the stripes just stuck the woman in the face … at least I think he did."

"Go on," said Moss.

"Now they sort of tumble back into the alley and disappear … and now here's your tilt down to the bag … Moss, where did that bag come from?" When his only answer was a testy gesture Owen took the hint. "OK … OK … now you're tilting up to the street sign ... and the video ends."

"What the hell was that?" said Nat. "It's like a double exposure on a film, but you can't get double exposures on digital imaging."

"No, you can't," said Moss and his voice trembled.

They watched it again, then again, trying to make visual sense of the blurred images, the chaotic motion.

"I see now it's definitely a shorter guy in what looks like a striped blazer," said Owen at last, getting a clearer cognize with repeated viewings. "Think he's wearing a snappy bowtie and a flat-brimmed hat, but he loses the hat during the struggle with the woman in the green dress."

Rewatching it and rewatching they were soon convinced the man in the blazer had stuck the woman a fearful blow.

Nat silently put her hand to her mouth as the two men, wide-eyed and white-faced, watched the woman in green once more dragged into the alley by the man in the striped blazer. The scene tilted down and zoomed onto the bag on the footpath, lingering a moment before slowly tilting up to the street sign: *Morgan Alley*.

"Two raisin toasts, two flat whites and a Pepsi 'n' goat milk." The woman behind the counter tapped up the price. Moss flourished his card with a hand visibly shaking. While they waited for payment to be electronically confirmed she added, "Are you filming something about the murder in Morgan Alley?" She glanced out the café window to Nat and Owen in their period clothes staring down at the phone on the table.

"The murder … yes," he said like a man whose thoughts were elsewhere.

"You know, you've got her dress wrong."

It took Moss a moment to pick up on what she'd said. The video was playing over and over in his mind. "Sorry. The dress is … what?

"The wrong colour. She wears green, not the grey-blue number that lady's wearing. Her hat's wrong too."

He fixed her with a hard look. "How do you know this?"

"Her ghost still walks that alley."

When Moss emerged from the café a minute later, Owen remarked on his fixed gaze, his twitching mouth. All three were disconcerted and nervy by what they'd seen, but now Moss looked bewildered as well.

He stopped by the table and gripped the back of his chair as if needing support. Then he turned his head and stared down the laneway in the direction of Morgan Alley a few shop fronts distant. Owen made to stand but Moss laid a hand on his shoulder and pressed him gently back into his seat.

"I need to check something." he said, more to himself than to the others. Scooping up his phone he headed down the lane with a hesitant step as if not really wanting to arrive where he was going

From their table Nat and Owen watched him stand at the entrance to Morgan Alley where he seemed to peer into its depths. They heard him say in a loud but quavering voice, "Jinny Lee … Jinny Lee … Jinny Lee …" He drew his phone to his eye.

"This has gone too far," said Owen with decision. He stood. "It's getting weird and dangerous."

"Yes, it has," said Nat, understanding what he meant on a purely emotional level.

She stood and joined him and together they carefully approached Moss still muttering the dead woman's name with his phone focused on the alley's shadowed interior. They craned their heads around its corner, inwardly terrified at what they might see. It was very empty, very still, very innocent of its dark past.

"What are you doing, Moss?" asked Owen, trying to keep his voice calm.

"The camera sees more than we do. I want to see what it sees."

"Do you think that's wise?"

"No. But I want to see it anyway."

Moss continued to work his camera, stills and video, all the while intoning, "Jinny Lee … Jinny Lee," panning, zooming, snapping, "Jinny Lee … Jinny Lee …"

Nat watched the alley in anticipation, desperately wanting Moss to stop. He was provoking and provoking and something would surely respond. Owen had to fight down an urge to snatch the phone and throw it into the gutter, half-convinced Moss was being irrational, sure he was meddling with things better left alone.

Moss dabbed at his phone, stopping the video. Nat and Owen began to breathe again. The shadows had brought forth nothing.

Their breakfast plates and cups had not been cleared from the table when they returned and they didn't notice the waitress watching them from the café window. Moss, holding his phone up for all to see, activated the still photos on a fast slide-show.

The green spectre appeared almost at once.

The rapid flickering series of shots animated her. She looked left, looked right in a stutter of movement, twitching to stare at the camera, raising her arms, head blurring to left, to right, shaking "No" and "No" then stepping forward, mouth agape sobbing "No" coming close, coming closer, filling the screen with her dead round face, her crying eyes …

The video began at the corner where there might've been something standing, shaking its head, lost as the view panned across to the right bringing in sharp and clear the back of a man's head, hair slicked and topped with a straw boater. He stepped forward to bring himself fully into shot as if in awareness of his viewers. And deliberately he turned and grinned from a scratched face, the man with the striped blazer and snappy bowtie. His eyes were wide in a lustful leer. Then out of nowhere thrust out his hand, fingers splayed jabbing through the screen. Moss and Nat and Owen jumped back in their seats, grabbing at their eyes, palming at the sudden gouging pain.

The phone clattered to the ground and went dark.

The first few moments were exclamatory as each sat in their own personal darkness, their hands over their tightly closed eyes. Cautiously they drew their hands away and opened their eyes to a squint, fearing the worst. They were not blind, though their vision was unfocused and clouded. They barely registered the presence of the waitress, gripping their shoulders, touching their faces.

"What have you done? What is it? Oh for god's sake, what is it?"

At once the pain eased from their eyes and their vision cleared.

Moss looked up through involuntary tears, grateful to see the woman, the street, sunlight. "It's all right, Miss," he said, though he sounded far from all right. "We had a moment with your ghost. Please let us be. We'll be fine in a moment."

Dubiously the waitress left them. Reluctantly Moss searched for his phone under the table, what it might show, what might reach for him as he reached for it. He found it with its screen a cobweb of cracks and smelling of burning. He threw it in a nearby bin.

Nat was the one who said it, though they'd all been thinking it.

"In the 1920s, a Sunday morning shop keeper wouldn't wear a striped blazer, a straw hat and a bowtie. But someone attending a Saturday night gala event with his lady friend would."

"Bet their argument was about sex," said Owen. "It'd explain a lot."

"Let's go," said Moss.

From the café door the waitress watched them disappear down the lane, then took a quick, nervous glance up at the entrance to Morgan Alley before withdrawing into the shop.

The seagrass matting deadens their footsteps as they assemble, a group of three outside the cell door, a group of several more at the other door further along. Those inside must not hear their approach, though they know they are coming. They know it like they know the sun has just risen.

Somewhere far above in the clock tower, a bell begins to strike the hour.

The cell door is opened with a jingle of keys and the warder in his prison blue uniform enters, followed by the hangman and his assistant in business attire. The man at the table is talking with the clergyman when they come in. He stands and faces them, a young man of stocky build, a little above average height . He has shallow cheeks that are clean shaven now and his black hair is neatly combed, though terror is still in his dark eyes.

The assistant turns him around and pulls his arms behind his back, binding the wrists with a leather strap, fastening it with a wooden peg. The warder has already slid aside the cupboard hiding the door into that other room. It has been hidden there unknown all these weeks of waiting. The hangman, the linen hood folded like a handkerchief in the top pocket of his suit coat, says, "It'll be all right," to the prisoner in his calm, professional voice. He passes through the erstwhile hidden doorway and into that other room where the prison governor, the under-sheriff, the doctor and other officials are waiting. Directly ahead is the noose positioned at head height, tied by light twine to two or three loose loops of rope. A warder stands either side on planks across the trap door, guarding against last minute surges of desperation. For safety's sake both have one hand gripping a length of knotted rope depending from the ceiling.

Touching the prisoner on the shoulder, the assistant says, "Follow him," and they move off in procession: the hangman, Josh Brannic, the assistant and the spectre in green, shaking her head, arms raised in despair and sobbing, "No …No …"

The Hungry Bones

LEE MURRAY

WITH THE TANG OF RECENT RAIN IN HIS NOSTRILS AND HIS BOOTS SINKING in the soft grass, Sergeant Taine McKenna of the NZDF skirted the group of mourners in the tiny cemetery of Rawene and climbed the hill to join the elderly Chinese couple near a large beech tree.

Turning up his collar, he slipped in behind the pair while they laid offerings of oranges and pears on the marble memorial. Already, someone had left a spray of bedraggled chrysanthemums…and a cold burger. Taine stifled a chuckle at that. His friend had always liked a good burger.

It wasn't the first time Taine had come to the far north to pay his respects to Corporal Jack Lui, or 'Coolie' as the soldiers in Taine's section had called him, the nickname earned not for the man's Asian ancestry but for his cool head in a crisis and his uncanny stealth. Although even those skills hadn't been enough to save Coolie from the enemy that had stalked them through Te Urewera Forest years ago. There had been no time to say goodbye. One minute Coolie had been there with them, and the next he was gone, his body never found, although the outcome was never in question.

Taine had been looking for closure ever since.

He looked up as muffled sobs carried from the crowd at the base of the hill. A woman cried out, her primal wail resonating across the bay.

Is closure even possible?

When he turned back, Coolie's mum was bowing before the memorial. Holding several burning incense sticks, she wafted the smoke over the headstone. It was a touching gesture, a message of love and goodwill sent to her son on the drifting swirls of sandalwood smoke. When she'd completed the ritual, it was her husband's turn to bend over the memorial. Taking out a lighter, he began burning pages of golden joss paper. An offering of prosperity to ensure Coolie wanted for nothing in the afterlife.

One by one, the golden leaves danced on the stone, the edges tinging red then black, the pages eventually disappearing in spirals of smoke. When the last one had shrivelled away, the old gentleman stood up and brushed the flakes of burnt paper off his trousers. He clasped Taine's hand. "Mr Taine. Thank you for coming." His dark eyes, so much like Coolie's, creased at the corners.

Did Coolie's parents have closure? Taine had delivered the NZDF's letter himself. Its tone had been clipped and the details sparse. A beloved son killed in active service. Distinguished conduct. Regrets, no further information at this time.

"Of course, sir."

At the bottom of the hill, the crowd was breaking up, the mourners dispersing in dribs and drabs for the car park on the other side of the road, but a small huddle, unable to tear themselves away, lingered near the gravesite.

Coolie's mum tugged on Taine's sleeve. So tiny that she barely reached his navel, Taine dropped his head to hear her. "How is Mr Trigger doing?" she asked.

For Trevor 'Trigger' Grierson, losing Coolie had been like losing his left arm. He'd quit the army, blotting out the pain with booze and pills and who-knows-what else. Taine had worried he'd lose him too, but the gods had other plans and Trigger had pulled himself out of it, cleaning up his act to become an intelligence agent at Wellington's Aitken Street HQ.

"Much better," he said.

"Hmm." Mrs Liu nodded, her eyes following the smoke spooling across the cemetery. After a long moment, she turned back and patted his arm. "You boys should talk more." She pushed the packet of incense into Taine's hands, then took her husband's arm, and set off down the hill. "Come for lunch tomorrow," she called over her shoulder. "I'm making my soya chicken."

When the pair had left, Taine took three sticks of incense from the packet, lighting them and bowing before the headstone as Mrs Liu had done. Setting the glowing sticks in the holder, he settled back on a nearby park bench to watch the smoke writhe and twist on the air. Spinning. Swirling. White wisps against a palette of grey…

"Boss."

What? Taine snapped his head up. "Coolie?" Taine clutched at the flattened blade of the *pūrerehua*-bullroarer at his neck, barely daring to breathe as his dead friend stepped through the smoky curtain.

Smooth-skinned and lean, Coolie still exhibited that same coiled tension he'd had in life. "Yeah. It's me. Sorry for ghosting you so long."

Same Coolie humour, too.

"Too long…"

As a *matakite*—Taine's gift of seeing from his Māori heritage—this wasn't his first brush with the dead, but in all the times he'd visited this cemetery, his friend had never appeared to him before.

Coolie took a seat next to Taine. "I need your help, Boss," he said. He pointed to a little girl jumping among the headstones. Taine peered through the smoke. The girl was six, maybe seven at most.

"That's Alice," Coolie said. "She drowned last week in the harbour."

Taine's heart clenched. Poor kid. Her life cut off before it even began. Was that why Coolie had appeared to him? To lead the child's soul to the stepping off place beneath the ancient *pōhutukawa* tree at the northern tip of the country?

Taine lifted the bullroarer. "Do you want me to sing her *wairua*-spirit home?"

Coolie ran a ghostly finger over the instrument's carved surface. "It's okay. I can do that. I'll be taking her right after we talk."

Taine cocked an eyebrow and smiled. "Another babysitting assignment?"

Coolie chuckled. "Just don't tell Trigger, mate. I'll never hear the end of it." He paused. Sucked silent air over his teeth. "The thing is, Boss, Alice's death wasn't an accident."

Taine straightened. "And you want me to find out who did it? Bring them to justice?"

Coolie shook his head. "It's not like that. I *know* who did it."

Taine got to his feet. "Tell me then," he said, his shout startling a lingering mourner, who looked their way. Taine returned to the bench and lowered his voice. "Tell me, and I'll take it up with the authorities."

"You don't understand. It was *them*," Collie whispered, and he opened his arms.

The ghosts emerged, maybe thirty of them, old Chinese men, coalescing from behind trees and headstones and out of hollows. They were withered and wizened, with limbs like gnarled branches that wisped to nothing at the extremities, yet their stomachs were swollen tight and veiny, like exposed fish bladders. The ghosts grinned cruelly, shuffling closer, and Taine shifted uneasily on the bench. But Coolie raised his hand, a signal he'd used a thousand times in the NZDF, and the horde halted.

"They killed her?" Taine replied, unnerved despite his friend's intervention. "How could they kill her? They're *dead*."

Coolie sighed. "Long story. These men were miners from China, who died over a century ago, their ghosts imprisoned on this island. They might have made it home, but the ship carrying their coffins foundered, its contents buried with it on the ocean floor."

Taine nodded. The story was well-known: in the early 1900s, the *SS Ventnor* had sunk off the coast at Mitimiti while carrying the remains of some five hundred men.

"The bones of some of the miners were buried here at Rawene,' Coolie said. "Their ghosts never made it home, but the tribespeople here understand *manaakitanga*, about how to care for the dead. They were welcoming, respectful of the men's *kōiwi*, so the ghosts were content enough…"

"Something's happened," Taine said.

Coolie exhaled slowly. "They say they're being robbed. Their gold is being pillaged from the wreckage. Taine, these men are estranged from their homes and families. Many of them have no descendants. Now, without their gold, they'll have nothing to nourish them, no way to feed themselves. Plus, it's August—" Taine must've looked puzzled because Coolie explained, "August is the seventh lunar month. Ancestor month. *Ghost Month.*"

The horde were edging closer now, scuttling towards them and brandishing their bony limbs like cockroaches.

Taine's skin prickled with their need, their meanness. "Let me guess. Ghost Month makes them bolder."

Coolie nodded. "Their hunger creates this surge of bad luck. A sour energy, it hovers around them and, because it's Ghost Month and the veil is thin, they can reach into the real world. They whipped up the currents with the force of their rage and pulled Alice under. She wasn't able to fight it. Taine, as long as their gold is being plundered, there will be more accidents. More misfortune..." Coolie glanced across at the dead girl, who was floating a leaf on a puddle. "More deaths of innocents like Alice. We have to do something, Boss. We're NZDF. It's our job to protect people."

Taine looked at his friend. "*Living* people."

"That's why I need you to help them," Coolie said, "before they kill again."

It was late afternoon when Taine left the cemetery. He climbed into his pick-up and pulled onto the road, heading for the holiday park he'd always stayed at, the weekends he visited Coolie's family. The day was bleak and grey, and the visibility wasn't great, so Taine switched on his headlights, the golden beams shimmering off puddles on the wet seal.

All this was so unreal. Coolie. Ghosts. Taine needed to get his head around it. He'd check in to his usual cabin, take a shower, make a plan.

Taine was slowing for the intersection when a sudden drift of fog rolled across the road, then cleared just as quickly, revealing the cohort of ghostly Chinese miners. They were lined up on the other side of T-junction.

What the hell? Were they smirking at him? Taine punched his brakes and jerked to a stop. All at once, a semi-truck hurtled by. In a slow-motion cliché, the semi hydroplaned through a puddle, then skewed sideways out of control on the slick surface, the back of the truck jack-knifing, then sliding, sliding...

Fuck. Taine was helpless. He leapt out of the pick-up anyway. Ran for the semi, while in the cab the driver fought to control the massive projectile. The wheels screamed. Metal groaned. The cab hit a fence and thundered on, the side door crumpling like tin foil. Still going…

At last, the brute shuddered to a stop. Taine jumped onto the running board and threw open the passenger door. The passenger airbag had deployed. He whipped out his tiny pocket-knife, sliced through the membrane, and climbed in.

In the driver seat, a shard of metal had already punctured the airbag. The driver was slumped over the wheel, his skull caved in and a smear of grey brain matter on the windscreen. Taine checked the man's pulse, only to feel his own heart thundering.

His hands shaking, Taine took out his phone, punched in the number for emergency services, then lifted the phone to describe the accident to the dispatcher. But his throat tightened, and his voice caught. The miners' ghosts were lurking around the truck, grinning with malevolence.

Coolie's words echoed in his head. *As long as their gold is being plundered, there will be more accidents. More misfortune…*

The dispatcher's voice crackled, "Emergency. What service do you require?"

Taine didn't go to the holiday park. After giving his statement to the police, he took the ferry across the inlet to Kohukohu and drove straight to Mitimiti, a windswept coastal no-place consisting of a *marae*, a church, and a dozen isolated farmhouses. By now, night was falling, and the beach was desolate, empty, and achingly beautiful. Tucking his phone and keys inside his jacket pocket, Taine shivered on the dunes, looking out to sea. Somewhere, beneath those grey waves, the *SS Ventnor* lay in its lonely grave on the seafloor.

But it wasn't just the cold making him shiver. Thirty dead men with their spindly limbs and distended stomachs had joined him on the dunes. Thirty *murderous* ghosts, the gruesome spectres hovered about him, their lifeless eyes fixed on the horizon.

There was nothing to see. Whatever Taine thought he might do here would have to wait until tomorrow. But as he turned to go, a flicker of light glinted off the water. Taine's spine tingled. He squinted into the distance. A boat. At this hour?

The light disappeared, and the ghosts howled silently. Taine's toes curled in his boots. What's got them riled up? Well, he was here now. Might as well find out. Taine hunkered in the dunes and waited.

Out at sea, lights flashed, illuminating a fishing craft before darkness engulfed it again. Now he knew it was there, Taine could make out its throaty chugging. Then Taine caught the higher-pitched buzz of another motor. A smaller craft coming ashore. When it had crested the breakers, the motor cut out, and two dark figures jumped into the surf, dragging the boat further up the beach. It was nothing, Taine decided. A couple of mates, late home from a fishing trip, who preferred to avoid the long drive around the harbour inlet.

But the ghosts didn't see it that way. They moved off, slinking down the dunes towards the newcomers. Taine followed them at a crouch, taking care to keep to the beach's dips and shallows, out of sight. He clutched his *pūrerehua*—his link to the spirit world—to his chest, but the ghosts' bitterness was oppressive, and Taine quickly released it.

Snippets of conversation reached him on the wind. From their tone, the pair were arguing.

"...where?"

"...dunes..."

"...how the fuck..."

"...trust...won't leave...our signal."

The men abandoned the boat and headed up the beach. The instant they'd moved off, the ghosts swarmed over the dinghy, clamouring excitedly. Then they turned in unison and beckoned to Taine. It was enough to make his blood freeze. But he'd made a promise to Coolie, so he crept forward. The ghosts parted to let him through. He peered into the hull. Ropes. Dive gear. A tarpaulin. Taine leaned over and lifted the canvas and was assailed by the stink of brine. He slumped. The boat was full of fish, including a small shark, and two smaller dolphins still flapping weakly.

For fuck's sake. What the hell did he think he was doing creeping around at night looking in people's boats like he was some kinda spy? And urged on by a horde of disgruntled ghosts no less!

Except why would a fishing crew risk coming ashore on this isolated stretch of beach? Why not just continue on to the harbour? And why, even without the aid of his *pūrerehua*, could Taine sense the *wrongness* of it all?

Somewhere in the distance, a car engine thrummed. It was coming this way. And without headlights. Why? What were they hiding?

Taine leapt into the metal dinghy and, ignoring the wet and stink, shoved aside the fish, discovering a large tackle box. Taine lifted the lid. The ghosts jostled to see. Inside, was a pile of misshapen rocks covered in barnacles. This was the ghosts' sea-cache. Their agitation left no doubt.

Evidence. Taine fumbled for his phone, but already it was too late. The car was here. The phone's flash would expose him, and the smugglers could be armed. Quickly, Taine closed the lid and covered the box, crawling over the side of the boat even as the vehicle pulled up.

Taine crouched in the shallows, the freezing waves buffeting his thighs. *Dammit.* He couldn't see the vehicle's registration plates from here. Out at sea, the fishing boat was moving off, the chugging heading north.

A door slammed. "Hurry up," a man barked. "Let's get this on the trailer."

A couple of the ghosts surged towards the voice, simmering with wrath. Taine waved them back, relieved when the ghosts melted into the gloom. If these men were stealing from the wreckage, Taine had no way of proving it. Not yet. He crept away, but not before noting the parent boat's name on the side of the craft: the *Isolde*.

Taine scrambled up the dunes in the darkness. The ghosts were gone, and he was alone. Still wet from the waist down, he slid into the driver's seat. Overriding the headlights, he drove the pick-up out of the carpark and headed south. About a hundred metres on, he pulled into a secluded driveway behind a line of scraggly *mānuka* trees.

This road barely saw any traffic. If a car went past, Taine would follow it. He stared into the gloom, looking for the faintest stirring in case, like him, they'd elected not to use their headlights. But after a half hour of shivering in his wet gear, he gave up. He'd obviously missed them. No doubt they'd driven a distance on the sand before hitting the road. They could've come up anywhere along the thirty-kilometre stretch of beach. Taine needed to go about this another way.

Trigger answered on the second ring. "McKenna. How goes it?"

"Trigger, are you at work?" It was nearing nine on a Saturday. What were the chances?

"Course not. I'm at a party. Free beer, pretty girls… Okay, you got me. I'm still at the office, working on a…never mind. Where are you?"

"I'm in Northland. Mitimiti."

There was a pause. "Ah. Of course. It's Coolie's anniversary. Is Jules there with you?"

"Not this time."

"Off saving the country's critters, is she? What is it this time? Penguins or geckos or something? Sorry, man. If I'd known you were on your own, I could've come with you. Made a road trip of it. I miss him too, you know—"

"Trigger, he needs our help."

Another pause. "Boss, Coolie's dead."

"Yes. I know he's dead."

Taine's friend gave a low whistle. "Is this more of your weird-arse *matakite* intuition?"

"Something like that."

Tigger mumbled what sounded like "Fuck me" under his breath, then Taine caught the thrum of a chair rolling on linoleum. "Right-o. What do you need?"

"The registered owner of a boat named the *Isolde* and its GPS whereabouts for the past 24 hours."

"Ten minutes," Trigger said, all business now. "I'll call you back."

Taine used the time to haul out his duffel bag, dry himself off, and put on fresh gear. He'd just finished lacing up his boots when his phone buzzed.

"It's a commercial fishing boat," Trigger said. "Owned by The Old Salt Fishing Co. Two trustees: guy by the name of IR Jones, seems he owns a few businesses, and the other is a big-shot Auckland lawyer, the Weir of Weir and Tolian. As for the *Isolde's* whereabouts, Northpoint Ship Tracking has her currently on the coast near you. She put to sea at 5am yesterday out of Whangarei. Looks like she's spent most of today near a protected heritage site."

"That's consistent with what I know. So Old Salt Fishing is based in Whangarei?"

"Yup."

Whangarei was on the other side of the island: as the crow flies just 120km, but by boat, it had to be triple that, maybe more.

"And those other businesses?"

There was the clacking of a keyboard, then Trigger came back on the line. "There's a high-end art gallery at Kohukohu. Hmm. Looks like that's run by the wife. A gas station and a dive and tackle store at Rawene, and a mini-putt course at Kaikohe. I'll forward the addresses."

"Thanks for this."

"No problem. Always happy to lend a hand. It's all public knowledge, anyway."

Except public knowledge isn't so easy to access if you're dead.

"Taine?" Trigger said.

"Yeah?"

"Watch your six."

While Taine drove back towards Rawene, he considered the information Trigger had given him, immediately eliminating the mini golf as the base of a smuggling operation. It was too far inland and too incongruous. By the same logic, the dive and tackle store seemed too obvious. The art gallery was intriguing, though. A business like that might offer a good cover for someone fencing stolen artefacts, for example. Since it was on the northern side of the inlet, Taine made a point of driving past it.

There were no cars parked outside the restored weatherboard cottage. No light filtering from a back room. No sign of activity at all. If the men in the boat had come here, they weren't here now.

What about the gas station? Taine pulled into the ferry car park and Googled it. He checked the satellite images and the street view. Typical of small coastal towns, the gas station was one of those one-stop shops on the main esplanade, forecourt and pumps at the front, and an automotive repair service operating from a garage at the back. And as the only service station around for miles, it was the kind of place that opened early and closed late—where it wasn't unusual to see vehicles come and go at all hours. Taine's gut told him that was the place. The ferry didn't operate at this time of night, so unless he wanted to wait until the morning, Taine had no option but to take the detour around the harbour. The men with the boat would have to do the same.

It was nearing midnight by the time Taine reached town. He left his pick-up at the holiday park, then walked the two streets to the gas station. The ghosts slunk in alongside him. While he'd been driving the coast road, they must've taken some cosmic short cut. They scuttled about him, dragging their bony limbs, the tension making his skin crawl.

The gas station lights shone into the street. No cars, though. And no cashier. Taine circuited the building to the automotive repair shop at the rear, checking for CCTV cameras. None that he could see, but there were two vehicles parked near a dumpster. Both white SUVs. This Jones knew his business. Anything out of the ordinary and the locals notice—folks here had sounded the alarm when two strangers came ashore to bomb the *Rainbow Warrior* in the 80s—but these cars would barely raise an eyebrow. Probably rentals. Taine clicked off a photo of the plates.

A hunch told him the gold was inside. The black bitterness coming off the ghosts was another clue. But opening the battered double roller doors wasn't an option. Not without waking the neighbourhood. He checked the side door. Locked.

There was a rattle above him. Taine snapped his head up. The ghosts were surging through an open window. Taine followed their lead, climbing on the dumpster to slip inside the garage.

Jesus. A line of glass windows revealed five men in the offices on the far side of the building. Taine dropped to a crouch on the bench, knocking a wrench off a shadow board. Caught it just before it hit the bench. Breathed out slowly.

He was clearly in the right place: one of the bays held the boat trailer containing the *Isolde*'s dinghy. In the other, a blue twin cab was parked over a service pit. A vehicle breaking down was as good a cover as any for being here.

He peeked over the boat trailer. In the office, two of the men, one wearing city civvies, were engaged in a heated exchange. So the other four must be hired muscle. Any guns? Didn't matter. He had to stop thinking like this was a NZDF mission and that those people were his enemies. Taine wasn't here to hurt anyone. Even smugglers. He was here to prevent the ghosts from killing again.

The spectres were crawling all over the building now, hanging off the walls, rushing along the aisles, and pressing their ghostly mouths to the windows. Their hunger was mounting. He'd seen the accident with the semi. The negative currents they'd caused. So far, they hadn't bothered Taine, but what might they do if they didn't get their way? Taine needed to hurry up. As soon as the smugglers had completed the transaction, they'd come for the gold.

Still holding the wrench, he slipped off the bench, narrowly avoiding a skate on a mechanic's flat-bed creeper on the floor.

"For fuck's sake, Jones. Who has a million to flash around?" a voice shouted. "The client agreed to cover the cash expenses, and we'd send you the real money after the sale—*and over time.*"

"What am I supposed to do with US dollars? This is New Zealand, in case you hadn't noticed…"

The ghosts were rabid with excitement now. They dashed past Taine, swarming around the dinghy. A battered baked bean can toppled off the bench. Had the ghosts caused that, or was it just a stray gust from the window? In any case, the can clanged to the floor, a handful of nails rolling every which way.

"What the fuck was that? One of you go look."

Shit. Taine ducked under the bench as a Russell Crowe-sort came out of the office, brandishing a Glock. The man edged around the front of the twin cab, past a fridge of ice and bait at the end of the aisle. Taine squeezed backwards as Crowe moved down the alley, stepping over the creeper, the ghosts swarming about him. Taine gripped the wrench. Any second and the man would see him. But that baked bean can rolled again, this time clanking against the metal roller doors. The man twirled. *Time to move.*

Fuck. SNAFU. Crowe clocked Taine's reflection in the fridge's glass door.

He was about to turn back, about to fire…

Taine charged at him, braining him with the wrench. The man slumped, unconscious. *Dammit.* So much for not harming anyone.

Scooping up the gun, Taine tucked it in his waistband and climbed into the dinghy among the fish. The two little dolphins were still alive, poor things, flapping their black fins limply in the water sloshing in the bottom of the boat. Collateral victims of the smugglers' greed.

A handful of ghosts appeared, peering over the edge of the boat, brimming with excitement. Taine opened the tackle box. The gold was still there. The ghosts crowed with soundless glee. Taine took out his phone, turned off the flash, and quickly snapped off a couple of photos. Then he latched the box, slipped his fingers under the base, and tested its weight. It was heavy, maybe forty or fifty kilos. Easy enough to squat at the gym, but the box was awkward and the surface wobbly. Taine breathed deep, bent his knees, and hefted it onto the edge of the boat. Part one. For Part two, he'd have to hang on to it, balancing it there while he clambered over the side. Only then could he lift it down.

All at once, the ghosts swirled around him, urgent and angry. Taine swatted at them. *Stop it. I'm trying to help you.* They were frantic, surging about him, clouding his vision. *No!* He overbalanced, the box slipping from his fingers…falling…

It gouged a chunk out of Crowe's leg on its way past, crunched to the floor, then ground forward, sliding on the concrete, the metal shriek resonating throughout the garage. When it stopped, Crowe's blood dribbled from a corner.

Taine barely had time to drop out of the dinghy before the second hired muscle appeared at the end of the aisle. Taine dived onto the creeper, coasting under the trailer as the man opened fire. Even with a suppressor, it was loud enough. Taine came up in the middle aisle, the creeper rolling away as he leapt to his feet. One of the goons in the office was pulling a gun, about the enter the fray.

Yanking the gun from his waist, Taine fired at the windows. The glass clouded with cracks and a rain of shards pummelled the men. All this noise. A hundred decibels or thereabouts. There are only so many gunshots you can attribute cars backfiring in a sleepy rural town. Soon enough, someone would call the police. If that happened, the smugglers would be caught, and the gold confiscated. And that was the best-case scenario.

The second man had reached the middle aisle. Nowhere to go. Taine backed away as the ghosts flooded the aisle. His eyes widened. The runaway creeper had been slowing, but all at once it surged forward, propelled by a wither of ghosts, and swept the shooter off his feet. The man dropped to his knees, firing wildly. Taine dived to the floor. A bullet ricocheted off the boat trailer and exploded in the shooter's leg. He stumbled sideways and dropped the gun. A ghost hunkered beside him and sucked at the wound.

Bad luck?

Taine wasn't going to look a gift horse in the mouth. Snatching up the weapon, he kicked the man under the truck into the service pit, then punched the button, lowering the vehicle. The man screeched. Taine figured he'd screech even louder if could see the ghosts hanging off him, hungrily lapping at his blood.

Three to go. All in the office. Taine whipped off his jacket and wrapped it around the lower part of his face. Time to finish this. His boots crunched on the broken glass as he entered the office, a gun in each hand. The ghosts crowded in around him, grinning and quivering with malice.

The muscle stepped up, his gun raised, while the guy in the civvies, Weir presumably, edged towards a pile of bills on the table.

Taine cocked his head. "You want to die? For what? A few coins? Just put the gun on the table."

"Don't," Weir warned.

The ghosts skittered about, hissing with agitation.

Slowly, the muscle raised his hands. "Okay, okay. Don't shoot." His eyes darting at Weir, he went to push the gun across the table, then suddenly swerved to the right. Fired. A frenzy of ghosts swirled in the small space. Struggling to see past them, Taine lunged and flipped the table over. The man rolled in the glass and sat up ready to fire, his face and hands riddled with bloody nicks.

Taine shot him in the shoulder. The blow barrelled him backwards, but to his credit the man hung on, his fingers twitching on the trigger. Taine shot the gun out of his hand.

Clearly, they weren't paying him enough because the man shuffled backwards on his arse, nursing his shattered arm and hand. He huddled in the corner, his head down, whimpering. Several ghosts poked wispy appendages into his bleeding wounds and tried to lick whatever they had for fingers. The man twitched as they touched him, then his eyes rolled back in his head and he slumped against the wall, obscured by the ghost cloud.

Taine kicked the gun out of reach in case he woke up. The masterminds hadn't moved.

"In the closet," Taine said, gesturing at a free-standing coat cupboard.

"The fuck?" Weir said.

The other, Jones, raised an eyebrow. "Let's just do what he says."

Realisation dawned. Jones figured Taine was a burglar. An opportunist. He would let Taine take the money because they would still have the gold.

"Get in!" Taine shouted.

Still, Weir couldn't help glancing at his precious bills. Taine raised the guns.

Weir blanched. He backed into the flimsy wardrobe, squeezing in beside his partner. The closet had a ridiculously teeny lock: smaller than Taine's thumbnail. He locked it anyway. Then, his back to the wall, he kicked the wardrobe over. It landed with a whump. Face down. Inside, Jones and Weir groaned.

Taine grabbed the money and the guns and sprinted into the garage. He had to go now, before the goons got their act together. He loaded the tackle box onto the creeper and threw the rest on top. Then, like an Olympic sprinter taking the blocks, he put his hands on the back board and hurtled for the side door.

The ghosts opened it for him.

Taine burst out of the garage and onto the darkened road. Which way? Left. Right. At two o'clock an ancient dinghy lay overturned the grass verge. Dashing across the road, Taine lifted the boat over the creeper, then rolled under the dinghy himself, letting it down slowly. More than a dozen dead miners squeezed in beside him, pressing against him with their swollen bellies and touching him with their wispy elongated limbs. He swallowed his horror and waited.

Ten minutes later, headlights glinted through the cracks in the boards and the white SUVs roared up the road. They must know he had the gold. Only they'd expected him to take the loot and hightail it out of town.

Instead, he planned to take it back.

Taine 'borrowed' a boat, one that was actually seaworthy, and an outboard motor from one of the boathouses, making a mental promise to bring them back before the owner woke up. He loaded the dinghy and set off.

The ghosts, strangely calm now, hovered on the beach, watching him go.

When he'd left the harbour inlet, Taine cut the motor and dropped the creeper and the guns into the inky depths. He sat back on his haunches. He was an idiot. Sure, so he'd stolen the gold and confiscated some weapons, but what had he really achieved? Jones and Weir would lick their wounds then come looking for more. And since Taine was putting the gold back, they would find it.

Would the photos be enough to convict them? Taine checked his phone. In the images, he'd captured the name of the boat, the dive gear, the tackle box, even the fish. The problem was the gold didn't look like gold. In the gloom and covered in barnacles, it could be oysters. Or rocks. Taine slumped. The ghosts would continue to haunt the region. People would die. *And I've let Coolie down again.*

The boat rocked on the waves. After a while, Taine took another look at the photos, then called his partner, the biologist Dr Jules Asher.

"Taine?" she said, her voice husky. The sheets rustled. "Everything all right with Coolie's folks?"

"Yeah. They're good. I'm stopping by later for lunch. Soya chicken."

"Sounds great." Silence. Taine knew she was waiting for him to tell her the real reason for the 3am call, wind whistling and water sloshing in the background.

"Hector's Dolphins have a black dorsal fin, right?"

"Uh-huh."

"I know they're endangered. Are they also protected? I mean, are there penalties?"

"Yes. There are penalties for people who knowingly hunt and sell them. Fines, prison time, revocation of commercial fishing licences…"

"So if I knew of someone who had two living dolphins in his boat, right now in the gas station at Rawene, someone whom I doubt has any intention of reporting them, could the Conservation Department step in?"

There was a click. *Her bedside lamp.* He had her attention. "Absolutely. If you have evidence, I could pull some strings, forward it to the right people. But wait, where was this? Hector's Dolphins are extremely rare in Northland."

"My guess is there could be a pod sheltering near a protected marine heritage site. I'm sending a photo now. You might want to check out recent tracking for the parent boat."

He heard her gasp. "Right, got it."

"You'll need to hurry, Jules. It's been hours since they were pulled from the water."

"On it." She didn't ask how he knew, just hung up.

Before Taine pocketed his phone, he checked the site of the *SS Ventnor.* Then he turned the dinghy and set course.

Hours later, when Taine had delivered the gold back to the deep and returned the runabout to the boatshed, he collected his truck from the holiday park and drove to the cemetery.

Alone on the hillside, Taine crouched beside the memorial. Removing the bundle of greenbacks from inside his jacket, Taine took out a lighter. He burned the bills in clumps, watched by the wilting chrysanthemums and the soggy burger. The linen notes glowed with orange flame, giving off a waft of grey smoke. There had to be a few thousand in notes here. He wondered what the exchange rate was in the afterlife.

For you, Coolie. Wishing you a prosperous eternity.

Coolie stepped from the smoke. "Thanks, Boss."

Taine smiled. "So did it work?"

Coolie shrugged. "Maybe. Without friends and family to nurture them, they'll always be hungry, but it might be enough."

"Will I see you again?"

Coolie grinned. "Never say never, man. Tell Trigger I said hi." He drifted off.

With the last of the money shrivelling to black, Taine leaned back on the bench and watched the sunrise glinting pink on the harbour.

Dangerous Specimens

ROBERT HOOD

'WELL, BASICALLY HE WAS HACKED TO PIECES,' SAID SERGEANT ERNIE STACE, a touch of malicious enjoyment lingering on his lips.

Lewis Burke raised his pen, wanting to write something clever, but nothing came to mind. 'Hacked to pieces?' he muttered instead.

'The examining medical officer estimated that, before and after death, the victim was stabbed maybe sixty times... Bit of a mess really.'

'Hardly routine stuff, is it?' Lewis commented. The routine nature of police rounds was why the *Tribune*'s editor had given Lewis the job. Generally, police briefings consisted of hanging about behind barriers decorated with promotional pamphlets and leafing through back issues of *Law Enforcement Gazette* and *Police News*, until Stace came and read off excerpts from his pile of duty summaries. Lewis usually returned to the office with a few notes on a robbery or two, a mugging, several minor drug arrests, or, if he were lucky, a routine murder. The latter often ended up as a story in its own right, as distinct from a paragraph under Police Rounds. Even so, the head journo, Trelawny Samms, reckoned crime was too trivial and sordid for her to worry about. She preferred political corruption. 'If an alderman gets done in, I'll take it,' she'd declared at the start of the year. Surprisingly, no alderman had ever been done in.

'Nothing routine about this one,' agreed Stace. 'The victim's head was removed afterwards and propped up on the lounge so it could watch the telly.' Lewis looked at Stace blankly. 'The telly was on when he was found,' the policeman added.

His editor, Jack, wasn't impressed. 'Why didn't he ring us yesterday, Burke? We could have had someone on the spot.' Lewis shrugged. Jack's cigarette smoke curled around Lewis as though trying to find a way to make him disappear. 'Never mind. Old news by the time our next issue's out, but we can do some localised coverage. Find an angle.'

'What sort of angle?'

'Blood and freaks, Burke. That's what suburban newspapers are about.'

So far as Lewis could tell, the victim's personal details, given to him by Stace and culled from reports in the Sydney dailies, weren't characterised by grime. His name was P. F. Mendez, 45, who'd lived alone in his unit flat on Warner Place for 18 months, until someone decided he should die there as well. He was a simple man—no political or business connections, no family ties that might make inheritance a motive, no drugs. No one seemed to hate him much. Or like him much either. Every day he went to work in a factory near the river, coming home at five-thirty, when he'd eat dinner, and then watch TV. Lewis thought his life sounded too dull not to be suspicious. 'What did he spend his money on?' he asked Stace, when he rang him later in the day, 'A girlfriend?'

'Sent what he earned to his mother in Brazil,' the policeman said in a bored tone. 'Hardly kept any for himself. Poor bastard.'

According to Stace, there were no clues as to the identity of the murderer; he wanted the *Tribune* to run an appeal for information. 'Someone must've seen him,' Stace snorted. 'Would've been covered in blood.'

Mendez' body was found at 9.35 on Wednesday night by a workmate who'd called by with a chook Mendez had won in a raffle. The workmate knocked on the door and it opened. Blood smears on the floor should have alerted him to the fact that something was wrong. But no one expects acquaintances to be hacked to pieces in their loungeroom, and he went in anyway, discovering Mendez' head absorbed in *Newsworld*. 'When he stopped spewing, he rang us,' Stace commented, 'The boys had to clean it up.'

The Homicide Squad took over after Stace and 'the boys' had clumped around the scene for a while, but so far they'd found nothing. Bloodsplatter patterns were consistent with out-and-out butchery; there were no fingerprints, except those of the victim; and though there were bloody footprints, they appeared to belong to the workmate only. 'The murderer was pretty careful,' Stace commented, 'considering how messy the whole thing was. He didn't leave much sign of having been there — apart from the body, that is.' Worst of all, the murder weapon was nowhere to be found. A team of searchers was still looking for it; and another was canvassing the area, door-to-door, seeking information. 'I can give you the address of the bloke who found him,' Stace added, 'But we've already ruled him out. That's it. There's nothing more.'

'It must have been a violent attack. Surely someone --'

'No one heard it. No one ever hears anything in those ant-hills— self-defence, perhaps.' He paused. 'There's one guy who says he knows what happened, but he's a crack-pot. T.G. Mephisto ... the T.G. stands for *The Great*. Fair dinkum, that's his name —The Great Mephisto. Ex-magician or something. Lives on the third storey.'

'He's a suspect then?'

'Hardly. Can't move from his bed. Been paralysed for yonks. And he's crazy.'

'Crazy? Well, whoever killed Mendez must've been crazy.'

Stace shrugged.

Lewis decided to check out Mephisto after he'd researched some paragraphs Jack wanted on the Council snake catcher—a small, weedy man who made a habit of picking up particularly dangerous specimens and gesticulating with them while he talked. 'Tiger snakes!' he yelled. 'They'll hide in anyone's backyard.' It made Lewis very nervous. He was glad when the interview was over, though investigating mutilation murders had a similar effect on him, and as he and Eric, the staff photographer, drove out to see this Mr Mephisto, Lewis was feeling rather like taking a holiday up the Gold Coast instead. He couldn't, of course. When Jack wanted blood, there was no help for it but to bleed.

Warner Place was a '70s horseshoe road lined with multi-storeyed red-brick edifices, whose units differed from each other only in the colour of their curtains and the type of rubbish accumulating on their balconies. To get to T.G. Mephisto's place Lewis and Eric had to pass the scene of the crime, which was on the ground floor. Mendez' front door was guarded by a uniformed cop who recognised Lewis and waved him away impatiently. 'I'm going to number 32,' Lewis said.

The cop grunted. 'Why?'

'What's it to you? Isn't the press free anymore?' snapped Eric.

Lewis dragged him off. 'His girlfriend just left him,' he said to the cop apologetically, as they went on up the stairs.

A surly woman only slightly smaller than a bus opened the door of T.G. Mephisto's flat when Lewis knocked. 'I'm a reporter,' said Lewis, holding up his notepad by way of confirmation. 'I'd like to talk to Mr Mephisto.'

'He's sick.'

'Yes, but I want to talk about the murder.'

For a moment, Lewis thought the woman was going to strangle him, but instead she nudged him aside and glanced down the corridor. 'Look,' she said, 'Mr Mephisto's a bit funny in the head. You don't want to make a big deal out of anything he says. He's always taking responsibility for crimes he didn't commit.'

'The police said he had some information --'

'It's crap, that's all.' Her face became more sponge-like as annoyance screwed it up.

'You his wife?'

She snarled. 'Just a nurse, darling. And I wasn't here on Wednesday night.'

'I see.'

'At my sister's,' she added, as the clincher.

'Will you ask Mr Mephisto can we talk to him please?'

She looked at Lewis and then Eric. The photographer made to take a picture of her and she covered her face. 'Put that bloody thing away or I'll shove it up your arse, buster,' she growled. Eric grinned.

'Please?' said Lewis.

'He's asleep.'

As the words left her mouth, fast like the flicking of a snake's tongue, another voice, old but powerful, echoed from inside the flat. 'Send them in, Miss Argant, send them in.'

The nurse turned, frowning at the invisible source of the voice. 'Just troublemakers from the newspaper!' she yelled.

'Send them in!' the voice repeated, determined to be obeyed this time.

'Might as well come in then,' the woman snarled. She pushed Lewis in front of her. 'If you insult him in your crumby newspaper, I'll make you eat it. Okay?'

Lewis nodded.

Mr Mephisto was a dapper old gent, propped up in bed in a threadbare silk dressing gown and wearing a fez. He had a sad, elongated face that made him look bewildered. He fingered three rubber magician's balls, swiveling them around his hands with distracting dexterity. The room itself was gloomy and cluttered; there were shelves to roof level on every available wall and on most of these there were books and odd ornaments. The shelves on the wall above the bed were covered in strange, coloured bottles that seemed to have objects surrounded by liquid in them. Lewis couldn't tell what the objects were, but they appeared disconcertingly nasty and perhaps biological.

'Thank God you've come,' cried Mr Mephisto, when the nurse shoved Lewis through the door. He got Lewis to drag a chair over to the side of his bed and began talking immediately, too full of the need to communicate his secrets to require prompting. Eric wandered about the room, eying everything with a view to effective background for a picture. Once or twice he snapped a shot of Mephisto in full flight. His flash lit up the room eerily.

'I've been beside myself with worry,' Mephisto cried. 'The poor man ... the poor man.'

'Mr Mendez?'

'Yes. It's my fault, you see. Perhaps the police told you?'

'No.'

'I should explain ...' He gestured toward the wall covered in bottles. 'I'm an exorcist. Over the years I've fought with many demons, you see, for possession of some unfortunate soul. It's vital work, Mr Burke. The world would be a much more dangerous place if it wasn't for me.' Lewis tried to look impressed. 'Just minor demons ... I wouldn't know how to deal with the Princes of Hell.' The old man patted his legs, which lay unseen beneath a patchwork blanket. 'It was Beelzebub himself who crippled me. Struck me down with a single blow, for interfering in his business. I haven't been able to walk for twenty years.'

'I'm sorry.' Lewis glanced at Eric, who was making faces off to the side, out of Mephisto's sight.

'But that's another story. Perhaps you'd like to hear it some time?' Lewis smiled and shrugged. 'This latest crime ... we must speak of that. You see, in these bottles I keep the demons I've captured --'

'In bottles? Sort of like genies, eh?' Eric strode over to the bed and reached up at one of the bottles. 'Don't touch them!' Mephisto shrieked.

Eric jerked back. 'Sorry.'

'If they escape there'll be terrible bloodshed!' While Eric and Lewis waited uneasily, the man calmed himself by reciting incomprehensible words that might have been Latin. 'The danger ...' he said at last, slumping into his pillows. 'A terrible burden. Such responsibility.' His mind seemed to drift off, dammed into inaction by the weight of some memory. 'I failed that responsibility on Wednesday evening. I was worried ... I don't know why, perhaps because I'd been thinking of writing my memoirs, of committing my life to paper, and was deep in contemplation of the struggles I've undertaken over the years. One of the bottles ...' He pointed at a burnt-umberish specimen, tall like a spaghetti jar. Lewis couldn't see what was in it. '... containing a demon I trapped thirty years ago in a Brazilian village, kept drawing my attention. I was weakened by my melancholy. I reached up to check the stopper ...' He sighed theatrically. 'Suddenly pain shot through my legs, and I knocked the bottle from the shelf ... The stopper came off and the demon was loose.'

'What happened then?' said Eric eagerly.

'I gasped out words of protection ... they were all I could remember in that moment. Folly! I should have used words of restraint instead, to force the demon back into the bottle, not simply drive it away ... But I was panicked, and age has worn me down.'

He began to choke. Lewis was worried he was having an attack. 'Perhaps we should come back later.'

The old man reached out and touched Lewis. 'No. I'm fine.' He settled back. 'It's just that the consequence of my ... lapse was so terrible. The demon sped from this room and soon I heard — heard clearly, in my mind — the awful cries of someone being butchered. I had to use the strength of my will, reaching out over the distance to Mr Mendez' room, to drag the demon back to me kicking and screaming. Once I had it before me, I forced it into the bottle. *You're too late*, it said as it went in, *Death has visited you and I have fed on it.* But your victim, I wept, he was innocent. *I left him as I found him*, the demon replied, *watching TV*. I shall never forget its laugh.'

Lewis swallowed a nervous chuckle that was itching in his own throat. He couldn't think of anything coherent to say. Eric was more lucid. 'So the murderer that did in that bloke downstairs is in this bottle?' he asked, pointing. Mephisto nodded and Eric took a picture of it. 'There's your scoop, Lewis — a murderer in a bottle. It's great.'

Again Lewis wished he were on the Gold Coast.

The rest of the interview was much the same. Mr Mephisto got more emotional and Eric got more satiric, but all in all there wasn't anything said that indicated Mephisto knew more about the killing than any other harmless oddball inhabiting the building. There was nothing suspicious in what he said — it was just craziness. By this stage Lewis was desperate to leave. It was obvious Stace was right: Mr T.G. Mephisto was a looney.

When Lewis finally dragged Eric away, the nurse, alerted to their departure by the old man's shouted farewells, came to see them out. 'He's harmless,' she whispered at Lewis, gripping his arm so tightly it ached. 'Leave him alone now, eh?' Lewis nodded and squeezed through the doorway.

Cynthia was absorbed in *What's On* when Lewis and Eric got back to the office; Trelawny was nowhere to be seen. *Thank God*, thought Lewis, feeling that somehow the whole episode was humiliating. He tried to creep to his desk before anyone saw him. 'Jack's after you,' muttered Cynthia, not stopping to look at him. Lewis was convinced she snickered.

While Lewis explained what happened at Warner Place, the editor involved himself in grinding a cigarette between his teeth. 'Maybe we can use it,' he said as Lewis finished.

'He's a looney, Jack ... you know, pathetic.' Lewis shuffled through his mind to find a reason Jack would appreciate—something more tangible than his own vague disquiet. 'It'd look like blatant exploitation. Cheap.'

'Maybe,' Jack said warily. 'Write up what you've got on the killing, including Stace's plea for information. Add a par or two about the old man—human interest. Tell 'em his demon story, it's sort of poignant. In the meantime I'll think it over.'

'All the gory details?'

'Up front. Hit them with the head bit. General public loves decapitation. Make them feel like they're walking a tightrope. No one's safe, even in front of their telly—that sort of thing.'

Lewis nodded reluctantly.

In the end Jack added his own details to the story of Mr Mephisto and the bottled nasties, giving a mocking tone to his account of the demon's malicious rampage. There was no picture; he'd told Eric to forget it. Didn't warrant the space, he said.

On Thursday, after the paper had been on the streets for a day, Lewis was sitting in his lounge room, watching TV and juggling bits of pizza past a greedy cat and into his own mouth, when he thought he heard a noise. Wind had sprung up, and the darkness he knew was out there was scraping nervously at the windows. The cat glanced toward the door, then leapt, its claws gouging into his knees. It disappeared into the laundry. Lewis' pulse quickened.

His eyes latched onto the handle of his front door. *My God*, he thought, *I didn't lock it.* He started up, but a sliver of darkness had run down the doorframe. The door opened. A figure tumbled out of the hallway gloom, so fast Lewis couldn't focus on it. It rushed toward him. It was waving something long and whitish, like a knife raised to slash down at him. Lewis registered bulk and nothing more as he jerked himself backwards, intending to scramble to safety. But the figure, a flickering shadow lit by the light from the TV, was over him in an instant. A fist beat against his chest, smashing the pizza he'd been clutching there; he stumbled and collapsed helpless onto his back. The white length held in the figure's hand was striking at him. 'No!' he screamed. Something blunt and yielding prodded his flesh.

'You bastard!' yelled a voice back at him. That it came from his looming attacker seemed an impossibility—the thing was too primal. But Lewis blinked and it took on a semblance of humanity: Mr Mephisto's nurse. Her face was distorted by the TV news and by anger. She was poking him with a rolled-up newspaper. 'What's this shit you put in here, eh?' she roared.

'What are you doing?' Lewis gasped.

'I told you not to write about him... he's sick. You wanna destroy the man? You think he has no dignity?' The newspaper was digging into him.

'Stop that!' Lewis said, trying to sit up; but she pushed him down again.

'I should fracture your skull with it, mister big-shot reporter.'

Lewis held up his palms submissively. 'Look, he's hardly mentioned in the article, and not by name.'

'You think he doesn't know it's him you wrote about?' Her grimacing mouth struck at him like a rattlesnake's. 'He's a sensitive man ... a great man. If he says there's demons, then there's demons. What call you got to laugh at him, eh? You think it's all crap, then just ignore him. You make him out to be a nut-case ... in his mind he's turned into a nothing by that.'

Lewis tried to smile reassuringly.

'Let me tell you something.' She stepped back now, glaring at him, but from a distance. Lewis sat up, somewhat relieved, but still anxious about what she might do. Her gestures exuded a strength he knew he couldn't fight, and a fierceness that would leave him in shreds if it became physical. 'He's been good to me, he's been nice ... not many people ever have been. But he's sick, tired ... a man of belief, you know, always struggling to do the right thing, to make a difference. I hated seeing him disappointed, not believing in himself anymore.' She moved into the shadows beyond the flickering blue light. 'Watch your TV, Mr Newsman! You're lucky that tonight I'm not the demon that did for Mendez ... or you'd be part of the news, like him.'

In the next moment she was gone.

The following morning Stace called. At first Lewis thought there'd been a breakthrough in the Mendez case, but Stace said no, not exactly. 'Related, sort of—but the plain clothes boys still haven't come up with anything, not even the knife. Pity about that. They always reckon they can wrap up a case once they've found the murder weapon.' He laughed. 'I called about that T.G. Mephisto character, remember him?'

'What about him?'

'Jumped from his bedroom window and broke his back on the footpath outside Mendez's place. Bizarre, eh?' Lewis was speechless. 'The thing is, Burke, he left a note, addressed to you.'

'Me?'

'Yeah. Says he was very disappointed you decided not to take his demons seriously. Goes on about danger to the public and all that. *No one'll listen*, he says. Poor bugger seemed really cut up that we all thought he was cuckoo. He was, of course. Nutty as a fruit cake.'

'I suppose --'

'*Can't handle the responsibility*, he says. *Everyone laughs and you treat me like a fool. The humiliation weighs on me*. Weighs on me? You like that?'

'Not much.'

'No. Anyway the coroner'll be after you to make a statement about the old codger's state-of-mind.'

'Oh, yeah?' For a moment Lewis thought of the bottles above the old man's bed, seething with demons left now without a guardian. 'What'll happen to his bottles?' he asked.

'Bottles? I don't know. The nurse said she'd get rid of them. Listen, Burke, come down the station like a good boy and make a statement, eh? Tomorrow?'

'Sure.'

'Waste of time. But that's the way it goes.'

How does it go? thought Lewis, his imagination suddenly spinning out into a whirl of speculation. *Could the old man actually have been the killer? Maybe. But why? How about this: Mephisto, nothing much left in his life, becomes desperate to prove this important thing, his collection of demons, is not only real, but vital. It means, at least, that he's a somebody. He hears Mendez talking about Brazil, remembers his Brazilian demon, and in his mind accidentally releases it. But the demon's him, a sort of displaced alter ego. He goes downstairs and deals with poor Mendez in a way that'll show everyone how serious these demons really are. Later he tells all, even takes the blame, because it makes him important. And because his story's so potty, no one takes any notice, no one suspects him. He's just a harmless looney, they say—and look elsewhere for a ruthless sadist that doesn't exist.*

Lewis frowned. *Could be true,* he thought, *except for one thing.*

'Stace? Where was Mephisto's bed? I mean, in his room, sure—but was it near the window?'

'The bed? Who cares?'

'Where was it, Ernie?'

'I dunno. Oh, against the inside wall, across the room from the window. Why?'

'If the old man was a cripple,' Lewis said, 'tell me how he got to the window, so he could throw himself out of it.'

'What?'

'Was he really crippled, Stace?'

'According to the nurse. And there's doctors' reports.'

'So how'd he get to the window?' There was silence, except for the distant sound of policemen shouting or laughing.

'The nurse carried him?' asked Stace shyly.

Lewis took a deep breath. 'More than that, Stace. I reckon she might be Mendez' killer as well. She came to my place last night. Threatened me. She compared herself pretty obviously to the demon that killed Mendez.'

'Why should she do that to the poor bugger? I grant you she's got the right physique for it, but why bother?'

'She would've done anything for that old man ... she adored him. And he needed to believe in his demons, Stace. He was close to the edge. Maybe she wanted to draw him back from the edge, give him a sense of importance.'

'But it backfired, eh? Made him feel more humiliated and he lost it. But if she adored the old man so much why murder him?'

'As I said, she'd do anything for him, and he wanted more than anything to die. Not murder. Euthanasia.'

More silence. 'Sounds a bit elaborate, Burke, but I'll check out her alibi—if there's anything dodgy about it I'll get 'em to bring her in. Don't hold out any hope though.'

'Why not?'

'All speculation. And she doesn't seem the type to cave in and spill her guts. Pity we can't find the murder weapon somewhere incriminating. Make the blokes in Homicide happier.'

'Having her walking around free makes me pretty nervous, Ernie,' Lewis said.

'Don't worry, Burke. If she carves you up, we'll get her for sure.'

Two days later, while Lewis was writing another story about the Council snake catcher, who'd been bitten by a brown snake on the back of the neck, Eric came up to his desk with a pile of prints and nudged his shoulder. 'Hey, Lewis,' he said, 'You know that looney with the demons?'

'T.G. Mephisto? What about him?'

'Did you ever find out what was in his bottles?'

'No. Why?'

'I just developed a roll of film I had lying around—the stuff I took that day you talked to him. Hadn't bothered before, 'cause Jack didn't want them. But look at this.' He tossed an enlarged print in front of Lewis. 'That's a picture of the bottle he reckoned killed Mendez. How's that for a demon?'

Lewis breathed out languidly. What he could see was not a demon, but confirmation that a demon had passed that way. Eric's flash had lit up the contents of the bottle, highlighting a long metallic sliver.

A knife.

Remnants and Bad Water

KAARON WARREN

ONE

THE RAIN SHOWED NO SIGN OF LETTING UP. AFTER AN EIGHT YEAR DROUGHT and the worst bushfires ever suffered, no one wanted to complain, but the relentless downpour was oppressive.

Sally stood on the back step of the small house she shared with Andy (he tried to be 'Drew' but it never stuck), Charlie, and Jules. The small courtyard was flooded and rising higher.

"Go for a swim," Andy said, pointing at the courtyard that was practically a pool. He sucked on his 6th or 8th beer of the day but she liked the way he smelled. He tapped his watch. "I'll time you, see how long you stay under."

Sally discovered she could hold her breath for a long time the day a bully from school held her head under water at the public swimming pool. Her head was down near his shorts and there were holes in them that made her feel sorry for him. She reached over and pulled his shorts down, tugging out his dick so it floated free like a dead fish. He let her head go and she bobbed to the surface. The stricken look on his face made her pity him again, and she leaned over and kissed him while he adjusted himself.

He changed from 'that bully' to 'Andy', just like that. They'd been friends and occasional lovers since.

The rain bucketed down.

Jules arrived home from work, soaked to the bone. Makeup streaked her face, making her look like a clownish tiger.

"You okay?" Sally asked. Jules shook her head. Always stylish, even soaking wet she looked good, with dark purple ankle boots, black leggings, a classic tartan skirt she'd cut ragged so it sat mid-thigh, and a sleeveless men's shirt. They were always finding scraps and strips of material all over the house, remnants from Jules' creations.

"Sacked. Fuckers," Jules said.

"How can they do that?" Sally asked.

Jules smiled. "Thanks for not saying 'what for'. But it was because I told a customer to fuck off. He deserved it."

"Of course he did," Andy said. "What, did he call you 'miss' or something? Ask you out? Evil."

Both women gave him a look that made him shrivel.

"The rain is making everyone cranky," Sally said.

They all headed inside. It was stuffy and close, the walls damp from leaking windows they'd tried and failed to seal with Blu Tack.

They crowded into the small kitchen, leaning against the benches and eating potato chips straight from the packet.

Andy handed Jules a beer, which she drained. She dropped the can, squashed it under foot, then lifted it as if to throw it.

Sally held her arm.

"I want to break something."

"Not in here. Go do it up the road. Throw stones at the lights or whatever."

It was Charlie who'd introduced them to the joys of smashing stuff. His arms were scarred high and low. Letting the sorrow out, he called it. Charlie was a poet at heart but not by talent. He'd learned that breaking things let that sorrow out as well.

Charlie was useful. He seemed to know stuff, and people, always a party invite, an opening, a launch, who had what for sale. So when he got home an hour or so later, buzzed and barely noticing the rain, it wasn't surprising when he said, "Kids, I have the solution to all your woes. Winery party!" His friend (while his definition of friend was loose, as long as they provided entertainment no one cared) had a winery just out of town, something given to them by rich parents looking for a tax loss. It was running okay; Charlie's friend was smart enough to hire expert staff. Tonight was the Grape Release celebration, something Charlie had been aiming for an invite to for ages.

Jules said, "Nah, too depressed. I'll just call my main man to come over to cheer me up." But her current boyfriend didn't answer messages or calls, so the others convinced her to shower and dress up.

The winery was right on Lake Penelope, a vast terminal lake that filled and emptied into the ground rather than the sea. It hadn't been full for years, so when they drove past and saw the water starting to rise, it was enough to make Andy stop the car so they could get a good look.

They saw sheds, huts, fences, farm equipment, troughs, old cars. All out there in the expectation the dry would continue and this space, covering many kilometres, would remain usable farmland. With the waters reaching closer, it didn't look as if anyone was coming to protect it.

A flock of sheep clustered near the water's edge a kilometre or so out, as did many hundreds of birds, drinking as the sun set. Usually saline, the water was sweet at present. Sally wouldn't tell the others, but she thought she heard her name, SSaalllyssssallly

Silly.

"Kinda beautiful," Jules said. She sparkled in her evening wear; they all did. Sally wore a skin-tight, hot pink dress that reached her ankles, but it was stretchy so she could walk. They all wore sensible thick down coats over the top that they'd throw off once they were inside.

"Come on, you lot. Wine is waiting," Charlie said, clapping his hands.

Cars were lined up along the driveway so Andy dropped them off at the entrance, then headed off to find a parking spot, earning a kiss and a promise from Sally. They handed their coats to the person at the door then Charlie led the way in. It was an over-dressed, rain-bedraggled crowd, talking loudly in posh voices as if to justify being in this place at this time, as if any of it was important.

The flatmates drank as much wine as they could grab, even Andy who joked about taking the backroads home when there was just the one road in and out. Charlie worked the room, making people laugh and blush. A group roared with laughter and Andy and Sally rolled their eyes at each other; he really wasn't that funny.

The other guests bored them but the wide windows gave them a great view into the vineyards and beyond. The snacks were good but the wine, quite honestly, was mediocre. At least it was free.

Jules chatted to a tall, handsome man who seemed to be wearing a singlet under his jacket coat. She rolled her eyes at Sally; *rescue me.*

"Beryl! It's time for your ointment," Sally said loudly to Jules, taking her elbow. "Good evening," to Mr Singlet, and they spluttered with laughter once they were out of earshot. Andy was the drunkest of them so Charlie took the car keys. The party had been far less fabulous than he'd hoped and he was ready to go. They grabbed a cheese platter each (not a soul else touching them) and a bottle of wine (they had to be subtler about that) and headed out. Andy had parked way down at the end of the driveway and the muddy walk made all of them laugh. It was still raining at a steady gentle pace and by the time they got to the car they were all soaked.

"Jeez, the water's coming in now," Charlie said, looking out at Lake Penelope. They walked to the road's edge.

Jules fidgeted with the fence. It was unstable where they stood and she pushed it back and forth like she was wriggling a loose tooth. The others joined in, feeling a sense of satisfaction as the posts lifted out and eventually fell. Jules stepped over it.

"Hey!" It was Singlet Guy. "What's happening?"

"We're going to have a picnic out there," Sally said. "It's what you're supposed to do as the water comes in. It's a tradition!" She was making it up on the spot, feeling wild at the sight of the lake rising, wondering how it would feel to dive in. "You go down there and let the water fill your footprints. Bad luck for the year, otherwise."

Jules shivered. She whispered, "It's bloody freezing, Sally. This is dumb," but Sally was already shoes off and running so Jules followed.

Singlet Guy said, "It's also tradition that this is the night the drowned walk out of the water looking for help. I saw one of them, last year. Might see him again. And if you eat a slice of a giant fish and throw him back, you'll have good luck for the year." He was clearly making shit up as he went along. "Only in Winter, otherwise don't bother. He'll taste sweet when it's cold; any other time he'll literally burn your tongue."

"Literally," Andy said.

"They say it sounds like a yearling calf, starving for its mother."

"Well, I'm shit outta luck, I'd take a bite out of that sweet motherfucker fish. Anything to change my fortunes," Jules said.

The moon was high and bright, the ground hard after years of drought. The rain had stopped. Everyone followed Jules and Sally out to one of the small shacks, a corrugated iron structure held up with old farm equipment.

Jules picked up a metal pole and banged it against the old machine. The sound rang out across the water and the land, almost bouncing. Andy whooped and ran down to join her, reaching down for his own pole and slamming it against the side of the structure, which shuddered.

"I didn't know there was a live performance," Singlet Man said. More to get away from him than anything else, Sally ran down to join Andy and Jules. She gave the door of the hut a kick. Already off its hinges, it fell sideways with a clatter. Inside was dark. It smelled like hay, like machine oil, and like something else. She thought perhaps old seaweed, or dried fish. Outside Andy, Jules and the others banged and whooped. Something shattered, a window somewhere, and they toppled a small water tank.

Sally lit her phone torch to look in the hut before they knocked it down. She heard someone say, "The water will smash all of this over anyway, we might as well enjoy it." She saw a sleeping bag, rolled up neatly but stained and torn. Beside it, a plate and a fork, food long since dried. She guessed it was an occasional sleeping place.

They wouldn't be sleeping here once the water came in.

Sally saw an old blanket in the corner, with a small, neatly stacked pile of empty sardine tins, rusty but still faintly giving off an aroma. A bent fork rested on the pile, its tines clean. The ground underfoot was sandy or it could have been salt, and fallen over under the small table was a candle. Sally picked it up.

The walls shuddered as the people outside began to hammer with fists and poles. "Hey!" Sally called. She pushed her way through the door. Jules screamed, as if she'd forgotten Sally existed. Sally wiggled her fingers and weaved towards Jules, whispering loudly, "I'm the ghost of a dead virgin raped in that there hut. I'll haunt you if you take my love shack away."

All this did was set off a chorus of "love shack", everybody dancing in the mud, even Singlet Man who clearly liked to be the cool one. He and Jules spun around together, flashing in the moonlight.

Sally found the sight annoying so walked out further. Her feet felt like ice blocks and she knew she should get back to the road, the car, dry off, but the water, the lake, was so beautiful.

Her feet sank further into the soft ground and she felt firmness on the sole of one foot. She looked down and saw something; in her phone light, it looked like desperate fingers reaching up, someone in a shallow grave. If she hadn't had so much wine she would have laughed it off but she was suddenly sure someone was buried and she fell to her feet and began to dig. She heard a sucking sound and saw what looked like a mouth, filled with dirt, gasping for air.

She dug harder.

Charlie and Andy joined her and she loved them for that.

"That's not where the bodies are buried. They're back there, under the stones," Singlet Man said. He lit a cigarette and smiled.

There was no body, of course.

Sally cleared her eyes, blurry in the cold night and she didn't have her glasses on, hated wearing them.

"Come on! We wanna smash!" Jules called out, her voice sounding deeper in the thick, moist air. Sally stepped away as the others demolished the next hut with yells and shouts, grunts, and a cry as someone hurt themselves, shedding blood. No one cared.

Singlet Man said to her, "Did you see some tins of food in that other hut? Last meal before he died."

"Who?"

"The guy I mentioned. The ghost I saw last year. Poor guy. Kicked out by his wife for drinking and she didn't even know the rest of it. His plan was to come here to dry out, lose weight, sober up. He had an exercise routine, dragging big trunks around the place to build a fire pit. He was about as bright as anyone who stays out here. They don't really believe the water will come back. And they don't know how many sink holes there are. He drowned and no one even noticed."

The hut proved sturdier than they expected and they gave up. The rain started again and Singlet Man said, "That puts a dampener on proceedings."

"How many kids do you have, anyway?" Jules said. "Because that's a good Dad joke."

He walked ahead as if he didn't hear her, hands thrust tight into pockets. Jules danced in puddles and Sally took off her shoes, the two of them spinning like fairies, the moonlight shining through clouds and making them look like magic.

Charlie had found a tarp from somewhere and wore it like a cape. They all crowded under it as the rain pelted down. It smelled of old water and little else.

Sally bent down and dug her fingers into the sand. This time she pulled up a strange grey bone.

"I wouldn't," Singlet Guy said. "Shit loads of cows and sheep died out there in the water. God knows what's in it."

Charlie said, "Will they be back to haunt us?" and someone mooed. Laughter broke up the dark mood and someone called out they should head back to the winery to drink.

Jules didn't move. "Can't you hear them?" she said. "I swear I can hear something crying out there."

"I'm gonna catch you a fish," Singlet Man said. No one had any interest in watching him do that, so they traipsed up to the road, then along the driveway to the inviting-looking winery, glowing bright and warm in the dark night.

They were all pretty dirty so they gathered in one of the outer rooms and the party went on all night, the mood far improved now they had been out on the lake.

Singlet Man did indeed catch a fish, which he cooked and fed to Jules. The others were a bit sickened but copious amounts of dessert wine helped soften the blow.

Andy had sobered up enough to drive as the sun rose, but they sat in the car and watched the rain fall in sheets and the water rise towards the roadside.

TWO

APPARENTLY JULES LIKED SINGLET MAN BETTER THAN THE REST OF THEM because she started seeing him. He'd caught her a fish, so she thought he was good luck. His name was Ryan Churn, which cracked them up. "It's like the name for the star of farm porn. *He's Ryan Churn, he gonna churn your butter*," Charlie said. Made Andy and Sally cry with laughter. It felt like a year had been compacted into that single night, as if all the seducing, convincing, talking, stalking, spoiling, had all happened and Jules finally relented.

Ryan Churn would roll up in some big fancy car (the boys knew what it was, Sally didn't care) and Jules'd float out the door, perfume left in her wake. They didn't mind. Charlie had plenty of parties for them to crash. Crash parties is what they called them; they became addicted to ones held in condemned buildings, where they could rip off wallpaper, smash through walls, tear up the floor, paint on the walls. It helped keep all of them balanced, on track to succeed, but no one could truly say why. Andy got himself sorted and found a job in a surveyor's office and Sally finished her uni degree in water management but was putting off getting a real job because that would mean she had to move and she wasn't ready to leave. Andy would always be there but she had a feeling that once she lost touch with Charlie and Jules, she'd never be invited to another cool party again.

Ryan Churn ended up buying the Lake Penelope winery and they'd find bottles of half-drunk wine about the place.

He and Jules were still together a year later when, as new owner of the winery, he invited them all to celebrate Christmas in July. He changed the name of the winery to Penetralia, which was ridiculous. The invitation told them it meant 'a secret and hidden place' which, firstly, his winery wasn't, it was there for all to see and second, it sounded like a porno company. They all told him this.

He smiled in a way he had, as if they were foolish children. "Not only is it a word in its own right, but it brings together Penelope, as in the lake, as in the wife of the man who discovered that lake, with Australia. IE where we live."

He actually said 'IE'.

Jules said "Pretty sure the lake was already there," but to Ryan Churn, there was no one living in the region before white man arrived.

There were only a dozen at the lunch, including some of his friends and a couple of movie types. Most of the evening was spent making fun of Porno Ryan. He tried to talk to them about the winery, and his vision, but the more they drank, the more hilarious it all was.

"But listen," he said. Jules wasn't; she was holding court with two musicians at the other end of the table. They were trying to convince her to join their band (*we need beauty*, one of them said, *we need your pure beauty*) and Ryan Churn was ignored. "But listen," he said, his voice louder. "The most glorious lakes in the world are full of colour. Lake Natron is pink! And Lake Hillier bubblegum pink! Lake Takap is turquoise blue, have you seen it? Listen," he said. "I want our lake to be the most beautiful in the world."

"Ryan, mate, stick to porn. You're an idiot. You have no idea where the water goes when it goes out. You can't send dyed water wherever," Charlie said.

"Think how beautiful it would look!" Ryan said. They all gazed out. The water had risen all the way to the road for the first time in decades. It had taken a year, and now it threatened to rise even higher. He called his latest wine High Tide, and it wasn't a bad drop. They were in a large room he'd had added on; high ceilings, high angled windows, one whole wall a glass door. He wanted to be able to see Lake Penelope whenever the fancy took him. The large piles of rocks were almost submerged, just the tops of the peaks showing.

He'd bought a huge old printing press that he used as a table, and it was here dessert was served, all of them standing around it, eating the gold-leaf truffles, drinking his dessert wine. A large bowl of perfect grapes sat at the centre, with a small covered bowl beside it. The walls held a printer's box, filled with letters they made crude words with, and a large black and white picture of a religious scribe.

"This place used to be a monastery," Ryan Churn said. "Hundreds of years ago."

"Nah, mate. It was a porno film studio. That's why you got it so cheap, right? All the stains? All the ghosts of murdered porn stars?" Charlie laughed. Sally almost felt sorry for Ryan, as deluded as he was.

"What sort of religion was it?" she asked him.

"They were bible bashers. Printed their own version of the bible, one where Christ doesn't rise. He stays buried under a pile of rocks."

No one bothered to correct the many incorrect things Ryan said. They were tired of him.

"Let's go out to the lake," Jules said, taking his arm. "It's time to catch a fish!"

Ryan nodded and picked up the small covered bowl. Jules rolled her eyes at the others.

"He *loves* his rituals. That he makes up. He's added some shit about feeding the fish mouldy bread."

She was tired of him, too.

They had to walk along the road for a bit to find an area where the water wasn't all the way up to the bitumen. They wanted to leave footprints, have the water fill those footprints. They settled on a place and Ryan began to talk about the importance of friends, and rituals. Sally tuned out, listening instead to the soft SSSSS of the water.

"Grenache, do the honours," he said, handing the bowl of bread to Jules. The nickname was one they hadn't heard before; it sounded childish. Manipulative.

Jules tossed the bread out but shook off his kiss. She was clearly bored with him and had something else going on. She danced around at the water's edge then waded in up to her ankles, singing angelically as she kicked water at them.

Sally felt envious of this carefree traipsing of Jules. She was both annoying and entrancing.

"Nothing to smash this time," Sally said. The roof of a hut showed above the water line and she pointed at it. "Although I guess we could throw rocks at that."

"I think that might be the small part of Lake Penelope I own," Ryan said. "So please don't smash anything!"

"You don't own it," Jules said. She meant because land was never ceded, an issue she often mentioned but never actioned.

The group wandered off then, to cars and to home. Sally, Andy and Charlie waited for a while for Jules, but she was in a deep conversation with Ryan, the two of them up to their knees in the cold water, Jules spinning slowly.

"She's dumping him," Sally said.

"Should we wait, do you think?" Andy said. "Because I'm quite bored."

"Jules! Jules!" Charlie waved at her.

She called, "I'll see you at home." She took a good swallow of wine from the fancy bottle Ryan had pulled out of the cellar then he took one, wiping his mouth, his eyes never leaving her.

When you have a friend who disappears, your life changes.

THREE

Sally had the terrifying idea that Jules was trapped in one of the broken huts under the water, that something had fallen on her, but she wasn't there. Search parties looked everywhere, police divers swimming far out in the lake. When the water subsided, crowds of people searched, the disappearance becoming a public mystery, something each person wanted to solve.

Suspicion fell on the three friends for a while, because Jules was seen leaving the winery and heading for home, and Ryan Churn had a text from her saying she missed him already. He was beyond suspicion; his grief too real, his witnesses at the winery too many.

Having a friend disappear makes you famous.

As the days shortened and Winter approached again, Sally, Charlie and Andy talked about heading out to Lake Penelope, to commemorate their friend, gone almost a year. As if by some kind of magic (but really not at all), an invitation arrived for them all.

The Lake Penelope Long Table Christmas in July affair

50th Anniversary Gathering

In the year since we lost Jules, Lake Penelope has emptied out again, and we at Penetralia wines would like to invite you to dine at our long table. The vineyard in winter is quiet times, in soul as well as in body, and we would like to wake up!

Please observe a fast in the day before as we will feast to celebrate and this requires a deep hunger.

It was the worst nonsense any of them had ever read, but that didn't mean they wouldn't go.

Andy drove them to the winery. Andy and Charlie both had girlfriends, who were best friends from school but tried to include Sally, so she didn't feel like a fifth wheel. She wasn't jealous, either; she and Andy hadn't hooked up in over a year.

As they approached the winery turn off, they saw the long table set out for the feast on the bed of Lake Penelope. Around it, huts, small sheds, stacks of rocks and piles of wood stood as if they had never been damaged. Many of the structures had been rebuilt or repaired, and there were more, surely? There was something about the structures that made Sally feel queasy and uneasy.

Blackberry bushes lined the driveway, laden with fruit. Three teenagers with green t-shirts (Penetralia Long Table Feast!) picked the fruit.

"You all came! Magnificent!" It was Ryan Churn. He wore a turtleneck jumper in a soft brown fabric and had a haircut that made him look even more like a porn star. "Welcome to Penetralia!" All five of them laughed. The name would never not make them laugh. "You're a bit early," he said. "Come on, have a look at what I've done to the place. And we can get started with the booze, ay? I've got a bubbly mixed with brandy that will knock your socks off. If you're wearing any! Barefoot down on the lake!"

The wine was very good; sweet, solid, smooth.

Sally said this, putting on a posh critic's voice, making the others laugh. Ryan said, "Like a good muscat," and gave her a smile she could only describe as sexy.

On the walls were framed certificates, proof of ownership and insurance. Charlie said, "Most people just file these away."

"I know. I know. Most people frame their first dollar, or their first cheque. These are the meaningful things to me. My family has lost everything in the past for want of a bit of paper; that isn't going to happen to me."

"What if there's a fire?" Andy said.

"There won't be. The gods of cold and wet will look after me."

Charlie and Andy cracked up. "Ryan Churn, you are the porniest non-porn star I have ever met," Charlie said. "The gods of cold and wet!"

The day would be short and night would fall sooner rather than later, so they made their way down onto the lake bed. A group of perhaps 100 had gathered. The idea came from the Long Table lunches at wineries. Ryan had been to one once and said it was the greatest meal he'd ever had.

"But they didn't have this setting," he said. It was beautiful out there. The sky vast and blue. The lake bed covered with soft grass, fishweed, and tiny yellow flowers. Birds surrounded them, feeding at the water's edge, flying in swarms overhead, calling and swooping as if putting on a show.

The ground was firm enough, although the table legs sunk in a few centimetres and the chairs were effectively set in place once they sat on them. They'd all carried their own chairs down there, 'to make them feel a part of the whole venture', Ryan said. The 'them' was annoyingly flattering and Sally tried not to fall for it.

"Too scabby to pay your staff to move the furniture," Charlie said.

The chattering of the guests rivalled that of the birds. Everyone was rugged up; boots, coats, scarves, hats, but the walk down there, and the winter sun, and the good red wine, all warmed them, so they stripped off layers and hung them over the backs of their chairs.

The table was set with glittering glasses, huge white dinner plates, linen napkins the same shade as the lake when it was blue, solid cutlery that sat well in the hand. Mounds of golden bread, and salads in all the colours of the rainbow, sat in the centre of the table. Small vases were placed there as well, filled with flowers all found growing on the lake bed. Sally bent over for the scent, but there was none.

Ryan asked Sally to sit next to him. She gestured the others desperately to sit on the other side. Ryan said, "I've been fasting intermittently all year. I keep hoping she'll return, she's been somewhere and she's back, but…" he shook his head. He lifted a bottle from the table. "I give you my new wine variety. A mix of grape I call Jewels. May it sparkle on the tongue."

"Like she did," Andy called out.

Charlie and Andy teased and mocked Ryan Churn until their eyes streamed with tears of laughter. He didn't seem to mind. He was pleased with himself and his table of food. Many of the raw ingredients were harvested from the lake itself, he swore, or foraged. Jules had been a great believer in foraged food. She'd argue with other foragers she ran into at dumpsters, out the back of supermarkets and other places; she said she was doing it out of need, and that should take precedence over those who were doing it out of principle. The fact she had a paying job and others contributing to the household didn't matter.

There was mushroom soup, served in small antique tea cups. "All from the lake," the head waiter announced. "As in 1932, when picknickers filled their car with such mushrooms." The man made a performance of what would otherwise have been an awkward announcement, and Sally admired him for that.

"Jules would have loved this," Sally said to Ryan. He'd really made an effort, and the wine was plentiful.

"Drink up!" He called, "drink up! The Bible says give strong drink to the heavy-hearted, so they can forget. So drink up!" He said in an aside, "The Bible also says strong drink leads to babbling, so mind your ears!"

His workers brought out great platters of meat, prepared in a dozen different ways. They brought out bowls heavy with dark fruit, and baskets of bread made with ancient grains.

Ryan said he'd love to have a restaurant under water; his dream. Andy said, "You can have Sally as your maître'd. She can hold her breath for fucken hours."

"I heard about that," Ryan said. "That really is cool as! Does anyone know why? How? And have you ever thought of trying to monetize it?"

"Well, I kinda do. I'm big in the water world, you know." Her research was beginning to 'make waves', as the joke went, but she usually kept her ability quiet.

It was never explained *how* but the story was told (by her mother, often on Christmas Day or other special occasions, or on the anniversary of her father's death).

She was an only child. Her father drowned in the backyard swimming pool. Her mother an alcoholic ever since and talked on and on about the drowning and how she swore (but no one believed her the timing of it) that he came to her dripping wet and still warm and made love to her like she was a goddess, and left her asleep. She woke to screams; he was drowned, had been for hours. A neighbour found him.

"You were born with a caul, that's why you're so special," her mother always said. Sally was born drowned in drink, the neighbours said. That was what they said about her.

She didn't feel like sharing that, though.

The waiters delivered cocktail popsicles (daiquiri, tequila sunrise, pina colada, all on a stick) and Ryan stood up. "Explore!" he said. "Go anywhere you like. I own more than I was saying before. But please, stop by the statues over there. My testament to Jules, my memory of her, in the place she was lost to us."

The crowd moved that way but Sally held back. She didn't like the press of bodies and wanted to explore in her own time. Once she heard the exclamations, though, she had to see.

Ryan had commissioned a statue of himself as well. It stood far taller than he did, strong, masculine, blocky, naked, in the pose of the thinker. It was clearly his face, with the strong, high cheekbones, the cleft chin, the good hairline.

There were four statues trailing along behind him, like the disciples. The first three Sally didn't recognise. Two young women and a young man, draped in marble cloth, gazing down at the lake bed. The young man had his arms raised as if about to dive, and the young women both were on their toes, heads bent back as if holding their heads out of water.

Behind them was what Sally assumed was Jules.

"He's made a giant vagina for our Jules," Charles said.

"Vulva," Sally said, at the same time as Andy. He'd been reminded enough times.

"It's a flower," Ryan said. "A cala lily. Her favourite. I thought if it represented her from the body down, then her face would stand for her."

"It looks like a vagina," Andy's girlfriend said.

"Careful at the edge of the water. Lake Penelope will suck you in," someone called out.

Charlie muttered loudly, "And Ryan will be there with his vaseline-smeared camera," and he and Andy joked around, pretending to film porn. Their girlfriends ignored them.

They were all drunk as they explored the rebuilt huts, the sheds, the small towers.

"Remember how we smashed these?" Sally said, pushing at one of the walls.

"The farmers fixed them," Ryan said. "I think. I mean, I got some of them rebuilt. But the others were like this."

"The ghosts did it," the head waiter said. Sally realised his performance wasn't an act; this was who he was. "The ghosts who come out when the water is full. It's all those whose bodies were never found. They come and they repair the buildings as if they don't know they are dead."

"Like who?" someone said, as if the man needed any encouragement.

"Like the two young girls who drowned clinging onto a rowboat. They were out there with a priest when they capsized, and he said, Hold On! Don't Let Go! and went off for help, but help was too late. If they cling onto you they won't let go, so shake them off."

The whole crowd shook like dogs after a bath.

"Like the three cadets who were out here in the boat shed. For no good at all, no good. Perhaps they started with four; that part is a mystery. Three murderous nasty teenagers whose bodies have never been found. Those are some angry ghosts.

"Like the mother and child, who lived in that house over there." He pointed way out to a larger structure. "Water took them like it came in a flash. She just wants to see her child grown, like any mother would. Cooks good meals."

People disappeared in pairs to explore, and while the afternoon was cold, they warmed themselves up with close personal contact.

In the boatshed, the air smelt salty and a bit fishy, and further investigation showed marine creatures, left behind as the water receded, dead and drying in the corners of the hut. One corner saw them piled up in a way that looked deliberate, but that didn't seem right to Sally.

There were piles of tiny fish bones

Andy called for Sally and drew her into one of the smallest sheds. Again, she felt uneasy to look at it. It was too perfect, perhaps, the wood unmarked, the nails invisible. Inside, there was a small bed, the pillow dented as if recently slept on. Sally wondered if homeless teenagers still came out here. There was no evidence of take away containers or cheap wine bottles, nor cigarette butts or any other evidence of a young person staying. Somebody must have been, though. There were scratches on the floor underneath the one chair, signs of a person sitting and rising at the table many times. There were remnants of material around the place; tied to the chair, to the door handle, scattered on the floor.

She and Andy exchanged looks. She tugged at one piece, a dark corduroy damp and soggy, but he said, "Leave it."

Outside, someone shouted. "Look at this! Careful!" They'd found a kind of well, a hole in the lake bed that gurgled and bubbled. Someone had piled stones around it, perhaps as a warning. Dusk was falling and the gurgling made Sally nervous, as if the water was calling, getting ready to draw them in.

There were more piles of stones than the last time they were there. Someone said they'd heard there were bodies buried underneath, that maybe Jules was there, and so they tried to pull apart the piles of stones. They found police tape halfway down; the police had done this and found nothing, but how far down did they go?

Charlie lifted one of the smaller stones and threw it, landing a direct hit through one of the sheds, smashing the glass. He lifted another and the rest of them followed, sucked into a sudden frenzy of destruction, like the last time but filled with misery and despair. Ryan stood on a pile of wood and told them good. Good. Let's destroy everything so no one can live here again. Cut down all the trees, fill the wells, mar good land with stone.

He winked at Sally. "I'm a good Catholic boy. I know my Bible," he said. He called out, "Leave somewhere for the homeless kids to sleep."

Charlie, putting on a voice, said, "I'd rather sleep on the side of the road, mate."

"No need for that. Always a place to sleep up at the winery. On a hot day there's a cool breeze through those vines, best place in the world. Apart from the rats." Ryan seemed to glow with good intentions.

They ripped off enough wood for a big bonfire and lit it. The warmth of it made Sally feel sleepy, and when Ryan put his arm around her, she happily snuggled into him and closed her eyes.

"Have a rest, Muscat," Ryan said. Sally smiled. The wine nickname was no more ridiculous than her own actual name, Salacia.

"That is vaguely obscene but I'm not sure why," Charlie said. His girlfriend snuggled up to him and he seemed happier than Sally had ever seen him.

Muscat. Sally found it stupidly sexy. Ryan had gone from wannabe to actually is. They all had; Ryan had spoken at lunch of a sacrifice giving them all success.

"We didn't ask for that," Andy had said, and Ryan said, "And yet you've got it. I've had some lean years, let me tell you. I've been a farmer and seen crops fail, I've been a shopkeeper and see that boarded up. I've never had a more fruitful year than the last, I hate to say."

Ryan Churn was actually pretty cool and Sally began to understand what Jules had seen in him. He had a directness of focus that almost burned when it was on her, and he was strong, confident but also emotional. And rich. Lots of money helped.

The first time they slept together he took her to a fancy resort. It was a winemakers' convention and he brought her along to discuss water purity and management. He was upfront saying, *this is business but I can't promise to stay professional, just letting you know*. She knew she was second choice. Replacement Jules. The second Mrs de winter. And she didn't even care.

The swimming pool was beautiful. Fake rocks lined the base, smooth and colourful. Sally dived down to touch them, and the peace, the quiet, the way the sun looked through water, filled her with such a sense of relief from sadness and from guilt that she stayed down there.

She didn't realise how long it had been until someone dived down to save her.

Her presentation went incredibly well. "So young, so gorgeous, so smart," one man said, and she realised they were hovering around her like flies, all of them wanting a piece of her, as if what she had could rub off on them.

Or they just wanted sex, plain and simple. Ryan didn't leave her side, buying her drinks, pinching her cheeks, calling her 'Muscat', and if she was drunk enough she'd miaow. She licked his face once, like a cat, but he tasted of river water. He sweated a lot, even in the air conditioned room, and had a suitcase full of singlets. He'd throw damp ones out; he didn't care.

She wasn't sure why she ruined it, or if she did it on purpose. But when he caught her giving a blow job to one of the men (that man looking at her, open-eyed, staring, *Have you taken a breath*?) it was over.

FOUR

It was two years before the water came in again to Lake Penelope. Then it came in quickly, almost overnight.

Sally was travelling for work, testing remote water sources for ore material, but Ryan managed to deliver her a bunch of flowers and an invitation to the next Grape Release celebration. The thought of going back to Lake Penelope was an attractive one, although she'd thought she wouldn't be welcome at the winery. Too much water under *that* bridge, she told herself.

She placed the yellow roses in an ice-bucket and called Andy to see if he'd been invited as well.

"I didn't get any flowers, though. Don't think Charlie did, either. You're the lucky one."

In the usual style, the invitation was almost a letter. Ryan Churn did not understand brevity.

"Please join me at Penetralia for Christmas in July. It will be cold so please come and celebrate by the Yule Log with me. We will remember lost friends who still haunt us, the herd of cows who drowned, and we will remember all others who drown here and in other waters."

Andy drove the three of them. He always liked to drive. He negotiated Sally to sit in the front seat and he kept telling her how good she looked.

"It's been a long time between drinks for our Andy," Charlie said. He was off his face on something. Charlie had lost a baby to stillbirth and was not the same. "Andy still loves Sally."

The water had come in higher and faster than ever before.

"Drowned some kids," Charlie said. "Hanging out there, smoking or whatever. Four of them or five, no one really knows." He still lived close by; in fact he barely left his home now.

Sally had been to the lake many times, alone, without telling anyone. She was drawn to it (Ssssssallly, SSSSSS) and she thought if she went often enough, she'd find a clue to Jules, find her there. The Jules statue moved around, but she could see drag marks and thought perhaps Ryan did this, trying to find the perfect place for it. She knelt in the wet sand, poking her fingers into the holes. Jules was down there, she was sure. Finger-like bones thrust up from some of the holes, looking like mushrooms, but when she tried to pluck them, they sank down out of reach.

Ryan wore baggy pants, the type they call fisherman's pants. Loose, linen, beige, and he still wore a singlet. His hair was longer and he carried that friendly manner many people in the alcohol business have. The winery was thriving with people. Rather than a long table, he'd set up dozens of smaller ones, with staff in similar clothing to him breezing about. It was to be a traditional Christmas feast

"You've been working out," Charlie said, squeezing Ryan's muscles.

"I carry a lot of boxes of wine," Ryan said. "Here, let's raise a toast. To the missing, the lost, the long beloved gone from us."

His latest wine used groundwater from the lake, water he claimed to be thousands of years old. It sounded like it had to be bullshit but none of them called him on it. He said it was named for the drowned children; he called it Precious Bubbles. It saddened Sally that none of them laughed at that.

She stood gazing out of the large window that looked to Lake Penelope. Ryan came to stand beside her.

Sally said, "I've always had this idea that she's stuck out there. Under the dirt or whatever, in a hidden cave. She's got her sleeve caught, you know she always wore her sleeves too long. If I dive under I might find her. I feel like she's somewhere you can only reach when the water is high."

"Why do you think I want to own so much of the land? Buying it when it comes available? I think I'll be searching until the day I die. Well, and I admit the rumours of hidden treasure don't hurt. Wallets and purses dropped down there over the years. I keep hoping I'll come across a goldmine of goodies."

"Well, but the property isn't actually yours, is it? I've been doing a bit of investigating," Charlie said. He worked for the local council and had access to papers and applications.

"If you're talking about indigenous land rights," (Ryan made air quotes here) "that's another matter."

"I'm talking about what Jules was talking about. That you haven't actually made a legal deal for any of this, even the winery."

Ryan shook his head. He made a gesture to one of his staff, who came over with more wine. "Come on, Charlie. I know you've suffered. I know. It's terrible. Come on. Let's just enjoy this day together. Maybe later we'll go down and try to catch that fish."

"You think you're gonna get lucky?" Charlie said, winking. His heart wasn't in it, though.

A call went out amongst the rest of the visitors to catch the fish. The tradition was only a few years old (invented by Ryan, surely they knew) but they all pretended it was hundreds of years older. That the fish had lived a long time and travelled the world.

"Let's do it," Sally said. "Let's dive under."

There were only two wet suits, so Sally and Andy were the only ones to make the dive. It felt a bit ridiculous and uncomfortable but the water would be cold. Sally struggled to get hers on and allowed Andy to zip her up because the long zipper strap was broken.

Andy struggled into his own suit, shivering. He spun his arms as if limbering up for an Olympic swim, then lit a cigarette.

"Andy! Let's go!" Sally said.

Charlie sat on the broken brick wall and opened a bottle of beer. "I can do it, mate. I like a deep dive." Charlie tossed back his beer, opened another. Andy fixed the face mask in place.

Andy stepped clumsily into the water ahead of her. He'd always been awkward in the water and spluttered and choked the minute his head went under. He wanted to do this, though.

Charlie stood at the edge, chucking rocks in to freak Andy out.

Sally headed down, seeing the roof of a small shed. It was harder to navigate than she'd thought. Nothing looked familiar. She wanted to find the building where remnants of material had been found.

The water churned above. Andy, startled, headed for the surface and Sally followed, annoyed.

"There's something down there," Andy said, spluttering, wildly waving.

Charlie stood laughing on the shore.

"It's Charlie chucking stones. Come on, Andy. He's a shit-stirrer. Come on. Or just wait there and I'll go. If I see anything I'll call for you."

With no argument, Andy swam for shore. Charlie kicked off his shoes and snatched the face mask from Andy. He handed him a camera. "Keep filming, even if nothing's happening."

The water was murky but not so much that Sally couldn't see. She wore goggles Ryan had handed her. Charlie told her horror stories about tiny hooky worms that sucked onto your retina and you didn't really know until it ate your eye from the inside. "The retina has no pain receptors," he said. She wasn't sure if she believed him but wore the goggles anyway.

She headed back down towards the standing shed. The sun was out but the water was freezing so she wanted to keep moving. She regretted not waiting for summer but you never knew what the water in Lake Penelope would do from one week to the next. And she felt some superstition about the timing, wanting to search around the same time of year Jules disappeared.

They popped up for air every now and then, Sally only doing it when Charlie did, not feeling the need otherwise.

Trails of bubbles filled the water, shedding debris. Fish swam in the sunlight, a trail of them, like sparklers in the night, like the memory of light left behind to create an image. Sally pointed them out to Charlie and he gestured at his eyes, grinning.

There was no sign of the big fish. They peered into one hut, possibly glimpsing movement. Then Charlie gestured. He waved his arms wildly and when she reached him, his eyes were panicked behind the mask.

The glass was broken. Sally wagged her finger; *be careful.* Inside was much as they'd seen last time. Sally leaned in to see better because inside was a woman.

Her hair floated around her head, a greenish halo that made her look like a sad angel sitting at a table, tearing at raw meat with bare hands, sinking her teeth into it.

The woman turned towards them. Sally's heart beat so hard it deafened her. Charlie panicked, kicking for the surface. The woman swam through the door, as fast as the tiny fish, and up in front of him. She reached out and touched his face and chest. Sally saw tears open in his wetsuit as he kicked away, swiping at the woman desperately, churning up the water.

She slashed at him, catching his face again.

Sally couldn't tell if Charlie was swimming or floating. If he was floating she should help him, but she didn't want to draw air, she didn't want to rise to the surface yet. That was a kick; he was all right.

The woman turned to Sally

It was Jules.

Jules.

Dancing around, bones all white and clean, poking through mottled flesh. Her rotting shoulder missing something, as if a large fish has taken a bite. She opened her mouth; it was all black in there, and Sally thought *poisoned by those blackberries or something* but her throat gaped open as well and if she still had blood she'd be bleeding.

Sally glanced up where Charlie was. She needed confirmation of what she was seeing. Jules opened her mouth again (nothing in the eyes, eaten by fish, but it didn't matter) and tucked fishweed in there, and in her pocket.

She swam towards Sally, followed by a giant fish. Sally turned and headed for the surface. She could see others in the distance, heading towards her, so she swam for shore. She hadn't taken a breath.

There was a commotion above, splashing. Someone reached down a hand to her and pulled her out by the hair.

They told her she was dead and returned to life. That she'd been in a near-death dream state. No, she swore.

She was certain all of it was real.

She was desperate to get the wetsuit off because little fishes were in there, in the cuts.

Andy led her up to the winery. She shivered with cold, her feet like iceblocks even in the Ugg boots she'd laid out ready.

Ryan had mugs of spiced wine ready and she drank three, not thinking, until her brain was fuzzy and she was warm. An open fire blazed. The sun went down as they sat there.

"And so the fake Christmas Day came to pass," Charlie said. His hair had dried in spikes. He had a long scratch on his cheek he said was from a branch or sharp corner. "Underwater fences and stumps can be dangerous, cause injury," he said. "You should have been more careful."

"You saw what I saw. It was Jules."

He wouldn't look her in the eye but unconsciously touched his chest where he'd been scratched.

Andy was unscathed. He seemed to feel guilty about this, but moreso relieved.

"We saw Jules. Charlie?"

He denied it.

Ryan said, "I always said she was a witch. You can't drown witches. I guess that makes you one too, Sally. Witches float."

"People float, you idiot," Sally said. She patiently allowed Ryan to disinfect her cuts, and to give her more spiced wine. She curled up in front of the fire, a blanket wrapped around her, the sound of the lake reaching her, and she slept.

She woke up in the morning, a glorious, crisp day. Andy and Charlie were gone.

"I can't believe they left me here!" she said as Ryan handed her a large cup of coffee.

"They knew the better man won. We should get back together, Sally. Things are falling into place, money-wise. Land-wise. You won't have to work again."

He faced the fire, putting a log on. She thought of Jules, her black mouth, her wounds. He turned, holding the poker in both hands.

She said, "I can help you with the wine. I'll take water samples, I'll take some now." She ran outside and he followed, going at his own pace. He knew she couldn't get far, barefoot, only a t-shirt on. Very little traffic this early in the morning. She heard him singing Christmas Carols.

She climbed over the fence, tearing the flesh behind one knee, and ran down to the water. As she plunged in she glimpsed Ryan on the shore. He'd taken the time to grab a folding chair and a bottle of wine and he sat there, waiting.

It was calm under the water. Looking up the surface seemed wild. Suddenly choppy and dangerous. She swam down further, but not in the direction of Jules. She headed for the boatshed, thinking she could sit in there for a bit, wait Ryan out, emerge further down the shore away from him.

She felt seaweed clinging to her legs and reach down to swipe it off but there were two young girls holding on for dear life (not life, long gone), their skeleton fingers digging into her calves, their soft-flesh faces rubbing up against her. She shook them off, wishing she could save them. On an overturned table a man sat eating sardines from the tin, using his fingers, as if he was fully formed and not a blackened mess of a man, ragged of skin, grey of bone. He tilted his head as Jules passed and gestured; join me?

She swam on.

She saw a woman bending over a stove red with rust and a child at her feet, swimming in tight, somehow terrifying circles. As she neared, mother and child sank into holes in the lake bed.

As she reached the boathouse she paused. Her ears hummed. Even underwater she heard the noise of something breaking. Bones? Wood?

The boatshed seemed complete, with a few palings missing and the windows broken, but otherwise rebuilt. There was no sound apart from the beat of water. As she approached the beat increased, as if there was more activity. She held onto the window frame and peered in.

There were three of them (the unfound cadets George, Harry and Matthew, she thought, and she could read their badges). She wondered if she was unconscious and dreaming. How could she see so clearly in this murky water? They were working on a boat. One was hammering (with no hammer). One rhythmically swiping as if painting. And one did something she couldn't understand. They all had their backs to her.

They were fully clothed, the material almost blurry after so long in the water.

They noticed her in the window and swam to the door, which swung open. She turned to swim to the surface, scared now as they came at her with their fists raised. Fingers like claws. Fingernails like knives. Weird puffy pale peeling lips. Lips swollen, white, nibbled in places by the tiny fish that swarmed, almost invisible. She felt them nibbling at her.

She felt bubbles in her blood, warning that she should swim to the surface.

A moonlight shaft reached her underwater. A long time had passed.

Sally rose at last, floating to the top as if filled with air.

She opened her mouth to scream, forgetting where she was. Her mouth filled with fresh water; it was sweet, and cool, and she swallowed that mouthful and took another.

She hit the surface

The first lungful of air hurt, like it came straight off a hot fire, ashen and dry.

Ryan was there in a moment, clutching her, holding her at the water's edge, trying to hold her under, calling her a witch. She grabbed hold of him, arms and legs around him, then spinning around like a crocodile. She held his head under. He didn't grab at her, didn't pull at her clothing like she'd done, long ago, to Andy.

She imagined feeding him bite by bite to the big fish. She imagined the ghosts pulling him to pieces and using his bones for furniture. She waited until he was still, all breath gone from him, his face pale. Then she let him float away.

Sally was frozen to the bone. Ryan had left wine, a blanket, a chair. She wrapped the blanket around herself and sat curled on the chair, enjoying the wine, and the warmth, and the sound of the water gently singing her name.

Black Cohosh

GEMMA FILES

for Willow Dawn Becker

It begins where it ends, for him, for them. But not for me, or for us.

That's the whole point of the exercise.

Women take what's beautiful and make it horrible, they said, back in Salem Times...you know how we are, we just can't help it. We're weak and wicked, born sinful and inclining to sin; we can't be trusted, not even with ourselves. Our brains are small, wombs wandering and full of evil spirits. We steal men's penises and hide them in birds' nests. We smear ourselves with the fat of unbaptized children while masturbating with broomsticks.

So if churches or state (or church-states) led by men have to arrest us, to save us from error—scare us straight, as it were? Make us confess our lies through torture, or threat of torture? Well, then, that's better in the end, isn't it? Better than hanging, by far; better a dog than a bitch. Better to marry than burn.

Yes. And yet they expect us to believe they don't hate us, that they never really did. That everything they do to us is *for* us, for our own good.

It's enough to make you scream and keep on screaming, forever.

As I approach the border at speed, I am burning, burning—black cohosh in my veins, at least metaphorically; bugbane, snakeroot. Invisible letters printing my skin like scars turned inside out, poison-etched. I ride a dizzying path of visual effects, lungs so heavy I can barely pant as the sun stares down twinned while shadows loop and spit, snarling like yarn around me. And the pain of what I carry inside makes me want to puke, but I laugh instead, out loud and long, shocked by how much the sound of it frightens me. Then hear it echoed back to me in the car's roar, ragged-harsh as some carrion bird's cry, shaking the ground below.

There's an army already massing within me, drunk with rage and high on hate, and all of them more than ready to riot. More than ready to *kill*.

The signs show me where to go, exactly as they're designed to. So soon enough, I find myself slowing to join one of the lines where they wind through a shiny forest of steel-slicked holding cages with low-level electric haloes: Immigrant-criminals on the one side, citizen-criminals on the other. I can't stop to sympathize, though, even if I was still capable of it. Simply travel on, scanning the crowds inside, looking for my chosen people.

And here, at last, I spot them, all massed together; two cages set facing each other, for maximum psychological cruelty—"smugglers" versus "kidnappers," those caught travelling with extra cargo. The pregnant ones.

They don't sort out the unviable, not here. That'll wait until the camps. Which means the sizzling threads of pain I glimpse snaking their way through the huddled forms who clump away from the bars, hugging themselves or each other, could easily come from someone already miscarrying, someone fever-bright with internal decay, someone whose ectopic malignancy could never survive her death but still manages to produce a bare shadow of cardiac action. Could come from some ten-, eleven- or twelve-year-old just trying her best to breathe away incipient panic, well aware that when her burden comes to term the result might rip more than just her perineum apart, or a woman five times her age whose geriatric system somehow beat the odds in a way she might have thought miraculous, under other circumstances. Or from someone whose truth doesn't match their biology, not even now they've been trapped into performing said biology's supposedly most natural function .

The thing I carry inside me is equally improbable, crude and dreadful in its flailing grotesquerie, a boiling, tornado-sized freak of supernature. It took thirteen of us to put it together, let alone inflict it upon ourselves—thirteen witches, sworn to revenge ourselves or die, scattered in thirteen different directions. Thirteen magical suicide bombers whose black intentions gripe us like gut-acid, scouring away all our empathic impulses, our much-lauded softer parts, our misguided capacity for mercy. Removing our regrets in service of a path that turns everything from this point on to nothing but grief, and bile, and awfulness.

A working like this takes blood, too, like everything else. Like all magic. (Re-)balance through sacrifice; blood for blood, for blood, for blood, for blood. It's only fair in that it's not, at fucking all.

Yet I've never, in all my life, anticipated giving blood over anything else with *quite* such a fierce and savage joy.

Three guards at my checkpoint, two male-presenting, one female-. I'm not surprised: Uniforms really do change everything, don't they? Powerless to powerful, in one small step. All it takes is a willingness to be the stamping boot for once, instead of the face it grinds down on.

They ask me where I'm going, and why.

(*Across. To visit friends.*)

They ask me if I have anything to declare.

(*No, officers.*)

They ask me if I'm sure.

(*Why wouldn't I be?*)

And here they exchange glances, all three of them—two smug, one kept carefully blank, only guilty by association. Or so she thinks.

Come with me, ma'am, one of the men tells me, as the other one fails to hide a grin. Pulling out the blood test kit.

We all know the story—how it happened slowly, almost imperceptibly, until it didn't. Until, all at once, it was already too late.

I remember straight, cishet men complaining how hard it was to get women to date them, let alone fuck them, and wondering why. Conversations with my straight and bi female friends about how everything was taken as an invitation, a secret signal: Talking to a man means you want sex, dinner means you want sex, stopping on the street when someone yells at you means you want sex, meeting someone's glance means you want sex. That constant frantic baboonish obsession with their own genitals every prospective patriarch seems to share from adolescence on, almost to the moment of death: There's a reason we used to call it "acting like a dick," before they made that illegal.

Women won't engage with us, they thought, so we'll force them to. We'll pass laws saying they have to be married to access what few rights we leave available for them, then make them have kids with us in order to buy the rest back...and they'll stay with us because they love those kids, because it's genetically encoded into them *to* love them. Because no one can ever physically be a mother without automatically feeling *motherly*.

Sure, the same way all cancer patients can't help loving their disease, or anything else life-threatening they might want—need—removed from their bodies, in order to survive. Fetishize our tumours by giving them a soft skull and a nice smell, love-drunk eyes, little latching mouths to siphon off the discomfort. Call it Cronenberg's Law, and leave it at that.

At some point, it was decided to replace all adult women unwilling to be involved with this process with children, who have no choice but to accept it: Tiny blank slates dependent on the same injustices that created them, ripe for brainwashing. And if childbirth doesn't kill us the first time, they'll just force us to keep on having children until it does: Force generation after generation of children to be born motherless, instruments of their own half-orphaning, splashed out into the burning garbage heap of this dying world on a tide of pregnant people's blood.

I can take this, we told ourselves, over and over; I can take this, if I have to. The same way we did about every other fucking thing. But we can't, and we don't. Not anymore.

On the one hand, sacrifice isn't sacrifice when there's no other choice, self- or otherwise. It's murder.

But you know what? I'm good with it, at this point.

We're good with it.

When the border guard sees my blood test's the result, he turns it towards me, so I can see it too. Leans close and murmurs, obviously lying: *I could help you, you know.*

(*Oh, could you, officer?*)

He was someone's baby once, I think; he had a mother who loved him, who he loved. Then his father taught him he was more important than her, and she said nothing to contradict him.

But he wasn't, officer, and neither are you. You just don't know it yet.

You will, though.

For me, the plan went like this: Get pregnant, reach a border, try to cross. Find a guard willing to usher me across in return for favours. I knew it wouldn't be difficult, especially if I offered him unprotected sex—I mean, I was pregnant already, right? Soiled and soul-dirty, core-ruined, illegal on every level. Just like they like it, predators like whoever *this* particular predator would turn out to be. This fellow victim of the system so bought in he truly believed he wasn't a victim at all, that he never had been, and never would be.

(Outside, there's no way the female doesn't know what's happening, too. But she won't say anything, or interfere. Not with the other one looking at her and sniggering like it's all a big joke while waiting for his own turn, later on. How many times do they do this a day, usually? Impossible to say.)

(Well, never mind.)

No need to go over the details, aside from the fact that I don't shut my eyes, or bother to pretend I don't enjoy it. Just meet his gaze full on, nurture my own scant pleasure like a lit fuse, a tiny spark. He'll never notice, probably, grunting and sweating away above me, greedily chewing my breasts like something born with teeth...or *not* like one, not really.

As they'll see soon enough, all three of them, and more.

And ahhhhh, you wittering idiot G-d I refuse to believe in even now, but I hate them all so savagely—all the men and women who ever cooperated in putting this roundabout of stupid, brutal zealotry in place—for making me hate *anyone* this much, any real and actual other human being, that I'm willing to do what I'm about to. For making me so happy to anticipate his suffering once the spell I carry inside me is unleashed. But I made my decision miles back, years back; I suck it up, I nurture it, I turn it inside out, excoriating myself as much as anyone else involved. I ride a cyclone of rage and desire, bucking and snapping and snarling as I chase my own climax, knowing full well that it's key. How it's the final ingredient that will turn my child—however potential—into my weapon, my black miracle, my blood-magic atom bomb.

From cell-swatch to baby to monster set free to ravage and avenge, in a single squirming, painful, red-soaked forward surge.

See him start to hunch and lock my shaking thighs, making it impossible for him to pull out. The process starts here, with his ejaculation, my orgasm: A flash-paper split second of bodily joy before he feels something turn irretrievably *wrong*. Too tight, too *hot*, pain ratcheting sharp up the scale from arousing to anything but; oh Christ, oh *no*. Like sticking your cock in a pool drain by accident and feeling that sudden tug, that *rip*—blood in the water, bastard, gouts of it, dizzying-fast. Yes, that's right.

I see it reach his dumb animal stare, that fear, which makes me grin. And I—

—*I* can feel it too, now, my child, only mine. Swelling between us, reaching out with claws fixed, with mouth wide open.

Feel it start to salivate at the very taste of him and bite down, *hard*.

Things happen fast, from then on. Exactly the way they need to.

My child tears through my would-be rapist from the bottom up, starting with his dick. It slips from me in a mess just as he begins to shriek, uncomfortably large enough to bruise my groin but not break my pelvis; I rise without bothering to pull my pants back on, slipping off my shirt as the placenta spills out as well, then catches fire and spreads upwards, hardening into armour. The door bursts open; I hear the shouts, feel bullets bounce and skitter off me, ricochet to spin the other male sidelong while my child finishes with his partner and leaps on top of him instead, still growing. It's going through puberty now, suddenly rabid to breed, spiked penis jerking up to spear him straight through the guts and spit on contact with his gooey-hot insides; it jackhammers him to the point of death, then hurls him aside and swipes the female across her throat even as she punches the alarm, freeing a bright crimson gush, a wail that never seems to end.

And: Yes, I tell the rest of the border guards, come now, keep on coming. My child wants to meet you.

My child, and *its* child.

The placenta reaches my face and closes over me, a bruise-coloured glassine helmet, tinging everything around me with rot. I step over the male guard as my child takes off down the hall, lope-brachiating, noting the way his perforation has already begun to swell: Tiny claws scooping up and outwards to free my first grand"baby"'s bloody muzzle, its jaws of multiply-rowed teeth that twist and root their way from its "father"'s pink-splayed intestinal nest. Then step past the female guard, her up-rolled eyes empty, thinking how this might so easily have been *her* fate, too. Since some of us hated collaborators enough to want to go that far.

(We took a vote on it, six to seven; you can thank us for our commitment to democracy, if you want, when it's all over. Those of you who manage to survive.)

Birth a monster, set it free, let it pave your way—this sloppy trail beneath my feet, wet with slime and screams. I follow its track outside, down the road of cages, hands raising to cast smaller workings as I walk by: Make the electrical charge-boxes overload, the locks melt away, the doors fall open. Let loose new crowds of siblings, friends, parents and kids that *my* child's children were all born knowing to stream around, to leave untouched in their wake, smelling their relative innocence. Immigrant-criminals, citizen-criminals...my business is not with them. My business is with the system, and those who want to join me in its downfall.

At last, I reach the same cages I passed on my way to find that first sacrifice, dead Officer Idiot, my blithe sexual extortionist. Pause outside as the doors spring free to make my pitch, before they all go running: *Here's what happened, what I've done, what* we*'ve done, my co-conspirators and I. Here is what I can do for you too, if you're so inclined.*

Revenge always digs two graves, they used to say. Perhaps so; no, *probably* so. And yet.

And yet.

Will it hurt? Someone asks.

In this world of ours? I think. And hear somebody laugh, long and bitter, before realizing it must be me.

What doesn't? I reply.

Some nod, some don't. Some shake their heads and shoulder through, leaving the rest behind.

Take each other's hands, then, I tell those who remain, not watching the others go—run to find their families, made and otherwise. To spit on the remains of their captors or sob with disgust at the carnage, grab the ones they love and head for the open border's lights, together. *Hold on tight. I'm going to cast the spell again now, pass it on to all of you, to do whatever you want with it. And then I'll be done.*

(At last.)

Because: *Blood's what it takes,* I say, *and I still have some left to give, thankfully. So here's the deal.*

You can have it all, so long as you promise to use it.

They think a minute, longer than I did, my first time. And then, then...

I do, someone says, quietly.

I do too, says another.

I do, I do, echoing through the group, rippling outwards. I feel my eyes sting. I've never been so proud. Black cohosh in my veins, at least metaphorically; hatred's poison, anger's bite. All the pain I've ever felt, or ever will. A hunger for justice I trust to never die, not even if it kills me.

I breathe out, one final time. Transmit it to them like a virus, its lettering inscribed on all their flesh at once, scarred upside-down. That rush of nausea, tight chest and doubled vision, colours exploding outwards on every side. A toxic, tropical frogskin bloom.

Everyone doubles up, screaming, shaking. Everyone gives birth together, rips wide in a splash of blood, heals perfectly in the trauma's wake. The babies burst like bombs, bloat like leeches and claw the dirt, mouths slavering. The electricity only makes them bigger. No bars can keep them in, or out.

I fall backwards, already cold, and stiffening. Peer upwards and search the sky for stars, even as my sight starts to fade.

Soon we're alone. I can hear women crying around me; women, people, mothers. I understand, though I can't help but feel impatient.

You would have had to trade your children for freedom eventually, I tell them.

I know, one replies again, barely able to whisper. And *yes, yes, I know as well,* I want to snap, but don't. I mean—what would be the point, exactly?

We've always known.

Other children are coming, now, for the ones who have them—half-siblings running with arms out, calling. *Please,* they say. *Come with us, please. Don't make us live without you.*

Go, I tell them or try to; I can't tell anymore. *There's only so much time, so go—find a new country, one that isn't this one. Just go, go...*

...and don't look back.

The Infinity Effect

JOANNE ANDERTON

BARBARA HAD ATTENDED MANY CRIME SCENES IN HER LONG CAREER, BUT this was among the most disturbing. Not because it was particularly gruesome, every murder was visceral in its own terrible way, but because it looked so… *staged.* Someone had gone to a lot of effort to imbue this death with a twisted kind of meaning, and that was never a good sign.

A small rural cemetery on a hazy, moonlit night was an appropriately atmospheric setting, even with spotlights illuminating the scene and the forensic team busying around the graves. Barbara circled the body slowly. Early twenties, she thought. Dressed head to toe in a white sheet with holes cut out for his eyes, he'd been tied to the worn-down stone of a raised grave. Forensics had removed the costume to uncover a deep and ugly gash across his throat, and the word 'truth' cut into his chest. And yet, there was little in the way of blood anywhere at the scene.

'I probably don't have to tell you he was killed elsewhere.' Neil, the forensic pathologist, crouched beside the body. 'And then set up here like a cheap Halloween decoration.'

'All looks very clean,' Barbara said. 'Considering the damage done to the poor kid.'

Neil nodded. 'Someone's being fastidious, that's for sure.' He was not the most exciting, or even empathetic, pathologist she'd ever worked with, but he was reliable.

'You got here quickly, sir.' Kam hurried across the graveyard, still pulling their suit-jacket into place. A young and earnest assistant detective sergeant, they had been a little hard to take at first, but after three years together Barbara was used to them. Relied on them, even. 'Sorry to have made you wait.'

A small crowd huddled at the hastily erected line of police tape. Barbara tipped her head towards them. 'Wish I could take credit, but just bad luck I'm afraid.' Her wife Joyce and their daughter Laura were in the group, anxiously watching. 'We were already here.'

Kam lifted eyebrows in an unasked question.

'Ghost tour.' Barbara couldn't stop herself from rolling her eyes. 'Actually, give me a minute.'

The ground was muddy and clutched at Barbara's shoes as she approached the cordon.

'So sorry, my loves,' she said to her small family, blue and white plastic flapping in the chilly breeze between them. 'You'll have to go on without me.'

Joyce gave her a resigned smile. 'I don't envy you,' she said. Leaned across to kiss her.

'Be careful, Mum,' Laura said, and gave her a tight hug through the tape. Not quite a teenager, her daughter was a tumble of uncoordinated limbs attached to a quiet, serious personality.

'Always.'

Barbara stood for a moment longer than she should have, watching her family disappear into the night. The village of Raynhaven had a reputation for the ghostly, which was a fascination Barbara simply couldn't understand. But for Joyce and Laura, she'd do anything — even put up with stories of a spectral astronaut in the local bakery or a singing nun who floated around the train station. Her wife and daughter had, quite literally, saved her life. Years on the force had led her down a rabbit hole of alcohol and overwork, a path she knew led to darkness and an early grave but seemed unable to escape — until she met Joyce.

The woman was a beacon of hope, a lifeline, the mother of her child, and more. Being together had given Barbara the strength to drag herself out of a cesspit of depression and self-loathing, and away from her career in the city. They'd relocated to the small county of Chestershire, and a simple life.

'Despite the occasional truly bizarre murder,' Barbara muttered to herself as she returned to the crime scene and tried to get her mind back on the job. That moment when she switched from family-woman to detective chief inspector always felt a little jarring.

'Cause of death seems self-evident,' Kam was saying to Neil.

'You'd think,' Neil answered. 'And yet…'

Barbara and Kam shared a glance at his hesitation.

'Time of death wasn't that long ago, sometime this afternoon I'd say. But his bloodless wounds, the sheer *cleanliness* of the scene.' He seemed distracted, which wasn't like him either. 'I need to get him back to the lab. Until then, I hesitate to come to any real conclusions.'

Before Barbara could begin to instruct Kam on the next steps of their investigation, a scream echoed across the cemetery. 'Lee?' A man's voice. 'Oh my god, it is! Lee!'

A small group of people were pushing their way towards the scene while the uniforms attempted to hold them back. Two men, one woman, carrying cameras and a fluffy grey mic. Kam and Barbara rallied immediately and hurried over to reinforce the blues.

'Stop!' Barbara put on her best *I'm a DCI don't fuck with me* voice and held up her badge. 'This is an active crime scene and you will not go barging into it.'

It worked like a charm. It usually did.

'But he's—' The man carrying the camera had anguish written all over his face. 'That's my— it's Lee.'

'You know the deceased?' Kam asked.

'We do.' The woman took over. Though visibly shaken, she seemed to be able to keep it together better. 'He's doing the documentary with us. We were scheduled to shoot at Ezekiel's grave tonight, and he wanted to double check the set up.' She drew a shuddering breath. 'That was this afternoon. We waited, but he didn't come back, so we figured he was going to meet us here…' Her voice broke.

'What's your documentary about?' Kam asked.

'The hauntings of course. Why else would we be here?'

Barbara nodded. Ghosts, again. 'The town's specialty.'

'Not everyone was happy to have us here.' The third man in the crew, carrying the mic, hadn't spoken until now. He stared at Lee's body with an impenetrable expression. Reading people was most of Barbara's job, and she didn't usually find herself having so much trouble. Another thing that worried her.

'What do you mean by that?' she asked.

'Some of the people in town don't like the reputation. We've had some… trouble.'

'Nothing serious,' the woman hastened to clarify. 'There's this bunch of oldies who call themselves the *sensible sceptics*. They've been following us around, trying to get in the way of our camera and ruin the shots.' Her expression hardened. 'You should talk to them.'

Seemed like as good an idea as any.

'Know where we might find them?' Kam asked.

'It's a small town,' the woman answered. 'I suggest you try the pub.'

Barbara nodded. 'One last thing. You said Lee came back here to check the site? What's so special about that grave? Who was it?'

A communal look of surprise. 'This is where it all began,' the woman said. 'The death that brought the ghosts back, at least according to legend. This was just a normal town until, well, until him.'

Barbara hadn't paid much attention to the name on the grave where Lee was lying. Now, as she returned to the dead man's side, she peered at the words etched into stone: *Here lies Ezekiel Dudgeon, 1952-1992. Man of science. Atoms to atoms, and nothing more.*

The drive to the pub was less than five minutes, but at least it was warm and dry inside the car.

'Why truth?' Kam mused as they drove. 'If you carve a word into someone it usually means something important.'

'Hardly a neat, specific word either,' Barbara answered. 'Could mean a lot of things.'

'People who make documentaries are interested in truth.'

'So are sceptics.'

A small, white building with a thatched roof and a swinging sign out the front, the *Stranger Comes to Town* was an archetype if Barbara had ever seen one. A wooden bar with large beer taps, complete with an elderly couple to man them, the only thing off about the place was how quiet it was. When Barbara and Kam entered, most of the tables and chairs were empty, the only exception a knot of people deep in discussion and drinks up the back.

Barbara had a strange feeling these were the people they were looking for. 'Which would be almost too convenient,' she murmured to herself, as she and Kam approached them.

A group of five, most in their forties to fifties, dressed in a whole lot of cargo pants and camouflage jackets. They all appeared nicely sloshed, too.

'Excuse us,' Kam interrupted a particularly raucous-sounding story, told from the head of the table — a woman, probably in her fifties, with a neat salt-and pepper braid.

'Yes?' She was smiling as she looked over Barbara and Kam, even taking their badges into account. Didn't seem put off or intimidated in the slightest.

Barbara liked her instantly. 'Might this be a meeting of the Raynhaven sensible sceptics society, by any chance?'

The woman laughed, deep and throaty. 'Indeed it is.' She stood, offered her hand. 'The name's Fiona. Fi.' She had a strong, sure grip. 'How can we help you, detectives?'

'We wanted to ask you about the documentary being filmed here,' Kam said. 'We had some reports that you've been harassing the filmmakers.'

'Oh, come now,' Fi scoffed. 'I'd hardly call what we've been doing *harassment.* This is our village, we're free to wander its streets and graveyards as we please. If we happen to get in the way of some uninvited cameras, well, so be it.'

The group thumped the table in agreement.

This was getting them nowhere. 'One of the documentary makers was found murdered tonight,' Barbara cut to the chase. 'Perhaps you would all like to confirm your whereabouts this afternoon and evening?'

Fi, so cocky just a moment before, instantly paled. 'Murdered?'

'I'm afraid so.' Barbara scanned their faces. Shock. Surprise. One guy who looked like he might throw up. Easy enough to fake, but they did look a little too drunk to do so effectively.

'Oh god.' Fi slumped in her chair. 'They're kids, silly kids. Who would do that? We've been here since lunch, detectives. The owners can vouch for that.'

'Since lunch?' Maybe they weren't drunk *enough* for people who'd been here that long.

'There aren't many activities for middle aged singles in a village like this.' Fi's lips were shaky as she tried to re-establish her smile. 'We try to honour Ezekiel and his memory but really, we do this for the socialising.'

'I see.'

'Ezekiel and his memory?' Kam asked. 'We keep hearing — and *seeing* — this name everywhere. Who was this man?'

Fi turned to one of the other members. 'Phil, do you have—'

Phil nodded, fished a manila folder out of a weathered briefcase, and opened it on the table. A collection of papers and photos. He flicked through, selected one, passed it to Fi. A small group of people in what appeared to be a laboratory, if the beakers, Bunsen burners, and computers were anything to go by. Fi pointed to a middle-aged man in a lab coat in the centre.

'Ezekiel was my mentor and friend,' she said, then moved her finger over to a younger version of herself. 'He was a doctor and a scientist, a true sceptic who believed only what could be measured.'

'Not a fan of ghosts then,' Kam said.

Barbara picked up the photo. The picture had the over-saturated, faintly blurred look of an image taken in the 90s, so he wasn't the easiest to make out. She squinted, brought it closer, and his eyes…his eyes were black, like the night was black.

You.

Maybe it was the poor-quality photo, the way it smudged his gaze, made his pupils so large and dark they seemed to be trying to seep out of their sockets and swallow him whole. Swallow her.

Here.

And the world seemed to rotate around his image. To slip, briefly, from its axis.

Finally.

'Ghosts?' Fi made a rude, frustrated noise. 'There were no ghosts in the village in my day. Not even stories about them. This was just a normal village. It all started after he died. After—' a hesitation '— the accident.'

Find me, Barbara.

'It was a gas leak, nothing more. The lab was in the basement of his family's manor, and his only mistake was asking too much of the plumbing.'

Let me show you the truth.

'Ezekiel was looking into the substance of matter, into particles and sub-particles, nothing freakier than a little backyard quantum physics. Nothing occult, nothing about raising the god-damned dead. When the sightings began, people tried to blame him, anti-scientific hysteria whipped-up by the hippie crowd. But that was thirty years ago, detectives, and the world moved on. As it should.'

Barbara's hand was shaking as she placed the photo back on the table. She cleared her throat. 'Well, then. Thank you for your time.' Did her best to pull herself together while Kam approached the bar and corroborated the group's collective alibi.

'What now, sir?' Kam asked when they returned. 'We seem to be at a dead end.'

'So we are,' Barbara said slowly. She felt a little like she'd been drinking all afternoon herself. She should be mulling over their words, teasing out connections between the *truth* on Lee's chest and the *truth* the documentary crew were talking about and the *truth* that had so obsessed Ezekiel and now his little gang of groupies, but also...

...*Let me show you the truth.*

Barbara rubbed her eyes because the world still looked blurry. Saturated. An old photo in itself. As they gradually focused she realised there was someone standing in the doorway to the pub, a figure that couldn't be real.

'Barrington?' she breathed the name of her predecessor.

He looked exactly the same as the last time she saw him, almost a decade ago. Dressed in a dark blue, ill-fitting suit, middle-aged and slightly pudgy around the middle, beginning to go bald, but it suited him. Entirely nonthreatening and easy to underestimate.

She'd only known him a few days before he died, but she'd never forget him. And here he was, catching her eye then tipping his head to the side in a clear 'follow me' gesture, before walking out the front door. Barbara was after him so quickly she was virtually running, leaving Kam gaping and surprised near the bar.

As soon as she stepped outside she realised something was wrong. The streets of Raynhaven were not the same as they were little more than fifteen minutes ago. They were… layered. That was the best word she could come up with. At once a dark and drizzly night, but also the middle of the day, and if she blinked or turned her head too fast, then it was snowing and bright, but also arid and empty. People were moving past her — or, at least, the faint outlines of people. Like old school photography, laying negatives over negatives as she had in her high school days, before it all became digital.

'What the fuck?'

'Now, now. Language.' In the middle of it all, stood Barrington. 'We don't use words like that, Barbara.'

Barbara approached him, trying not to look down at the snow she just stepped in, no the puddle, no, was that sand? 'Barrington, sir?' she whispered. 'How is this possible? What—' it was all starting to make her feel a bit nauseous '—what's happening?'

Barrington pinned her with a look between fear, and disappointment. It was the disappointment that ate her. 'Don't listen to him,' he said, gruff and sensible as always. 'He nearly destroyed us all, don't scratch at the scars he left behind. Get back on the case and maybe the world will forgive you. And forget.'

'The world will what?'

Neil chose that moment to appear, his car racing down the narrow street and skidding to an un-Neil-like halt.

'Ah, there you are detective,' he said, getting out of the car, holding an iPad. 'I have information on the cause of death for you.'

Barbara tore her gaze from the impossible man in front of her. 'And you came here to tell me?' Neil *never* did that. Neil waited in the lab for her to come to him. And more importantly, *couldn't he see the shit going down around him?*

'Yes, well. I knew you'd want to get on this immediately.'

'You did?' Something about the whole thing seemed off. Too convenient. Rushed. They needed a new clue, and here was Neil hand-delivering one?

'What have you got for us?' Kam emerged from the pub, business-like and taking Neil's presence in stride.

'Take a look at this.' Neil was trying to shove the iPad under Barbara's nose. 'It does indeed appear that the wounds on Lee's neck and chest were made after he died. See this puncture mark?'

'An injection?' Kam was holding their chin and nodding thoughtfully in a completely unnatural way. 'Was he poisoned?'

'The world has no sense of mercy, Barbara,' Barrington was saying over the top of it all. 'It has been kind to you — instead of PTSD and alcohol dependence you have a wife, a child, a normal life. You might be able to push it further than Ezekiel did, but even that has its limits.'

'What do you think, sir?' Kam struggled to get her attention.

'Solve the case, ignore Ezekiel, and just pray the narrative doesn't change its mind and take it all away.' Barrington flickered, for a moment, like the image on a dodgy TV. 'Like it did to me.'

'*Can no one else see this*?' Barbara finally found her voice again.

Kam didn't startle easily, but even they looked shocked by her outburst. 'Sir?'

'Can't you see—' she waved her hand at the world, the village, and the layers rippled like paint on water '—all this. Whatever the fuck it is?'

'Ah.' Neil looked decidedly uncomfortable. He wasn't a heartless man, but he wasn't great at dealing with human emotions. 'Well, um, Barbara, are you alright?'

'Perhaps you should sit this one out?' Kam wasn't big on the feels either, tending to lean on their strengths of practicality and logic.

It's what made them a good team. Neil for the details, Kam for the logical connections, Barbara because she understood what motivated people to do the shit they did.

She'd never really thought of it that way. They made such a perfect trio of crime-solvers, it almost felt… designed.

'I'm sorry,' Barrington said. He was looking at her with an expression like wet paper, a collapsing mess of grief and humiliation.

Barbara might have a better understanding of matters of the human heart than her assistants did, but that did not make her prone to hysterics. She rolled her shoulders and took a breath deep into her diaphragm.

'Neither of you can see the man standing beneath the sign, can you?' she said. 'And the streets are dark, yes. Damp from the earlier rain?'

'Still drizzling,' Neil said as an answer. 'Technically.'

Strange, she couldn't feel the icy water anymore.

'Come now, sir.' Kam placed a reassuring hand on Barbara's shoulder. Things must be bad. 'Let's go find out what kind of poison killed Lee, and who might have access to it. I'm sure that will lead to a break in the case.'

But Barbara shook her head. 'Thank you, Kam.' Slipped her shoulder out from the DS's touch. 'But no. We're going to Ezekiel's manor.'

'Well, this is my cue.' Neil nodded to them both. 'I'll let you know when we have results.' He drove away at a much more traditionally-Neil pace.

'Sir,' Kam pushed on. 'I really think we should—'

But Barbara already had her phone out, and it took thirty seconds worth of Googling to find a map to Ezekiel's manor.

'I told you to leave this alone,' Barrington said, apparently following her. He managed to sound entirely unsurprised.

'I need to find the truth, and all signs are pointing towards Ezekiel and his experiments. So that's where I have to go.'

'I'm not sure how Ezekiel's manor fits with Lee's death.' It took Barbara a moment to realise Kam had fallen into step beside her. 'But if the past three years of working with you have taught me anything, it's to trust your hunches. Sometimes, what seems logical isn't the right answer. But listening to you and following your instinct always is.'

Ezekiel Dudgeon's manor wasn't far, and was in better condition than Barbara had expected, although the term 'manor' might have been a stretch. A large house compared to the rest of the village, sure, but even burned and neglected she could see it was nothing more than one of those ugly mass-produced McMansions popular in the 80's. The second story seemed to have copped most of the damage — the roof was simply gone, and several walls were crumbled and blackened. The ground floor showed some evidence of a fire, particularly around the windows, but had retained more structural integrity. It looked like no one had lived here since the accident. The windows and doors were boarded up, and a chain link fence hemmed the structure, dotted with rusty 'KEEP OUT' signs.

At least, that's the impression Barbara got of the place, but it was difficult to tell. The building was at once a ruined house in the village, a ghetto-style apartment block, and a lonely shack on a wind-wracked beach.

'Here,' Kam said. They crouched by a hole in the fence, lifted and peeled it back like skin. Together, they crawled inside.

'Looks empty,' Kam said, as they pushed open the plyboard used as a door, its chain cut and lock rusted over. They turned on the flashlights on their phones, illuminating a damp corridor scrawled with graffiti. 'Maybe the odd kid or junkie hangs out in here, but nothing more.'

'Fi said the lab was below ground,' Barbara said, and strode ahead.

The accident had blown the basement door off its hinges. Barbara and Kam climbed over soggy, splintered chipboard and made their way down narrow, dark stairs. Slippery with mud, tiled walls thick with greyish-green growth. Empty light sockets protruded from the ceiling, connected by ropey wiring. A dank scent rose to meet them: wet earth and fungus, closed-in airlessness, and something else, something Barbara's mind seemed to balk at rather than identify. Not the smell of something dead, neither rot nor decay — those, she knew well. This was something chemical. It burned in her sinuses. It added an unsteady spin to the already unstable world.

The basement — or lab, or whatever — was disappointingly mundane when they made it down. The tables remained, empty but for a layer of dust and mould, but the Bunsen burners and glass vials from the photo were gone. Something large was covered in a tarpaulin in one corner, a stack of rusty filing cabinets filled another. What there was not, however, was any sign of an explosion or fire.

'I thought the accident happened in here?' Barbara mused, aloud. 'Why isn't there more evidence?'

'Because the accident story is a lie.'

She spun. A man emerged from the shadows, and even though he looked like footage from an old movie — grainy, colours washed-out and flickering — Barbara knew immediately who he was.

'Ezekiel.'

'Welcome, detective,' Ezekiel said. His voice had an odd, fuzzy sound to it, and there was a slight delay between the movement of his mouth and his words. 'So nice to meet face-to-face.'

Barbara couldn't help but recoil as Ezekiel approached. Not because he was dead and really shouldn't be standing in front of her, but the way he moved. He... stuttered. Again, she was reminded of the old TV she had as a child. When the signal was bad it used to do this.

Kam was staring at her like she'd grown a second head. 'Um... sir. Are you okay?'

'No one else can see me, certainly not your trusty DS, I'm afraid. I'm not, after all, even here.' A pause, in which he looked strangely thoughtful. 'Strictly speaking, none of us are.'

'What?'

'Don't play dumb, detective, because I know you're not. I have shown you the true reality of this world. Or, perhaps I should say, it's unreality.'

Barbara fought the urge to close her eyes against the crowding. The way the laboratory was also a batman-like cave and the bridge of some alien spacecraft, complete with purple-skinned humanoids.

'It's difficult, at first, when you realise there's something wrong with the world you thought was real. It's a kind of grief, I suppose. I thought of myself as a rational man of science, but my measurements, my recordings, even my maths they, well, they weren't adding up. One day up would be up and the next it would be down and I thought, for a while, that I was going insane. Particularly when no one would listen to me. But numbers don't lie, and I refused to give up. Instead, I tried something...unorthodox.'

Ezekiel pointed to the tarpaulin-covered lump in the corner.

'I refer the court to exhibit-A,' he said. 'If I could dramatically remove the cover with a flourish, I would. As I can't interact with anything physical at all anymore, I will leave that to you.'

Making her way over to the tarp felt like walking through water, maybe even quicksand. Every part of her screamed not to touch it. Not to listen to him. Whatever truth this was, her body and some deeper lizard part of her mind weren't sure it should be uncovered.

But she wasn't about to let that stop her. Barbara used no flourish to drag the tarpaulin off a mountain of large mirrors. Behind her, Kam sneezed.

'Do you know,' Ezekiel said. 'That every time you observe something, you change it. Every time you try to measure the world, you influence that measurement. The act of being seen changes not only who we are, but the stuff we are made of.'

'I am aware that such a principle exists,' Barbara answered. 'But I'm not sure that's what it means.'

The mirrors were mounted on steel frames but were surprisingly light. She gripped the edge of the top one and dragged it aside, resting it against the wall. Then did the same for the next two. There were sockets and brackets on the frames, like the whole lot had slotted into something larger.

'I spent so much of my career observing the world, measuring it, but that wasn't helping. So I turned the principle on myself.'

'With mirrors.'

'Reflections of reflections of reflections. It's called an infinity effect. I saw more versions of myself than I had ever imagined seeing, and I recorded and I measured and in doing so the very stuff that I am made of began to change. Do you know what I discovered, as I pushed the boundaries of the atoms that hold me together?'

'What?' Why was this filling her with such dread?

'That I am hollow. I am not a person, Barbara. I am the shell of an unimportant character.'

Barbara stared down at the mirrors, the image of herself staring back. At the same time there was an emergency on the alien spaceship. And Batman appeared to be taking a nap.

'All the world's a stage, and I don't even have a speaking part. But you on the other hand, with your plucky sidekicks and your difficult past and your character arc, you're something else. You might be the heroine herself. For now. Ask your predecessor how stable that job is.'

'Sir?' Kam, behind her, sounded small and uncertain. Very unlike them. 'Are you okay?'

Barbara realised there were tears in the eyes of her reflection. She couldn't feel them on her actual cheeks.

'But now you've seen the truth too,' Ezekiel was saying, and there was an unholy glee in his voice but a look of relief, even hope, on his face. 'You have no choice but to finish the experiment before the story that runs the world catches on, and casts you into limbo with me. Trust me, however much this hurts right now, it's nothing compared to eternity trapped between the stories, neither real or unreal, neither living or dead.'

'What do you think, sir?' Kam, behind her, was a pensive reflection in the mirrors. 'Does this have anything to do with Lee?'

'I was a nobody,' Ezekiel continued. 'I scratched the surface and left the tiniest scar. But you could free us all.'

Free us all? What would that even look like?

What would happen to Kam if Ezekiel was right? Or Barrington, dead but apparently not gone. And more importantly, what would happen to Joyce and Laura? Were they hollow, the way Ezekiel thought he was hollow?

Like he could read her mind, he said, 'We did not choose to be here, puppeted in a world that revolves around you, for the amusement of some invisible entity or whatever the fuck is controlling this story. Hell, maybe it controls itself. Either way, we are prisoners here. Everyone you've ever met, everyone you care about, trapped in our meaningless half-lives.'

'What happens next?' Barbara whispered the words, watching her lips move. Did she change what they were made of simply by watching?

Kam twisted, looked back up the stairs. 'I guess we could call Neil to come take a look, if you think the mirrors are important. But I have to say, I'm more inclined to interview the documentary crew again. Something about their story didn't sit right with me.'

Ezekiel, meanwhile, shook his head. 'I don't know. Perhaps we die, our thin skins dissolving to dust. Or maybe we learn the truth about the story that has trapped us? Either way, isn't that better than slavery and illusion?'

Did he realise the moment he lost her? The instant the beacon of *truth* always so bright inside her dimmed. She hated the idea of Joyce and Laura trapped, manipulated, yes, of course she did. But even if they weren't real, even if she wasn't real, she knew she preferred that illusion to loneliness. Having Joyce and Laura in her life had saved her. She would never let them go.

So, without saying anything, she scanned the room. Found a piece of old piping. Marched over to collect it. Gripped it tightly.

Only then, it seemed, he understood.

'Barbara, no!' He launched himself at her, slipped through her like the reflection on the surface of a pond. 'Please don't!' He screamed and thrashed and beat his fists into her head, but she felt nothing. 'This is our only chance.'

Kam was staring at her, stunned. 'Sir, what—'

'Don't leave me trapped like this!'

And she smashed the mirrors, slamming the pipe into them until all that remained were large shards of sharp glass and twisted frames. Then she tossed the pipe aside and turned to Kam.

'The film crew, you think?'

Her detective sergeant couldn't have looked more shocked if she'd suddenly turned into a unicorn. 'I— ah—'

'I'm not so sure I agree. I rather think we should interview the sceptics again. One at a time, maybe, rather than as a group.' Anyone who had access to that photo of Ezekiel, for a start.

'What about the lab?' Kam asked, looking very carefully at everything except the mirrors their DCI had just destroyed.

'This was a dead end, I'm afraid. Nothing useful here.' Barbara gestured to the stairs. 'Shall we?'

A smile settled on Kam's face, an expression of comfort. Like they'd slipped on a well-worn jacket. Rightful order had been restored. 'Sir.'

'It's too late,' Ezekiel cried out after her. 'You've seen behind the curtain and that will never go away. This is your new reality, detective. How long can you survive life like this?'

Barbara didn't bother answering. He was a shadow of a character, after all.

'Let's find our killer, Kam,' she said instead. 'Like we always do.'

But as she climbed the stairs and waded through a swamp and stepped into the darkness of space, then down the hallway which was also a cathedral and an alien plateau, and Barrington was waiting for her and Kam was too, and they were both talking but she could hear neither, and she felt none of the drizzle outside or the sun or the wind, she wondered.

For Joyce and Laura, she could endure anything. Even an infinite number of worlds and their stories, even all at once.

But for how long?

The End Will Emerge from the Filth

GABINO IGLESIAS

ALBERTO STEPPED UP TO THE TINY WINDOW IN HIS LIVING ROOM AND looked out as his coffeemaker gurgled its sad, wet song in the kitchen. Alberto had been renting this tiny apartment on top of the Chinese food joint for more than a decade, and the view of the Gowanus Canal and the Union Street Bridge never got old. He knew the owner had kept his rent the same because there was a story between them, one that involved a lot of blood and a man who was never seen again, but he didn't mind. The place served him well, and with no kids or wife, he was ready to spend the rest of his days sipping his coffee and looking out at the canal every morning. After the shit he'd seen, it struck him as a peaceful existence and a nice way to go.

The aroma of coffee—Puerto Rican, of course, just like his mom had always drank—was starting to tickle Alberto's senses when the previous afternoon crashed through his bliss like a truck falling off a bridge.

Two cops had come knocking at Alberto's door. That was always bad news. Alberto had been out of the life for at least half a decade, but cops were still at the top of the list of things he disliked. He'd spent too much time running from some cops and greasing the palms of others to know that pigs at your door was always a bad thing.

The two cops—one tall with eyes like a snake, the other shorter, muscular, and with a face that made Alberto wonder if his mom had tied a steak to his neck when he was a kid so the dog would play with him—wanted to talk about the canal. They asked about "suspicious activity" and whether Alberto, who the cook at the Chinese joint had told them loved to walk around every day, had seen anything out of the ordinary. Then the cop with the snake eyes had noticed the ink on Alberto's arms and changed his whole approach, as if realizing Alberto could handle what they had to say.

"We've pulled some bodies outta the Gowanus in the last few weeks," said the snake. "Gangbangers, mostly. At least we think so. Some we don't know because they were too messed up to be identified."

"Messed up how?" Alberto asked. A bullet to the face would mean one thing, but missing eyes, destroyed heads sitting on top of untouched bodies, and things like words carved into their flesh could mean something much different. The former was something Alberto knew happened often, but the latter meant something darker and bigger than gang violence was at work. Snake eyes looked at Alberto and stayed quiet. When Alberto was sure he wasn't going to get an answer, the cop spoke.

"Eaten," said snake eyes. "No other way to put it. Chewed up. Mangled." The shorter cop coughed. It was fake. Probably trying to tell his partner to shut up. Snake eyes ignored him. "The bodies look like they were given to animals before they were dumped in the Gowanus. Animals with big teeth and a healthy appetite. Either that or we have sharks or piranhas in that water, and I have a hard time believing anything could survive in that poisonous soup."

Alberto nodded. He told the cops he hadn't seen anything out of the ordinary, but that he would keep an eye out. Snake eyes left like he'd been dying to run out of Alberto's tiny apartment. The shorter cop stayed back. He plucked a business card with a number on it out of some pocket and placed it on the table.

"I know about you, Mr. Vázquez," said the cop, his voice low. "My pops was NYPD back in the day. He told me all about Los Dragones. I know you left that stuff behind, but if something's happening anywhere in Brooklyn, I'm sure you know about it. My partner thinks it's all gang stuff, but we've pulled some bodies outta there with regular clothing and no tattoos. Some women, too. People who worked in offices or local businesses. Some of them may have been sex workers, maybe not. We don't know. Point is, this isn't just gang business. If you find out anything, please let us know."

Alberto hated the man for what he was and hated his father for what he had been. Once a cop, always a cop. However, there was honesty and concern in the young man's voice, and it reminded Alberto why he'd left the life behind, why he'd stepped away from the money, power, and women he loved so much to spend the rest of his days in a tiny apartment above a Chinese joint. Alberto didn't say a word, but he reached across the table, grabbed the card, and nodded. If the cop knew anything about him, he'd know that was more than enough.

The coffeemaker was no longer making noises. It was time to get a cup and come back to the window to look out at the world and plan his day. Alberto knew he had to run some errands. Laundry. Groceries. Visit Doña Janet to make sure she was taking her pills, which he had been doing for almost twenty years, since his homie Rodrigo got shot right in front of his place.

Nah, he could do all that the next day. Or maybe the day after. Today he had to see if he could figure out what was going down in the Gowanus.

The stocky cop had said he knew about Alberto, but there were a million things the man ignored. Some of them were dark, but others were somewhat normal. For example, the man couldn't know Alberto had quit the streets because he refused to sacrifice kids to the dark god the leader of Los Dragones was convinced would help them rule the city. There was also no way for him to know that Alberto had fallen in love with the internet after quitting the gang. He had always been curious by nature, and the internet allowed him to get information immediately. One of the things he became obsessed with, in part because he moved right next to it, was the Gowanus Canal.

Alberto had read about the pretty unremarkable beginnings of the

1.8-mile long Gowanus Canal, which started as the Gowanus Creek. That part of it didn't interest him. What had made Alberto develop a small obsession with the Gowanus was its current state as one of the most polluted bodies of water in the world. While the water was dark and some places of the Gowanus smelled awful, just looking wasn't enough to understand exactly how bad it was. More than a century of industrial use, garbage, oil slicks, raw sewage, and continuous dumping of god knows what by chemical factories and gas plants had made the Gowanus a deadly soup of bacteria and harsh chemicals in which nothing could live. Stories of fishermen pulling out strange, mutated creatures abounded. A dolphin that got stranded in the canal a few years back had died pretty quickly and made the news. That was the last push, the last bit of bad publicity the city needed, so in 2020 they teamed up with the Environmental Protection Agency to dredge the entire length of the canal. The project was supposed to take at least a decade to complete, but it didn't last a year. The dredging buckets came out full of a poisonous sludge unlike anything the EPA folks had ever seen. The smell became a problem. The city called in more scientists to help them find ways of cleaning up the canal. The scientists came, analyzed the sludge, which everyone was calling black mayonnaise by then, and the results went viral. Every news station and newspaper in the city reported on the sludge, a lethal combination of drug residue, unknown chemicals, raw sewage, oil, pesticides, rotting debris that included human bodies, and a collection of heavy metals that included mercury, arsenic, chromium, benzene, and lead. The project was abandoned.

Alberto had always known a fair number of bodies ended up in the Gowanus Canal, but what the cops had told him was different. Hearing about it had woken up a memory he'd worked hard to put to sleep.

Los Dragones started out as a group of Puerto Rican youth trying to survive. They'd come together under the leadership of Alana, a brown girl with a big mouth and an attitude to match who made a name for herself cutting off the hands of anyone who touched a woman against her will in the barrio. At the beginning, Los Dragones protected each other and made sure no one messed with the old folks who ran the local bodegas. Then things got complicated because if you wanted to run a street, that meant running everything in it, and that included drugs. And the money was good. Then came the rest: odd jobs for the Bonanno crime family, gambling, deals with local pimps, greased cops, and a lot of drugs. Alana took to it like a fish to water, and her attitude turned her name into something people spoke proudly or whispered in fear. As the bodies piled up and the money rolled in, Alberto became one of Alana's right-hand men. He did as he was told, and she loved him for it and rewarded him nicely. Then Alana went crazy.

Alberto wasn't sure crazy was the right word, but it was a word that made sense to him when he thought about Alana. She'd become obssessed with, in her words, "owning New York City." She wanted to run the barrio and take over Brooklyn, but also the other four boroughs. She talked about systematically killing the five families and any gang that resufed to join Los Dragones. Alberto went with it for a while. Then Alana asked him to take her to see a lady in the back of a pizza joint in New Jersey and things went south.

The lady was waiting for them at a table when they arrived, smoking a hand-rolled cigarette and sipping on some amber-colored drink she had in a red coffee mug. Her eyes were missing, the flesh inside her eyes a raw pink that unsettled Alberto more than he thought it could. Despite not having eyes, the lady, whose name Alberto never caught, complimented Alana on her red pants, seemed to look at her cigarette from time to time, made a comment about the demon tattooed on Alberto's right forearm, and told them to look at a bird who'd flown into the power cables oustide the pizza joint's window and said, "It's a black bird. Always pay attention when you see a black bird." Alana told Alberto to wait at another table. He did as he was told, only catching bits and pieces of their conversation. Before they left, the lady gave Alana a book and Alana slid a thick envelope over to the lady, who picked it up as if she could see it.

The weeks that followed were the beginning of the end for Alberto. Alana became obssessed with the occult. "We can do whatever we want," she'd told Alberto more than once. "All we need is a bit of help to get it done." But the help wasn't easy to get. First, their murders took on a ritualistic nature. When they had to kill someone, Alana would come along and carve strange words into their flesh, light candles around their bodies, or whisper prayers in a strange language over them before someone else pulled the trigger. Alberto hated it, but he went along with it because Los Dragones was family, and doing what he did was all he knew. That changed when Alana told them to kidnap some kids. She needed two girls. Twins. For a ritual. She needed their blood. Alberto said no. Alana threw everyone out of their meeting place and yelled at him, threatened to make him disappear. It was the straw that broke the camel's back. Alberto talked back for the first time in his life. "I know everything about you and about everyone out there," he told Alana. "I'm out. For good. If you decide to come for me, I'm gonna take all of you down with me." Then he turned around and walked out, leaving Alana, Los Dragones, and the only life he knew behind.

The thing about the Gowanus Canal had him worried because the onslaught of memories had pushed something to the forefront of his thoughts, something crazy Alana had been saying a lot in the days before he called it quits: "The end will emerge from the filth." She was convinced they had to paint the streets with blood, that they had to make Brooklyn a rotten place so that the help Alana wanted would finally come. She spoke of a god of filth, Javasasgot—a name Alberto hadn't been able to forget—who would only help them if she found a place for him to live, a foul environment in which he could thrive. The things the cops had said were mixing with the memories now, clicking into place with a clarity that sent a shiver down Alberto's spine.

The day came and went. Alberto got another cup of coffee right after lunch and then spent some time on the internet, playing pool and reading about the history of tattooing to kill the time. Throughout the whole day, phrases and images popped into his mind, all of them reinforcing his fears, all of them screaming that Alana was behind the bodies being pulled from the Gowanus Canal. Finally, when darkness fell over Brooklyn like a wet towel, Alberto pulled his old gun from under his mattress and headed out.

Staying close to the water wasn't easy, but Alberto knew how to pull it off. If the situation had gotten so bad that the cops were asking people like him for help, chances were that he would find something going on that night. The cops were cowards, so they wouldn't go where he planned to go.

Alberto walked for hours. He went to the Gowanus Waterfront Park and stayed in front of the water, sometimes breaking into private property, all the way down to the end of Smith St. Then he crossed right under the Gowanus Expressway and started heading back up to his place on that side of the canal. He broke into the Baxter Metalworks parking lot and stuck to the edge of the parking lot. At the end of it, right next to some abandoned barges, there was a small patch of green. Alberto walked up to it and looked out at the dark water of the canal. He was about to turn around and keep walking when he heard splashing. He stood still and paid attention. Across from him was an empty construction site with a few trucks left there for the night. On the canal's wall right in front of it there were some rusted pillars, and Alberto saw a figure there, holding on to one of the pillars. It looked both humanoid and reptilian and—

Steps.

Alberto froze. His heart slammed against the side of his neck. Someone was next to him. He was reaching for the gun before he was done turning his body toward the sound.

The figures stading there were just like the one in the water. Up close, Alberto was surpised at how big they were. They were the same color as the sludge—the black mayonnaise—from the bottom of the canal. They were both taller than him. Their bodies made Alberto think of big men covered in dark, wet chunks of leather. Their eyes were black orbs with no pupils, their mouths ragged holes stuffed with glistening black teeth the size of daggers. He pulled the trigger.

The sound of the blast and the creature on the right jerking to the left were simultaneous. Then something slammed against the back of Alberto's neck. Something wet that smelled awful. The gun flew out of his hand. His body toppled forward, momentum carrying him to the grimy floor. A second later, four creatures were on him, their powerful hands grabbing his arms and pulling him up. Alberto screamed. A wet hand twice the size of his face covered his mouth. It smelled like dead fish that had been left in the trunk of a car for a week. Alberto gagged.

The end will emerge from the filth.

Alana's voice came to him and the chaos around him suddenly made sense. These creatures had been summoned or created or brought here from somewhere else to help her. They were going to turn the city into a place where Javasasgot could thrive. There were more bodies coming. A lot more. And then…well, Alberto could only begin to imagine what would come next.

The end will emerge from the filth.

The creatures had carried Alberto to the edge of the water. He realized he had to do something or he was going to become one of those mangled bodies. *Eaten.* That's what the cop had said. Alberto tried to scream. The sound became a desperate animal trapped in his mouth, its power thrumming against his throat.

The creatures reached the edge and took a final step, their bodies dropping to the fetid water below. The water was colder than Alberto expected. The hand covering his mouth disappeared. He felt long, thick teeth dig into the back of his right shoulder. He opened his mouth to scream and the Gowanus Canal invaded his mouth. It tasted like death wrapped in something chemical and sour.

Strong hands pulled him down, deeper than he thought possible. Everything was dark. The taste of the Gowanus was overwhelming.

The end will emerge from the filth.

Alberto felt a deep ache in his lungs. He battled it, the fight making him ignore the creature chewing on his shoulder and the one now doing the same to the back of his left leg.

Finally, Alberto's body ignored his orders and inhaled. The cold, foul water flooded his system. His body stopped fighting, but his brain could still hear Alana. *The end will emerge from the filth.* She'd been right. This was the beginning of that emergence, and he was dying submerged in its filth.

The Invited

MARIA LEWIS

"Kia whakatōmuri te haere whakamua." – Māori proverb

TUI WASN'T A MONSTER. SHE ONLY ROBBED THE PLACES OF THE DEAD. SHE was very specific about it: the more haunted the place, the better the loot. And there were few cities in Australia more top-to-bottom haunted than Adelaide. From the moment she had rolled into town six months ago, she'd felt uneasy, like death was waiting for her around every corner. Yet with each day that passed, she realised that was just how this place *felt*. It was the perfect hunting ground for her very particular type of break and entering. 'Burglar' was such a dirty word. She preferred curator … with force.

She applied that force to gently and carefully removing the screws that had been hidden behind Encyclopedia Britannica volumes in the study of Brighton's Dunluce Castle. From the outside, it looked out of place wedged among the micro mansions and bougie beach houses of Adelaide's most expensive suburb. It was built in 1912 by some Reverend guy, Macully something. Tui could never keep the names straight. It was always 'Mc' this or 'Mac' that. What was important is the good Reverend modelled the joint on the Dunluce Castle of his homeland in Northern Ireland, which had its peak in the 1500s but now lay in ruins.

Few people had an appreciation for history like she did, especially not the current owners of Dunluce. They had made it big in the world of finance and snapped up the notorious property when it had last gone on sale in the eighties. A gay couple who thought the idea of owning and living in a recreation castle was camp. They even held monthly murder mystery nights, enabling dozens of lookey-loos to walk the hallways of the allegedly haunted building in costumes that could be from any period you wanted, basically. Tui had attended as a flapper in a bobbed, blonde wig, with a white powder beat to tone down her ethnicity. If anyone tried, it would be hard to remember the woman she looked absolutely nothing like among the crowd of some fifty people dressed as everything from Austin Powers extras to a Brontë sister. It was the nonsensical scope of the costumes that annoyed her the most, but it was worth it.

It was one thing to study the floor plans inside and out, but to walk the space was another thing entirely. She saw what they didn't because she was willing to. The study was larger in the original design of the house, aligning with the castle it drew inspiration from. Somewhere along the way, the size of the room had been halved. Time had passed. So had various owners. People didn't notice how the length of the outer wall didn't line up with the interior.

"How much longer?" Plummy asked.

"Just hold the torch still," she hissed at him. She pocketed the screws. They'd be going back where they belonged once she was done. If they did their job right, no one need know they had ever been there, let alone that they had been robbed. Tui leaned forward, blowing away the dust. The outline of the false wall was barely visible, but she felt the tingle of excitement as she ran her fingers along the ridge. It was fitted perfectly against the wooden frame that passed the whole thing off as shelves built into the walls themselves. A gust of stale air blew against her face as she exposed the entrance to the hidden room.

It was dark in there, blacker than black with no natural light to penetrate the space. Plummy was muttering with excitement next to her, but Tui was still. Cautious. This is exactly what she had been looking for, exactly where it was supposed to be, but something felt … off. Her grandmother would have called it kohimu, a whisper from the ancestors, a warning.

"All our wāhine can feel them," she would say to Tui when she was a child. "Just the wāhine. It's a reminder."

Tāua had lived poor and died poor. Tui would do neither. Whether it was a murmur from the ancestors or a bloody yell, she was going in. By the time she snapped back, Plummy had removed the remaining two shelves. Tui stretched her body through the dark square and into the room. The beam of light from her headtorch bounced around the space, inches of cobwebs and dust coating everything.

"Yuck," her offsider muttered, looking to her for guidance. Tui was the brains, Plummy was the brawn. She preferred it that way. She was smart enough for the both of them, but what she wasn't was big. She could wiggle, she could twist, she could contort and bend herself into almost any small space if she needed to. Plummy could headbutt someone unconscious and that was its own kind of useful.

"The books," Tui said, pointing. "This was part of the Reverend's original library, so books first. Wrapped in—"

"The tissue paper, I know, boss. *First editions are valuable, Plummy. Not just smelly, heavy tomes.*"

His impression of her caused a smirk as she brushed dust off the cover of one such tome.

"Alice's Adventures In Wonderland," she murmured. "Published in 1867."

"A first edition?" he asked, looking hopeful.

"A second, well, technically third. Still valuable."

"Yeah, but *how* valuable, aye?"

"A few grand," she lied.

His eyes lit up and she immediately felt better about the fib. In truth, it was closer to a dime if she found the right fence. It was safer to tell Plummy a mistruth. He'd been her go-to on the last four jobs and she kept him well and truly fed, but she also kept him in the dark. They worked fast, filling ten bags of books and an additional one of antique knick-knacks that screamed old money. Plummy left her as he started moving the loot, which would take a few loads, and Tui did a final sweep. She didn't want to leave as much as behind as she was, but they also only had a limited window of time with the owners at a Christmas In July function in Glenside. She had eyes on them there, so the second they left, her phone would buzz in her pocket and she had thirty minutes at best. That hadn't happened yet, but it was close to midnight. Their window was closing.

She hesitated to leave the room within a room. She didn't want to, knowing the money she was quite literally leaving on the table but also the opportunity. *Fuck it,* she thought. She'd seen greed bring down lesser thieves and that wouldn't be her. She began lifting the remaining bags out, before inching her body back through the entry point until she was settled on the other side. A cobweb brushed against the skin of her neck and she hurriedly slapped it away, feeling phantom tendrils of hair she knew hadn't escaped her tight bun.

Without a word, Plummy grunted back and forth between the study and the vehicle parked down a nearby alley by their driver. Tui retrieved the screws, carefully getting one panel back in place and the shelf, before starting on the last. Plummy had to hold it while she worked on the final section, their faces inches from the wood. That's why there was no mistaking what they heard as four loud, firm knocks rung out from the other side.

Plummy jumped, dropping his torch and scrambling for it just as quickly. Tui froze, eyes wide as they stared at each other. They turned back, looking hard at the wooden panel, as if trying to stare through it, even though it was now tightly in place.

"The wind," Plummy said, knowing full well it was a windless night. "These old places are draughty as hell."

Tui nodded, but didn't say what she was thinking. The wind didn't make four clear, concise *knock, knock, knock, knocks.* The space on the other side was more empty than ever before thanks to them, but just because there was no one in there didn't mean there was *nothing* in that room. Unease prickled up her skin as she moved back from the wall, checking the image she had taken of the books stacked on the shelf previously. Tui moved hastily, returning them in the exact same order they had been before and quickly wiping down any errant dust or clues of their presence. Satisfied, she nodded.

"Let's move."

On the drive back, she couldn't help but think of the knocks as her phone vibrated four times in her pocket. It never did that. Usually it was just the once. *Nerves,* she convinced herself. Every job had them and even if part of her value was keeping her small team steady with her calmness and confidence, that didn't mean adrenaline couldn't manifest in unusual ways.

They're en route, the message said. It was inconsequential now as they pulled up in the loading bay at the rear of an old pub on the outskirts of the CBD favoured by old, white people and young, white people who played cricket. The Seven Stars Hotel shut at eleven, with only the caretaker remaining at this hour. Tui nodded at her brother, Te Kohe offering a wave in response as he disabled the building's alarm and propped open the back door. There was no need for their wheel woman Nunda to keep watch, with high walls and even higher overgrown vines blocking out any view from the alleyway as the four of them moved the bags inside and up the creaky, narrow staircase that had once led to the publican's quarters back in 1818 when the place was first erected.

A locked door at the rear of the pokies area was the only access point and that's where they confined themselves for the next several hours, cleaning and cataloguing every item they had obtained over half a carton of James Squire pale ale. The entire second floor of the pub was empty, too rundown to feasibly have paying tenants. Whole chunks of plaster dangled from the ceiling and water damage had left stained trickles down the walls that made the place look like it was bleeding inky grey. There were even gaps wide enough in the floorboards that Tui could see down into the pub below.

The owners had used it as storage for years now, with her clever little brother negotiating an additional role as caretaker on top of his one as bar manager if it meant he could live upstairs for free. There were eleven rooms and he had the sole one with functioning electricity. When Tui had arrived, he was able to clear out the second, less gross room for her but it could only be illuminated by candlelight. She didn't care. It was free. It was off the radar. It was safe. They had a functioning bathroom with four toilet cubicles and a kitchen with electricity that became their centre of operations. More than enough.

"Wait, so I don't understand," Nunda huffed, gloved hands wiping down one of the last books they'd stolen. "If this Reverend didn't murder anyone there, why is Dunluce a *haunted* castle? Like, it just looks creepy?"

"Isn't that enough?" Plummy chuckled. "You should've heard what Tui and I did."

"It was his daughter," Tui remarked, taking a reference image of a candelabra.

"She died there?" Plummy questioned.

"Technically she died at Brighton Pier," she answered.

"Murdered?" The hulking man was clearly intrigued.

"She was teaching swimming lessons to kids, dived off the pier into the water and was snapped up by a Great White Shark."

"Shut up!" Nunda squealed. "You lie!"

"Became South Australia's first recorded fatal shark attack."

Plummy coughed as he took a sip of his beer, half-laughing, half-choking. "When was this?"

"March, 1926," Tui said, plucking the date from her mind. "And it's said to this day that the disgruntled spirit of Kathleen 'Kitty' Whyte still haunts the halls of her father's old mansion."

"What's he saying?" Plummy questioned, pointing at her brother who was signing quickly.

"Unless she was eaten by a shark on the grounds," Tui said, reading the sentence Te Kohe was putting together with his hands, "it makes no sense that the castle itself would be haunted."

"In simpler terms ... " Nunda chuckled, emphasising the final word with one of the few sign language phrases she knew. "Bullshit."

Te Kohe beamed in response. He had been born deaf, completely, but he missed nothing because of an ability to read lips and pick up those inaudible, subtle cues in human behaviour that bordered on supernatural. Their grandmother had raised them, learning New Zealand Sign Language (NZSL) then teaching them both - along with their native tongue - so that there was no barrier between their whānau, no obstructions to the way they communicated at all, no problems until the first time Tui was arrested for stealing. Then the second. The third. The—

"It was haunted though!" Plummy exclaimed, interrupting her guilt trip and earning a scoff from Te Kohe. "It was! Tui, tell 'em about the knock."

Her brother was still grinning and it encouraged her, just a little, so she told the story. Nunda leaned forward as she spoke, Plummy muttering his agreement and adding details to her anecdote, but Te

Kohe's smile slowly began to drop the longer she talked. She signed and spoke simultaneously, her own grin compensating for his lack as she drew the others in with the story.

"And then there was a *knock, knock, knock, knock* against the false wall," Tui said, rapping her knuckles against the wood of the table to demonstrate the sound. She was on the last knock when Te Kohe reached out to stop her, but it was too late.

"Could have been a possum," Nunda commented.

Plummy scoffed. "A possum with knuckles?!"

"I'm just saying, your explanation of *wind* doesn't make any sense. I don't believe in this spooky juju crap—"

"Spooky juju! This operation literally relies on that spooky juju and people being too freaked out to delve deeper into the places we wanna rob!"

"It relies on Tui's research, actually."

She wasn't listening to them bicker, instead her focus was on Te Kohe, whose hand was still outstretched in hesitation.

"What?" she asked.

"You shouldn't have done that," he signed.

"Bit late to flag a moral quandary. The bounty is tallied."

"Not the crime. The knock."

"This?" She did it again, her brother's hand slapping down on hers before she even got past the second.

"Stop it."

"Why?" she mouthed, tilting her head.

"It's an invitation."

His stare penetrated hers, his dark brown eyes almost black with their intensity.

"To who?" she croaked.

"To what?" he responded, swift.

Tui let out a heavy sigh, the expelled breath causing a loose curl in front of her eyes to flutter with the gesture. "You sound like tāua."

"And you should listen," he cautioned. "What did she always used to say, Tui?"

"*Kia whakatōmuri te haere whakamua*," she recited.

Te Kohe nodded. "I walk towards the future, with my eyes fixed on the past."

"Then how do we make money, huh? They steal from us, we steal from them."

"And you're still not listening. I'm not saying stop what you're doing, I'm saying use your mātauranga Māori."

He tapped his skull for emphasis, but it was clear from the expression on Tui's face that she still didn't understand.

"Indigenous knowledge," he signed, casting a look at Nunda and Plummy who were still arguing with each other. "We're not them. You're not them. Our understanding is not theirs."

Te Kohe took the pencil from her hands, drawing a line down the middle of a freshly turned blank page she had been using to list every item they acquired.

"They view life and death as a straight line," he signed. He tapped one side of the line. Life. He tapped the other. Death. Te Kohe quickly began scribbling, using the pads of his fingers to smooth out the lead so it blended from light to dark and back again in seamless motions on the page. He tapped his work, letting the pencil drop.

"Us," Tui murmured, looking down. Te Kohe's chin lifted in a firm yes.

"The truth," he signed. Tui felt that unease spreading back through her limbs, echoing over her skin, the whisper of a mistake she had made but couldn't undo. She ripped the page out of the book, scrunching it up and hurling it into the bin across the other side of the kitchen.

"Kobe," she smirked as it landed in the basket. Te Kohe didn't return her grin, instead his expression remained just as grave. His eyes never left hers.

"I gotta ditch the van," Nunda said, slapping her hands down on Tui's shoulders in a subtle enough gesture but one that made her jump. "You right?"

"Yeah," she nodded, not wanting her brother to see that she was rattled. He'd never liked what she did, but he respected how she did it and he respected the coin. "You're keeping it, right?"

"Totes, just change the plates, lose it in the parking garage, wait a week and if things are still cool then pick it back up, paint it, use it for the next job."

"I'll leave your cut in the drop box," Tui said, tossing Nunda the keys.

"Love ya, leave ya."

She blew them a kiss as she disappeared down the stairs, Plummy watching her go.

"She's my lift so … "

"Chase it, then." She held up her hand to high five the giant as he trotted after Nunda, his footsteps echoing through the building as he fe-fi-fo-fummed his way to the back door.

"They're shagging," Tui said to her brother the second she heard the van leave. He rolled his eyes at her, annoyed as he pushed up from the table. "What? Oh come on, you know it too!"

He was annoyed at her. Mad, even. She could tell by the way he huffed around the kitchen, collecting empty beer bottles. *Fine,* she thought, pissed off right back as she snatched up the paperwork and stormed to her room. Only when she heard his door shut did she make a move for the box of matches next to her bed, striking one, she used the illumination to find the candles around the room. Yet the wicks wouldn't catch. She held the flame right next to them, each having caught perfectly the night before. Now the flame just inched along the wood of the matchstick until it singed her flesh.

"Ah, shit," she said, dropping the match and stamping out the flame with her foot. She sucked the tip of her finger where there was a small burn, annoyed as she tried another candle and then another. One flickered like it was about to catch, then went out with a depressing *pfft.*

"The fuck?"

Tui stood in the room, surrounded by the dark, physically alone but not feeling it. Her eyes had adjusted to the gloom and the space was bare, yet still she scanned every shape as if she was looking for the threat her body was telling her was there. Nothing. She grabbed the switchblade from the back pocket in her jeans and flicked it open as she settled on her bed. It was little more than a mattress on the floor, but the sensation of linen against her skin was somewhat of a comfort as she crossed her legs and waited.

She was exhausted. The adrenaline had waned some time ago. She was in desperate need of a shower. Yet fear kept her stuck in place as she listened to every creak, every whisper of a breeze, every car that backfired on the street out the front. Tui would never say it out loud, maybe she didn't even realise it consciously, but she was waiting for the knocks.

Knock, knock, knock, knock.

Only the faintest relief greeted her when the walls shifted from black to grey as the light of dawn eventually broke. Te Kohe nudged at her door with his toe, bringing a cup of tea as a peace offering. She barely noticed his arrival as she made notes against a set of blueprints that were stuck on the wall, checking her markings against information on her laptop screen. He placed the mug at the edge of her bed, noting the wet wipes she'd used to clean herself up and the pile of dirty clothes that had been swapped for silk pyjamas in pounamu green.

"Did you sleep?" he signed. She didn't see his message at first, nor his wave to get her attention. He rapped his knuckles against the wall she was pressed along, knowing she'd feel the vibrations. Tui leapt back, eyes wide and wild as she stared around the space with terror.

"What the fuck did you do that for?!" she snapped. "Hell, Te Kohe!"

He pointed at the steaming beverage. She sighed with relief, reaching for it with shaking hands and taking long, slow sips as she crouched at the base of the mattress.

"Thank you," she murmured. "Sorry."

"Did you sleep?"

She shook her head. Tui jerked her chin in the direction of her notepad, Te Kohe examining the calculations there.

"It was a *good* haul," she said. "Really good. It's the most Nunda and Plummy will have made on a job."

"And us?" he questioned, hands moving through the air.

"It's a good haul."

"Good?" he reiterated. "If we're careful, this combined with the past few jobs … it's enough to quit, Tui. Go back to school. Study history. Do something you love."

"I love this. I get to study history as it is."

"You know—"

"It's not enough for both of us, not yet. But that will be."

Her brother followed her gaze to the plans on the wall, some meticulously sketched out and others in the indecipherable scrawl fuelled by whatever kind of brilliant mania drove Tui when she had an idea she couldn't let go of.

"This is big," he signed, frowning as he took it all in. "Too big, Sis. Adelaide has no shortage of haunted buildings that are much lower risk."

"Yeah and we could do another ten *or* we could do that one and be done. Forever."

Tui could tell he didn't like it, neither did she, but suddenly the compulsion to be out, to be done, was one she couldn't ignore.

"No," was Plummy's immediate response when she pitched him the gig.

"No?" Tui pushed. "Are you kidding?"

"Do you know what that place is?" he asked.

"Of course, the South Australian Film Corporation."

"And before that?"

"An insane asylum, but every second building in Adelaide is an old insane asylum—it doesn't make sense. There were more asylums than people. I mean, the botanical gardens were the site of an insane asylum, for fuck's sake."

Tui was rambling, she knew it, but she wanted him on the job.

"No," Plummy repeated. "This place is different. Parkside Lunatic Asylum was hell, Tui. You're not from here, you don't get it. Ten per cent of their patient population died every year, there were stories of lobotomies and Z Ward … don't even get me started."

"That's why it's perfect," Tui insisted. "There's only one security guard and they struggle to find cleaners because people are too scared of the place. Our entrance is completely forgotten, through one of these old cellars that were used for storage—"

"Lobotomies," Nunda corrected. "They were used for conscious lobotomies. There are fingernail scratches down the walls. Still."

"I thought you didn't believe in that spooky juju?" she countered.

"My auntie was one of those cleaners who quit," Nunda whispered, having stayed unusually quiet for most of the meeting. "Said she got pushed into a cell and locked in there by a child. It was past midnight, there were no kids about. I'll be your wheels, but I'm not stepping foot in there."

Tui turned to Plummy, who crossed his arms. "I'm out. I haven't been feeling right since the last job and the more I think about it—"

"Since when do you think?" Tui's response was harsh. She didn't like the way she sounded and neither did Plummy, who held his hands up in truce. When he left the kitchen, Nunda followed. Tui was left alone, glaring at the bin. Angrily she pushed her chair back, grabbing the piece of paper long buried. Unwrapping it, she wasn't sure why she needed to look at Te Kohe's illustration. Some fluid has seeped into the paper, warping it further so that it appeared like an insidious oil spill as the grey and white and black shades rolled together. No line. She tossed it back in the bin, jumping as she spun around to find her brother watching her from the top of the stairs.

"Your toxic trait is you think ghosts can't get you because you're Indigenous," he signed.

She laughed, appreciating the joke because it lightened her mood in the moment. Only when Nunda pulled around at the rear of the South Australian Film Corporation building several nights later did it occur to Tui that her brother had never cracked a smile. It wasn't a joke to him. The rumble of the engine puttered rhythmically, a *grack grack grack grack*. Tui shook her head slightly, trying to ditch the memory of the knocks from her mind. She was strung out, stressed, pressed, that's all it was. She'd been hearing the knocks everywhere.

"Circle back in thirty," she told Nunda, sliding out of the van. Forward motion would leave little room for fear. At least that's what she told herself as she cut through the dark, dressed like the night itself in all black. The strategically placed lights at the base of the building did their best to make the looming structure feel more inviting, but it was a failure. It looked like the kind of asylum drawn in the pages of a comic book, with three wide storeys spanning the length of a football field. To complete the look was a clocktower that shot up from the middle of the structure like a blade.

Her spine was ice, but Tui didn't stop. She paused briefly to confirm the one, lone security guard was at his well-lit station watching whatever free-to-air crap played on the television at two in the morning. He was. It wasn't lost on Tui that he choose to man the reception desk, the brightest and lightest spot in the old asylum and the one closest to the exit. She moved around the back, closer to the empty studios where they'd shot movies Te Kohe loved and Tui tolerated. There was a huge iron fence there, a card reader displaying a red light that would usually be green during the day. Red meant the building was in overnight lockdown, all cleaners and other tenants having emptied out for the evening.

A viable security pass wouldn't have been that hard to obtain—i.e. steal—but what was the point? She deftly scaled the long, iron bars with the grip pads of her gloves providing the extra assist she needed and took several seconds to stretch herself over the sharp edges. This spot was out of the range of any cameras and she was able slide down to the courtyard on the other side easily enough. Tui eyeballed the lock set within the wooden door, reaching into her kit to grab a feeler pick and double ball rake. Switching on her headlamp, she listened carefully 'for the clicks that would indicate the lock was successfully picked.

Click, click, click, click.

Don't think about it, she told herself as the door popped open faster than she expected. *Don't think about it,* she repeated as the digital alarm began counting down from ten seconds. She only heard the first four, naturally, as she quickly snipped the power wire.

Beep, beep, beep, beep.

Shutting the door behind her, she watched the seconds tick by on her wristwatch until they hit two minutes. She reconnected the alarm. It was a hard reset. No alerts. Everything would look and appear perfectly normal. A long hallway stretched out in front of her, the ceiling arching in unusual shapes that began to disorient her as Tui moved through the building. This place was a mirror of itself, a true labyrinth that she'd studied in theory but walking between the walls was something else entirely. She knew the lights were rigged to motion sensors and they should have snapped on as she moved, but they didn't. An incidental assist? She wondered. There were footsteps behind her and she froze, but so did they. It wasn't a man's shoe, it was the sharp *clack* of a high heel against a hard floor. When it didn't continue, Tui decided to. *There must be someone else here,* she reasoned, but the *clack clack clack clack* was faint as it faded away in the opposite direction. The question of who would be working in their office in the wee hours of the morning in high heels should have concerned her more than it did, but she was focused on the crime at hand.

She paused, re-examining the map she'd made for herself and comparing it against where she guessed she was. Right. Then two lefts. She'd be one stairwell away from where she needed to be. Yet somewhere on that route, she got disorientated again. It was something that never happened to her, but there she was: spun around and turned about in one of the Corporation's disused corridors. Film posters and boxes were stacked on top of each other, raw concrete floors exposed underneath as doors sat open at precisely one metre apart. No, not doors. Cells.

This place was illuminated by synthetic light coming through huge, rectangular windows that cast unnerving shadows against the hollow doorways. It was a bad place. Tui could feel it clearly now, although maybe she always had and just ignored it. The end of the hallway was an impenetrable blackness and she pressed her back against the wooden door she had just come through, comforted by the solid shape behind her.

BANG.

She jumped, the cell door furthest from her slamming shut. Tui stared, silent, open-mouthed, willing it to be… the wind? A gust that was just as unlikely to exist here as it was in Dunluce Castle? A cleaner she had overlooked?

BANG.

The next cell door violently snapped back. Locking. Secure. Permanent.

BANG.

Tui was fumbling at the door handle now, desperate and scrambling to get out of there but unable to take her eyes off the cells behind her as the fourth clanged shut.

BANG.

She screamed as the wood of the door she was trying to get through vibrated, throwing herself backwards as four unmistakable and deafening knocks rung out.

KNOCK, KNOCK, KNOCK, KNOCK.

She saw a shadow moving against the door frame, something illuminated on the other side through the crack in the door. Tui scuttled away on all fours, flipping over as she stumbled into a sprint. She streaked along the corridor, towards the inky black. There was nowhere else to go. She knew in the core of her being – just like she knew tonight had been a mistake – that she needed to get as far away from the knocks as she could.

An invitation.

The movements of her brother's warning danced in front of her vision as she pumped her arms, willing her body to move faster. Four knocks banged against each cell door as she raced past, her breaths coming out in frantic sobs.

KNOCK, KNOCK, KNOCK, KNOCK.

Her lungs burned as she took the stairs upwards, leading away from the sound, not knowing where she was going but chasing as much distance as she could put between herself and the invited. Bursting into a tiny, circular room that smelled like pigeon shit, she slammed the door shut behind her. There was a slab of rotting wood nearby and Tui shoved it with all her might, using it to block the one entrance she'd come through. There was a huge window behind her and above, an even larger circular one. She slammed her hands over her ears, trying to block out the deafening sound as she looked up at it.

TICK, TICK, TICK, TICK.

"No," she whispered, feeling the heavy steps reverberating up towards her, closer and closer.

DUNT, DUNT, DUNT, DUNT.

"No!" Tui screamed, watching as the wood shuddered against the door.

KNOCK, KNOCK, KNOCK, KNOCK.

She dashed towards the only exit left to her, sprinting at the window. Tui couldn't have been more than a storey up at most, she was certain of it. And she was certain that if she didn't escape the knocks behind her, something worse than death waited. Te Kohe was right, he was always right. She scrunched her eyes shut as she smashed through the glass, shards cutting her skin as she tried to remember what it was that had driven her to this gig, this building, this city in the first place.

The cold night air stung her cuts, but it was a second of blissful relief as Tui felt herself soar. She went to curl her body into a ball so she could roll into as much of the impact as possible, land in a bush or hard on the dirt ground outside. Te Kohe was going to be so smug when she recounted this –

"Ack!"

The hard iron pierced her body in several spots all at once, the height of the clocktower from which she'd leapt doing most of the work as gravity forced her flesh down the bars like a human kebab. Tui barely made a sound as she died, the life dripping out from her as blood snaked down the gate she'd so deftly negotiated only seconds earlier. Or was it minutes? Hours? It was a windless night, but the locked iron gate slid apart easily enough as it banged open and shut in her final moments.

Clang, clang, clang, clang.

Ghost Gun

JOHN F D TAFF

THE TRITEST WAY TO OPEN A STORY IS TO SAY "I AWOKE IN A DARK ROOM."

Well I ain't a writer, so I awoke in a dark room.

I was disoriented and sweaty. What had roused me? I felt *so* tired. Another late night in another shit bar, getting liquored up with some floozy I wouldn't toss a nickel to if it were daylight.

I reached over, expecting to find curled warmth next to mine, but the bed was empty. I fumbled on the side of the bed, but there was no nightstand, no lamp to turn on. I musta knocked it over coming into the room last night. Or during our drunken escapades, because I still thought I'd ended the evening with *someone*. She must have left earlier. Probably felt the same way I did when she saw me in the morning.

I yawned, stretched. Damn, that felt good, felt right. I did it some more, then swung my legs over the bed, put my feet on the cold floor. Still groggy, I stood, tried to decide which direction to move. I thought the bathroom should be first after a night of drinking. Who knew what kind of greasy food I'd eaten, either before the alcohol started or after? Hamburgers or meatloaf or maybe steak and eggs. I thought a good shit would be in order to start the day right.

Trouble is, I felt neither. My bladder wasn't full, nor my bowels.

I stood there, seriously thinking I'd shit the bed and that was why the girl had left. Wondering what to do next.

When the door opened.

I jumped, feeling naked and exposed, with no idea where the nightstand with my gun in the top drawer was.

"Here," said the man-shape backlit in the doorway.

This obviously wasn't my apartment. That missing broad musta slipped something into my drink to get me here. Wherever *here* was.

He threw a parcel that struck me in the chest, fell to the floor.

"Put those on and come downstairs. He wants to talk to you."

Where was I? And who the hell was *he*?

The shape flipped a light switch, closed the door.

In the light, I noticed I really had been naked and exposed. The parcel at my feet was a leather suit bag. I picked it up, put it onto the unrumpled bed, unzipped it. Inside, I found a pair of shoes, socks, and underwear. A nice dress shirt, tie, and a three-piece worsted-wool pinstripe grey suit.

My clothes. Atop the hangers the clothes hung from was a rumpled grey fedora, a little worse for wear having been smashed inside the bag.

There was no mirror in the room, but I tied the tie as I'd learned as a boy, cinched it tight against my neck. The vest, then the suit coat, then the hat. Even without a shower, I felt refreshed, energized. The clothing smelled newly laundered, but still retained a memory of some cologne. *My* cologne, I knew. Some fancy shit a lady had bought for me after a particularly trying escapade. Expensive. I treated it like liquid gold, applied it sparingly. But it had soaked into my clothes, my very soul.

The door opened again.

"Good, you're dressed. He's wondering what's taking so long."

I nodded when what I wanted to say was *Tell whoever it is to hold their water*. I still wondered where I was, who was asking for me. But I figured all that would come out in the wash, so I followed the guy out the door and down a long hall hung with garish art and framed photos of fat, smiling faces captured at various moments—eating, vacationing, dancing. Children with the same fat, smiling faces.

We went down a broad, marble staircase to a terrazzo-floored foyer, crossed back under the stairs, through the center of the house—bright and airy and utterly unlike the décor I'd seen upstairs—out to a sunny veranda at the back of the house.

A pool, a big one, reflected the clear blue of the sky. No one swam there, no fat smiling kids, no children's toys.

Under a canopy, there was a single round table set with four chairs. The day was breezy and warm-cool the way some mornings here are, with the false coolness of night giving way to the true heat of day.

At that table sat a man in a silken robe, the flaps of which fluttered in the breeze. He wore house shoes and a cravat at the open throat of his robe, and I instantly knew I disliked him, though I couldn't quite place his face.

Why was I here?

"Well, well, well," he said, returning his dainty coffee cup to the saucer set before him. "It's about time. Were you gonna sleep all day?"

"Whatever's going on here, I don't appreciate being awakened by one of your goons. I don't appreciate doping me or whatever it is you did to get me here. I should say, though, thanks for the twenty-four-hour laundry service. My clothes smell daisy fresh."

The man smiled. I saw him roll his eyes at the escort behind me.

"Mick here thinks we slipped him a micky." He chuckled, sent him away with a tiny wave of one hand.

Mick? Was that me? I instantly hated that name. I also instantly realized I had no idea *what* my name was. Whatever they'd slipped into my drink last night had packed a punch.

"Can I get you anything?" he said, offering a seat at the table. There were two folded newspapers atop a silver tray, a carafe of what looked like grapefruit juice, another of coffee. A half-eaten croissant was on the guy's plate.

"Just coffee maybe…and a few aspirin," I said. "I feel as if I should have a headache. Or I'm about to."

The man nodded to a server I hadn't seen, standing in the corner of the pavilion.

"And bring me a less dainty cup of coffee," I shouted after him.

"You never change, I'll give you that," the man said.

"How's that?"

"The snide comments, the disrespect. It's entertaining, really, after all these years."

"All these years, huh?" I said, reaching behind the carafes to the fruit bowl there and grabbing a clutch of grapes. "Excuse me, but who exactly are you? You look familiar, but I can't place the face exactly."

"I'm saddened you don't remember me," the man replied just as the server returned. He set a large, clunky ceramic mug in front of me, motioned to the cream and sugar on the table, then disappeared just as efficiently as he'd appeared.

"You're Sid Carmichael," I said, pouring cream into my ridiculous mug of coffee, rattling the spoon as I stirred it in. "Big Sid. Though you look better than I remember. Younger. Thinner. You been hitting the gym?"

The man smiled. "Let's just go with Sid why don't we?"

"Big Sid," I said, thinking back to just who he was. "Been a while."

"You have no idea."

"Why am I here, Sid?" I popped a grape in mouth, chewed, washed it down with a swig of the best coffee I'd ever tasted.

Sid watched me with a kind of morbid curiosity. "You might regret that."

"What? This coffee is amazing. And the grapes."

"Let's just say the way I got you here will make all that a little difficult on your stomach."

"Wait, you *did* slip something into my drink last night. Why not just call and ask? Why complicate things?"

Sid smiled. Seemed all his smiles were thin, too. I wondered who the fat-faced family pictured in the hallway were. Sid was thin as a nun.

"Because you're complicated, Mick. Always have been. But I need you, so you're here. Let's dispense with all that and get down to brass tacks."

Again. My name. Mick. Mick what?

"Sounds good to me. Hey, I'm suddenly famished. Can you have your people rustle me up something more substantial than a croissant and fruit?"

I wanted to buy time to get my head straight. And I really was famished.

Sighing, Sid motioned to the kid, who jogged away to bring me breakfast.

So, the start-of-the-day shit I was anticipating when I got out of bed that morning?

Yeah, well it happened after about four bites of the best omelette I'd ever had, with peppers and onions. Big Sid, smiling as always, directed me to a downstairs bathroom, to which I literally raced with the napkin still tucked into my lap.

It all came out in a stream, left me breathless but feeling better. Like the gentleman I am, I flushed without looking, washed my hands with rose-scented soap, and returned to the table.

"Everything copacetic?" he asked on my return.

"Yeah," I said, conspicuously pushing the plate with the omelette and fruit away and taking a long drink from a glass of water that had appeared in my absence. I drained the contents, refreshingly cold, thunked it empty onto the table.

"I guess you brought me here for something more than to take a shit in your very nice bathroom."

"I did," he said, rocking back in his chair. He eyed me for a moment, measuring me in some way. When he came to a decision, he motioned slightly, and the invisible man appeared again, this time with a folder thick with papers.

Lots of paper receipts, pages from accounting ledgers, financial stuff I found hard to follow, so I nodded sagely as I leafed through them.

Some pictures. A dame. Nice-looking, smartly dressed. Big Sid must've liked her because he'd popped for color photos.

"The woman is Catherine Woodman. A bunch of my money is invested in her business," Sid said, watching me closely. "Kinda think she's been skimming a little here and there, sending it off to private accounts."

"Why involve me? Fire her and be done with it."

"Not that simple. I can't, for an entire host of reasons too boring to get into. I'm not even one hundred percent sure it's her."

"That's where I come in, I suppose."

"Yep."

"I should tell you, financial stuff is not my thing. Never did well in math at school."

"You don't need to pore over papers or even do math. Just do your thing, get close to her. Figure her out. Figure out if she's the one."

"And when I do?"

Sid said nothing, remained motionless.

The invisible man appeared at his back, proffered a wooden chest about the size of a cigar box. Highly polished, its woodgrain sparkling like the pool. He lifted the cover, and Sid waved a hand.

Inside, nestled in dark navy crushed velvet, was a gun. A thirty-eight. Made entirely of glass.

Everything looked so different in the light of day. So bright and shining. I was finding it hard to focus. The streets were crowded with people, with cars, taxis, delivery trucks. Steam hissed from grates embedded in the street and the sidewalks. Everything seemed so clean.

I did most of my business at night, so was unfamiliar with the city under the direct glare of the sun. Everything seemed too bright, too loud, too chaotic. Maybe that was whatever they'd slipped me last night, still playing havoc in my system.

I told the driver Big Sid had provided to take me to the corner of 11th and McPherson, on the fringes of downtown. I needed someplace familiar to get my bearings.

There was a bar there I frequented, with the forgettable name of Pat's Place. I told the driver to park or circle or whatever while I ducked in. He was a big slab of beef, poured into a dark suit and crammed behind the wheel of the car. I suspected he was less a driver and more of a minder. He glowered at me, but eventually pulled over. I got out of Big Sid's sleek black car, ducked into the bar, whose door was wide open onto the sidewalk.

Inside, it was dark and cool. Smelled of cigarettes, spilled beer, and old wood. A quiet pool table, a few circular chairs, unfamiliar music blaring from a small radio behind the bar. A thin man with ridiculously long hair eyed me as I approached. He was wearing a t-shirt and a pair of dungarees. I was ridiculously overdressed.

I leaned against the bar, pushed my hat up.

"Where's the prom?" he asked.

"Ain't you a gas?" I said. "Johnny around?"

"No one here by that name."

"How about Marty?"

The man frowned. "Marty DeSalles? You kidding? He's been dead since Nixon was president."

Dead? Who the fuck was Nixon?

"I'm looking for two things. A drink and a guy who *knows* things."

The bartender chuckled. "You for real, man?"

"Real? Yeah, of course I'm for real."

"Well, you're *in* a bar. What do you want to drink?"

"Something that won't strip the paint off a car. You know, some real illegal, off-the-books, good stuff."

He shook his head, plunked a glass onto the bar, tipped a bottle of amber liquid into the glass. I took it, sniffed. It smelled pleasantly of burnt caramel and smoke. I sipped it, and it was mellow all the way to the center of my bones.

"Wow, that's some good hooch."

"Well, you said you wanted the good stuff. Now what else?"

"I need to talk to someone who knows things. Know anyone to fill that bill?"

"Yeah, how about me? I know shit."

I pulled a folded sheet from my pocket, slid it across the table.

"You know this girl?"

The man turned the paper around, then turned it back to face me.

"No."

"Thought you said you knew things."

"I know plenty, just not some rando girl on a piece of paper."

I flashed a sheaf of money in his direction.

He saw the money, smiled.

"I might know a little more, sure."

"I thought you might."

"Looks like she works for Luminescent Tech, downtown on Walnut. Probably find her over there, nine-to-five, unless she's working from home these days."

I made a note of that. Might be a call girl, too.

"But Luminescent, man. I'd stay away from them. Bad news, man. Bad news."

"How so?"

"Strange shit for a tech company. At least that's the rumor around the 'net these days."

"The what?"

"Internet. You know. All the social media sites, Reddit. That kind of stuff."

I thanked him, flicked money across the bar at him, downed the rest of my drink, went to leave.

"Thanks…I guess," I heard him say as I stepped back out into the light.

Amazing what ten dollars can buy.

I'd never seen anything like the building I stood in. Mr. Gorilla, my driver, had dropped me off, told me he'd be nearby when I was ready.

The lobby was open and airy, the ceilings at least two stories up. Elaborate woodwork and gleaming marble. Huge pendant light fixtures. Whoever built this pile had a stack of cash, that was for sure.

I went to the bank of elevators, doors of burnished brass reflecting the doors of the other elevators across the corridor, creating a strange, gold-colored illusion of infinity. A directory on the wall listed Luminescent Technologies LLC on the sixteenth floor, Suite 100.

An elevator door opened, and I went in on a wave of other people, some curiously dressed, especially the ladies. Very casual, very sexy, which seemed odd in a business setting. But what did I know? I'd never worked a desk job, pushing pencils around, watching the clock.

The elevator car had no operator, which was fine, but it zoomed from floor to floor, moving so fast it unnerved me.

When sixteen arrived, the doors swooshed open, and I was in the lobby of a business. A reception desk dominated the space, a wide arc of wood with a pert blond perched inside like a bird in a cage.

I watched my elevator companions flash badges as they walked past the receptionist, and she smiled as she acknowledged them. I thought about why I was here, what I was supposed to do, how to achieve it.

I felt in my jacket pocket, my hand bumping the cold grip of the gun in its shoulder holster. I found a pack of cigarettes—Lucky Strikes!—and a box of matches from a barely remembered place called The Lion's Den. I knocked out a cigarette, perched it on my lips as I fumbled with the matches.

Struck, I smelled the comforting smells of sulfur and burning tobacco, and I inhaled greedily as I stowed the pack and the book back in my pocket.

I leaned against the wall, trying to appear inconspicuous, dragging the butt, when I heard someone distinctly clearing their voice.

The cute receptionist glared at me, her face twisted as if I were kicking a puppy or slapping a kid.

"You can't do *that* in here," she said, her lips as tight as a noose.

"Loiter?"

"No. *That.* You're not allowed to smoke in the building."

"Oh," I said, wondering at the daintiness of a place that didn't allow smoking. "Alright."

I looked around for an ashtray or garbage can, couldn't find one. So, I pinched the end of the butt, burned my fingers a bit, slid the rest of it into the other suit pocket.

"Can I help you with something?" she said, now clearly irritated.

I went to her, put my hands on the cool swipe of wood surrounding her. She leaned back in her chair a little at my encroachment of her space.

"Yeah, I'm here to see Catherine Woodman."

She appeared skeptical. "Is she expecting you?"

I played a hunch. "Yeah, I believe she is."

The doubting Thomas touched some buttons on her elaborate phone set up. "Excuse me, Ms. Woodman, but there's a man here to see you. Yes, ma'am. His name is…"

She put her hand over her headpiece. "What's your name?"

That stopped me for a minute. I had to drag around in some dusty places in my memory, stalled me even more.

"Michael Riley," I said. I remembered most people called me Mick. Big Sid had. I hated that diminutive.

She repeated my name and there was another pause, but this time it wasn't me.

I could hear a faint voice on the connection, telling the receptionist what to do. She furrowed her brow a little, but ended the call with a "Yes, Ms. Woodman."

The receptionist let out a little blat of air. "Someone will be out soon to escort you. You can take a seat over then until they arrive. Is there anything I can get you in the meantime?"

I slumped into an overstuffed couch the color of window putty, thought about what I'd make this woman get me. "Just water, if you have it."

She reached under her desk, and I wondered what the hell she was doing. One hand instinctively went for the gun tucked away under my suit, gripped its smooth, glass handle.

Coming up with a bottle, she placed it on the lip of the desk.

I rose, took the bottle. It was cold and had a picture of a snow-capped mountain on its label. Water. I twisted the cap, took a long, refreshing drink, sat again.

Minutes went by, a lot of them. When I was beginning to think she might have hoofed it out a back door, down into that glorious lobby, and out into the blinding sunlight, a severe young woman appeared. She was pencil thin, hair pulled back, black clothes. No jewelry.

She contemplated me with the veneered look of someone trying to be polite to someone she clearly didn't give a shit about.

"Mr. Riley? If you'll come with me."

I stood, drained the rest of the water, put the bottle on the desk of the receptionist who whisked it away like a pesky fly.

The escort led me around a rabbit's maze of offices, some just small cubicles not much bigger than a drugstore phone booth. People darted here and there. Nothing that I saw made any sense, what the people were doing or wearing. The little panels they sat in front of, typing away. The sounds, the glare of the lights. I began to think all this might *not* be the aftereffects of some drugs at all. But I pushed that thought aside for the time being. It had to be the drugs. Because if it wasn't, that just left reality as the answer. And I wasn't prepared to deal with that.

Around another corner, and the corridor ended in a wooden door. There was an engraved placard at eye level: Catherine Woodman, COO.

I had no idea what the *COO* meant, but the prim woman knocked on the door, opened it. "Mr. Riley to see you, ma'am."

I pushed past her into an office that, frankly, took my breath away. Windows on two sides, floor to ceiling, showing an awesome view of the city skyline, lots of blue skies and clouds reflecting in the broad swath of the lake.

The office itself was as airy as the lobby, high, coffered ceilings, bookcases covered the wall opposite the windows, blonde furniture sat on delicate legs seemingly too thin to support much weight.

"Please come in, Mr. Riley," said the lady rising from behind a large, plain desk, completely open to the floor. I saw a few wires and a fantastic set of legs.

"Take a seat. Did they offer any refreshments? Coffee, tea, water? Or did you just want to get to killing me?"

That stopped me on the way to sitting in a low chair with a decorative blanket as insubstantial as the furniture's legs thrown over it. "Excuse me?"

"That is what you're here for. Correct?"

I stared at her, words unwilling to spill past my suddenly frozen lips.

"Come, Mr. Riley. I have a busy schedule today. If you're going to murder me, let's get to it."

She came around to stand near me. She was all blonde hair and legs and curves, and I had trouble reconciling all that with what I was sent here to do.

"Let me help you," she sighed. "Sonny Carmichael sent you. Wanted you to kill me. Probably gave you an unusual weapon. A slithering knife or a diamond-crusted garrote."

I shook my head, as much to gain some clarity as to say no.

"Big Sid sent me," I said, trying to figure out why I was telling her this, why I was being honest with her. What the hell was I doing? This was a simple job, and I was fucking it up. Royally. This was clearly going to get me a snug hole six feet down.

"Big Sid?" she said, laughing. "Oh you poor man. Where'd he dig you up, anyway? The first Big Sid has been dead for nearly ninety years. In fact, his son, also called Big Sid, has been dead for fifty years. *His* son, also called Big Sid, because why not, has Alzheimer's, so *his* son, curiously not named Big Sid, is currently running things. His name is Sonny. Sonny Carmichael. He sent you."

She sat on the couch opposite, stared at me.

"How do you...how do you know all that?"

"You really have no idea, don't you?" she asked, leaning in to me. "Nothing about what you must have seen on the way over, the people, the cars for chrissake. Nothing struck you as strange?"

"It all strikes me as strange, sure," I shrugged, hiding the fact this all had indeed bothered me. "But who cares? I guess this city cleans up well for the light of day."

She sat back, giggled. "And how...how does he want you to do it? To kill me?"

I reached in and brought the gun from out of my shoulder holster.

It gleamed in the bright light of the office, showing hazy, carnival glass images of the place in its crystalline shape.

"Ahh, the Transparent Gun, I see," she said. "I'll give him this, he's classy. That's an expensive weapon, hard to get. I guess I should be flattered he's willing to use it on me."

"Why? Why you? What'd you do to him?"

"What's this Scooby-Doo shit? You want me to regale you with my devious plan before you paint the room with my brains?"

I didn't get the reference, and that stymied me again.

"Oh, you poor man. You have no idea, do you?"

"About what?"

"Being dead."

I blinked a few times, felt my gut rumble with the water and whisky sloshing inside it. "*Dead*? What're you talking about?"

"You're some dead gumshoe the Carmichael family keeps on its payroll. Probably died sometime in the Roaring Twenties, from the look of you. But they kept you on ice, used some pretty hardcore rituals to keep you here, tethered, ready for them to use. And no one could finger you or trace you because you're dead. Not even a print in AIFIS or any DNA on record. Crafty motherfuckers."

"I have no idea, darling, what you're talking about."

"Well, of course you don't, you poor thing. Out of time, caught between life and death. I can see the spell, the caul wrapped around you like a twisted aura, all purples and blues, like you're at the center of some bruise in reality. You've got to feel it. You don't feel it?"

"You got something to drink in this fancy office?" I asked, more to change the subject. She unfurled her beautiful frame to her feet. I kept the glass sight of the gun trained on her as she did.

"You do feel it. Charming."

She drifted across the carpet to a shelf, which she opened onto a small bar. Two highball glasses, a generous pour from an unfamiliar squat bottle. She carried both back, handed one to me, reclaimed her position on the couch.

No ice, no water. This was a woman I could love. The stuff was mellow, like sinking into a comfortable bed.

"What is this?"

"Patron. You've never heard of it. Tequila. After your time."

I squinted at the pale, buttery liquid, took another swig.

"Whatever this is, whenever this is, I'm liking it."

"Well, then, I'd best inform you when you complete the task Sonny sent you to do, it's all over for you. Back to sleepy time until he needs you again. And who knows how long that'll be. A year? Ten? A century? You're like a family heirloom, a sword handed down through generations. How's that feel?"

It didn't feel great, though it was hard to get my head around what she was saying. It made sense. It didn't make sense. It was the drugs. It wasn't the drugs. My head ached from all this.

"I have a daughter," came out, and I almost put my hand over my mouth to trap the words, like some ditzy dame.

"I'm sorry, she's likely dead," Catherine offered, her sincerity striking. "Grandchildren perhaps."

I took another swig.

"How would you recommend I solve this problem?"

She shifted on the couch, drained her drink, set the glass gently onto a nearby table.

"Well, the only way to break the *geas* is to kill him."

"Excuse me…the what?"

"The spell. He's ensorcelled you."

"What are you? A fucking witch or something?"

"Well, kind of. I'm a data cruncher. We stumbled onto the fact spells and almost all magic are a basic rundown of the right things in the right order—words, ingredients, manipulations. Programmed into our computers, we can easily access exactly what we need a spell to do."

"And where'd a gamook like Big Si—Carmichael learn that?"

"From our firm. Luminescent Technologies. Look, the stooge's great grandfather stumbled onto something, an artifact, probably stolen. He wanted it deciphered. We worked on it for fifty years before we cracked the code. Once we did, it opened a whole new world, a way to control certain aspects of it. We built this company off that. Sure, we develop security software, but just to bring in cash to support our real efforts."

I considered all that, or at least as much as I understood, set my own empty glass next to hers. Maybe it was the spell that caused all my mental fog, not a drug at all?

"He still has this…artifact?"

She nodded enthusiastically.

"Then it seems to me my job is to kill him and retrieve it."

Her smile was incandescent with sincerity.

"You mean *our* job."

I walked through the lobby of the building to the revolving exit doors. Early evening sunlight slanted between the skyscrapers, gilding the edges of the buildings, the cars. Standing on the corner waiting for my ride, I felt a renewed sense of purpose, but not a greater appreciation for what was going on.

This wasn't *my* world, even though it was my city. And it wasn't just whatever spell I was under. Things had changed. People had changed. The job had changed. But Catherine made me feel as if there was a new life for me here, a new sense of purpose.

Mr. Gorilla showed up with the car. It purred to a stop, and he rolled the window down.

"I ain't getting out to open the door for ya, so just get in," he said.

I climbed in, closed the door behind me.

"He's anxious to hear back from you," he said, rolling the window up and pulling out into traffic. "Did you finish the job?"

"I'm finished with his job, yes," I said, slumping in the seat.

"What the fuck does that mean?"

"You can ask him after I finish talking to him."

Traffic was lousy, so it took a while to get all the way out to Big Sid's... *Carmichael's* place.

I lowered my hat over my eyes and feigned napping, my hand curled around the handle of the gun nestled against my side.

As the car approached the mansion, Mr. Gorilla entered a code into some kind of device, and the ornate steel gates parted like angel wings. He steered the car down the long, straight driveway leading to a roundabout in front of the main house, looping under a portico.

No grand entrance through the front door for me. No, we circled to the side of the house, to what I guess was the service entrance. All the better.

Mr. Gorilla parked the car, turned the engine off.

"Get out," he said, fumbling with the keys.

I slid the gun from my suit, placed its barrel against the back of the driver's seat. I didn't exactly know what to expect. I mean, sure, it was a gun, but it was a *glass* gun.

Bracing myself for the deafening report of a .38 in the close confines of a car, I was surprised when the thing made a slight, tinkling sound, like bangles jingling in some fancy chandelier.

The bullet, glass, too, I assumed, punched through the seat, through Mr. Gorilla's remarkably thick torso, through the dash, the engine compartment, and out of the car. For all I know, it's still ripping through trees and underbrush on its way to Wisconsin or who knew where.

Mr. Gorilla turned to me, surprise on his face.

"Well, fuck you, too," he said, then spit some blood, and collapsed against the steering wheel. I was relieved he didn't set off the horn.

I exited the car, which had begun to smell like copper pennies and day-old beef, crept toward the house, gun held before me like a dog on a leash. I didn't know how many bullets I had left, but I knew it was probably no more than four or five rounds.

I hoped Carmichael's men were having a late dinner.

The back door was firmly locked with some device where the doorknob was. I twisted and grunted, but the door wouldn't budge. I thought briefly of shooting the thing, but that would deplete my slim supply of bullets.

Sighing, I returned to the car, searched Mr. Gorilla's very heavy, very bleeding body. He had a sleek little pistol I borrowed. In his jacket pocket, he had a small rectangle of plastic with a black strip on one side, a ribbon looped through it.

A little loose change, a lighter, some chewing gum, his wallet. That was it, aside from the single car key still in the ignition.

This little card must gain access to the door.

I went back to it, stared for a moment, going through various plans of action. Finally, I settled on swiping the card through the narrow slot on the door device. After several attempts, there was a satisfying click, and the door popped open.

A small antechamber with another door on the opposite side. A series of cubbyholes along both walls, with coat hangers and shelves, what looked like shoe storage underneath, and a narrow bench in front of each locker. A bin to one side held what looked like tiny hair nets. Couldn't figure out what they were.

I pushed open the other door and found myself in an unadorned hallway lit by sconces. Pausing here, I fished from my pocket the coin Catherine had given me. One side bore all sorts of unrecognizable symbols, the other a star within a star within a star, circled in a kind of text I couldn't read.

The Seal of Solomon, Catherine had told me. A powerful talisman that would allow me to penetrate any of Carmichael's defensive wards.

"I designed all of his defenses, set all the wards in place," she'd told me. "But there are times you might need a backdoor. This is my backdoor."

I rubbed the coin between my fingers, felt the inscriptions ripple under my touch. A little unnerving, but whatever.

I slipped it back into my pocket, went quietly down the hallway.

It led to a huge foyer, all marble with columns and statues of ladies with upswept hair wearing togas and spilling water from enormous urns. Tall, crushed sky-blue velvet curtains fell over the windows, and an enormous crystal chandelier dangled from the high ceiling.

Refreshing to know the family still had no taste.

The house was all dark and quiet. It couldn't have been too much later than eight p.m. The Carmichaels must turn in early.

I could see two huge magillas standing outside the front door. Obviously, they hadn't expected anyone to get inside from the backdoor. Eying them cautiously, I crept up the marble stairs, careful of the sound of my footfalls.

Get rid of him, she'd said. *It's the only way both of us get to live. If he's dead, I'm safe. If he's dead, he can't hold you any longer.*

I still didn't really understand what was going on. Was I really dead? Did he somehow keep me on ice until he needed me? If that was so, where was I when I wasn't creeping around with a gun for him? Purgatory?

That thought made the little Catholic hairs on the back of my neck stand up. I thought of being an altar boy long, long ago. All the stories I'd learned in parish school.

You know, when I grew up, I always knew I'd go to hell for the things I'd done. The yucks I'd murdered. The dames I'd strangled. The families I'd left to mourn, to carry on.

Somehow, though, the thought I was caught in limbo between Heaven and Hell, well, that seemed worse. Seemed unfinished, and I hated to let a job go unfinished.

The halls were decorated with a heavy, florid hand, like I was stuck in an opera. I half-expected some fat, Viking clad broad to burst out of one of the doorways screeching some ball-shattering song. I dunno, would have been interesting at least.

The household was quiet as a mouse. Catherine told me his bedroom was at the end of the hallway on the second floor, two enormous iron doors barring entrance.

The doors are the sum of his protection, the things he relies upon most to keep him safe.

Standing before them, I couldn't tell if they were ancient, burned wood or cast iron, or maybe something different. Twisted human shapes writhed across their surface, and at the top, split at the seam where the doors met, the image of a huge, spiraling shape rising from ocean waves.

Like an octopus grafted onto the torso of a human, but with many, oh so many more arms. These writhed around it, some reaching down to shatter the earth, others uplifted to snuff out the stars.

I almost lost my nerve there. Never seen anything like that, never contemplated anything like it. More than the graven images there, though, the door exuded something, gave off a strange feeling, like a humming I could feel across my skin, down through my pores and into my veins.

It felt electrical, but also greasy, like when you fry bacon and the rendered fat of it hangs in the air. It felt dangerous. It felt *wrong*.

Catherine had said the coin would allow the doors to open for me, and they did. I didn't have to do anything but grab their enormous handles and push.

The room behind the door was enormous, almost a dancehall ballroom. A few pieces of furniture scattered almost indiscriminately; two low, plush chairs, a loveseat with clothes thrown over its back. There were shoes scattered everywhere, like a department store had exploded.

The room had a weird smell, too, off-putting. I'd stood on the beach up near Boston once or twice, and it smelled like that now. Salty with a background tang of fish and watery rot.

A huge bed at the back of the room attempted to dominate the space. It was an imposing four-poster, easily the size of two king mattresses pushed together. The posts held a canopy over the bed, with bunting hanging from it.

I crept closer, saw there was a dark bulk under the satin covers of the bed. In the darkness of the room, the shape seemed odd, though. Too bulky even for Big Sid… I mean Sonny Carmichael.

Too many limbs.

I tiptoed to the bed, silent across the deep pile carpet. I'd stood over many men in many beds. Sounds weird, I know. But there was none of that. Getting them in their beds made my job easier. And their deaths.

Only people who lost out in this arrangement were those who had to clean up the messes I made.

I lowered the glass gun, the barrel sight twinkling like a falling star.

The shape in the bed squirmed, seemed to gather itself under the covers, and I froze as it rose, the bedclothes falling away.

"You here to kill me, Mick? She send you?"

Shit. He wanted to talk. I wanted some answers to what was going on, so I let him.

"Yeah," I said.

"She's playing you. You know that, right?"

"Could be. Broads do that when they want something. And they always want something."

"How'd you get in anyway?"

"Seal of Solomon."

"I meant how'd you get in to see *her*? She's like the fucking Wizard of Oz. No one sees her no how."

"I walked in. Can we just get through this?"

The thing moved over the bed to me, and I recoiled, grabbed at the bunting over the bed to steady me. It was thick and wet, and that sea odor rolled off it when I touched it.

It wasn't cloth but streamers of seaweed.

And he was not a man.

In the dark, it was hard to see where the shadows ended and the… thing began. Its head was grotesquely large and swollen and it pulsed a little, quivered when it spoke. But it was the arms that made my skin crawl. So, so many of them, all weaving back and forth around its head.

"What the hell are you anyway? You're certainly not Sonny Carmichael."

It laughed, a squelchy, liquid noise like a drowning man.

"I certainly *am* Sonny Carmichael. And Sid Carmichael III. And Sid Carmichael Jr. And Sid Carmichael Sr. And so many, many more."

Well, that made no sense at all, and I told him so.

"I'm also the bar at the door, the lock on the gate. I prevent what you want kept out from getting in. Understand?"

"Nope."

"Well, Catherine Woodman does. She understands. That's why she sent you to kill me with that same damned gun I gave you to kill her."

"Why'd you want her dead? And why does she want to return the favor?"

"Because she wants the door open. She wants *it* in."

"Who?"

That laugh again.

"A thing so ancient its name is meaningless."

"Try me."

He coughed out a string of consonants, and he was right. Meaningless.

"If you do this thing, it gets in. It destroys everything, this entire world. Reality."

I shook my head to clear the greasy sheen left behind by the nonsense name he'd uttered. "And if she dies?"

"If she dies, I continue to keep it at bay."

"What happens to me?"

"You? Well, you stay safe. You return."

"I return where?"

"Mick—"

I ended the sentence myself with a few gunshots. They boomed in the room, struck the writhing thing. I watched it deflate into the bed, like a melted scoop of ice cream. When it was over, it was reduced to a puddle in the middle of a tangle of sodden sheets.

Something dripped from the edge of the mattress onto the floor, and I stepped away.

"I hate that name."

I went around to the nightstand, found the phone there, dialed the number she'd given me.

"Is it done?" she asked, just the slightest quaver in her voice, as if she couldn't believe what she was about to hear."

"He's…it's dead."

"Are you sure?"

"He's nothing but a puddle on the mattress."

There was a sharp intake of breath, a great sigh.

"Where's this artifact thing?"

"Oh, don't worry about that now," she said, a bit airily for my taste.

"What about me? What happens now?" I asked.

"You? Well, darling, you're too valuable to give up. You get to sleep for a while. Then, we'll discuss your future."

She whispered a few words into the phone, and it was like the end of a movie, when the projector stops flickering and the screen goes dark.

Everything was pink.

I realized I was seeing the sun through my closed eyelids.

I opened them, closed them almost immediately. The sun was insistent, and I shaded my eyes from it. The salt smell from the sea was overwhelming, and for a moment I feared I was back in that bed, back with the seaweed and that thing. But the smell was overlaid with coconut, and the glass in my hand with its frothy, creamy drink was ice cold.

I almost dropped it, expecting to see that gun in my grip, its transparent shape jutting from my hand.

"Wha…where's it at? Where?"

"You're awake," came a voice, feminine. "Finally."

I turned, expecting to see Catherine, but it wasn't her. She looked familiar but very much younger. "Who the fuck are you? Where are we?"

The sun was so bright, the air crisp and clean. I shielded my eyes, could see the horizon was a shifting line of greys and blues.

"We're on my yacht, the *Herself*."

"And you are?"

"Miriam," she said, brushing a strand of hair from her forehead. "Miriam Woodman."

"Catherine… is your mother."

She nodded, much of her face shielded by oversized sunglasses.

"Where is she?" I asked, expecting to see her, long legs in some French cut swimsuit, elegantly holding a drink.

"Mom? She died a few years back. You really don't know, do you? I mean, where you are, *when* you are."

Those words sounded damnably familiar. "What...," I asked, fumbling for words. "...do you want from me?"

"Got a job, something I need your skills for."

I sighed, set the drink onto a small table between us. I noticed I wasn't wearing a three-piece, just swimming trunks. My hand, which had been going to my shoulder holster, changed course to the table the drink occupied.

"What are you looking for?" she asked.

"The gun," I said. "The ghost gun."

"Oh honey, I thought you understood at least that much. She lied to you long ago. They've all lied to you. That silly glass pea shooter *wasn't* the ghost gun."

She turned, wriggling her tight, tanned flesh as she reached over to touch my chest.

"You are."

Spool

DAN RABARTS

I FOUND HER THERE, CURLING INTO HERSELF, WINDING DOWN TOWARDS THAT terrible, final conclusion. The same outcome I had seen long before and from which, so I thought at the time, I'd had the wisdom to hide. But truths cannot be hidden forever. They rage, they scream, they beat against their walls and their chains. They shine, like souls burning in the dark.

But I'm getting ahead of myself. There is a time and a place for beginnings, for the outermost point of the spiral before it winds inexorably inward, or perhaps the innermost point before it spools out to infinity.

"The further you take the calculations, the more they start to break down," she said.

We were in the decrepit old house the mathematics department had allocated to obscure points of study like ours. The buildings had been bought by the University five years earlier, in 1922, and refurbished into classrooms and library nooks, though the place never lost the sense of what it used to be. The walls oozed the stale odour of its unsavoury past, madness leaching through the plaster, down corridors where despair lay like dust across the worn floorboards. Before the war, it had been an asylum for outcasts, madmen, savants. A decade ago, the shell-shocked returning from the godawful nightmare of mud and trenches and piled corpses that had been the Western Front had been nursed here, and the walls still heard their dismal screams. The weight of history bowed the eaves, made crooked the lines of stair and lintel, remembering those horrors and the madness of those who had ended their days here before that. The creak of ancient timbers echoed choked voices.

Maybe she heard those voices, like I once had. Those echoes folded down upon themselves and never quite fell silent. I had learned to ignore them, to play the role of dutiful mathematics professor, teaching bright young talents in the art of higher arithmetic, for there is little as pure or as perfect as the concurrence of numbers, how they roll across each other, feed upon each other. How they begin as problems, and once posed, demand to be resolved. Like music demands to be made complete. So too is the mathematical discipline an art requiring inspiration, creativity, dedication, sacrifice.

How much sacrifice, I could never have calculated.

Magdalena was my protégée, the protégée I had never wished for. She had a true scholar's intellect and inquisitiveness, and she consumed my every lesson like a candle burns wax. Every day she arrived with more questions, boring deeper into the fundamental rock of mathematical science, seeking not just solutions but the layers beneath the numbers, the foundations of existence, all hidden in numeric secrecy.

"The numbers don't lie," I would tell her, knowing this for a half-truth. They may not lie, but they can certainly deceive. They can suggest truths which are not there, and thus we fail to quantify the actuality beneath. So we entertain the illusion of our enlightenment, rather than suffer our ignorance.

I'll never know if Magdalena saw the mistruths in the calculations for what they were, or judged them for her own errors, or simply felt the wrongness of them, just as the oppressiveness of the old house weighed upon her, but never was she satisfied. Had I been thirty years younger, and thrice more self-assured, and somewhat more handsome than my greying years allowed, I may have found other ways to distract her from her course. Sadly, the cruder path of romance was not an option, with its convenient blindness, its willing acceptance of imperfection which afflicts those fated to the idylls of love. No, the best I could do was guide her progress, and in so doing attempt to misdirect her from that which I had nearly fallen into. Would that it had been so simple. But she was so much stronger than I. Her will to persevere was second only to her demands for perfection.

Besides, on the matter of romance, I do not believe Magdalena would ever have looked at me with so much as a sparkle in her eye, even had I been an oil magnate or a star of the moving pictures, for in that regard her attentions belonged to Reginald Davinius, rising star of the University's Conservatory of Music, something of a virtuoso on all manner of stringed instruments as well as a talented composer. His *Concerto for Viola and Cello in G Minor* had drawn praise in drawing rooms from London to Vienna to Paris, and his future seemed predestined. Personally I did not care for the piece's dissonant descents, its shrill crescendos, and the obtuse silences which were characteristic of his work.

Perhaps, if not for Davinius, my Magdalena would never have fallen so far. Because if there is one thing worse than a perfectionist, it is two perfectionists in love. Worse again is perfection harnessed to genius, and when the energy this synchronicity creates takes on its own life. Which was, of course, the crux of the problem.

A stronger man than I would've made these calculations sooner, extrapolated the end result, and taken action at a point when something might still have been achieved. When something might have been saved. But I did not find my strength until it was too late, when the spiral had turned too far to cycle back.

"They are calling this mechanics," she said to me that day, when the clouds glowered down and the timbers groaned around us. "But numbers are not mechanical. Mechanisms are defined by numbers, yes, but they are fixed, inflexible, dependent on their functions and parameters. To suggest a mathematical theory is a mechanism is ignorant at best and arrogant at worst."

"They use the term broadly." I tried to appease her, concerned then with how close she trod to the precipice of madness I had once walked. "An imperfect use of an insufficient language to capture a sense of what quantum theory means."

Quantum theory. It was *la mode du jour* among scholars in many fields, this idea that beneath the measurable physical world lay another, more complex set of laws which did not obey those we had previously observed. The implications for the realms of physical science and astronomy were beguiling; the ramifications for higher mathematics were potentially more extreme. Concepts that risked unwinding centuries of learning; these false truths concealing unseen laws beneath. What Watson and Crick had begun by unravelling the genetic code, and Einstein with his fatal elucidation of the relativity of light to mass to space had continued, all flew in the face of Newtonian absolutist mathematics. I had read Max Born's paper when it was published in 1924, building on the work of Bohr and Planck and others, and it had sent a cold knife through my belly. All these visionaries suggested the deeper you look, the more complex the universe becomes. All life, all existence, all experience, could be calculated and codified to exponentially greater degrees of complexity. Rather than breaking down the components of the universe to their smallest possible building blocks, the maths only turned on itself and became infinitely more complex. The spiral turning in, only to spool out again, infinitely. To pursue the problems thus presented warped into deeper, darker arguments, with no answers in sight, every solution exposing more unknowns.

"They are numbers," she insisted. "They cannot defy calculation simply because we do not have the language to qualify them."

"And yet," I said, as rain obliterated itself against the windowpanes, "here we are."

My turning point, for all that it came too late, was at the concert hall. As Magdalena had no family in London, it was my pleasure to accompany her to the Royal Prince Albert Concert Hall to listen to the premiere of Davinius' newest abomination of scale and melody, being performed by the London Philharmonic. A musical atrocity with an unpronounceable name which the intelligentsia and social elite were anticipating as the *avant garde*, the very cutting edge of modern composition. If not for the company, I could not wait for it to be over.

Dressed to the nines, we swirled in with the milling masses and made our way to the reserved gallery box from whence we would experience this new aural travesty, and made polite conversation as was suitable for a young student and her elder teacher. This was, for me, the most pleasant part of the evening, though all the while a decided cloak of unease lay upon me, as if that which was to come would throw my world into darkness. The fear that nothing I knew would ever be the same again.

The lights dimmed and the conductor, Davinius himself, stepped onto the podium to uproarious applause. The violins trilled to life, quavering across an ominous chord like rain threatening on the horizon, then were joined by the thunder of the kettle drums, and the scraping of violas in bright harsh rips that broke against my ears like sheet lightning. Thus was the storm unleashed. I glanced at the programme:

Der Untergang
The Downfall

Clearly, Davinius fancied himself something of a Wagner, evolved. So *this* was the *magnum opus* Magdalena had been so excited by these past months, when not buried in the intricacies of quantum mathematics. Barely thirty, and the lad had the world at his feet for scoring music that set the teeth on edge; music of which I, inexplicably, wished to hear more. It was like watching a ship burning on the harbour, dreading the hopeless screams of those caught in the blaze yet unable to intervene, unable to look away as the wreckage slips beneath the slick black water, all the while fearing the darkness, the silence, that will follow.

Magdalena leaned into the awful rise and fall of the strings, the drone of the brass. Moved with it like it carried her somewhere. Her fingers twitched as if yearning to play those strings and her eyes fluttered, more closed than open, her lips slightly parted in an ecstasy only music could bring. She did not fight this, like she fought numbers. She lost herself in it. Watching her, something like hope turned brittle and cold in my breast, and broke. I was her mentor, not her suitor, yet I had lost her. The anger was unexpected, inappropriate, inarticulate. I interlaced my fingers and donned my most sincere mask of appreciation, continuing to take in the performance as the first movement became the second, became the third, and then silence before the opening bars of the fourth broke across the auditorium like a storm surge lashing a seawall.

Suddenly Magdalena sat upright, her fingers gripping the balustrade, her eyes open in a look I knew too well: Epiphany. She turned to me, eyes searching mine, mouth opening and closing as she searched this crude, insufficient language for words it did not contain. Behind it all, the violinists drew their bows across their strings while they slid their fingers down the fingerboard, a minor descent like a cat's howl falling away, wave upon wave, one bank of strings after another, an echoing slide into despair, a spiralling descent twisting into shadow. Like our calculations, turning ever in and upon themselves, diminishing with every cycle but suggesting something darker, more vast lurking beneath.

"The numbers are not absolute," she breathed, and though I did not hear her words over the discordant spiral of cellos echoing the cries of the violins, I saw them well enough. Knew them. For I had said them myself.

Magdalena grabbed my hands, leaned close to me. "Listen to the notes, how they don't step, they slide. Between each step, an infinity of notes, all *there*, all pressed up against each other, but sound is numbers. It can be measured, frequency and decibels. Keep breaking it down, it's still just numbers. But it's not, at the same time. Because when you run it all together, it *changes*. It becomes inconstant. It becomes fluid. That's why it's not right to call it mechanical. Numbers are a flux, and all the systems we use numbers to measure are fundamentally flawed because we treat them as rigid. Do you see?"

I knew exactly what she meant, and where it would lead her. I did not look away from her face, so full of the fervour of discovery. Such a tragically beautiful moment, like the flare of that half-imagined, burning ship on an unforgiving sea. I knew then what I would have to do, were I to have any chance of pulling her from the wreckage.

We joined Davinius and the orchestra in the reception hall after the performance, sipping champagne and exchanging pleasantries, congratulations, and the rest. I made rather an effort to ingratiate myself to this architect of cacophony, ostensibly for Magdalena's sake but in truth to serve my own ends. It was merely a calculation, an expression in the equation towards the solution I had mentally plotted. A variable to weight the odds in my favour. Davinius was a gregarious fellow with a quick wit and a generous smile, not at all the moody type his aesthetic mores suggested. I shook his hand and we conversed amiably for a suitably polite stretch of minutes before I excused myself, stepping aside so Magdalena might have some hint of a private moment with her suitor. I drifted in an ever-widening circle away from the eye of the storm, quelling the emotions that threatened to ripple outward through this algorithm and all its unknowns.

Shortly thereafter, I escorted Magdalena through the London night, back to the boarding house operated by the University where young women living abroad stayed while conducting their studies. As we walked, we talked, or to be precise, *she* talked. Of the collision of science and nature and mathematics, of how for everything in existence there was a measurement, and within each system of measurement existed further layers, and of how those systems pulse and ebb like the tide, or the beat of a heart. How these systems are like music, carried along by that pulse, always shifting, never the same. Of how we are fools to pursue an understanding of mathematics as absolute when clearly the fundamental structure of archaic numeracy fails to capture the infinite complexity that lies between every decimal point, no matter how far out towards infinity we quantify our degrees of accuracy. Because, if there is an infinity of space between every whole number, then mathematics as we understand it must necessarily collapse under the weight of its own over-simplicity. This Magdalena espoused with a delight that smacked of zealotry. I could not dissuade her from it, hoping the final calculations were beyond her prowess, yet doubting it. But I would deal with that by other means.

Bidding her a good night's rest, I turned and retraced my steps through the gloom of London's fog and the sporadic pools of light thrown by the gas lamps, until I reached the alley behind the Royal Albert and spied the dim glow of an electric bulb above the stage entrance. There, I sank into a pool of shadow and waited. I had not misjudged my quarry's egotism nor his ability to revel in the praise of his peers, while partaking of the good spirits of celebration, both literal and figurative. For sure enough, as Big Ben tolled half past eleven, Davinius and several of his entourage stumbled from the door in the height of good cheer. There was much carousing and slapping of backs as all and sundry bade each other farewell. They dispersed, and I trailed after, taking care not to be seen, until at last Davinius walked alone. I knew he would, for Magdalena had spoken of his penchant for long strolls along the Thames after dark, seeking inspiration.

I caught him up, hurrying to meet his stride, and was pleased when he recognised me and greeted me with a wolfish grin. "Professor," he beamed. "Lovely evening for a stroll, isn't it?"

"Indeed," I agreed, though the fog threw everything into murk.

"You have quite a dedicated student in Magdalena," he went on. "She speaks very highly of you and this journey of discovery upon which she has embarked." He waved his hands around in a manner at once vague and yet full of meaning, as though he still brandished the conductor's baton.

I nodded. "I could not agree more. So few have both the desire and the aptitude to learn as she does. To an old man like me, she is a thing of rare beauty."

Davinius' smile grew even hungrier. "As she is to a young man like me." His eyebrows waggled in a manner I found most unbecoming. The fog grew colder around us. We had reached a point equidistant between two gas lamps, where the shadows lay deepest, as the Thames sluiced the stone dock below. A place I had walked many times in both the light of day and on nights cold and still and clear. I knew it well, even cloaked as it was by fog. When I pushed, I judged where best to apply my weight and motion to his mass so his momentum would carry him over the stone railing and send him in a curving arc, headfirst, toward the intersection of pier and river. His cry of surprise was muffled by the fog, but I clearly heard the crack of his skull meeting stone, and the soft sucking plop of the river taking his body under her care.

I walked on.

I had calculated grief. When he never arrived home, when he didn't show at the conservatory or in any of his usual haunts, there was distraction, and worry. Fear, in small doses. But Magdalena, constantly and doggedly optimistic, refused to entertain the notion that anything untoward or indeed sinister may have befallen Davinius. He was wont to indulge in liquor but not to excess, so it was more likely he had found a pub near the river to his liking where he had been struck by the urge to compose, and where he was even now scribbling furiously as the day waned, unaware his presence would soon be required at the concert hall. She clung to this, and buried herself in her equations, driven by the previous night's epiphany.

"Everything," she declared, waving her fountain pen, "right down to the functions of life itself, the process of death, everything in between. If only I could simplify the variables into a base formula, then the totality of life could be condensed into a core algorithm, from which anything could be extrapolated. But that formula must account for the flux variable, which is defined by the science and within these each subscience, each discipline. This, my dear professor, could be revolutionary."

She turned her notebook to face me, so I might assay her notations. "I've nearly got it, but something's not quite fitting. What am I missing?"

I looked at the string of numbers, variables and symbols. She was right. She was painfully close. I could see the void in her work. It would come to her soon enough. My ploy to derail her may have come too late.

A knock at the door. It echoed through the old house like the hammering of coffin nails.

There was nothing to suggest foul play, the constable said. It appeared Master Davinius had been walking alongside the Thames and had slipped on wet cobbles, hitting his head before going into the river. He was probably unconscious when he drowned, though the blow to his head may have killed him first. All this the constable recounted while Magdalena sat, unblinking, in the drawing room. Mingled dread and satisfaction washed through me as the officer explained how no witness had come forward, that Davinius was last seen walking alone, he had been drinking, and there was no evidence of a struggle. He still had his possessions, including his billfold, suggesting it had not been a robbery. A slip, a fall. A tragic accident.

For a long time after the constable left, Magdalena sat, wringing her hands, staring at the floor. Here was the grief I had counted on. Here, to my great shame, was the breaking of the spirit. The snuffing of the light. The echo of those lost voices susurrated through the walls, pain and grief and madness brought to life by the soughing of wind through the timbers. I waited for her to buckle. I had seen how the breaking of a heart could ruin a mind and, however abhorrent, this was a fate more merciful than that which waited if she solved the infinity equation.

"I..." she said at last, "I need to walk." She scooped up her books and pens and fled into the long late afternoon shadows. The windows clattered with mocking laughter as she slammed the door. Yet there my calculations failed me, or perhaps failed her, for I had never predicted what Magdalena would do next.

Grief is a powerful thing. Perhaps too powerful. I always said she was stronger than me. I tried to break her, but I failed. Or, to be clear, I didn't break her the way she needed to be broken.

It was much later that evening as I was checking over the old house in preparation to retire to my humble room on the top storey when there came a knocking. It was the constable, looking rather more haggard and harried than when he had visited earlier. He queried me upon Magdalena's whereabouts, for she had not arrived at the boarding house and the matron feared for her wellbeing. I confessed to not having seen her since she departed this very doorway, and in that instant I too feared my student may have come to harm, perhaps by her own hand. Inwardly, I withered. If this were so, I would bear the guilt for all the long turning of my days. Yet I pressed the constable for what more he knew, upon offer of tea to drive back night's chill embrace. Somewhat reluctantly, he advised there had been a break-in at the mortuary.

The body of Reginald Davinius was missing.

The Chief Inspector now questioned if the disappearances of Magdalena and Davinius' body might be related. The old house banged and clattered dully, though there was little breeze and the river fog lay thick upon the dark.

His visit proving fruitless, the constable trudged away, vanishing quickly into the gloom. Agitated, I closed and bolted the door, the many unseen presences of the old house sighing their questions, prodding me back towards that madness I had once defied.

Magdalena missing, and Davinius' body gone! I returned to the drawing room and paced, hands clenched tight behind my back.

Had Magdalena indeed stolen his body? To what end? Surely she didn't think...?

There came again the banging of a shutter in a wind, nearby. Yet there *was* no wind. Uplifting a hurricane lantern, I moved through the dark hallways, shadows weaving by me like devils out a-haunting, until I came to the back door. Beyond lay the small cluttered yard that backed onto the river, its gate ajar. Gingerly I stepped onto the stairs, sweeping the lantern's pale luminescence about. I was halfway down the steps before I noticed the cellar door, unbarred, as it rose and fell, a little, then a lot, the source of the odd clattering. It pulsed, like someone was lifting it, letting it fall...or as if the house itself drew breath, and exhaled. The old house, with its secrets and its ghosts and its madness.

Trembling, I descended the stairs and stood for a long time—too long, I fear—watching the wooden doors lift and fall, the chill of the unholy wind pulsing up from the bowels of the building, down there among the dust and bones. Down among all the detritus of old years, so much furniture and dross laid to store in case it may one day be needed, but truly just forgotten. From through those doors, from inside that seething maw, came the sounds I dreaded. A voice reciting numbers and formulae, and the scratching of chalk on a blackboard.

Before my courage could flee me altogether, I hauled open the cellar doors and descended, choking on the dread of what I would find below. The chill wind pulsed against my skin, and in it I could taste... uncertainty. Possibility. Probability.

A foreign yet familiar taste, recalling another time, my own moment of clarity, when the shrouds concealing the workings of the machine had fallen away and I had seen...*it*.

The door at the foot of the stair stood ajar, banging against the wall with each flow and ebb of the breeze, and overlaid upon the creak of wind and timber and the precise numeric recitations worming into my ears was *music*. Notes sliding and scaling and falling, reverberating in my skull as if they reached me from somewhere vastly distant yet simultaneously originating inside me. This music had no melody, only tone, the song capturing both the great empty wastes between the stars and the seismic clash of breaking atoms. I was once again hearing the fabled music of the spheres.

My plan had turned against me, like a snake biting its own tail. Some people crumple under pressure, while others thrive and find greater inner strength when faced with ruin and devastation. I was the crumpling sort. Magdalena was not. Davinius' death had merely driven her over the brink of discovery, inspired her with bloody resolution. I had fuelled her final descent.

Magdalena had cleared a space in the centre of the cellar, around which stood blackboards all covered in chalk scrawls. On the floor, Davinius' body, pale, bloated, the side of his head a bloody crushed mess. His hands lay folded across his chest and his eyes were shut, as if laid out for viewing by the bereaved. Magdalena knelt at his feet, eyes half-lidded, swaying gently. She did not see me. She was looking far beyond something as insignificant as a withered man cowering in the cellar of a decrepit house. In one hand she held a piece of chalk; in the other, Davinius' baton. She moved like she was at once conducting an unseen orchestra while writing on an invisible blackboard.

Actual blackboards formed a pentagon around the dead body. When I looked directly at the complex weave of symbols they were static, but in the corner of my eye the numbers shifted and changed, flowing. Solid but unstable. All in flux. Scanning the writing, I saw it.

Fixed in the centre of a tight cluster of letters, numbers, parentheses, and algebraic symbols on each of the five boards was a character, a spiral loop that turned outwards from itself or, perhaps, sluiced inwards like a whirlpool. The divine integer; the *spool*, as I had dubbed it. That number which defined rationalisation because it was all numbers at once; it was zero and infinity and negative infinity and every possible point in between. The number that was the engine that drove the universe, Alpha and Omega. Every time I looked from board to board the numbers had changed, though I did not see them move. The spool could never be observed, could never be measured, not rationalised. Only the unhinged could grasp its portent; broken minds like mine, like Magdalena's.

I looked back at the girl who had cracked the infinity equation. Her clothes hung off her in bloody, filthy layers, the consequence of ghosting Davinius' cold corpse down the river and into our cellar. For what purpose?

At last, Magdalena saw me, her pale eyes flaring in the lantern-light, deep and dark and haunted. "You see?" she whispered, her voice sharp as the cold wind that swirled around us. "There is flux in the core of everything. I just needed to open my eyes to see it."

"Magdalena," I mumbled, edging closer, uncertain how I could stop what she had started. "You must forget this. Nothing good can come of unlocking this secret."

"They told me," she hissed. "They told me it was there to be found, if I but had the courage."

"This is not bravery," I said, my voice unexpectedly harsh. "This is madness."

Her gaze hardened. "They told me you knew. That you were keeping the truth from me. That you *lied*."

I recoiled, knowing who she referred to. The voices in the roof, in the walls, in our heads. "I never lied to you," I said, "but nor did I tell you, because this has the power to unravel the fabric of space and time. The spool is the thread that stitches everything together, keeping everything in constant motion. It is the heartbeat of the universe, and it hangs in a balance so fine that even to look upon it has the potential for ruin." The wind caressed me, and it smelled of birth and decay.

"I have calculated this with considerable accuracy," she breathed, equal parts perfection and insanity. "I can control it."

"The spool cannot be controlled," I pleaded.

"Yes!" she shrieked. "I can. I will. I *have*."

Movement caught my eye, and I flicked a glance at the nearest blackboard. Had the spool character inverted? I looked from one to the next and yes, I could not deny, the spool had changed from clockwise to anticlockwise, and as I shifted my gaze, that symbol seemed to spiral, twisting like a vortex, drawing me in. The bitter wind turned and rushed back into the cellar, the doors booming shut, blowing hot and sour and falling to where, I knew not.

Magdalena swayed in time with the soaring tones of the spheres, which had taken on a discordant, howling air. I stumbled back, preparing to flee from this portal which was opening for all I knew unto hell itself, when something wrapped around my ankle.

Davinius' dead hand had clamped hard around my leg, his pale bloody eyes shining as his lips cracked into the hollow wolfish grin I had last seen moments before I sent him plunging to his death. The voice that cracked from his throat, however, was not that of the murdered composer. Rather it was layer upon layer of the voices of the mad who had perished within these walls, all falling over each other in an endless, twisting echo. "Welcome back, Professor," they cried. "We've waited for you so very, very long."

I wrenched my foot away, falling, sending one of the blackboards toppling. As I gathered myself Davinius arose, looming over me, Magdalena at his side. The hot wind whipped at their ragged garments amid a discordant symphony, music and voices shrieking, the resonance of infinity grinding down.

I cowered. Magdalena touched her dead lover's cheek, turning his face towards her. "So tell me, darling," she said. "How did you die?"

I scrambled backwards, but they did not turn on me. It was revenge enough to see me, a man of merit exposed for the common street criminal and murderer I was, reduced to a quivering wretch. She had unravelled the universe to find her answer. She had claimed her victory, and now it would claim her, claim all of us. Perhaps, were I a stronger man, I might have told her why I had no choice but to do what I did, because the consequences of failure were not an acceptable sum. But she was beyond reason. She was spinning now, locked in the spool, whirling out of control into the chaos she had unleashed, Davinius turning with her.

Behind me, the music swelled. I had to find a way to undo the equation. Somewhere, over the screech of hellish choirs, a bell tolled midnight. The roof, the upper stories, and the floor of the old building tore apart, whirling into the sky in a shriek of splintered timber, leaving only a gaping wound of walls and the basement itself. Shards and splinters and tattered books rained down upon us. The stars arced overhead, rushing closer, filling the night with their cold blaze.

This was what the voices trapped in the walls had whispered in my dreams. To know the unknowable; to quantify that which defies all counting and rationale, is to undo the threads of the universe. At last, I knew why they had never let me be, why they had whispered to Magdalena and twisted her so. I heard their cries, saw them as blades of light that lanced out, spiralled into darkness and were gone, while the universe threatened to break apart at the seams. Those ghosts had been trapped for so long, and were willing to destroy our world to end their own suffering.

This was all my doing. My fear, my jealousy. My desire, my pride. Perhaps I had simply feared that Magdalena would indeed succeed where I had failed, that she would be capable of controlling the spool like I had not. Perhaps I had only seen the negative space of that infinite number, where she saw both sides, the spiral in and the spiral out. The mathematics and the music. She understood, where I had not, that both sides of the spiral are the same scale. Descent and ascent.

It may have been too late to save myself, too late to undo what I had done, but I did not have to let the world die for the sake of an old man's shame.

The lovers, reunited, whirled in their falling spiral dance, leaving this forgotten killer to the same fate as the collapsing reality falling upon

London. I found a hunk of broken chalk, dragged myself towards the fallen blackboard. My head burned with the sheer effort of seeing the numbers move on the edges of my vision. The spool spun hypnotically within a maddening sea of numbers, but it would not take much to break it.

Like that most low-brow of all artists, the street urchin who scrawls names and slogans on city walls in stolen paint, I defaced the eternal spiral into a static, meaningless smear of chalk, starting at the end of the spiral, bisecting the whorled loop to connect the tip to the tail. What remained looked like nothing less than a nautilus shell bitten in twain by a hungering cephalopod. Something once living, now dead.

Like Davinius. Like the ghosts in the walls. Like my soul, or Magdalena's soaring spirit.

The singing of the spheres diminished, the stars burned less brightly. The numbers ceased their devilish dance. I could still taste hell on my tongue, for the damage was done, but perhaps this might be enough to save the rest of eternity. Snatching up a shard of broken glass, I placed the edge against the soft flesh of my palm, that scholar's hand, that killer's hand, and cut deep. Blood welled, bringing pain and a wave of terror, as I twisted the edge in my skin, marking myself with the spool.

As the blood ran down my arm and soaked my sleeves, I pushed my mutilated palm into the blackboard, where the spool should be. The mechanics of the universe rushed through me, a madness so utterly divine no mortal could survive their revelation. In that moment I felt my body perish even as my mind broke free. I willed the spool to turn back upon itself, to close the hellish gate it had opened, making myself a part of the equation.

London was now elsewhere, and Magdalena would be, once again, alone, her love torn cruelly from her arms back into the death's eternal prison. She may try again. She had the knowledge, the power, the passion. But I would be here, waiting. A voice, a bad dream, trapped within the remains of these walls and the streets of this festering city, holding tight to the secrets of the spool.

Here, the spiral would end.

She Sleeps, nor Dreams, but Ever Dwells

CYNTHIA PELAYO

She sleeps, nor dreams, but ever dwells.

I THINK OF THOSE WORDS OFTEN WHEN I PASS A CROSSROADS, TRAIN STATION, or the lakefront. I wondered for a long time why were these the points they appeared, the lake front, connecting streets, train platforms and terminals at O'Hare International and Midway Airport. It took years, but once the answer was given to me, I almost felt silly that I did not discover it on my own much sooner. Some things are not meant to be understood. Some things just are, no matter how brutal the crime.

After I retired as the Chief Medical Examiner of Cook County it felt like the right thing to do, to tattoo those very words beneath my collar bone. This was the very place where they had the same words inked. I did it so that I could be reminded each time that I look in the mirror of what I allowed myself to keep secret.

She sleeps, nor dreams, but ever dwells.

I knew I could never forget them. Even if I wanted to ignore what had happened so long ago, it's impossible. They're everywhere now, moving carefully to their destination in order to live. They first appeared here in Chicago, and I was one of the very first people to be blessed by the presence of their beautiful death.

One sometimes wonders how do we right a wrong? How can we undo and erase injustice? There are crimes which sit at the top of our collective consciousness. Acts so heinous and vile that we often wonder how can another human being calmly jab, cut, slice, thrust, disassemble and ultimately obliterate another? I thought of this for a long time, because for much of my life that is what was often brought to me, battered and broken bodies. Humans as puzzle pieces.

My job was to rationally examine this postmortem existence, to determine not just the cause but the manner of their death. It's difficult to comprehend what miracles we humans are, the biological processes it takes to create life, to sustain life, and support life. We are all walking mysteries.

She sleeps, nor dreams, but ever dwells.

The first one reminded me of Sleeping Beauty. She was perfectly positioned, flat on her back and her hands folded just beneath her breasts. She wore a white dress made of dreamy layers of chiffon. She looked ethereal, airy, as if she was floating there on the prairie grass surrounded by bright milkweeds, blazing stars flowers and wild quinines.

Those words tumbled from my lips as a breeze from Lake Michigan just a few yards away joined us and blew strands of her golden hair across her eyes, "Sleeping Beauty." So beautiful that even the expanse of water behind us wanted to kiss her beatific face.

All of them were found in a similar condition and position. All of them were dressed in flowing and delicate gowns with their hands folded, their feet bare, and their eyes closed.

It was as if they glowed in the moonlight, and that's when we found them all, always at night. The sleeping beauties were not found together, but appeared across the decade, one by one. Officially they were Jane Doe numbers one through ten, but unofficially, they were named after the princess who fell into a death sleep caused by a curse.

There was the Sleeping Beauty of Northerly Island, a man-made stretch of land with a view of silver and steel skyscrapers on one side and Lake Michigan extending into what seemed like forever on the other side. Another was named Sleeping Beauty of Clark and Lake, her corpse found resting and serene on the Blue Line platform heading West. There was Sleeping Beauty of Milwaukee and Armitage Avenue, Devon and Western Avenue, Stony Island and South Chicago Avenue, Cicero and 127th Street and more.

I had never seen faces so serene, and at peace. I know now it was something else, not peace. In that grip of death and in the magic of their beauty, the threads of revenge were born.

Our tenth Sleeping Beauty marked the beginning of the end of so much. I named her the Sleeping Beauty of 31st Street Beach, and that day remains with me, etched into the very fabric of my being.

It was 2010, and our killer returned to the lake where it all began. When my phone rang in the late night, I knew I would need to get dressed and to the morgue quickly. The call however asked that I arrive first to the scene to analyze the corpse there. When I asked for more detail, I was told by the official that I would know what to expect only when I looked at the body.

It was then I knew another beauty had appeared.

We gazed in silence out there on the lakefront, our flashlights pointed downward trying to rationalize how a woman so perfect, without a single blemish or smudge or visible injury could be there dead. I knelt to check her pulse. Her skin was cold and stiff to the touch, but as I stood and was assaulted by the strong wind pushing me back and the crash of waves just yards away, I could have sworn I saw her eyes flutter beneath her lids.

One of the uniforms stepped out of view for a few minutes and I heard the whir of the Keurig I kept around only for them. I preferred my coffee brewed in a French Press. It's more time consuming, but I preferred my brew that way because I could control the taste. They often turned to the coffee machine as a distraction, a few safe minutes to step away from the decomposing. This was uncomfortable for many of them to witness, a human being laid out and open, but I didn't care. My job was not to comfort them, but to expose what was done so that they could do their job and find who had committed this crime.

There were four of us in the autopsy room—me, two uniforms, and a homicide detective. The room was cold and sterile. Freshly cleaned metal and white plastic gleamed around us. It smelled of disinfectant solution. New latex gloves and surgical equipment had been laid out for my next steps.

It was early and quiet otherwise. Early morning or late night? At this hour it felt as if we existed in an in-between thin place where anything could be possible.

"That's the tattoo they all have then?" Detective Cortez observed.

I adjusted my glasses. "That's the very one." I watched as eyebrows arched around the room.

Officer Liu was still beside the Keurig, blowing over the top of a mug while his partner stood near the table. I could tell from the corner of my eye Officer Torres was the type to not want to make it known she was nervous. She would shift her body weight from one leg to the other. Cross and uncross her arms, not knowing what to do with her own form as she gazed upon one that could not move.

I knew the look of unease on their faces. It was the same look many medical students had when they first came into contact with a body in this environment. Some people think if they know someone who died and have been to a funeral that attending an autopsy might be manageable. It's just meat on a metal table, right? No, it's not. This was someone once. They were all someone once.

Bright lights shone down on the naked body of a beautiful young woman. Her face was serene and still, while her chest cavity was open for us to gaze at all of her secrets.

Officer Torres crossed her arms once more. "And you've autopsied all of them?"

I gave a nod before continuing my duty, unraveling the cause of death. Was it homicide, suicide, an injury, caused by a hazardous substance, something else?

Detective Cortez said, "He can't keep getting away with this."

"Why do you assume it's a he?" I asked. "The killer can be anyone."

It was their job to investigate. My job here as an ME was to translate the story of the body before us. That was all. But still, they needed to understand that anyone was capable of monstrosity.

Although, this was now the tenth body I could confidently say was a

Sleeping Beauty. Ten women across ten years and in those years, there was not a single arrest or viable suspect. When asked during press conferences about the Sleeping Beauties, all law enforcement would say was: "We are investigating all leads." But what were the leads? Missing persons databases were scoured. Families checked in on loved ones. However, no one had come forward to claim any of the bodies. Of course, there were those who tried to mislead us, stating that they were a brother, sister, friend, anything, but no one could accurately describe any of the Sleeping Beauties, including their tattoo.

Officer Liu finished his coffee and joined us around the table. His color turned once again. "I heard it was from a fairy tale," he nodded toward her collarbone, and then covered his face.

"The rest room is just outside to your right," I said.

Officer Liu rubbed the back of his neck. "I'm fine. Thank you."

"It's a quote from the poem," I said as I slipped on the fresh pair of latex gloves. "Alfred Tennyson's "The Sleeping Beauty." It's the second-to-last line." They all looked surprised I knew this. It was something a simple internet search could have pulled up years ago. This should have been a part of their research and investigation when the first princess was discovered, but I was not surprised they still knew little to nothing. It was meant to be this way.

Our Sleeping Beauty's skin was smooth, blemish free, perfect. Her face, like all the others, looked like a child, but she was no child. Youthful and full of hope and purpose once. Her nails were clean, and without polish. Her hair was thick, dark and luminous and fell down her shoulders and to her waist in soft, sweeping waves. The bridge of her nose was dotted with tiny freckles that reminded me of the stars punctuating the nighttime sky. When I lifted her eyelids to confirm her eye color, black, they reminded me of the galaxies above, of black holes, impossible magic, and violence.

"What year do you think she's from?" Our detective finally asked the question we were all wondering.

"That will take me a little bit of time to confirm. We'll radiocarbon the dental enamel and that should give us a good indication of the date of birth."

Our detective's eyes moved to the dark channel that I had carved down her middle. The large opening had dried along the edges of the incision into a reddish black crust. The peels of flesh were pulled back and away and held there, exposing her insides. The organs had been removed, weighed, examined, and set aside. Her brain would soon be removed as well, but not yet.

The collection of fluids and chemical analysis were still needed, even though I knew from the previous cases nothing out of the ordinary would turn up, other than their age.

"They've only ever been found within the city limits," Officer Torres said, hands now on her hips, her head shaking side to side.

"Only in Chicago from what we know," the detective answered. "The killer could be local or not. They've been found almost every month of the year, consecutive order, from January through to her, October."

"Do you think we'll have a November next year and a December the following year?"

Detective Cortez took a deep breath. "This serial killer sure likes order. I'd imagine so."

At first, I thought it must be poison. Cyanide, arsenic, pesticides, something else. Combinations of poisons and potentially harmful substances were checked and rechecked by leading toxicologists, but nothing was discovered. The contents of their stomachs could not tell us anything as they were always empty. Besides being dead, our Sleeping Beauties were perfectly healthy women once, a long, long time ago.

"The first one I read about was born in 1960, but she was found in 2010 and her recorded physical age was 18," Officer Torres said.

Officer Liu turned to her. "How's that possible? If she was born in 1960 then she should have been 50 in 2010."

"That information is not to be shared with the public," Detective Cortez told both officers.

Officer Liu's face went blank and then he returned to the Keurig to find comfort in something that made sense, bad coffee that tasted like melted plastic.

"So, she was really born in 1960?" Officer Torres asked, once again not knowing what to do with her arms. They were behind her back now. "I thought that was just department gossip."

"I'm not staying with absolute certainty as a medical examiner that she was born in 1960. To me, physically she was a woman aged 18-24 who was found dead in Northerly Island in 2010. All that I can confirm about her date of birth is that the results of the radiocarbon analysis concluded the birth year was 1960. Obviously, I can't stand by the radiocarbon testing, because what I saw, what I autopsied was a young woman."

Officer Torres turned to me. "Are you saying the tests are all wrong?"

"I'm saying that something does not make sense. An anonymous girl has appeared every year for the past nine years, and now today this marks ten years. They have appeared throughout the city, at various major transportation sites, Union Station, O'Hare International Airport, Midway Airport, major street intersections and more. They are all dressed the same. They all appear around the age of 18. None of them are showing any signs of violence, and for all of them the cause of death has been inconclusive. It makes no sense. They make no sense."

I turned to Detective Cortez. "Do you think this will ever be solved?"

"We've checked street cameras. Searched for witnesses. Staked out various locations where we think another will appear next. We have nothing but ten bodies and seven tattooed words."

Officer Torres shifted her weight to another leg again. "Where are the others buried?"

I felt a pinch in my chest when Officer Torres asked this. No one had asked me that before. "They're buried in unmarked graves at Homewood Memorial Gardens."

"We haven't needed to exhume any of them so far," Detective Cortez added. "We have their DNA, clothing...but if there's no family to come forward, I just don't know how we can identify them."

Perhaps the real tragedy of our existence was that there were some things we had to accept that had no answers, no matter how horrific the consequences. What I did know was that this was a homicide, that I was certain, but I had no scientific or medical evidence to support it. So, I would go through my motions, required checklists and tests. Then, once the autopsy was complete, I would write another report that ended with cause of death, inconclusive.

"Why Chicago?" Officer Liu asked.

Detective Cortez shrugged. "Why not?"

I wished I could have answered that, but I remained silent, digging through a body that could not give me or them any of the answers we have seen time and time again that explained the abuse women sometimes endured before a painful death—sexual assault, domestic abuse, concussions, stab wounds, mutilation and more.

In my head I answered: *The land is taking what was killed and giving it back. What greater defiance to murder than rebirth?*

A phone began to ring. Another hour. Another murder. Detective Cortez stepped out of the room to take the call.

Beneath her breath, Officer Torres said, "If we don't catch the killer, then where's justice?"

And there was the question that should be asked. Killers were able to kill, to continue to kill, because many of them knew they could easily evade and charm their way out of the grips of handcuffs. Killers knew they could avoid detection by being nice or looking acceptable. Murderers are skilled in the art of getting away with murder, why else are there so many unsolved cases?

"Let's get going. Doctor's gotta finish her work." Detective Cortez waved the blue uniforms over.

"What will happen to the body?" Officer Liu asked on his way out.

"What always happens to the body. We will hold it for some time, and if no one comes to claim her then the county will proceed with the burial. Everything will be noted and recorded. Good luck. I hope you find the killer…"

They left. The door closed behind them with a clang, followed by a click. Automatic locking doors.

I walked over to the trash can and removed my latex gloves. I then moved over to my desk, removed my glasses and took a seat in my chair, facing her. It would happen soon, and as soon as I had that thought, I heard her fingernails rapping against the metal table beneath her.

I walked over to Sleeping Beauty's side, shushing her like a newborn baby. Letting her know that, like the others, she was safe and that all would be well.

Sleeping Beauty's eyes opened, a reanimated corpse with her chest cavity open, her organs in various containers around her. I removed the clips that exposed her insides and positioned the flaps of skin back onto her as she gasped.

"I'll get you cleaned up," I said as the eyes followed me around the room. I gathered the materials I would need to pull her back together again.

She remained silent and still as I sutured the skin together. They felt no pain, that I knew after doing this for the others.

I reached for her hand and squeezed it tight. "I'm going to get you some clothes now and things you will need."

She nodded, letting me know she understood why she returned.

In my locker I kept a bag, waiting for when another would return. It contained clothes and money, and a phone.

She dressed and as I looked at her sitting on the table, in one way dead, but in another wonderful way very much alive, I handed her the bag with all of the things she needed to start a new life.

"But first, you have to find your killer."

She nodded, and before she left, I asked her "Why do you appear at places like railroad stations, airports, intersections?"

Her voice rang like a bell. "They're access points, portals, and we all have a destination to make."

The Sleeping Beauties were murdered women who returned somehow, sprouted from the Earth, fresh and new. I could not explain why they returned, but they did. Detectives had never thought to check old unsolved murder cases, but I did, and there they all were, women who were murdered, their cases unsolved. Women who wanted first revenge, and second to live the life they deserved, before their first life was taken from them.

Later that month, another appeared, and then another. Soon they were sprouting up all across the country, like beautiful summer wildflowers beaming in the sun. It soon became clear what they were, and the guilty could not hide from something that could not be killed again.

And now, as I look at my tattoo in the mirror, "She sleeps, nor dreams, but ever dwells", I know they are what we needed, our Sleeping Beauties. For nothing dissuades a killer from killing, quite like knowing that one day their victim will rise to kill them.

Men Without Faces

J ASHLEY-SMITH

DAZ WAS MUNTED. RIGHT OFF HIS TITS. SO MUCH WHIZZ RIPPED THROUGH his system he hadn't slept in three days—now it felt like he'd never slept, would never sleep again. Things moved in the corners of his vision that weren't there when he looked. He swayed in the queue outside Romero's, half leant against Banger.

Around them, clubbers shuffled in the cold and dark. Chatter, tension, anticipation hung with plumes of breath and cigarette smoke in the autumn night. The walls of the club—a semi-industrial concrete box as charming and adorned as an electrical substation—throbbed as though some creature of bass were pounding against them. Light pooled around the entrance. Two bouncers loomed either side: a squat bald-headed ogre, wider than he was tall, and a pro-wrestler type with a blond ponytail. They ushered in a gaggle of shivering, bare-shouldered girls, who bopped and swayed as the music drew them inward. Behind Daz, the queue dissolved in writhing shadows. The orange traceries of cigarette tips hung in the air like some occult script Daz could almost read.

"Come on, mate, pull it together." Banger gave his arm a tug as the queue sidled forward. "You've got to at least *pretend* to look straight, or they'll have you in the back room with the rubber gloves on."

"You what?"

Banger laughed as Daz turned with exaggerated slowness, bulge-eyed and stuporous. "Fuck's sake, Daz. You are the original Lost Boy."

Daz glanced around, over Banger's shoulder, off into the seedy night of the club car park. His head jerked, eyes panicked.

"Where's Fallon?"

"You for real? That was only, like, five minutes ago. He fucked off, all shifty like. Thought he saw one of the Oxmoor lot. You don't remember?"

The queue took another step forward. Daz continued to scour the shadows and Banger rolled his eyes. He tipped out two cigs from his ten pack of Embassy, lit them both, passed one to Daz.

"Go on, mate. Better you have something to do with your hands or they'll know you're off it."

They stepped into the light of the doorway and Daz squinted it was so bright. The bald-headed bouncer gave them a look, gestured through the door with his thumb. Ponytail led them into the stairwell and pointed at the wall.

"You know the drill, lads."

Daz leant against the wall with his palms flat, fingers splayed. Ponytail patted him down, emptied his pockets, ran a finger along the inside of his trainers. Daz tensed. Bass thrummed from the bricks. Hi-hats clattered and echoed off the metal stairs. Patterns formed and reformed in the unpainted breezeblock.

"Alright," the bouncer grunted and nodded them up.

Daz and Banger merged with the flow of ascending ravers, stepped into the fug of dry ice, sweat and cigarette smoke. Daz felt as much as heard the music, a pounding as deep and alive as his own heartbeat and so loud it swept him up with all the force of a tidal wave. Romero's was heaving, the bar swamped, the dancefloor jammed. Banger made a drink gesture, but Daz shook his head, mouthed the word "bog" and nodded towards the toilets. Banger nodded, turned for the bar. Daz pushed through the crowd and into the Gents.

Locked in a cubicle, the walls breathed. Daz fumbled with the laces of his right trainer, tugged it off. Reaching in with two fingers, he slid out the clear plastic coin bag enclosing his last few wraps of whizz, all that was left of the ounce. He slipped them out of the bag and into his pocket.

The door to the Gents opened and music spilled in. Voices. When Daz unlocked the cubicle, two blokes were crouched over the sink, racking up lines of speed or coke. Avoiding eye contact, Daz made for the door, pulled it open and pushed into the club, right into the one person he'd hoped not to find.

Sadie grinned. Her gold tooth gleamed. She pointed at the door to the Gents and pushed Daz back through.

"You," she gestured at the blokes by the sink. "Out."

"Fuck off," said one. "Who d'you think you—"

The door opened behind Sadie and a seven-foot Yardie stooped to enter. He towered behind her.

"I said," Sadie pointed a thumb at the door, "out!"

The blokes scarpered. The Yardie chuckled. Sadie turned to Daz.

"Funny thing, bumping into you like this." Under the fluorescents, Sadie's tied-back hair was as red as a traffic light, her leather trench coat vast. The crow's feet beside her eyes tightened. "And here of all places. I can't help but feel we had an appointment this week, Darren. One that you failed to turn up for."

Daz stammered. "Sadie, I can explain."

"Save it. You made a commitment—one you have yet to deliver on. Now me, I'm a big old softy. It don't bother me none if you don't pay up when I tell you. Trouble is, it's not me you're messing around, is it?" Sadie gestured behind her to where the Yardie leant against the toilet door. "It's my boyfriend, here. And Ace and his posse don't take kindly to people—even sweet little boys like yourself—who try and do them over."

Ace yucked. Daz quivered. Sadie's look hardened.

"So why don't we just skip straight to the part where you give me the money."

It had been a mistake to get the ounce. Daz had known it even before he asked. But he was showing off, puffed with the braggadocio that possessed him every time he was around Fallon. The older boy—man, really—had a hardness about him, a coldness, that set Daz on edge, made him do dumb shit just to impress. But impress who? Banger? Fallon himself? Daz didn't know why he did it, only that it was like a seizure. He'd come round to find he'd talked himself up into something mad or dangerous or foolhardy.

They were up past dawn, pulling buckets in Banger's room, a squalid little upstairs bedsit off the Minton Road, littered with Rizla packets, unboxed mixtapes and half-roached rave flyers. Banger was Daz's oldest friend, a jug-eared goon with bushy eyebrows and puffy panda-ringed eyes, a cheeky side-grin like he'd eaten one too many French Fancies. He'd left school at sixteen, got a bedsit and an apprenticeship at the Kwik Fit tyre place in town. One year later, he had a tidy little life with a banged-up Nissan Micra and just enough from his apprenticeship to stay perpetually stoned, with maybe a little something for the weekend. Daz had been crashing at his place for months, paying his rent in weed and the occasional wrap of whizz. A spliff hung from the corner of Banger's mouth, dropped glowing blims on his baggy jeans. He hammered on the controller of a Sega Megadrive, giving beats to some thug in *Streets of Rage 2*. His eyes—like all their eyes—were wide as plates, nothing but pupil.

Fallon flamed Daz's lighter over the empty, two-litre squash bottle in the bucket, began with careful tugs to draw it upwards. The mounded clumps of hash in the tinfoil gauze embered. Grey-brown smoke roiled and thickened behind the clear plastic. He slipped the lighter into his pocket.

"Banger." Fallon nodded towards the bottle. "Time for your punishment."

Fallon was two or three years their senior—nineteen, easy—and a "*proper* criminal." Or so Banger worshipfully described him. An Irish rando Banger had picked up at some warehouse night, a refugee from the Oxmoor estate. He was scrawny and mean-looking, his eyes sunken and shrewd, missing nothing, his mouth an expressionless line. Fallon had been kipping over Banger's since that night—hiding out more like it, though from what he'd never mentioned. And when it came to Banger's bedsit, two was company and three was a fucking nightmare. Daz and Fallon were right up in each other's business, all day every day. And Fallon made him nervous, made him show off, do dumb shit like say he could get hold of an ounce of uncut speed.

Fallon gave him a look of bland disdain. "Yeah," he'd said. "Right." And gone on pulling buckets like nothing had happened.

The thing was, Daz *could* get an ounce. More, probably. And that was the problem.

Daz was still too young to claim the Jobseeker's, so he'd been making a bob or two of a weekend running whizz for Sadie at illegal warehouse dos. Sadie didn't look like much of a dealer, a middle-aged raver from Kings Lynn with tied-back hair that changed colour every other week. Turned out she had access to a near-infinite supply of the best speed on the market. The only other dealers around with speed that good were the Yardies, and Daz was too scared by far to be messing with that lot. He ran for Sadie every Saturday night, selling on her wraps to make one or two of his own. A bit of personal for him and Banger. Enough spending money for a sixteenth of sticky black and a packet of fags. It was a sweet deal. And Sadie trusted him.

She'd raised an eyebrow when he asked for the ounce. And when he asked for it on tick she sucked her teeth, gave him a look. Still, she told him a time and place to make the pickup. Gave him a deadline for the payment due.

"This is a big commitment, Darren." She never called him Daz, only Darren, just like his mum. "Don't you fail me."

Daz had nodded solemnly, made his vows. But even as the words were spilling from his mouth, his gut was churning. He knew he was going to fuck it up, that this was the biggest mistake he'd ever made in his life.

The weekend he picked up the ounce, they hadn't gone out at all. They sat up in Banger's room marvelling at the mound of gleaming, pinkish powder on the mirror on the bed. The look on Fallon's face then had been worth it. Not admiration exactly, but something like it—something less than disdain. That moment, that look, was almost better than the whizz itself. They'd had a fat line each. Then another. In amongst the powder, Daz found a rock the size of a walnut that he kept aside for personal. The whizz—pink champagne, Sadie called it—was so gorgeously pure, it seemed a shame to cut it with the glucose Fallon pinched from the Co-op across the road. By the end of the weekend, more than half the speed was gone and their eyes bulged in their heads like snooker balls. Daz hadn't sold a single wrap. Still, he had the glucose and a week to flog the rest before he had to pay up. Daz rang around, sold a wrap here, a wrap there, spent the money on cigs and strawberry Ribena and a quarter of soap bar.

Come Monday, Banger was back at the tyre yard, Daz was imagining all the wraps he was going to flog and Fallon was getting on his tits. He could feel himself building towards some other dumb shit. Come Wednesday and another O.D. of Fallon's scorn, Daz couldn't take it anymore. He necked the rock in one pop, just to wipe the look off Fallon's face.

He'd not eaten since, nor slept a wink, spent two tortured nights wired in the dark, chain-smoking and playing *Sonic the Hedgehog* while Banger and Fallon snored. That first night he'd thought he was dying, that his heart would give under the strain of its pounding, that his brain would tear itself right out of his head, or his eyes pop like crushed grapes. By the end of the second night things had calmed, but his hold on reality was untethered. He was seeing things, imagining things. Kept glancing around to catch—something that was never there. His fingers were stained yellowy-brown. He'd chewed his lips ragged.

Fallon wasn't impressed. If anything, Daz's little display had cranked up the derision to even greater heights. Fallon started actively fucking with him. Mocking him openly. And Daz was too blasted to do anything about it.

He was so wrecked, he'd skipped the meet with Sadie. Hadn't even phoned. He figured he'd make up the losses at the weekend.

He figured she'd forgive him.

"You figured *what?*" Sadie was incredulous.

Ace's monstrous fists were bunched against Daz's ribs, pushing him back and up against the tiled wall. Daz's head pressed the ceiling. He could see his legs flail in the mirror. Below him, Ace grinned, eyes twinkling.

The door to the gents opened and some bloke in a cap and glasses staggered in. He took one look at the scene on the far side of the bogs and couldn't get out again fast enough.

"Now I'm only going to say this once, Darren." Sadie's lips puckered, a mother berating wayward offspring. "Don't fuck with me. Ace don't like it. It makes him unhappy." Ace's grin widened. His knuckles dug deeper into Daz's chest. "So be a good boy and fetch what you owe."

"I don't *have* it," Daz was almost in tears. "Here. *Here*, I mean. I've got it all, and all. Just... not here. I'll get it you, I promise."

Sadie considered. "Alright," she said. "Monday. I'll give you to Monday, on account of your age and you being such a nice boy. Ace?"

Ace dropped Daz to the floor. He put his arm round Sadie's shoulder, stooped. They kissed loudly.

As they left the toilet, arm in arm, Sadie turned back to Daz. "Monday," she said, "or—" She drew a thumb across her throat. Ace yucked.

Daz lay heaped beneath the hand-dryer in a mess of wet paper towels, empty Jiffy bags and Rizla packets, the butts of unsmoked cigarettes. He lay sobbing, snot bubbling from his nose. He wanted to get up and run, but all the strength had left him. The pleasant derangement he'd arrived with, the blur of colour and sound and feeling that swaddled him like cotton wool, had been torn away the moment Ace stepped forward and lifted him against the wall. His blissed-out numbness transfigured into a kind of fractal terror, an infinite fall down a black chasm of snarling, snapping teeth.

He staggered out into the sweat and sinew of the nightclub, the clouds of cigarette smoke and dry ice now suffocatingly close. The deafening thump of the music seemed filled with interstices, abyssal spaces out of which poured mockery and laughter. All eyes were on him. Every face twisted with contempt. Over by the bar he glimpsed Fallon, his arm draped around a short bob-haired girl in a Puffa jacket. But Fallon was the last person he wanted to see. Where was Banger? All he wanted was to find Banger and get out of there, get in the car and drive. But though Daz stumbled through the crowd, he couldn't find his friend among the swimming faces.

Daz hunkered down in a dark corner beside the club's massive sound system, knees to his chest. He smoked cig after cig, desperate only for the night to end. On the dance floor, lights juddered and sprayed, ravers jerked in the zoetrope flickers of a strobe. Bottomless bass hammered like some incessant industrial machine. Shrieking lead lines warped and twisted, carving up the night. The mad play of darkness and light fed the panic that gripped his limbs, the slow-motion supernova detonating endlessly inside his skull. He was losing it, proper wigging out.

The music turned to mush, to an angry edgeless drone that seemed to emanate from deep inside him, from some vault of bottomless dark. The strobe slowed, pulsed in time with the pounding of his heart, each flash a silent still life of dancers in ecstasy, frenzy, madness. His skin crawled. The lights liquified, the crowd blurred, and the darkness beyond grew solid, sharpened, pulled suddenly into focus. From within the dim a figure coalesced. Pale. Crouching. Wrong somehow—the perspective—as though viewed from many angles at once. Now distant. Now close. His head was as smooth and featureless as a skinned almond. The man had no face.

When, after an eternity in hell, the lights came up around Daz and the clubbers began to shuffle out in a cloud of smoke and ugly fluorescence, Banger found him wide-eyed and drivelling, wittering on about some rubbish. Banger led him back to the car park, where Fallon was waiting by the car. They drove in convoy into the night, out to some wood where a straggle of ravers carried on the party. Halogen headlights. Car-boot bass bins. And Daz, fully gone.

He lay half-foetal among tree roots, staring into the inky black. In that lightless forest, *no one* had a face.

When at last he slept, drugged senseless by one of Fallon's wickeder buckets, Daz dreamt turbulent, uneasy dreams. Banger and Fallon, Ace and Sadie, every one of them faceless, a featureless blob where the face should be. He woke in the dark, disoriented. The faint glow of the TV tinged the darkness with crackling purple. Nothing was where it ought to be. He stumbled to the bathroom, pinged on the light, ran cold water into the sink to splash his face. When he looked in the mirror, water dripping from his forehead and cheeks, he saw nothing. No eyes, no nose. Naked terror unspooled in his gut. He made to stammer, to gibber, to scream. But he had no mouth. As he stared at the pale blur in the mirror, a reddish seam began to unstitch from right to left. A lipless fissure yawning open—

This time when he woke, he really was in the room. Sweating, disoriented, near sick with fear and the kick-drum thump of his heart. But there. The bedsit's familiar odour of unwashed sheets and stale hash smoke was unmistakable, comforting almost. The light outside was dusky and sombre. Voices echoed from the shared kitchen downstairs. Then it came back to him. Sadie. The money. His stomach knotted.

In the kitchen, Banger and Fallon were sitting at the cheap laminate table. Their empty plates were smeared with brownish sauce—Fallon's piled with fag ends; Banger's wiped clean, the cutlery together. Their downstairs neighbour—Hannah? Joanna?—was over by the microwave, pretending they didn't exist. She was pressed into the corner by the microwave, staring at the green digital clock, at the seconds ticking down. Her Lean Cuisine ready meal turned and turned in the sickly light. The moment it pinged, she popped the door and pulled out the steaming tray with a tea towel, vanished with it into her room. Banger laughed and shook his head.

"We left you a little," he gestured towards the stove, to the grimy aluminium pot spattered with reddish brown. "But there's another tin in the cupboard you could stick in."

"I'm not hungry," said Daz. He poured squash into a glass, filled it at the tap. It tasted like sugar and metal.

"Bollocks," said Fallon. "You've not et in what, three days? You'll be needing all your strength for tonight."

Daz looked blank. "Tonight?"

Banger peered round the table, down the corridor to where Hannah-or-Joanna had disappeared. "You know," he said, then whispered. "The *robbery*."

Daz felt his bowels loosen. "The robbery?"

"That's right," said Fallon. "Now you just need to tell us where it is we're going. Where we'll find this old biddy of yours."

Daz stared at them from across the kitchen, his face a blank.

"Fuck's sake, killer. Don't tell me you've forgotten already. Rich old biddy from your village? Priceless, historic medals? Life savings under the bed? Ring any fucken bells?"

"Yeah," said Daz. "Yeah. Course."

Though it didn't. There were flashes. Murky scenes of Banger's admiring looks, Fallon's raised eyebrow. And Daz banging on and on about... something. A *robbery*? A rich old lady from his village? Mrs McRae's husband had those old World War Two medals, but surely... His gut churned. Automatically, he dropped two bits of bread in the toaster, opened the remaining tin of Heinz Spaghetti Bolognese and shook it into the pot with the leftovers.

Daz spread marge on the toast, glopped warm spag bol onto each piece. He took his plate and the glass of squash over to the wobbly table.

"Right then," said Fallon. "We'll be heading out around eleven. Banger'll drive us over to this village of yours. How far is it, killer? From here to the old biddy's place?"

Daz stared back at Fallon, a mouthful forgotten on the end of his fork. It was all moving too fast.

"I dunno," Daz shook his head. "Twenty minutes or something. But we can't just drive right up to the house—"

"That's right," said Fallon. "You're going to show us where to park, then you're going to show us where to find the house. You'll show us to the buried fucken treasure and then out we fucken go. Easy peasy."

"But—"

"Don't you go all liquid shit on us now, killer." Fallon's eyes were hard, his mouth an expressionless line. "Don't forget, it's for you we're doing all this. Getting you out of the hole you dug for yourself."

Fallon pushed back his chair, squeezed past Banger, leaving his plate and glass on the table. "Get it the fuck together, killer. We need you compos fucken mentis by eleven at the latest."

As Fallon strode down the hall to the stairs, Banger cupped a hand beside his mouth, leaned towards Daz and whispered. "For the *robbery*."

Daz lowered his fork, the mouthful untouched. He pushed the plate away and exhaled queasily. The robbery.

The motorway was quiet, near empty, bleak with pools of orange light beyond which lay the dark expanse of the fens. It didn't seem real—none of it. The road. The car. The electric night. Banger up front, Fallon riding shotgun. The cool glass of the passenger window against Daz's forehead. White lines disappeared beneath the bonnet of the car, each blurred line drawing them closer.

But to what?

Though Daz had been awake now for hours, the dream still clung to him like mould, all knotted and tangled with flashes from his encounter with Sadie, and mounting panic about 'the robbery'. He'd dreamt it before, or something like it. As a kid of—what? Six? Seven? This nightmare, the same one night after night. He'd wake in his room, his own *actual* room, the clock radio blinking redly. He'd wake, unable to move, as though heavy hands were pressing down on his chest. He'd freak, try to rise. But the invisible hands held him down. Then the shadows would solidify, a figure cohere. A faceless man, crouching over him where he lay frozen with terror.

That was around the time his dad fucked off. Or rather, when his mum kicked him out—finally sick of his shit, always pissed or AWOL, draining her wages to pickle his liver. Useless as the old fuck was, Daz loved his dad. He'd never forgiven his mum for what she did, cutting him out of their lives. To make ends meet she'd taken on extra hours, got herself promoted at the haulage company where she'd worked since Daz was a baby. They never went hungry and he never wanted for nothing. Only she was never there, always at work.

Mrs McRae was an elderly Scotswoman who lived out towards the northeast of Fenmorton with her wheelchair-bound husband. Every day after school and through the holidays, Darren would be looked after by the old lady. She wore glasses on a chain, tartan skirts, tan tights and buckle shoes. Around her always hung the smell of Elnett hairspray. She did a lot of work for the church, for the W.I., always busy. But she adored and spoiled Darren as though he were her own grandson. Daz remembered the long strange days of summer, playing by himself in her garden, or with her cranky Yorkshire terrier, Simon. Or sitting with her in the dining room, sipping milky tea from smoked glass cups and doing the crossword.

Mr McRae was a still, silent presence throughout these visits. He spent each day unmoving in his wheelchair, tucked beneath a woollen blanket, mouth open, lower lip drooping, his eyes fixed permanently on some scene far beyond the room. And yet the sense of him hung throughout the house like an unacknowledged ghost. Mr McRae was a war hero. Had been, at least—it was near impossible for young Darren to connect the slumped figure in the wheelchair with the black and white portraits of a smart young infantryman, with a shrewd expression and immaculate toothbrush moustache. The medals laid out in a frame above the fireplace: the France and Germany Star, the Distinguished Conduct Medal; the coveted Victoria Cross. Young Darren spent long quiet hours in the living room, gazing at those medals, trying to picture the acts of extraordinary courage of the man whose stertorous breath rasped from the wheelchair behind him. He couldn't bear to be there, though, when Mrs McRae came in to "see to Frank," feeding the old man mush like a baby, or wheeling him to the downstairs toilet "for his business."

But it wasn't the medals Daz pictured as the car plunged into the night. The images of his mum and dad, of Mr and Mrs McRae, wisped and swirled, but did not settle. The spectral drift of his three-day jag and the spliff Fallon was passing round the car could not still the cyclone of anxiety, the poison mantra that looped in his head. He'd gone and done it again. Fucking Johnny Two-shits, always having to go one better, always having to prove... what? And to who? Banger's looks of worshipful admiration. That single moment of surprise when Fallon's disdain was, for just a second, dimmed. Were these reward enough for what lay ahead? Even the prospect of paying off Sadie with whatever spoils they could make away with was nothing in the face of the tsunami of dread now looming above him, casting its shadow over everything. The certain knowledge that he could not unfuck the disaster he had wrought and was now hurtling towards.

Daz stared through his reflection in the rear window, beyond the face that blurred and vanished into the dark void of the rolling fens.

Banger pulled over on the south side of Fenmorton, in the backstreets near the motorway footbridge. He got out, then Fallon, all business. Daz popped the door, but didn't move, just sat there. It was freezing out. His muscles were stiff with fear, bones aching from the cold. When at last he dragged himself up and out of the car, his breath hung in the air. Banger passed round fags and they all lit up. Fallon took a backpack from the boot and they set off over the footbridge. No one said a word.

The village looked different by night. Everything silent and empty. Beneath the orange street lamps the thatched cottages along the high street looked like a deserted film set. Daz could hardly connect it with the village of his childhood. They turned off the high street and into the newer estates behind. They passed his old street, past the house where his mum still lived. The old anger, that sense of injustice, flared distantly within him. Fallon's backpack clanked faintly as they walked.

He couldn't remember the last time he'd been to Mrs McRae's—years, easily—but his feet led the way. In the orangey glow, nothing seemed familiar. That was good. He didn't want it to. When they got to her cul-de-sac, he paused and Banger and Fallon fell in beside him. All the houses were identical, pebble-dash duplexes with recessed porches, stacked bay windows and mock-Tudor gables, low-roofed garages off to one side. Daz scrutinised each house, his breath pluming in the frigid air. Something about the fourth along drew him: the garden, its fussy neatness. The white and red roses along the wall—orange and black in the streetlights—sparked some vague memory. The closer they drew, the more certain he was. He pointed, and Fallon took the lead up the pebblecrete path to the frosted glass front door. He gave it a gentle push, but it was locked.

"Worth a try," he whispered.

"Now what?" Daz whispered back.

Behind him, Banger hissed. "I got to take a shit."

He ducked into the bushes beside the front door and dropped his jeans. Fallon shook his head, disappeared around the back. Daz felt watched from all sides, like eyes in every darkened window were on him. The sound of Banger's farts was an outrage in the silence. Daz shifted restlessly, then followed Fallon round beside the garage.

He found him inspecting the kitchen window. "It's no good," Fallon whispered. "There's locks on everything. Double, triple locked. Fucken loopy old biddy."

"Well that's it, I suppose." The whiney sound of his voice made Daz squirm. "We'd better—"

"Back round the front. We'll try the garage."

Banger was doing up his belt. Fallon crouched by the garage and rummaged in his backpack, handed them each a torch. He drew a coat hanger from his bag and untwisted it to a length of strong-ish wire with a hook at one end. The hook end he slid through above the garage door, fumbling with tiny movements till, with a faint click, it latched to some mechanism beyond. Still holding the wire, he stood back a little, gestured to Banger.

"Grab the handle and get ready to pull," he hissed. "Quietly!"

When Banger got a grip, Fallon tugged the wire, Banger pulled, and the garage door swung open to reveal a stuffy darkness beyond. They piled into the shadows and Fallon made for the inner door.

"Moment of truth." Fallon turned the knob and the door swung open without a creak. He disappeared into Mrs McRae's house and Banger followed. Torch lights strafed the darkened hallway.

Daz stepped in behind. The smell of the house, a kind of homely melange of Elnett and floor polish, rooted him where he stood, transporting him in an instant to his childhood. At any moment, Mrs McRae would come out of the kitchen with a plate of flapjack and tea steaming in those smokey glass cups. His bowels turned liquid. Banger and Fallon had already disappeared into the house. He heard the faint clatter of their rummaging. Daz forced his legs to move. He felt swollen, dizzy, disoriented, like his whole body was shutting down. He faltered towards the lounge, every step an effort.

Even in the dark, Daz could tell nothing had changed. The room was exactly as it had been last time he was there. The heavy shadows of the lounge set. The same springy shush of the carpet. Only Mr McRae's wheelchair was missing. He remembered the torch in his hand and flicked it on. The disk of light roamed, floating over the chintzy couch, the pleated curtains, to the mantelpiece above the fireplace where, pinned within their frame, the medals gleamed. A silvery coin beneath a blue and red ribbon. The coppery-gold star beneath the red, white and blue. And the Victoria Cross, unmistakable. The proud British lion, the crown, and the words: FOR VALOUR. He heard the stairs creak and his heart stopped. Footsteps, going *up*stairs. Banger and Fallon, going deeper into the house. He snatched the medals in their frame and crept back to the hall.

Whatever thrill had been holding him together fled. He hopped restlessly from foot to foot, waiting for the others to come down. He had no idea what they'd find—if there even *was* anything to find but an old woman asleep in her bed—but he couldn't bear the thought of looking further. Couldn't bear to stay here another moment in this house with its familiar shapes and smells, the memories it forced on him. He'd found the medals. He was done. Daz tiptoed down the corridor to where garage door lay open—a portal of deeper dark within the gloom. He swung the beam of his torch ahead of him, lifted it to the door and yelled. The torch slipped from his hand.

The stark beam had lit up a figure in the doorway, blocking his exit. A figure half-eaten by shadows, by the relentless dim of the garage. A pale almond-shaped head with absolutely nothing where its face should have been.

The torch hit the parquet floor with a smash. The plastic shattered and batteries skittered across the polished wood. The light in the hall clicked on, blindingly bright. Then the light in the landing. A silhouette appeared at the top of the stairs.

"Hello?" A reedy, frightened voice. "Whoever you are down there. I've called the police. They're on their way now, so... so you'd better just go."

Daz glanced towards the top of the stairs, where Mrs McRae stood in a long nightie. Her grey-white hair hung loose around her shoulders. She looked terrified. His mind yelled at him to run, but some older instinct—some childhood memory of this house, this woman—rooted him to the spot.

"Darren?" She leaned forward, peered at him through her little round glasses. "Darren, is that you? What are you doing here? It's the middle of the night."

She began to descend. Carefully, one step at a time, gripping the banister tight in her bony white fingers.

"How did you get in?"

Daz swallowed. His mouth was gummed shut. A door opened silently and Fallon crept onto the landing, his movements silenced by the carpet. All the old woman's attention was on Daz.

He tried again to swallow, croaked, "Mrs McRae...?"

"Oh for fuck's sake," Fallon hissed and charged forward. He pushed.

Mrs McRae pitched forward. Eyes wide. Mouth an O of terror and surprise. Her hair billowed as she fell, and for a moment her head was coronaed by the landing light above. Her nightdress fluttered. She looked like an angel in flight.

Daz put out his arms—a pointless gesture. The frail body struck him obliquely and they both fell backwards. His head hit the parquet, hard. The last thing he heard was the shatter of glass as the frame he was holding crashed into the floor, scattering medals about the hall.

That dream again, the old dream. The weight on his chest, pressing him down. Paralysed, yet awake. Horribly awake. The shadows turned solid and the faceless man loomed. Bony, many-jointed fingers stretched towards him...

Daz gasped awake. He tried to move and wailed to find himself still pinned. The hall lights blared above him, hurt his eyes. The smell of old-lady hairspray was overwhelming. He choked, gagged to realise the weight was not a dream but the body of Mrs McRae. Her grey-white hair spilled around him, tickling his face, his neck.

All the tension and terror and disgust erupted from his throat in a primal groan. He toppled her from him, shuffled backwards on his hands and gasped as he leant his full weight on broken glass.

"Fu-uck," he hissed. "Fuck! Banger? Banger, you there? Fallon, mate?"

He propped himself against the wall and gingerly tweezed the bloody shards from his palm. "Banger? Fallon?"

The house was silent. The only sound a melancholy gurgle from the radiator pipes, the vague drone of the motorway. "Banger? Mate?"

The old woman lay crumpled beside him. Her wide-open eyes locked on his. Her mouth hung open, the tongue protruding dumbly, like some hideous cut of meat she'd failed to swallow. Her glasses lay strewn among the bits of frame and glass. The medals were gone.

Leaning against the wall, he pushed himself upright. His hand left a bloody print on the magnolia paint that glistened redly in the hall light. His palm was cut badly with tens of small incisions, all bleeding. When he dropped his hand to his side, the blood pooled at his fingertips, dripped on the polished wood floor.

He glanced down the hall towards the kitchen. He could wash the cuts in cold water, wrap his hand in a clean tea towel. But hadn't she said something about the police? How long had he been out? They could be here any moment.

Even in the bright light, the door to the garage was a void. And though he knew it was his imagination, a deranged remnant of too much speed and too little sleep, the image of the faceless man looming in the doorway remained fresh, as did the terrible weight of that bony hand on his chest. There was no way he'd take a step towards it. He made for the front door instead, slid back the top and bottom bolts, removed the chain, unlocked the deadbolt and staggered out into the night.

The cold was in his bones, marrow-deep, and his cotton jacket and baggy jeans were no protection from the wind. It howled down the alleys between houses, whistled over fences, through street signs. And in its moans, surely that was a siren? Even as he stepped up onto the footbridge, across the motorway, he knew they wouldn't be there, that Banger's car would be gone. And what the fuck was he going to do then? What about Sadie? And the money? Teeth chattering, the wind roaring in his ears, he crossed, descended the ramp, traced up and down the dim backstreet. The empty cars stared back at him through faceless blank windscreens. All of them dark, blank as the eyes of the dead old woman.

In despair he walked on to the squalid playground the village kids called 'the tubes.' An expanse of dirt, tufted with unmown grass and feral cow parsley. A swing-set and trapeze that hung on chains from a bare metal scaffold. An ancient metal slide, a roundabout set in cracked concrete. And the tubes themselves—the heap of concrete sewerage pipes abandoned with the completion of the village's last housing estate.

Daz crawled inside the nearest, still freezing, but grateful to be out of the wind. Back curled against the wall of the tube, he fumbled for his cigs. He tugged one out, held it upside down and shook the pack till a nugget of hash at the bottom fell into the fold of his jeans. He tore off one, two, three Rizla papers from the half-roached packet. His hand shook as he gummed them together, crumbled in the tobacco. Cupping his lighter against the gusts from both ends of the tube, he heated the hash, pinching off piece after piece until the spliff was loaded. His bloody hand was almost completely numb by this point, stiff and useless, and rolling that spliff with only one hand seemed insurmountable. But essential. As though success or failure in this small endeavour was for Daz a turning point, and its outcome would decide some grander question hanging in the balance.

By the time he'd twisted the paper back over itself and gummed down the flap, he was almost in tears. The spliff was a piece of shit, the worst he'd ever rolled. But it flared when he held the lighter to its tip and the smoke when he drew it into his lungs was everything he needed it to be. When he exhaled it was almost a groan. He wiped tears from the corner of his eyes. His hand ached.

The police would be there by now. At the old lady's house. They'd find the body and the broken glass. His handprint on the wall. He tried to think what he was going to do, where he was going to go, but all he could picture was the old lady's face. Not as he'd known her, bustling and busy, fussing over him with her remote warmth. Not *that* Mrs

McRae. It was the wide goggling eyes, the meat tongue, the bird-like skull beneath parchment skin.

Daz began to cry. Heaving, self-pitying sobs that shook from deep in his belly. He wanted above all things to be home—not back at the bedsit where Banger and Fallon were no doubt already getting wrecked, divvying up the loot—but *home* home. His mum's house. He wanted nothing but to be warm and safe and held, wrapped in her arms, her forgiveness. She'd make it alright. She'd make it go away. All of this.

But even as he thought it, he knew he couldn't go back. He knew he was his father's son—the fuckhead, the screw up—and not hers. That she'd never forgive him, not now. Not in a million years. He snorted, sniffed away the tears, relit the spliff and stared blankly at the hole at the far end of the tube. At the parallaxed darkness of chain link fence and fens and the distant orange seam of the motorway.

A shadow passed across the end of the tube, obscuring for a moment the faraway lights. Dry stalks of cow parsley rattled, the sound weirdly distorted.

"Hullo?" said Daz, his voice little more than a croak. "Banger? That you?"

The wind picked up and the cow parsley shook wildly. The air whined through the tube like someone blowing on a beer bottle.

"Hullo?" said Daz again and immediately wished he hadn't.

He fumbled in his pockets for the torch, then remembered where he'd dropped it. The shadow passed again across the mouth of the tube and this time did not move on. The wind moaned and whistled and whined.

Daz could just make out the shadow at the end of the tube, five feet or so from where he lay. The darkness solidified. A figure on all fours. Crouching. Silent.

The wind rose again, hissing through the long grasses and pattering the cow parsley stalks against the concrete. Then it dropped and all was quiet but for the distant sound of the motorway. The figure began to crawl. Into the tube.

"What?" Daz fumbled for his lighter. "What d'you want?"

He flicked at the striker. It sparked but didn't catch. In the brief white flash he saw the figure outlined. Adrenaline lit him up brighter and tighter than even the rock of whizz at its peak. His heart thundered in his ears, louder than the wind now roaring fiercer than ever.

Daz flicked and flicked. And though the lighter didn't catch, each spark lit the concrete pipe for an instant, a flare burst of magnesium white. And in each strobing flash, Daz saw him—*it*—the faceless man. Sickly, blue-white, almost translucent. Limbs everywhere. And crawling. Crawling.

Daz moaned, shuffled backwards, kicking desperately with his heels till his back came up against another tube that blocked his way out.

Again and again he flicked at the lighter, revealing in bursts of static the faceless man's approach. The hideous movements, now jerky, now fluid. And the thought passed through his mind that he'd been wrong all this time. That it had never been a *man* at all.

At last the lighter caught and, in the flickering yellow, shadows twitched. The featureless face of the faceless thing, so close now he could have touched it, was pocked and pitted and scarred and not the pale smooth surface he'd dreamt of for so many years.

A split began to form around the equator of that cratered moon. A thin red seam emerging left to right, as though the skin were pared by an invisible knife. Black-red liquid oozed from the cut. Daz was gasping, sucking in air but never enough. His heels scuffed uselessly against the concrete.

The seam widened as it grew and reddish bubbles burst around the opening. At last, it yawned wide and the head flipped back to reveal a sloshing bowl of black blood ringed with teeth.

Bony, many-jointed fingers reached towards him.

The lighter burned his fingers and he dropped it. And Daz was plunged into darkness.

The Varying Value of Graves

KYLA LEE WARD

WHY WOULD ANYONE BUY THE BURIAL RIGHTS TO A GRAVE AND THEN NOT be buried in it?

This thought increasingly exercised Vicky's mind as she neared her destination. At least, she hoped she was near. Rookwood Cemetery was the largest in Australia—according to their website—and her impressions so far bore that out.

It was a hideous November day in western Sydney, broiling hot and humid. From horizon to horizon, a blanket of white cloud pressed down upon the graves. Riding the bus in through the gates, she had viewed shaven lawns dotted with brassy plaques, the pretty All-Saint's chapel and next to that the office of the Cemetery Trust. The office had been air-conditioned, filled with lilies and helpful ladies. Charged with the day-to-day administration and maintenance of Rookwood, they checked their database and confirmed there was no record of any burial in the plot registered to Alma Ismay Diederich. It was in an old part of the grounds. They gave her detailed directions and she left the office on foot.

Now there was nothing *but* graves, up hill and down dale, broken only by the occasional palm tree or Norfolk pine. No overhead wires, no roads, no signs: from here she couldn't even see the chapel. It could almost have been mistaken for a rock-strewn field, except the stones emerged from the yellow grass at regular intervals and in vaguely traceable rows. Each capped a length of sunken earth, a patch of weather-bleached tile, or a slab overgrown with bracken.

The Diederich estate was likewise vast and overgrown. This, and a lack of immediate descendants, was why Alma had made the firm of Skelton, Carew & Co her executors. It had initially struck Vicky as profound that, in legal terms, she was one of three people who currently controlled the Diederich fortune, responsible for honouring Alma's exhaustive list of directives and bequests. But Alma had dealt mainly with old Mr Carew, and all Vicky really knew was she had been wealthy, had chosen cremation and the scattering of her ashes, and the anomaly of the plot was somehow Vicky's problem.

No, a phone call won't *do! What the hell's happened at SU if they're turning out graduates like this? Burial rights at Rookwood are worth six to ten thousand but if it hasn't been in use, then it could be overgrown or vandalised. I need eyes on that plot. Your eyes, Ashe, and back by one-thirty!* Skelton's grin had been vicious, displaying his unnaturally white and even teeth. He was broad-shouldered, with a head like a bolt, and his blue suit always seemed on the verge of splitting. Graduating in a year in which junior solicitors had reached plague proportions, the only job Vicky could find was at the boutique firm managing the affairs of a select number of wealthy families, occupying a cramped and ancient Chambers on Elizabeth Street. With a boss who grinned like that.

In a rare fit of temper, she kicked at the gravel on the path, then jumped back as that gravel boiled suddenly into motion. Huge, amber ants with black pincers swarmed in search of the threat. For the first time since leaving the office, she was glad she wore proper shoes.

Victoria Ashe did things properly. It became her defence while still at school, after the bullying set in. She was slight of build, with brown hair and pale skin, but she arrived at work each morning washed and combed, in a tailored black suit with shirt ironed and crisp. Her eyes were her best feature (so her mother said), so she added just the minimal make-up required to bring out the hazel green. So far as she could tell, nobody noticed—the receptionist, Ms Malik, didn't even look up as she went by, let alone greet her as "Ms Ashe".

Now (sidestepping the ant nest), her polished Oxfords were scuffed and coated in dust. She carried her jacket over one arm, but her shirt was soaked with sweat. From above, the cloud's view, she would look like an ant with a dishevelled, black carapace, crawling across the endless field.

The graves were numbered along their rows like houses along a street. Each had a little metal disc affixed to the kerbing, or spiked directly into the ground. As the helpful ladies had said, she just had to check her progress against them. Simple. But there were so *many* stones. It seemed inconceivable that this many people had died during the... she seemed to be walking through the early decades of the twentieth century, dates like 1923 and 1915, names like Hettie and Frederick. Some of the stones listed multiple names, suggesting there were three or four people stashed underneath. In that moment, nothing seemed more obvious than Alma had purchased the right to be buried here, then developed agoraphobia.

To distract herself as she walked, Vicky started running through the bylaws of the Crown Lands Act pertaining specifically to cemeteries. If her memory served, it was illegal to drink or possess any alcoholic or intoxicating beverage. It was illegal to conduct a business other than those directly associated with the operation of the cemetery. It was illegal to bring in or leave any kind of rubbish or refuse...

Something's wrong.

The thought came out of nowhere, with all the force of a slap. She snapped out of her fugue with pounding heart and sweat suddenly chilled, convinced she had passed into some immediate danger. Like an ant feels when a shoe passes overhead... All around her rose big, pink obelisks, a kind of dark, stunted pine had crept up unawares, the bleached grass was waist-high and *rippled*, the thorny bushes parted as though slashed by an invisible knife...

But nothing was moving. Not so much as a stem quivered in the non-existent breeze. If anything, the air was hotter and heavier than ever. She was overheating, that was it. And didn't she smell something off, like rotten fruit? That was one of her migraine symptoms. Oh great—if her vision went, she'd never find the damn grave. She dug in her satchel for the water bottle and ibuprofen.

Migraines were an unwelcome but familiar visitant. Her grandmother had suffered them badly, and even her mother had the odd episode. She sometimes wondered if that was why her father left, if having three of them lying around and groaning was just too much.

After drinking, she felt a bit better. But everything around her still looked odd, as though the light had changed, and some things were genuinely strange. Ahead, the path became less gravel and more a beaten strip of earth into which grass intruded and which the pine trees finally claimed. And the obelisks were the *only* monuments. They were all roughly shoulder-high and fashioned of the same pinkish granite. The inscription on the nearest was only a single word, SURGIMUS.

Vicky searched for a tag on that one. It was tangled around with one of those bushes—scraps of pink and crimson shivered as she jolted the branches. She found nothing. And there was no name, no date and now she looked, no row. The obelisks broke the pattern, they seemed to form a half-circle around the clump of trees. Forget "old"—this part of the grounds was rapidly degenerating into wilderness. She had clearly gotten lost, and it was already… a quarter to twelve.

Entering practice, she had expected dog work and insane hours, had been prepared to bear it all with the same dutiful sufferance as her studies. Now she was wondering why—really, truly questioning how she could have put in all those years of effort just to end up in the middle of a cemetery on the worst day of the year. It hadn't just been the need to have a profession, to secure her future and prove to everyone she wasn't just an ugly mole, or a smartass bitch who thought she was so clever. She had been dazzled by the idea that the law could be used to change things, to help people. And instead, it was *this*?

She wasn't wading into the grass to check another obelisk—the panicky feeling might be all in her head, but there could be snakes out there. And squinting, all she could see on any of them was that same word. *Surgimus* was Latin, it meant something like "we rise"? Why did she know this… oh, of *course*! There was an entry in the list of assets appended to Alma's will. Something like "Antique silver-plated dinner service, including soup tureens, fish platters, meat platters, fruit platters, inscribed with armorial and the legend *Surgimus Lege*." We rise by the law. It was the Diederich family motto.

She was in the right place, after all. Now she simply had to find the unused plot. She looked at the vanishing path and sighed.

Walking slowly, she pressed through thick and bristling pine branches. Thorns snared her sleeves and the legs of her pants. She smelt pine sap and yes, something rotten. Then the glare of the cloud was cut off by dark branches meeting above. Suddenly, she was cold again. Her eyes were dazzled, she couldn't see.

Everything moving past her, beneath her, icy currents running towards the centre—

A lungful of utter foulness and dizziness struck. Coughing, she lost her balance and was stumbling, falling—

She righted herself, still coughing. She had passed from the trees into a cleaner, brighter land, looking much like the cemetery had before she entered the Diederich zone. Weathered, grey stones marched along either side of a neatly gravelled path. The monuments closest to where she stood were obelisks of pink granite, but all that meant was, they formed a complete circle, around the central grove.

The nearest obelisk was nested in a rose bush, to which the last petals still hung. And there was a fresh scuff of feet and a few drops of water not quite absorbed into the dust. Just where they'd be if she'd been standing there, drinking, only a few minutes before. Could she somehow have gotten turned around in the dark and come out the same way?

It forced me back.

Her panic surged. Once again, the rippling patterns appeared around her, and it seemed that someone close by was screaming long and loud, without being able to make themselves heard.

Vicky hunkered down on the path in her torn pants and tried to breathe slowly, hands pressed to her temples, willing the tablets to kick in. Then without standing, she shifted around until she was staring back at the vista of hunching pines. What lay beneath the branches seemed blacker than normal shadow. Stop it, she told herself, it's the migraine. Which is bad enough. But you know where Alma's plot must be—the obelisks surround it, for whatever reason. Everything else, the smell, the dizziness, the panic, migraine. Unless it's the other thing…

That was a bad thought. A mad, bad thought to be tamped immediately down. Oversensitive, her mother had called her, when little Vicky suffered nightmares of her grandmother leaning over her bed and whispering, for months after the old woman died. When she refused to enter their house except by the back gates, or to step on cracks. Once, she had started screaming on a school excursion, after walking into an empty room at the old Darlinghurst gaol. And then Mum said, no wonder they tease you when you behave like *this*...

But the grown-up Victoria Ashe did things properly. She would stand up and push her phone through the branches. She would photograph whatever was in there and then find her way back to the chapel and wait for the bus. And if Skelton said just one thing about her being late, she would... She would find another job! It didn't matter what. As a conveyancer, or copyright monitor, she would have less to do with old families and their mottos.

She braced one hand against the ground. "But for now, I'm Alma's lawyer," she muttered aloud, to whichever Diederichs *were* buried here. "Maybe your motto should be mine. *Surgimus lege*." And she pushed herself up.

Pain burst in her head and she nearly fell again. Her vision spackled and blurred. When it cleared, things were even worse. The trees had pulled back from the path, branches falling away like curtains. A clearing lay there, roofed in branches, floored with dried, brown needles, and centred by an open pit.

And two pallid-faced men were staring at her in shock.

They appeared to be gravediggers or groundskeepers, for one had a big, old shovel with a wooden handle. Both were burly sorts, with hi-vis vests and hats. There was no reason for her heart to jump and start hammering, except that she *knew*. She knew that by speaking the motto out loud she had overcome whatever stopped her before, and this was the heart of it, where all the currents met and went *down*—

Which was *ridiculous*! There was nothing here but two gravediggers, startled that she'd broken in on them.

"Afternoon," she said brightly.

"Who are you?" the foremost demanded, stepping into the light.

You could always tell when people were bullies, and when they were sizing you up. This man had heavy, black eyebrows, that looked like they'd crawled onto his face, and he was cruel. He was the kind who'd assume authority because she was slight and female, and use it to make her squirm.

She swallowed dryly. The urge to squeak, "Sorry!" and just bolt was very strong, but she had a card, and she would play it. "I'm here from Skelton, Carew and Co, lawyers."

He stared, undeflected. "What are you doing here?"

"Looking for a gravesite. Hey—" Producing her phone, she called up the list of assets and thumbed down. "I don't suppose you can tell me if this is anywhere close by?"

The man with the eyebrows glanced back at the taller one, who stood behind him. "*Du schaust nach dem Hexenbier.*"

Vicky's German was as piecemeal as her Latin (and neither was as good as her French). But as the tall man turned obediently, she could swear that Eyebrows had just said something about "witch beer".

Eyebrows snorted as she presented the listing for the plot and bent forward to read it. As he did, a pendant slipped loose from his collar and dangled over the vest. The design, in gold inlay on onyx, resembled an eight-rayed sun, only the centre had been left black.

"There's nothing here," she continued. "No tags at any rate and I'm running late already." She rambled as he read, his defining features contracting into a scowl.

"You're her lawyer," he said.

"The late Ms Diederich's? One of them, yes."

"Why do you want to see the plot?"

"So we can get it cleaned up. Is that why *you're* here?"

"Perhaps it is." With the pendant, and the fact that his shoes were shiny, black winklepickers, Eyebrows no longer resembled a gravedigger—more like some kind of kooky magician. "Why does this concern you?"

"Ah… yes, well. As Ms Diederich decided not to be buried here, the rights will be sold."

"*Sold*? What do you mean, sold?"

"Along with the other assets of the estate." She withdrew the phone.

"Everything's fine," said Tallboy, smiling in a truly ghastly way as he loomed over his partner's shoulder. "The plot will be cleared, so you can just go on home. It'll all be fine." He made a shoo-ing motion.

If I turn my back on them, they will jump me. Was *that* all in her head? Just how far away from help was she? Fear sluiced through her but somehow, she kept her voice calm. "So, you work for the Trust?"

Tallboy nodded but then Eyebrows took another step towards her. "I think," he said, "the question is who do *you* work for? The truth, now." Tallboy made a frustrated noise. "Oh come on—*she broke the ward.* Which coven is it, girl? Who dares intrude upon the territory of the *Buxen*?"

Vicky said, "I don't know who you are or why you're here. But if you have a legitimate claim on the estate, you should present it to the firm."

"A legitimate claim." He smiled. "Yes, I think we have that."

"Then it should all be fine." Despite her resolve, Vicky found herself stepping backwards, up the path. "Like he said."

"This ground is ours. Granted to us by Johann Alaric Diederich in exchange for fortune and a long life for himself and his descendants."

"That's not in the records," she said, readying to run as Eyebrows gripped his pendant with one hand. He raised the other, glancing not at her, but around at the obelisks. She had very nearly cleared them.

"By our ancient pact," he shouted, "I tell you that this stranger is not one of us! She had no right to enter, no more to leave!"

And Vicky found she could not move.

She was right next to the obelisk with the rose bush. She saw nothing, but both her feet felt cold and leaden from the ankles down. No matter how she tried, she could no more shift them than if she had sunk suddenly into the path. And now she felt the currents as though she stood in the stream.

There was no ignoring this.

She strained her neck past her attackers to get a better view of the pit. The interior was dark, but not so as she couldn't make out the motion inside. Seething, particulate motion, she could only think of a massive ant's nest. Stable amid the seethe were two shapes, resembling nothing so much as beer barrels. Big, wooden beer barrels.

They're brewing witch beer, she thought. *They really are.* Then, *I'm being held in place by some sort of curse.*

Which was even more ridiculous. But she couldn't *move.*

Steel flashed in front of her nose—she yelped and flailed but could not shift away from the blade Eyebrows had drawn, could not even turn as he tracked behind her. She squawked as his other hand dug beneath her shirt collar, as if seeking something.

"Which coven?" he barked.

"Carew, Skelton and Co! And you shouldn't be conducting business in a cemetery, even a microbrewery. Especially a microbrewery!"

"*Meister*." Tallboy hazarded. "She carries no sigil and didn't try to defend herself. What if she really *is* just a lawyer?"

Eyebrows sighed. "In that case, how did she open—"

"Well, she's representing old Alma. What if, somehow, that *did* give her the right to enter?"

I said the words, she thought, *and I got in. But with that speech he gave… he countered me.*

Eyebrows looked thoughtful. "Well, it certainly doesn't override our pact." He glanced at Vicky's feet. "But if she's no witch, what shall we do with her?" He chuckled. "Lawyers. They wouldn't have sent anyone important out on a day like this."

Can't run, Vicky told herself, so *think*. What if it's like an argument in Court—is he speaking for the Defence or Prosecution? Defence, he's defending his right to make witch beer based on permission received from Alma's father, or grandfather. How long since a Diederich *was* buried here? Has the plot just been passed down…

Eyebrows tapped one pointed fingernail against his teeth. "Why don't we give her what she came for?"

Tallboy sounded even more nervous. "I really don't think—"

"You shouldn't! It's like an acid test—if she's arcane, she'll be able to handle it. We'll take her to the sanctum, let the others join the fun. If not, then… she'll no longer be a problem, will she?"

Tallboy sighed but turned towards the pit. His back blocked her view of the barrels.

"I'm sure there's no need for whatever this…" Vicky stuttered. "I mean, it's like you say, the bylaws aren't much to worry about. If this is all cleaned up, then—"

Eyebrows chuckled. "I don't think so. *Hexenbier* takes decades to brew and requires exactly the right conditions to infuse. A man must cede his own grave and damn eight of his kin."

Pain sliced into Vicky's temple—not the knife, the migraine. The foul smell was back and she needed, quite desperately, to drink.

And then, as Tallboy turned back around, she realised that was the idea. "Oh, hell no! I'm not drinking that!"

The cup was bone. Curved bone, that held only a smear of the thick, black liquid. Blacker than shadow, blacker than ants—it was wrongness distilled and concentrate.

"You should appreciate this!" Eyebrows sniggered. He actually sniggered. "Even within the *Buxen*, few are granted this privilege!" And what was probably somebody's skull touched her lips and tilted.

A live wire forces down her throat, or a live and wriggling thing. Pushing through her stomach wall and into her lungs—even as her stomach convulses, it is too late. The pain in her head intensifies, then whoosh! It is gone, erased as the vapour makes new connections between flesh and spirit. Her eyes burn, then suddenly, she sees it all.

Eyebrows and Tallboy are ringed with vivid, roseate auras. The sigils and the blades of their knives glow purple. And behind them is the pit, boiling and throwing up motes of black light that it constantly sucks back into itself. The black infuses the objects lodged there, like the pit is choking on them. But it is surrounded by eight, tarnished yellow lines, radiating like a sun. An inverse sun, for these are the currents she feels. Each one runs from an obelisk.

("Look at her face. Well then, I guess you were right. She's a normie.")

Beneath each obelisk something curls like a huge, pale grub. Suffused very faintly with gold, they wriggle, pinned by the obelisk above. But these grubs are people, *human beings writhing beneath the ground… looking straight down, she sees the one that grips her tight. It is a woman, throwing both arms up to chain Vicky's ankles, as she lies flat in her grave. Vicky sees the pain inscribed in her large eyes and open mouth. Her pale hair spreads around her, but by the will of her brother, son or father, she cannot move. She cannot rise.*

Vicky sees this and anger fills her.

"I speak for the Prosecution."

("What's she saying?"

"Just babble. Come on, let's turn her loose in the Independent Section.")

"You claim the right to do this because Johann gave you permission. A blood contract or something. But you *needed* the permission. Every other law forbids this!"

("That's not babble.")

"Could Alma have just revoked it? She's a Diederich, the last of the direct line. She didn't, but she didn't transfer it to you either, just lumped it in with her assets."

("Well then, better crack her on the head, hadn't you!")

"She was scared of you!" *She is aware of Tallboy, moving forward with his shovel, but continues.* "Too scared to interfere. But I think she was hoping that after she died, somebody would." *She slaps her phone upon her chest and raises her left hand.* "As Executrix of the estate of Alma Ismay Diederich, late of Potts Point, Sydney, I revoke your pact and rights. Surgimus lege!" *The proclamation rolls off her tongue with a thunderous resonance and she feels quite smug.*

The ground shudders beneath her feet.

"What the…." Eyebrows looked around. His eyes widened.

"Fuck," said Tallboy.

Eyebrows gaped, then raised his knife. "Retrieve the barrels! Go!"

Tallboy drops the shovel as he dives but the black light is fading. Simultaneously, each of the yellow lines flicker. Against her legs, the motion becomes fitful.

"You are a witch!" Eyebrows levelled the blade at her. "Of some kind!"

"Lawyer," she corrects him.

"Whatever, you will die and be bound to us!"

Behind his back, pale figures unfold. Rising, up through the soil. As Eyebrows comes at her, the woman below lets go of her ankles, twisting like a snake to come between him and Vicky. She is gold now, rekindling, but breaking the surface she acquires a glistening drape of ants. Chalky soil become her face, she trails finger-sticks and dead, dry needles. Embodied, she advances upon him.

Eyebrows thrusts his pendant at her and she falters. Ants begin sloughing to the ground. He shifts the glowing blade from Vicky to her.

Vicky sees the shovel still lying there, beside the path. Though she can't feel her feet, it's but a step for her to seize it. "Poor lady," she says and swings, not at the knife but at the pendant. With a chink of snapping chain, it sails away into darkness.

As the spectre seizes him, biting with a million pincers, Vicky staggers back along the path.

When Vicky arrived back at the office on Elizabeth Street, the neatly garbed Ms Malik gave the faintest gasp.

The skin was peeling on her nose, which distracted some from the dilation of her pupils and bloodshot sclera. Her pants and shirt were in shreds. She had, however, brushed off as much of the dirt as possible, combed her hair and buffed her shoes. Slung over her other arm, her jacket was pristine.

"Are you *quite* alright?" Malik asked.

"Yes," she answered. "Are there any messages for me?"

"One from your mother."

The words that rose to Vicky's lips were *screw her*. But then she thought that maybe they did need to have a talk about her grandmother and the things that used to happen. "Thank you. Please let young Mr Skelton know I'm back." The receptionist turned to her keyboard, then realised Vicky was still standing there.

Malik swallowed. "Yes, Ms Ashe."

Vicky nodded, then proceeded to her desk and sat down.

That there were actual occult forces and she had somehow used them to save not just her own life, but eight people who were already dead, did not seem a suitable subject for a file note. She chose instead to record that she had discovered evidence of dumping and vandalism at the site of the Diederich grave complex and had spoken to the Trust about remedying the situation. The office ladies had denied all knowledge of the perpetrators but promised to have the pit filled in.

She was citing bylaws when old Mr Carew approached along the corridor.

Whereas Skelton was too bulky to really fit into a corner of the late 19th century, Mr Carew might have clung on here, like the plaster mouldings and fanlights over the doors, since the epoch itself. He wore an old-fashioned, grey pin stripe, with a genuine fob watch in his waistcoat pocket. His sparse white hair was combed across his spotted scalp.

"Ah, Miss Ashe," he greeted her. "You're back."

"I'm afraid it took longer than expected," she said, "But I have it under control."

"Good work," he said, "Very good work indeed."

Vicky blinked. The effects of the witch beer had faded now, to the occasional flare of aura, but what she saw around Carew was alarming to say the least. She said, "Thank you."

"Working in our particular area has special challenges," he continued. "I wasn't sure we should be sending you out into the field just yet. But even at our first interview, I could see your potential. Such a potential, untrammelled by any… preconceptions." Carew's old head bobbed, and once again, she seemed to see a glowing spirit form, pinned to the body by something she couldn't quite make out. "All the same, I think it might be best if you took the rest of the day off."

It would be rude to stare. "I might just do that."

He started to totter away, then paused. "But please, do keep on top of this. I want to know the instant the plot is ready."

"Of course, Mr Carew."

"It's quite important. We already have an offer for those rights."

Contributing Authors

GEMMA AMOR

Gemma is a Bram Stoker Award nominated author, voice actor and illustrator based in Bristol. Her traditionally published debut novel *Full Immersion* is out September 2022. Other books include *Dear Laura, White Pines, Six Rooms, Girl on Fire, Cruel Works of Nature* and *These Wounds We Make*. She is the co-creator of horror-comedy podcast *Calling Darkness*, starring Kate Siegel. Her stories feature many times on popular horror anthology shows *The NoSleep Podcast, Shadows at the Door, Creepy, The Hidden Frequencies* and *The Grey Rooms*. Gemma illustrates her own works, hand-paints book covers for other horror authors and anthologies and narrates audiobooks too.

Twitter and insta: @manylittlewords

JOANNE ANDERTON

Joanne is an award-winning writer of dark and weird science fiction, fantasy and horror – but also kids' books and creative nonfiction. Her most recent collections are *Inanimates: Tales of Everyday Fear* and *The Art of Broken Things*. She's currently doing a PhD at UQ, where she's attempting to use speculative fiction to write memoir and having far too much fun in the process.

You can find her at joanneanderton.com

J ASHLEY-SMITH

J. is a British–Australian author of dark speculative fiction and co-host of the *Let The Cat In* podcast. J.'s stories have been shortlisted for multiple awards, winning both the Australian Shadows Award and Aurealis Award. His first book, *The Attic Tragedy*, won the Shirley Jackson Award. His short story collection, *The Measure of Sorrow*, is due for release in 2023 from Meerkat Press. J. gathers moth dust in the suburbs of North Canberra, tormented by the desolation of telegraph wires.

www.spooktapes.net Twitter: @SpookTapes

ALAN BAXTER

Alan is a multi-award-winning author of horror, supernatural thrillers and dark fantasy liberally mixed with crime, mystery and noir. *This Is Horror* calls him 'Australia's master of literary darkness' and the *Talking Scared Podcast* dubbed him '"The Lord of Weird Australia'. He's also a martial arts expert, a whisky-soaked swear monkey, and dog lover.

Alan is the author of more than 20 books, including The Alex Caine series, The Eli Carver supernatural thrillers, and the Aurealis Award-winning *Tales From The Gulp*. He creates these dark, weird stories among dairy paddocks on the beautiful south coast of NSW, Australia, where he lives with his wife, kid, hound, and other creatures.

Find him online at www.alanbaxter.com.au You'll also find him spending far too much time on Twitter @AlanBaxter

AARON DRIES

An author, artist, and filmmaker, Aaron was born and raised in New South Wales, Australia. His novels include the award-winning *House of Sighs, The Fallen Boys, A Place for Sinners, Where the Dead Go To Die* (with Mark Allan Gunnells), plus the novellas *The Sound of His Bones Breaking* and the Australian Shadows award-nominated *Dirty Heads. Cut To Care*, released in 2022, is his first collection of short stories and was described by author Paul Tremblay as 'heartbreaking, frightening, and all too real'.

Aaron is one host of the popular podcast, *Let the Cat In*, and also co-founded *Elsewhere Productions*. His fiction, art, and films have been celebrated domestically and abroad. He is currently working on a new novel and a number of screenplays.

Drop him a line at aarondries.com, on Twitter @AaronDries or TikTok @aarondries_writer.

GEMMA FILES

Gemma is a Canadian horror writer, journalist, and film critic. Her short story, 'The Emperor's Old Bones', won the International Horror Guild Award for Best Short Story of 1999. Five of her short stories were adapted for the television series *The Hunger*.

Find her on Twitter https://twitter.com/gemmafiles

GENEVE FLYNN

Geneve is a fiction editor, author and poet. She is the co-editor of *Black Cranes: Tales of Unquiet Women* (with Lee Murray). The anthology won the 2020 Bram Stoker and Shirley Jackson awards and shortlisted for the British Fantasy, Aurealis, and Australian Shadows awards.

Geneve's short stories have been published in various markets, including Flame Tree Publishing, PseudoPod, Crystal Lake Publishing, and Black Spot Books. Her poetry appears in the 2021 Bram Stoker Award®-winning collaboration *Tortured Willows: Bent, Bowed, Unbroken*, and has been nominated for the Pushcart Prize, and the Rhysling and Australian Shadows awards.

Read more at www.geneveflynn.com.au

PHILIP FRACASSI

Philip is the Stoker-nominated author of the story collections *Behold the Void* and *Beneath a Pale Sky*. His novels include *A Child Alone with Strangers, Gothic*, and *Boys in the Valley*. His stories have been published in numerous magazines and anthologies, including *Best Horror of the Year, Nightmare Magazine, Black Static*, and *Cemetery Dance*. Philip lives in Los Angeles and is represented by Copps Literary Services.

For more information visit his website: pfracassi.com

ROBERT HOOD

Robert has been continually published in Australia and overseas since his first professional sale in 1975. His favourite genres are: horror/weird fiction, crime, fantasy and science fiction. His published works include over 150 short stories, a number of novellas, a few novels, some kids' books and other strange stuff. He has won several awards, including the 2014 Ditmar Award (Best Novel) for *Fragments of a Broken Land: Valarl Undead* and the 2015 Australian Shadows Award (Best Collected Work) for *Peripheral Visions: The Collected Ghost Stories*. His crime/horror novel, *Scavengers*, was released in 2022 with Clan Destine Press.

GABINO IGLESIAS

Gabino is a writer, professor, and literary critic living in Austin, TX. He is the author of *Zero Saints, Coyote Songs*, and *The Devil Takes You Home* and the editor of *Both Sid*es and *Halldark Holidays*. His work has been nominated twice to the Bram Stoker Award as well as the Locus

Award and won the Wonderland Book Award. His reviews appear in places like NPR, the Boston Globe, Locus Magazine, the San Francisco Chronicle, Vol. 1 Brooklyn, and the Los Angeles Review of Books. He teaches creative writing at SNHU's online MFA program.

You can find him on Twitter at @Gabino_Iglesias.

RICK KENNETT

Rick has recently retired after 42 years as a motorcycle courier – possibly a world record in this occupation – which is giving him more time to indulge his hobby of necrotourism -- wandering cemeteries. Rick won a Ditmar in 2008, and two Parsec Awards for podcast stories in 2013. He's had many stories published in magazines, anthologies and podcasts and has six books at Amazon: two novels, a novella and three collections, including one continuing the adventures of William Hope Hodgson's Carnacki the Ghost Finder.

MARIA LEWIS

Maria is a best-selling author, screenwriter and pop culture etymologist based in Australia. She's the writer of the internationally published Supernatural Sisters series, which includes the Aurealis Award-winning *The Witch Who Courted Death*, and the upcoming slasher, *The Graveyard Shift*, coming September 2023).

She's the writer, producer and host of audio documentaries *Josie And The Podcats.* As a screenwriter, she has worked across projects for Netflix, Stan, ABC, Marvel, AMC, SBS, DC Comics and many more. Her directorial debut, *The House That Hungers*, is due for release in 2023.

CHRIS MASON

Chris is an award-winning author who lives on Peramangk land in the Adelaide Hills of South Australia. Her stories have appeared in numerous publications, including the *Things in the Well* anthologies, and the Australian Horror Writers Association's magazine *Midnight Echo.* Chris has won Aurealis Awards for Best Horror Short Story and Best Horror Novella, received the Australian Shadows Paul Haines Award for long fiction, and been shortlisted for a Shirley Jackson Award.

Visit Chris at: facebook.com/chrismasonhorrorwriter or on twitter @ Chris_A_Mason.

LEE MURRAY

Lee is a multi-award-winning author-editor, screenwriter, and poet from Aotearoa-New Zealand, and a *USA Today* Bestselling author. Her titles include the Taine McKenna adventure series, supernatural crime-noir series The Path of Ra (with Dan Rabarts), fiction collection *Grotesque: Monster Stories*, and several books for children. Her short fiction appears in prestigious venues such as Weird Tales, Space & Time and *Grimdark Magazine.* A four-time Bram Stoker Award® winner and Shirley Jackson Award winner, Lee is an NZSA Honorary Literary Fellow and a Grimshaw Sargeson Fellow.

'The Hungry Bones' is a Taine McKenna adventure, featuring the NZDF sergeant on another uncanny mission.

Read more at leemurray.info

CINA PELAYO

Cynthia 'Cina' Pelayo is a three-time Bram Stoker Awards® nominated poet and author. Her novel *Children of Chicago* won the International Latino Book Award for Best Mystery (2021). She lives in Chicago.

DAN RABARTS

Dan, Ngati Porou, is an award-winning author and editor, living in Aotearoa New Zealand. He's a four-time recipient of NZ's Sir Julius Vogel Award and three-time winner of the Australian Shadows Award. His short stories have been published worldwide, and he is the author of the steampunk-grimdark-comic fantasy series *Children of Bane* (*Brothers of the Knife, Sons of the Curse, Sisters of Spindrift*).

With Lee Murray, he co-wrote the Path of Ra crime-noir thriller series: *Hounds of the Underworld, Teeth of the Wolf, Blood of the Sun*; and co-edited the anthologies *Baby Teeth - Bite-sized Tales of Terror* and *At The Edge.*

www.dan.rabarts/fiction

JOHN F D TAFF

John is the multiple Bram Stoker Award-nominated author of *The End in All Beginnings* and *The Fearing.* His short stories and novellas have appeared in innumerable magazines and anthologies over the last 30 years. Peter Straub once tweeted that he was 'mighty cool', which Taff will undoubtedly have engraved on his tombstone.

John edited two anthologies, *The Bad Book* (Bleeding Edge Books), and *Dark Stars* (Tor/Nightfire). Recent works appear in *Orphans of Bliss, The Hideous Book of Hidden Horrors, Human Monsters*, and *Shadows Over Main Street 3.*

You can follow John on Twitter @johnfdtaff or visit his much-neglected blog johnfdtaff.com

KYLA LEE WARD

Kyla is a Sydney-based writer, Ghost Host and former carnival attraction. Reviewers have accused her of being 'gothic and esoteric', 'weird and exhilarating' and of 'giving me a nightmare'. Her writing has garnered her Australian Shadows and Aurealis awards, she has placed in the Rhyslings and received multiple Stoker nominations. Her short fiction is collected in *This Attraction Now Open Till Late*, joining two poetry collections and the novel, *Prismatic*, co-written with David Carroll and Evan Paliatseas.

More may be discovered at www.kylaward.com

KAARON WARREN

A Shirley Jackson award-winner, Kaaron published her first short story in 1993 and has had fiction in print every year since. She has published five multi-award-winning novels: *Slights, Walking the Tree, Mistification, The Grief Hole* and *Tide of Stone* (all now from IFWG); and seven short story collections, including the multi-award winning *Through Splintered Walls*. Her novella, *Into Bones Like Oil* (Meerkat Press), was shortlisted for a Shirley Jackson Award and the Bram Stoker Award, winning the Aurealis Award.

Her most recent books are *Tool Tales* (IFWG0, and a writing chapbook, *Capturing Ghosts on the Page* (Brain Jar Press).

Clan Destine Press Anthologies

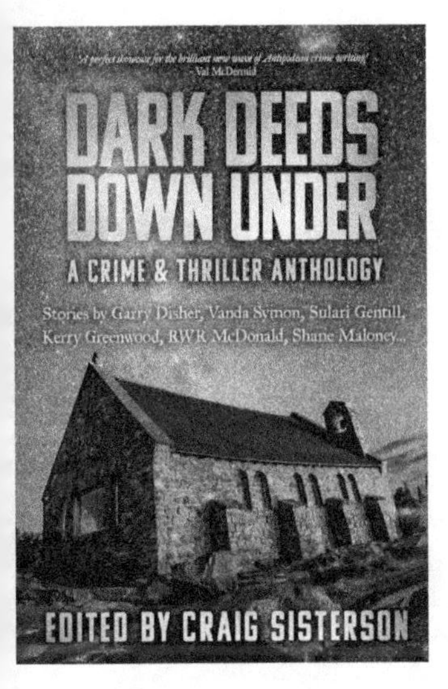

ISBNs: 978-0-6453167-9-7 (hc)
978-0-6453167-8-0 (pb)
978-0-6453168-0-3 (eB)

A Vibrant Southern Constellation of Crime Writers

Dark Deeds Down Under features the very best of modern Australian and New Zealand crime and mystery writing.

Spend time with some of your favourite Aussie and Kiwi cops and sleuths – Hirsch, Corinna Chapman, Sam Shephard, Rowly Sinclair, Murray Whelan – and the edgy stars of some cracking standalone tales.

Travel the criminal trails of two countries from the dusty Outback to South Island glaciers, from ocean-carved coastlines and craggy mountains to sultry rainforests or Middle Earth valleys, and via sleepy towns to the seething underbellies of our cosmopolitan cities.

The 19 dark deeds herein are perpetrated by: Alan Carter, Nikki Crutchley, Aoife Clifford, Garry Disher, Helen Vivienne Fletcher, Lisa Fuller, Sulari Gentill, Kerry Greenwood, Narrelle M. Harris, Katherine Kovacic, Shane Maloney, Renée, R.W.R. McDonald, Dinuka McKenzie, Vanda Symon, Dan Rabarts & Lee Murray, Stephen Ross, Fiona Sussman, David Whish-Wilson

ISBNs: 978-1-922904-16-4 (HC)
978-1-922904-17-4 (PB)
978-1-922904-18-8 (EB)

A clamour of rooks. A mischief of magpies.
A storytelling of crows.

All the corvids – rooks and ravens, jays and jackdaws, crows and magpies – have the best collective nouns: from tidings and titerings, bands and trains, to a parliament, a party, and an unkindness.

Clamour and Mischief is a veritable storytelling of adventures featuring corvidae, the bird family known for its intelligence, cunning and connection with folklore and urban legends.

Our storytellers come from around the world and include award-winners, and fledgling authors in their professional debut.

Herein are 16 striking stories imbued with the humour, darkness, wisdom and magic of the birds which inspired them.
Stories by: Raymond Gates, GV Pearce, Eugen Bacon, Geneve Flynn, Alex Marchant, Jack Fennell, RJK Lee, Lee Murray, Dannye Chase, Narrelle M. Harris, R.D. White, Jason Franks Katya de Becerra, George Ivanoff, Tamara M Bailey, Gabiann Marin.

CPSIA information can be obtained
at www.ICGtesting.com
Printed in the USA
BVHW041230221122
652522BV00005BA/117